THE MAKING

Christopher Mitchell is the author of the The Magelands and Masters & Makers fantasy series. He studied in Edinburgh before living for several years in the Middle East and Greece, where he taught English. He returned to study classics and Greek tragedy and lives in Fife, Scotland with his wife and their four children.

By Christopher Mitchell

The Magelands Origins

Retreat of the Kell
The Trials of Daphne Holdfast
From the Ashes

The Magelands Epic

The Queen's Executioner
The Severed City
Needs of the Empire
Sacrifice
Fragile Empire
Storm Mage
Soulwitch Rises
Renegade Gods

The Magelands Eternal Siege

The Mortal Blade
The Dragon's Blade
The Prince's Blade
Falls of Iron
Paths of Fire
Gates of Ruin
City of Salve
Red City

City Ascendant
Dragon Eyre Badblood
Dragon Eyre Ashfall
Dragon Eyre Blackrose
Dreams of Kell
God Restrainer
Holdfast Imperium
World's End

THE MAGELANDS DOMINION

Serpent Dominion
Demon Witch
Death Seer
Blood Burden
Kin Strife
Tempest's Edge
Creator of Worlds
Palace of the Almighty

MASTERS AND MAKERS

Fall Seldom Kings
The Making of Abigone
Whalebone King

Cover Design by Sasha Almazan and Gene Mollica, G&S Cover Design Studio. LLC.
Maps by Irina French

Brigdomin Books Ltd
First Edition, September 2024
ISBN 978-1-915978-43-1

ACKNOWLEDGEMENTS

I would like to thank the following for all their support during the writing of Masters & Makers - my wife, Lisa Mitchell, who read every chapter as soon as it was drafted and kept me going in the right direction; my parents for their unstinting support; Marilyn Hopwood for reading the books in their early stages; James Aitken for his encouragement; and Grant and Gordon of the Film Club for their support.

Thanks also to my Advance Reader team, for all your help during the last few weeks before publication.

THE WORLD OF THE MASTERS & MAKERS

Klef Mordain – A large port city on the eastern coast of the continent, north of the mountains that divide the old Northern Provinces from the former Central Provinces. Once the foremost port of the Elestian Empire, Klef Mordain secured its independence following that empire's fall. Ruled by a shadowy clique named the **Corse**, Klef Mordain is the latest target for the expansionist Sanctian Empire; and it is also the home of the Secret School – the last place on the continent that trains young Masters and Makers.

Upper Down – A small mountain realm between the old Northern Provinces and the old Central Provinces of the Elestian Empire. Historically part of the Duchy of Down, it gained independence with the collapse of the Elestian Empire, splitting away from what became the kingdoms of **Greater Down** and **Lesser Down**. Upper Down sits astride one of only three passes through the mountains, but its most significant attribute is that it remains the last realm still governed by Masters and Makers.

The Elestian Empire – Sometimes referred to **the First Empire**, the Elestians governed vast tracts of the continent for almost a thousand years. Ruled by an elite aristocracy of Masters and Makers, it eventually collapsed after prolonged rebellions and uprisings. Its collapse led to widespread massacres of Masters and Makers, reducing their numbers until few were left alive. The old calendar system ended upon the death of the last Emperor, and the years are now dated from this momentous event. ***The Making of Abigone*** begins in Year 108, i.e. one hundred and eight years since the fall of the Elestian Empire.

The Sanctian Empire – Centred around the island of Sanctos, the Sanctian Empire arose from the ashes of the Elestian Empire. Sometimes referred to as **The Second Empire**, the Sanctians have been re-conquering many of the old provinces, and re-uniting them under its rule. The Sanctians view Masters and Makers as wicked and blasphemous, and have pledged to hunt down and execute the last remaining survivors.

The Westlanders – Hailing originally from the great plains to the west of the old Northern Provinces, the Westlanders swept through those provinces following the collapse of the Elestian Empire. Seen as a primitive, violent people by the citizens of the old Central Provinces, the Westlanders are hated and feared. Known for their worship of the three moons as much as for their raiding and brigandage, the Westlanders are unrivalled in warfare.

Masters – Men who possess the ability to transmute elements.

Makers – Women who possess the ability to summon objects.

NOTE ON THE ELESTIAN CALENDAR

This calendar was devised during the rule of the Elestians, and is used in all lands that were provinces of that empire.

The world has three moons – the Big Red Moon (King Aloth), the Silver Moon (Queen Ninia), and the Little Red Moon (Prince Logar); and the months are organised around the orbit of the largest of these – the Big Red Moon, which goes around the world once every 33 days. Hence, each of the eleven months contains 33 days – creating a Solar Year of 363 days (with no Leap Day required).

Each month is named after one of the Emperors or Empresses of Elestia.

In the Elestian Calendar, each year begins on the 1st day of Pomana. The below list of months details the corresponding dates upon Earth. These dates are a rough guide only, as a year on the world of Elestia and Sanctos contains two fewer days than a solar year on Earth.

- Pomana– corresponds to 21 March to 22 April
- Saluna– corresponds to 23 April to 25 May
- Ara– corresponds to 26 May to 27 June
- Considera– corresponds to 28 June to 30 July
- Tempora– corresponds to 31 July to 1 September
- Desira– corresponds to 2 September to 4 October
- Lamenta– corresponds to 5 October to 6 November
- Minula– corresponds to 7 November to 9 December
- Quoma– corresponds to 10 December to 11 January
- Regula– corresponds to 12 January to 13 February
- Nova– corresponds to 14 February to 18 March

DRAMATIS PERSONAE

From Upper Down

Princess Abigone, Aunt of King Alfgang VI

Lothar, Commander in Mountain Rangers

Annalise, Lady-in-Waiting to Princess Abigone

Members of the Corse

Fyenna, Head of the Makers' School

Metrius, Leader of the Anti-Sanctian Bloc

Niscoll, Ally of Metrius and friend of Fyenna

Harrow, Pro-Sanctian Politician

Penny, Pro-Sanctian Politician

Asquith, Pro-Sanctian Politician

Makers' School

Rupert, Secretary

Vesta, Teacher

Raewyn, Third-Year Student

Stanza, Second-Year Student

Reath, First-Year Student

Nyli, First-Year Student

Masters' School

Drummond, Head of Masters' School

Tobold, Teacher

Constans, Fourth-Year Student

Aplin, Second-Year Student

Salus, First-Year Student

Ignatius, First-Year Student

Marlow, First-Year Student

Second Empire Association

Tain, Director of the Association

Ursula, Director of the Association

Petros, Scribe

Loryn, Notary

Adamnul, Former Secret Police

Other Citizens of Klef Mordain

Selanius, Fyenna's Husband

Mabda, Widow

Heston, Drummond's Brother

Eshia, Graduate Maker

Portia, Member of the Secret Police

Sanctians

Tertius, Ambassador to Klef Mordain

Assanio, Sanctian Admiral

Pontus, Sanctian Naval Captain

Geathians

Mor Galthide, Former Prince of Geathan

Mor Dennahelm, (Denny) Son of Mor Galthide

Ter Angla, Mor Galthide's Servant

Others

Amery of Yearl, Lawyer

The World of
Masters & Makers
The Westlands
Northern Provinces
Desert
Klef Mordain
Upper Down
Lesser Down
Estral
Greater Down
Campsie
Anster
Guran
Central Provinces
Jallin
Yearl
Elestia
Osbruck
Mylos
Anster
Dibain
Aubruk
Subnestia
Nessos
The Thousand Lakes
Sanctos
Western Colonies
Ocean
Geafhan
Ocean
Southern Provinces
N
W
E
S
Road
Town
Ocean

CHAPTER 1
CITY OF NO PRISONS

Great Northern Highway, Klef Mordain – 3rd Day of Saluna 108

'I want blood,' said the robed man. 'Tell the chef that I shall refuse to pay if there is none. I will not waste money on overcooked steak. Is that clear, girl?'

'Yes, sir,' said the waitress. 'Would you like something to drink?'

The man waved his hand. 'Anything red from Yearl or Campsie will suffice; but nothing from Subnestia – I cannot abide the stuff.' He glanced at the two men and two women sitting across from him in the alcove. 'In fact, bring a couple of bottles for the table.'

The waitress nodded, then she turned and made her way through the quiet tavern. The robed man smiled at the other occupants of the alcove.

'I hope I'm not intruding,' he said. 'I noticed that you were fellow travellers bound for the centre of Klef Mordain, while many of the other patrons of this establishment appear to be locals. Nevertheless, I should have sought your permission before sitting down next to you.'

A polite response flitted over Abigone's lips, but she stopped herself from uttering the words. The man had annoyed her by sitting in their alcove when there were plenty of empty places available in the rest of the tavern.

'It's quite all right,' said Amery. 'We four have been on the road for many weeks, with only ourselves for company.'

'That can test any friendship,' said the man. 'My name is Denon; who might you be?'

Lothar frowned. 'How did you know we were bound for the city centre?'

'Simple logic, my friend,' said Denon. 'There is a carriage parked outside fit for four travellers; you are dressed for the road; and your accents mark you out.' He pointed at Amery. 'Except for you. You are from Yearl, if I am not mistaken.'

'You are not,' said Amery.

'And what is your business in Klef Mordain?' said Denon.

'That doesn't concern you,' said Lothar.

Denon smiled. 'You carry yourself like a soldier,' he said, 'therefore, I would assume that your role in this little band is that of protector – but whom are you protecting? And that accent? Greater Down, perhaps, or further afield?'

'We have heard all about the secret police that operate in this city,' said Abigone. 'Why do you think we would share our personal lives with a stranger?'

'I am merely making conversation, young lady,' said Denon. 'I, too, have been on the road for a long time, with only my driver to talk to every day; and he is rather a dull man. Let me see if I can paint a picture of you with my words, from the little I have so far gleaned.' He pointed at Lothar. 'You are the soldier.' He moved his finger towards Annalise. 'You are this young lady's nurse or chaperone.' He pointed at Amery. 'And you? You are most certainly no soldier; you have the look of a clerk or a lawyer about you; therefore, I would hazard that you are also an employee of the young woman sitting opposite me. But why would three people be escorting a young lady to Klef Mordain? That's what interests me. It would most likely also be of interest to the famed secret police who watch over this city. Did you know that every citizen of Klef Mordain, from the youngest to the oldest, man and woman, also works for the Corse?'

'The what?' said Abigone.

'The Corse,' said Denon; 'the secretive little cabal that runs Klef Mordain.'

'The word means *guild* in the old language of the Northern Provinces,' said Amery. 'They took over the running of the city after a coup some sixty or so years ago.'

Denon smiled again. 'You have received an education, I see; although I notice that you failed to refer to the young woman sitting next to you as *my lady*, or *ma'am*. Am I to assume that you are travelling in secret?' He laughed. 'There is no need to look so anxious. I do not work for the Corse. I would advise, however, that you get your story straight before the real secret police decide to question you. The soldiers of Klef Mordain have a nasty habit of reaching for the noose if they suspect any double-dealing within their city. Did you know that there are no prisons in Klef Mordain? What does that tell you about their methods? What does it say about their approach to law and order?'

'We came into this tavern for some food and a rest,' said Lothar, 'not to be harassed by a be-robed meddler who thinks he knows us. Take your opinions to some other alcove.'

'Now you are starting to really intrigue me,' said Denon. 'What would necessitate coming to Klef Mordain in secret? That's the question. These are perilous times. The Elestian Empire is but a memory, while the Sanctian Empire has yet to cement its rule over the old provinces. Klef Mordain – the richest jewel of the old north – finds itself harried from all directions. Is it any wonder that the Corse have become a little paranoid, seeing enemies where there are none?'

'Klef Mordain is more than able to protect itself,' said Amery. 'I doubt the Corse gives much thought to affairs beyond its borders.'

'Then you would be wrong,' said Denon. 'As I mentioned before, every citizen of this city works for the Corse. Some fulfil their duty as reserve soldiers, others assist in the maintenance of the city's defences, or work as fletchers, to supply the city's archers; while others act as spies, reporting anything suspicious to the Corse authorities. You would do well to remember that.'

The waitress approached.

'Ah, here is our wine,' said Denon, then he frowned. 'I asked for two bottles of red, girl; why are you returning empty-handed?'

The waitress lifted a finger and pointed at Denon.

Eight armed men burst through a side door of the tavern and ran towards the alcove. Denon reached for the hilt of his sword, but the men were on him within moments. One was gripping onto a thin cord, and he coiled it round Denon's neck from behind, and pulled it tight. Another man drove the iron butt of his crossbow into the robed man's face, breaking his nose and spraying blood over the table. Denon was dragged choking from his seat, his hands trying to loosen the cord round his throat. Two of the men were carrying wooden clubs, and they brought them down onto Denon's legs, while others held his arms.

'Take the accused outside,' said one of the soldiers, a man with a grey band tied round his right arm.

'Yes, Captain,' said another.

The officer turned his glance to Abigone and the others still in the alcove.

'You, too,' he said. 'Outside. Orders of the Corse.'

'But…' said Abigone.

Amery raised his empty hands in the air. 'We'll do it!' he cried. 'We aren't resisting.' He stared at Abigone, Lothar and Annalise. 'Do whatever they say,' he hissed.

'We haven't done anything wrong,' said Lothar.

'It doesn't matter,' said Amery. 'These men have the authority to execute criminals without trial.' He stood, his arms still raised.

Abigone hesitated, then she got to her feet. To her left, Annalise also rose, and they followed Amery as he edged through the soldiers. Lothar cursed and joined them, as Denon was dragged across the floor of the tavern. A few patrons by the bar stopped drinking to watch, but none spoke or intervened, while the waitress gazed at them without emotion.

The soldiers led Abigone and the others out onto the street. It was almost evening, and the heat of the day had lingered. Wagons and carriages were lined up along both sides of the Great Northern Highway, and a multitude of taverns and inns lay clustered by the road. Beyond, the outskirts of the huge city spread away into the far distance, the red-tiled rooftops glimmering in the afternoon sunlight. More soldiers were standing outside waiting for them, and Denon's wrists were tied behind his back as he lay bleeding on the uneven cobbles.

Abigone, Lothar, Amery and Annalise were taken to the side of the road, and forced to kneel on the cobbles with their hands behind their heads.

'Remain calm, no matter what happens,' said Amery. 'This has nothing to do with us.'

The officer walked over to where the robed man was lying.

'Lord Denon of Sanctos,' the captain said, 'you are charged with the crime of espionage; of working for a foreign government to undermine the city of Klef Mordain. How do you plead?'

'Go fuck yourself!' Denon cried. 'I have diplomatic immunity!'

The officer smiled. 'Search him. He should have documents hidden on his person.'

Two soldiers knelt by Denon, and began rifling through his robes. A pouch of gold was removed, and passed to the officer; then the sword was unfastened from Denon's belt, and given to another man. A moment later, one of the soldiers searching Denon pulled an envelope from the man's robes and handed it to the captain. The officer broke the seal and opened it. He unfolded a sheet of fine paper, and read. After a few moments, he nodded, then he placed the letter into an inside pocket.

'Lord Denon,' he said, 'this letter has proved your guilt beyond all doubt. Do you have anything you wish to say?'

'Klef Mordain belongs to the Sanctian Empire!' Denon exclaimed. 'If you execute me, then my compatriots shall avenge my death. The Corse are doomed! The Corse can kiss my...'

The captain stamped his boot down into Denon's face, and the robed man fell silent.

'I hereby sentence you, Lord Denon, to death,' the officer said. He gestured to the soldiers. 'Gut him from neck to navel; then place a noose round his throat and hang him from the nearest lamppost.'

Abigone looked away as a soldier drew a long knife and crouched by Denon. She heard a gargled cry of agony, as the blade ripped down the robed man's chest, slicing him open. Another soldier tied a thick rope round Denon's neck, and tightened the knot.

'Prepare a sign,' the officer said. 'Mark it with his crime, and hang it over his shoulders.'

A wooden placard was produced, and a soldier began to write on it with a thick piece of charcoal. When it was finished, the soldier placed it round Denon's neck. A ladder was propped up against a lamppost, and the rope was slung over its top. Four men heaved on the rope, and Denon's body was lifted into the air, his feet twitching as blood flowed down from the gaping wound on his torso. Abigone gazed at the placard hanging over his chest. *Spy*, it read.

A small crowd had gathered by the side of the road to witness the execution, and the soldiers did nothing to stop them from watching as Denon gasped out his last breath. His eyes remained open, as though he was staring down at the watching soldiers and civilians.

'By the authority granted to me by the Corse,' said the officer in a loud, clear voice, 'Lord Denon of Sanctos has been justly executed for the crime of espionage. Let it be so recorded and witnessed by the citizens of Klef Mordain.'

The captain turned to Abigone and the others. He eyed them for a few moments as he approached, and Abigone kept her head down.

'I want your names, places of birth, and the reason you have arrived in Klef Mordain,' the officer said. He pointed at Amery. 'You first.'

'My name is Amery of Yearl,' he said, 'and I have come to Klef Mordain to seek work, I am a lawyer by trade; trained at the old Imperial College in Elestia.'

'We noticed your carriage cross the boundaries of the city this morning,' said the captain, 'and have been following you. Was your meeting with Lord Denon pre-arranged?'

'No, sir,' said Amery; 'I swear we met that man by chance alone. He approached our table without being invited, and we did not desire his company.'

The captain glanced at Lothar. 'And you?'

'Is this how you treat all visitors to your city?' said Lothar.

'Only the ones found consorting with known spies. Give me your name, place of birth, and your reason for being in Klef Mordain.'

'Do it,' whispered Abigone. 'Tell him the truth.'

Lothar glared at the officer. 'I am a commander of the Mountain Rangers in the realm of Upper Down, seconded to act as bodyguard to Princess Abigone of House Shiel, Regent of Upper Down. My name is Lothar.'

The soldiers quietened.

The officer stared at Abigone. 'You are a princess of Upper Down?'

'I am,' she said.

'What are you doing in Klef Mordain?'

'I was visiting my sister, Princess Nolan of Lesser Down,' she said. 'We were accompanying our friend Amery to this city, before returning to Upper Down.'

The officer narrowed his eyes. 'I assume that this is not an official visit? Are you part of a diplomatic mission to the city?'

'No. I was travelling in a private capacity. I didn't tell Denon my name. He had no idea who I was, just as we had no idea who he was.'

'I need proof of your claim.'

Abigone nodded, then she unclasped her hands from behind her head. 'I am going to reach into a pocket,' she said, as several soldiers kept their crossbows trained on her.

She withdrew her silver signet ring from her clothes, and held it out on her palm of her hand.

'That bears my royal seal,' she said.

The officer plucked the ring from her hand, and gazed at it in the fading light. 'Why was this not upon your finger?'

'I did not wish to attract any attention,' she said.

'My mistress has done nothing wrong,' said Annalise. 'The way you are treating her is an outrage.'

The officer smirked. 'And you are?'

'My name is Annalise of Upper Down,' she said; 'lady-in-waiting to the crown of that realm.'

'Upper Down is nothing but a tiny, backward mountain kingdom,' he said; 'one ill-renowned for harbouring criminals and raiders from the Westlands. I hear you bowed before Prince Valentino, the brother of the Sanctian emperor.'

'We did not bow before him,' said Abigone. 'We came to an agreement.'

'I also heard that Valentino's cannon were destroyed,' the officer went on. 'Is that correct?'

'We buried them under a rockslide,' said Abigone; 'hence the reason the noble prince was forced into making peace with us.'

The officer nodded. 'I will have to report this to the Corse. As a regent of Upper Down, you are a sovereign leader of a foreign realm. You should have sought permission from the city authorities before entering Klef Mordain.'

'I know a member of the Corse,' said Amery. 'I was intending to escort the princess to his home, and offer an introduction. If there is any fault in what we have done, the blame is mine alone.'

'Have you been in this city before, lawyer?'

'I have, sir. That member of the Corse I mentioned – I would consider him to be a friend of mine. I also happen to be familiar with the laws of Klef Mordain, and know that you cannot act against us without evidence of wrong-doing. Might I ask your name?'

'I am Captain Yenalt of the Third Regiment of Infantry, empowered to act as a magistrate. This section of the Great Northern Highway is mine to oversee.'

'What are you going to do with us?' said Abigone. 'If you intend to have me executed, Captain Yenalt, then I would ask that you stop talking and get on with it. I have no desire to be kneeling in a street gutter for any longer than necessary.'

The captain stared down at them, then a half-smile flitted over his lips. 'You are free to go.'

Lothar got to his feet, then he extended a hand to help Abigone up.

'My ring, if you please,' Abigone said to the captain.

The officer handed her the ring. 'For your protection and ours,' he said, 'you and your party will be followed wherever you go within the boundaries of Klef Mordain. You can rest assured that I will be filing a full report about your presence in the city... Your Highness.' He gestured to the other soldiers. 'Get back to your posts; these four are being released. Have two men assigned to trail them to the city centre.'

The soldiers saluted.

'Why was Denon here?' said Abigone. 'What did he want with Klef Mordain?'

'That is none of your concern,' said the officer.

'But he was from the Sanctian Empire?'

'Evidently.'

Annalise and Amery stood, as the soldiers began to disperse. The officer inclined his head a fraction, then he strode away, leaving the body of Denon swinging from the lamppost. Several children began throwing stones at the corpse, and a crow that had settled on his shoulder flew away, its harsh cry resounding over the roofs of the taverns lining the road.

'Are you all right, ma'am?' said Lothar.

'A little shaken,' said Abigone.

'We were exceptionally fortunate,' said Amery. 'Denon was at our table for a matter of moments. If he had been there for much longer, we would most likely be decorating the other lampposts along this street.'

'And now the Corse will know that I am here,' said Abigone. She shook her head. 'Kilbride will be furious. She told me to make sure I kept a low profile in Klef Mordain. Perhaps we should leave while we can.'

'That is your decision, ma'am,' said Amery. 'You are free to return to Upper Down, but I will continue on into the city.'

Abigone chewed her lip as she watched the crowd staring up at the body of Denon.

'I don't feel safe here,' she said.

'Klef Mordain has remarkably little crime, ma'am,' said Amery. 'As long as you do not break the law, you should be safe enough.'

Abigone lowered her voice. 'The reason I am here – the real reason – is that breaking the law?'

'No, ma'am,' said Amery. 'The school might be unknown to the majority of the population of the city, but it is secretly funded and supervised by the Corse. Becoming a student there does not violate any city ordinances. Furthermore, I know a member of the Corse, who will be able to enrol you into the school. If you decide to stay here as a student, the Corse will protect you.'

'Why?'

Amery smiled. 'Because it is in their interests to do so.'

'What does that mean?'

'Perhaps we should retire to our carriage before discussing this any further, Your Highness.'

'Very well,' she said.

Lothar cleared a path through the crowd of watching civilians, and the others followed him to their carriage, which was parked next to a line of others. Their two drivers were lingering by the outside tables of another tavern, and they ran back to the carriage when they saw Abigone approach.

'How was dinner, ma'am?' said one.

'A little too bloody for my tastes,' Abigone said.

'Did you see the execution, ma'am?' said the other driver.

'We had an excellent view. Get ready to leave, but wait for my signal.'

The driver opened the side door of the carriage, and Lothar assisted Abigone to ascend. When all four passengers were inside, the two drivers mounted the bench at the front of the carriage, and took hold of the reins.

'I feel that you have been less than honest with us,' Abigone said to the lawyer.

'In what way, ma'am?' said Amery.

'You told us that this school was a secret; and now you tell us that the government of the city runs the establishment.'

'Both things are true,' said Amery. 'Klef Mordain conducts much of its business in secret; that is the nature of the Corse. It is most certainly not in the interests of the city to openly advertise the fact that they are training a new generation of Masters and Makers; not when everyone knows that Emperor Antonio is trying to rid the Sanctian Empire of all such people.' He lowered his gaze. 'The Sanctians want Klef Mordain. It was one of the richest and largest cities in the old Elestian Empire – a rival even to Elestia itself – and the Sanctians long to incorporate it into their own empire.'

'Does the city have any cannon?' said Lothar.

'They do not,' said Amery, 'though not from want of trying. There is a hidden programme to develop the black powder required to operate such weapons, but the Sanctians jealously guard that secret, and the city's attempts have so far failed. That is another reason the Corse supports the school – a cadre of Masters and Makers would constitute a powerful defence of the city, if ever the Sanctians tried to use force to capture Klef Mordain.'

'Is that likely?' said Abigone.

'No, because the Sanctians must be aware that the school exists, even if their agents have never been able to find it.'

Abigone gazed out of the carriage window. 'I had been picturing a school that was a secret hidden from the world, not one funded by the government of a foreign city. If I enrol, would I be expected to fight for Klef Mordain?'

'I have told you all I know,' said Amery. 'Anything else – its location, the number of students, its rules – would be pure speculation on my part. I can take you to the member of the Corse that I know, and he might be willing to share some information with you. However, such is the secrecy shrouding the entire project, you might not be able to discover more unless you are prepared to commit yourself to becoming a student.'

'It's time for a decision, Your Highness,' said Lothar. 'If we press on into the heart of Klef Mordain, and meet with Amery's friend, then the Corse might not allow us to depart, even if you changed your mind about wanting to join the school.'

'In other words,' said Abigone, 'if we don't leave now, we might never be able to leave?'

'Lothar is probably correct, ma'am,' said Amery. 'If the Corse becomes aware that you are a Maker, they might decide to hold you here indefinitely.'

Abigone's temper simmered over. 'Why didn't you tell us any of this when we were in Upper Down?'

'I was asked if I knew of anywhere upon this world where you could receive training and education in the arts of being a Maker, ma'am,' he said, 'and I answered honestly. The secret school of Klef Mordain is the only place I know of that matches those requirements. It might well be the only place in existence that does so, at least in the civilised parts of this continent. Two hundred years ago, there were likely dozens of such schools, spread all over the Elestian Empire, but times have changed.'

'Then these are my choices,' said Abigone; 'to either return home in failure, or to place myself into the hands of the Corse? I wish Kilbride were here.'

The others said nothing.

'I miss Tulip,' she went on. 'I shouldn't have allowed my sister to persuade me to leave him in Upper Down.'

'It was a wise decision, ma'am,' said Amery. 'We couldn't have brought a cat all this way with us. Besides, there are plenty of them in Klef Mordain if you want another one.'

'There will never be another Tulip,' said Abigone. 'All right; here is my decision – I refuse to return home with nothing to show for it. I came to Klef Mordain to learn about being a Maker, and that is what I will do.'

She turned, and tapped on the little window dividing the interior of the carriage from the two drivers.

They turned to face her.

Abigone smiled. 'Take us to the centre of the city.'

CHAPTER 2
THE ASSOCIATION

Old City, Klef Mordain – 4th Day of Saluna 108

'I'm terribly sorry, sir,' said the clerk, 'but I am afraid Lord Metrius is too busy to receive any visitors at present.'

'Ah,' said Amery. 'Should I wait here?'

The clerk frowned. 'There would be no use in that, sir. His lordship will be extremely busy over the next few days.'

Amery glanced at the office door. On the other side of it was the only member of the Corse that he knew in Klef Mordain – a man he had referred to as a *friend* to the soldiers who had executed Lord Denon.

'My business will take a mere moment,' he said, 'and it is rather urgent.'

'You may not see him without an appointment, sir,' said the clerk. 'Those were his orders.'

'Then could you please pass him a message?'

The clerk sighed. 'Very well.' He gestured to a pile of loose leaves of paper.

Amery picked one up, and drew a pencil from his pocket. He leaned on the clerk's desk, and thought about what he was going to commit to paper. He hesitated for a moment, then began writing.

Lord Metrius, greetings. I have a Maker for the city. Your loyal friend, Amery of Yearl.

He folded the scrap of paper, despite knowing that the clerk would almost certainly read it on the way to see the lord. The clerk smiled as he took the piece of paper, then he rose to his feet.

'Please remain here, sir,' he said.

Amery walked over to the large window as the clerk knocked on the office door and entered. The view from the waiting room looked out over the streets of the Old City, and Amery could see the grand buildings that housed the headquarters of the shipping fleets that plied the ocean. Much of the city's great wealth came from its trade routes. Its merchants sailed the eastern coast of the old Elestian Empire, from Klef Mordain in the north, all the way to Sanctos and the old Southern Provinces far to the south. There existed vast shipyards on the eastern side of the city, that were among the few places capable of constructing the huge vessels that braved the journey across the far side of the ocean to the strange lands beyond – lands that sent their exotic goods all the way to Klef Mordain, and from there, to markets all over the old Central Provinces. The coffee he had drunk that morning was just one example of Klef Mordain's influence and power. Packaged for pennies on the other side of the ocean, small cups of the dark beverage commanded high premiums in the inns of Yearl and Sanctos.

Amery smiled. After the disturbing experience of working for Duke Hector in Upper Down, arriving in Klef Mordain had felt like a return to normality – a return to civilisation.

The office door opened, and the clerk emerged.

'Lord Metrius will see you now, sir,' he said; 'but I must ask that you be brief.'

'Thank you,' said Amery.

He hurried through the door before the clerk could change his mind, and closed it behind him. A robed figure was sitting behind an enormous oaken desk amid a sumptuous office, with wood-panelled walls, and long, overflowing bookshelves. On the right was a blazing hearth, and the room was stiflingly warm.

The figure stood, a wide smile on his face. 'Amery, my friend!' he said. 'How good to see you again. The last I heard of you, you were seeking fame and fortune in the wilds of Upper Down.'

'Lord Metrius,' Amery said, inclining his head. 'Thank you for seeing me without an appointment. I understand that you are very busy.'

The two men shook hands. 'More than merely busy, my old friend,' Metrius said. 'I'm up to my neck in Corse business. Of course, I cannot tell you any more than that. Sit. Help yourself to coffee. None for me, though, my head is already buzzing with the stuff.'

Amery sat down, then he reached for a silver coffee pot, and filled a small cup.

Metrius took his own seat, and eyed Amery. 'I read your note.'

'Did its contents interest you, my lord?'

'Indeed. It was a little indiscreet of you to have written what you did, so I took the liberty of tossing the scrap of paper into the fireplace.'

'Thank you.'

'Where is she?'

'She is waiting in a carriage in the street outside, my lord.'

'And how did you come across such a find?'

'This will be open knowledge soon, my lord, but we had a little run in with the Third Regiment of Infantry yesterday, on our way into the city. We had the decided misfortune of being in the same tavern as Lord Denon when he was arrested for espionage.'

Metrius chuckled. 'That is a misfortune.'

'Naturally, the soldiers there wished to question us; and, as it is always wise to be honest in these matters, we told the truth to a young captain by the name of Yenalt. We neglected, however, to mention the fact that my companion was a Maker.'

'That was probably wise.'

'Her name is Abigone, and she is a princess of Upper Down.'

Metrius fell silent, his eyes tight.

'She has received no training whatsoever in the arts of being a Maker,' Amery went on, 'but she shows tremendous promise. Do you recall the tales about Prince Valentino's cannon being destroyed? That was her doing. Were it not for that act, Upper Down would probably no longer exist as an independent entity. Prince Valentino had been planning to have the realm dissolved, and incorporated into Greater Down – no doubt with a view to having the place annexed to the Sanctian Empire. Princess Abigone prevented that outcome.'

'Is she Kilbride's sister?'

'She is, my lord.'

'And is Kilbride acting as regent for the young king?'

'Yes, along with the King's Champion – a man named Walter. Abigone is also a regent.'

Metrius shook his head. 'Are you telling me that a sovereign leader of Upper Down is not only in Klef Mordain, but that she is a Maker? Well, well. Thank you for bringing this to my attention, Amery.'

'She is hoping to enrol in the school.'

'I see. Was it your job to escort her to Klef Mordain?'

'Princess Kilbride requested that I lead her here, my lord. However, I intend to remain in the city.' He smiled. 'If I can find a suitable position, of course.'

'Ah. Unfortunately, I do not require any legal staff at present.' He took a pencil and scribbled something on a scrap of paper. 'Take this – it bears the address of an inn where the Corse lawyers often drink. A noticeboard hangs upon a wall, displaying any job vacancies. Be aware, however, that every lawyer working for the Corse will be extremely busy over the next few days. Actually, that might work out well for you, as there will probably be a few opportunities for work. You may use my name.'

Amery slipped the paper into a pocket. 'I am most grateful, my lord; thank you.'

'Now, what shall we do with this Abigone? I assume she is willing to commit herself to the school for at least a year?'

'Or longer, my lord. She understands the implications.'

Metrius nodded, then he pulled on a cord. A bell rang, and the clerk entered the room.

'My lord?'

'Send in Portia, if you please,' said Metrius.

The clerk bowed. 'Yes, my lord.'

'Tell me more about Upper Down,' Metrius said, once the clerk had left the room. 'Is the pass through the mountains now open for business?'

'It is, my lord,' said Amery.

'And were the Westlanders sent packing?'

'Those who survived have fled north.'

'That is good and bad for Klef Mordain,' Metrius said. 'Good, in that the raids upon the Central Provinces shall cease; and bad, as we here in the city were growing accustomed to receiving the trade that used to pass through Upper Down. Our tax receipts will be lower this year as a consequence. On the other hand, without the fear of a raid by the Westlanders, the wealthier classes in the Central Provinces might be inclined to buy more goods from us. It will take time to see if the events in Upper Down have a positive or negative effect on the city.'

There was a knock on the door, and a woman entered.

She bowed. 'You called for me, my lord?'

'Thank you for coming, Portia,' said Metrius. 'I have a task for you. My friend here has brought a certain young lady to Klef Mordain, and she needs to be escorted to the offices of Lady Fyenna.'

Portia bowed again. 'Understood, my lord.'

Metrius got to his feet. Amery took that as his cue, and also rose. He and Metrius shook hands again.

'If you would please point out the young lady to Portia when you leave,' Metrius said, 'I would be most obliged. Oh, and good luck finding yourself a job. Send me a note to let me know how it works out.'

'I will, my lord. Thank you,' said Amery.

Amery and Portia left the office, and descended the stairs to the ground floor of the building. Amery eyed Portia as they made their way to the main entrance, but the woman's expression remained guarded. They emerged out on to the busy street, and Amery led her to a carriage that was parked by the side of the road.

'The young lady in question is in there,' Amery said.

'How old is she?' said Portia.

'Eighteen.'

'That is a little old for Lady Fyenna, is it not?'

'The girl is guilty of neglecting her studies.'

Portia frowned as Amery opened the side door of the carriage.

'How did it go?' said Abigone, who was sitting inside with Lothar and Annalise.

'It went very well,' said Amery. He gestured to Portia. 'This woman will take you to where you need to be.'

'Step down from the carriage,' said Portia.

Lothar began to move, and Portia raised a hand.

'Not you,' she said. 'Just the girl.'

'Where she goes, I go,' said Lothar.

Portia turned to Amery. 'Is there going to be a scene? I presumed you had made things clear to these... people. The girl comes; the others stay.'

The interior of the carriage fell into silence.

'Do I need to call for assistance?' said Portia. 'Believe me, that would not turn out well for you. This matter is now under the authority of the Corse.'

'We should do as she says,' said Amery.

'If this woman takes her away,' said Lothar, 'then how am I supposed to protect her?'

'The Corse will protect her,' said Portia. 'This is your last chance. There are over a dozen men-at-arms in a room just inside my master's building. I will call upon them if you do not comply.'

'I will come,' said Abigone. 'Lothar, please trust me; and Annalise, thank you for all that you have done. I'm not sure when I will see you both again, but I will send word, if I can.'

Lothar glared at Portia, but he remained motionless as Abigone squeezed past him. She climbed down from the carriage, and eyed Portia.

'Luggage?' said Portia.

Abigone gestured to a small trunk strapped to the rear of the carriage.

'You will carry it,' said Portia. 'I have another carriage a few streets away; we will take that to our destination.'

'All right,' said Abigone. 'My name is...'

'I don't care. The fewer details I know, the better.'

Abigone unfastened the straps securing her trunk to the carriage, then she staggered a little under its weight. She glanced into the carriage.

'Farewell,' she said.

'This way,' said Portia.

Amery stood back as Portia led Abigone along the street. He watched them until they turned a corner, then he gazed up at Lothar, whose anger was palpable.

'We did what we had to do,' said Amery.

'If anything happens to her,' said Lothar, 'I will hold you partly responsible.'

'What shall we do now?' said Annalise. 'Our entire purpose for coming here was to serve and watch over the princess. Without her, we are simply strangers in a foreign city.'

'I will not leave Klef Mordain without Princess Abigone,' said Lothar. 'We should stay; she might need us at some point in the future. Amery, can you help us find accommodation and jobs?'

'I will do my best,' he said, 'but I will need to find a job of my own first. When I have secured myself a position, I should be able to help you both.' He withdrew the scrap of paper that Lord Metrius had given him, then he walked to the front of the carriage, where the two drivers were sitting. 'Can you take us to... *The Scriveners' Inn*, please? It's on East Norton Street, about half a mile from here.'

'No problem, sir,' said one of the drivers. 'With Lady Abigone no longer with us, will you be paying our wages from now on?'

Amery frowned. 'I can pay you to the end of the month, I suppose. After that, it depends upon me finding a job that earns enough to afford you. It would be nice to have a carriage to take me around the city. What will you do if I have to let you go?'

'We'd go back to Lesser Down, sir,' said one.

'Take me to the inn, and I will think it over,' said Amery. He climbed up into the carriage, and closed the door.

The carriage set off along the street, and Amery glanced out of the window.

'Where are we going?' said Lothar.

'I am trying to find a job,' Amery said; 'one that will pay for two drivers and the upkeep of a carriage, and one that might also find you both employment.'

'If you get a fine position,' said Annalise, 'then might I also work for you? I could housekeep, and Lothar could be your butler.'

Lothar snorted.

'It's not a terrible idea,' said Annalise. 'At least we know Amery. Think of the alternative. We might end up working for a rogue, or a ne'er-do-well.'

'I'll consider it,' said Lothar, 'if the pay is decent.'

'By all the blessed spirits,' muttered Amery. 'Are you expecting me to employ all four of you? Didn't Abigone leave any money to cover your expenses?'

'She had plenty of money,' said Lothar. 'The problem is – it was in her trunk.'

'You will lead me to poverty,' Amery said.

'Then you'd better make sure you get a good job,' said Lothar.

The carriage came to a halt after a few minutes, and Amery peered out of the window. A narrow alleyway led off from the main street, and a battered old sign was hanging from a pole – *The Scriveners' Inn.*

'That doesn't look very promising,' said Annalise. 'Perhaps Lothar should go with you, Amery, in case there is any trouble.'

'There is no need,' said Amery, as he opened the side door. 'I shouldn't be too long.'

He stepped down to the roadside, and made his way up the alley. He pushed at the inn's door, and it opened. Amery strode inside. He passed through a small vestibule, then entered a large saloon, with low ceilings and several dozen empty tables. A man glanced over from the bar.

'I wasn't expecting much custom today,' he said. 'What will you be having?'

Amery walked up to the bar. 'A glass of white, please. From Yearl, if you have any.'

'I haven't seen you in here before,' the barman said, as he poured some wine into a glass. 'That will be seven farthings.'

Amery grimaced at the price, then handed over the money. 'I was led to believe that a noticeboard hangs upon a wall somewhere in this establishment.'

'Ah, I see. That's why you here – you're looking for a job. Are you a scribe, or a notary?'

'I am a fully-qualified lawyer, certified by the Imperial College in Elestia.'

'All right; I meant no offence.' He pointed to a wall. 'The noticeboard is over there.'

Amery picked up the glass of wine and walked over to where a large board had been nailed to the wall. Upon it were pinned dozens of small slips of paper. Some were from lawyers looking to share accommodation, while others were offering positions with various law firms. The vast majority were for clerks and scribes, and Amery's eyes darted over the noticeboard. He moved a few slips, re-pinning them elsewhere, to take a look at some of the older offers. His attention fell upon one.

Experienced lawyer required, it read. *Must be on call at all hours and upon all days. An intimate knowledge of the Sanctian law code is essential.*

Written beneath was another address.

Amery smiled, then he ripped the slip of paper from the board and pushed it into his pocket. He returned to the bar, and placed his unfinished wine onto the counter.

'Are you sure about that?' said the barman.

'I confess I merely bought the wine out of courtesy,' said Amery.

'I wasn't talking about the wine; I was talking about the job offer you just removed from the board.'

Amery blinked. 'Was I not supposed to remove it? I'm interested in the position.'

'Intimate with Sanctian law, are you?'

'I have studied that subject in detail, yes.'

'Hoping they annex Klef Mordain, eh?'

'What?'

'That advertisement has been pinned up there for over a month, and not a single lawyer in this inn has ever expressed any interest in it. That's because the lawyers who drink here are patriots. What are you?'

'I… I'm sorry; I don't understand the question.'

'You're not from Klef Mordain; that's clear,' the barman said. 'On your way. If I see you in here again, I'll have you kicked out.'

Amery stared at the barman, then he turned and hurried from the inn.

Two hours later, Amery was led into a tall building hidden away in a backstreet of the Old City. The man at the door had eyed him with suspicion when he had knocked, and it had taken Amery some time to persuade him that his intentions were honest. The man escorted him into a large office, where over a dozen men and women were sitting round a table, the surface of which was littered with papers. One of the men immediately moved to cover some of the documents as Amery entered.

'We asked not to be interrupted,' the man said. 'Who is this?'

'He claims to have come about the vacant lawyer's position, my lord,' said the doorman.

The group at the table stared at Amery.

'Throw him out onto the street,' said another man. 'He's secret police.'

'I am not,' said Amery. 'I am from Yearl, and I arrived in the city yesterday. I went to *The Scriveners' Inn*, and saw your advertisement. Has the position been filled?'

One of the women smiled. 'He might actually be serious, brother. Should we interview him?'

The man across from her frowned. 'Let's make it quick; we have a hundred things to be doing right now.'

'And a lawyer would certainly help with some of it – if he can be trusted.'

The woman and the man rose to their feet.

'Let's take him into the meeting room,' said the woman. 'This shouldn't take too long.'

Amery walked with them to a door, and they passed through into a small room, whose sole window overlooked a brick-lined back alley. Amery was shown to a chair, and they all sat.

'What do you know about this job?' said the man.

Amery removed the advertisement from his pocket. 'Only what is says here, sir. I am fluent in the Sanctian law code, as well as that pertaining to the old Elestian Empire. I studied at the Imperial College in Elestia, and specialised in overlapping areas of jurisdiction.'

The woman gazed at him. 'What did the other lawyers say when you took that piece of paper from the board?'

'There were no lawyers present at the time,' said Amery, 'but the barman practically accused me of being a traitor.'

'It was the words *intimate* and *Sanctian* that caused his reaction,' said the woman. 'Besides, most of the lawyers in there would have recognised the address. Before we proceed any further, we will need to establish that you are not working for our political enemies. I would not put it beyond any of our rivals to have sent you here, in order to spy on us and cause dissension.'

'Who do you know in Klef Mordain?' said the man.

'I am a friend of Lord Metrius,' Amery said.

The man and the woman glanced at each other.

'I think this interview is at an end,' said the woman. 'Lord Metrius's political opinions are diametrically opposed to ours, and if you are his friend, then you will be of no use to us.'

'I don't understand,' said Amery. 'I am a professional lawyer. My patron's politics are of no concern to me. I have just returned from a job working in Upper Down, where I was employed by a dreadful brute. Regardless, I acted with integrity and diligence throughout the period of my employment.'

'And why did you leave Upper Down?' said the man.

'Because my employer was killed in the recent conflict there.'

'We need more than that if we are to trust you,' said the woman.

Amery nodded. If his suspicions were correct, he had stumbled upon a group in favour of Klef Mordain's annexation by the Sanctian Empire. He had a choice to make – flee at once, or press on, in the hope that any position with such a group could prove highly lucrative. It was time to play his best card.

'My great-grandmother was Princess Helena of Sanctos,' he said, 'the aunt of Emperor Antonio.'

'You are related to the imperial family?' said the man.

'Rather distantly, but yes.' He smiled. 'I am around thirty-ninth in line to the throne.'

'Would you say that you are a friend of the Sanctian Empire?' said the woman.

'Yes, in a manner of speaking. I happened to meet Lord Metrius when I was last in Klef Mordain, but our association is not close.'

'Something doesn't quite add up,' said the man. 'If you were trained at the Imperial College in Elestia, and are related to the imperial family of Sanctos, then what the blazes were you doing in a backwater like Upper Down?'

Amery took a breath. 'I shall be completely honest with you, even though it may cost me this opportunity. I had to leave Yearl in shame and disgrace, and I am forbidden from ever returning to the place of my birth. In effect, I was exiled.'

'Why?'

'I killed a fellow lawyer. It was an accident, but an accident caused by my anger. The man insulted my mother, and I struck him. Unfortunately, he hit his head when he fell, and expired before me. His family demanded that I be executed, but the courts granted mercy upon me, and commuted the sentence to exile. After that, I wandered the Central Provinces for a while, visiting Klef Mordain, before I was offered a position in Upper Down. Should I leave?'

The man and woman remained silent for a moment, then the man shook his head. 'Not yet. You might be what we are looking for. Are you prepared to work long hours?'

'Yes.'

'Would you be willing to take a vow of secrecy?' said the woman.

'Of course. Any work I carry out would be with the strictest confidentiality.'

'We do not do anything illegal here,' the woman went on, 'but we are well aware that the cause we promote is unpopular. If we were to offer you the position, you would be wise to keep it to yourself, or you might attract the ire of others, especially the secret police. They have been known to raid these offices from time to time.'

'May I know the nature of the cause you are promoting?'

'Why don't you take a guess?' said the man.

'Very well. You advocate for Klef Mordain to join the Sanctian Empire. Am I correct?'

'You are.'

'Let me make something clear to you,' Amery said; 'I have no particular opinion one way or the other regarding this cause. However, if you were to offer me a job as a lawyer, I would obey your instructions without question. I am, at heart, a consummate professional, and I would apply all of my abilities to assist you.'

'The job is yours, if you want it,' said the woman.

Amery smiled. 'Thank you.'

'We are offering three thousand sovereigns per month as remuneration,' said the man. 'Does that sound reasonable?'

'It is more than reasonable, sir. I accept.'

'When can you start?'

'I need to find accommodation within the Old City, but I could begin work tomorrow.'

'Can you begin tonight?' said the woman. 'The Corse is...' She glanced at the man, who nodded. 'The Corse is conducting its elections tomorrow. They happen every five years, and all five thousand members of the Corse have a vote. It is imperative that as many pro-Sanctians are elected as possible. Do you know how to operate a printing press?'

'I do.'

'Make your way back here to these offices at sunset this evening,' the man said, 'and we will put you to work. It will be a long night, and an even longer day tomorrow, when the voting takes place. And then there shall be the count, which we shall be observing, to ensure its fairness. It is likely that you will not be able to go to bed for a couple of days. Are you up to it?'

For that amount of money, Amery thought, he would do almost anything.

'I am,' he said.

'We have a contract for you to sign, and then we shall need to hear your vow,' said the woman.

'I am ready.'

'It is probably time for some introductions, sister,' said the man. 'This, Amery, is Lady Ursula; and I am Lord Tain. We are ship owners, as well as political activists. One of us is a member of the Corse, but we will not tell you which of us, not yet at any rate.'

Amery inclined his head. 'It is an honour to meet you both.'

Lady Ursula smiled. 'Welcome to the Second Empire Association.'

CHAPTER 3
DUTY AND PRIVILEGE

Old City, Klef Mordain – 5th Day of Saluna 108

'Name?' said the clerk.

'Fyenna of Liliacos.'

The clerk ran his finger down a long sheet of parchment until he found her name, then he marked the page with ink. He reached into a drawer and passed her a voting slip, stamped with the seal of the Corse.

'Is this your first vote?' he said.

'It is.'

'Write down a single name on the ballot paper, fold it in half, and drop it into the bell.'

Fyenna nodded, then she walked over to the side of the hall, where a dozen small voting booths had been set up. She walked into one, and picked up a pencil that was lying on a little table. She leaned over the paper, and wrote *Lord Metrius*, then she folded the paper in half. She set the pencil down, and walked out of the booth. Four soldiers were standing guard next to a huge upturned bell in the centre of the hall. Small stools had been arranged between the soldiers, and Fyenna stood on one, and dropped her voting slip into the bell's interior. She smiled to herself. After four years of being in the Corse, she had finally been able to take part in one of its arcane voting procedures.

Unlike most members of the Corse, she had no inherited wealth, nor had she built up any businesses, or owned any land or ships. She had been elevated through merit alone, after her performance in the famed Battle of Hader Pull, when the invading Westlander army had been annihilated. The proudest moment of her forty-seven years of life had been when she had received a letter informing her that she had been selected to take the place of a deceased member of the Corse. That was the way it worked – its membership was kept static at five thousand, and no one could join until someone died or left the city forever.

She strode out of the voting hall, and smiled as she saw a group of her friends waiting for her in the marble-lined vestibule.

'How did it feel, Fyenna?' said one.

'Good,' she said. 'After so many years of wondering what lay inside that hall, now I know.'

'Yes, a great, big bell!' said another.

'That bell is four hundred years old,' said a woman. 'It was cast for the Celestial Bridge, but the tower meant to hold it was replaced by the statue that stands there today.'

One of the men frowned. 'Did you all hear what happened to Lord Denon?'

'We heard,' said Fyenna.

'It was the out-going government's last act before it dissolved itself for the election,' the man went on.

'Everyone has known for a long time that Denon was acting as a spy,' said Fyenna. 'He shouldn't have tried to return to the city.'

'The Sanctian ambassador has submitted a formal complaint,' said the man. 'I worry where this will lead. If the Sanctians decide to move their fleet up to Klef Mordain, how should we respond? We cannot defend the city against ships armed with cannon.'

'I heard something else about the incident that claimed Denon's life,' said a woman. 'Apparently, he was sitting with a group of foreigners in a tavern when he was apprehended. The foreigners were released after questioning, and guess what? One of them was a damn princess. An actual princess, who had entered Klef Mordain without notifying the Corse in advance.'

'What princess?' said Fyenna.

'Her name is Abigone, I believe.'

'From where?'

'Oh, some remote mountain realm.'

'It was Upper Down,' said a man. 'I can confirm the story. Agents followed the princess after she and her companions were released, and tailed them all the way to the Old City. They found lodgings, and the agents waited outside all night, but nothing happened.' He smiled. 'Can anyone guess where they went yesterday?'

'Where?' said Fyenna.

'Lord Metrius's office,' said the man. 'Their carriage was seen parked outside, and a man entered the building. Twenty minutes later, the same man emerged with Portia – do you know of her? – and then Portia took Abigone away. The agents were then ordered to stop following them.'

'Why?' said a woman.

'Presumably because Portia knows what she's doing. She is a colonel in the secret police, after all.'

'I hope she didn't murder the poor girl,' said another man.

'If she did, then she would have had reasonable cause.'

'I should go,' said Fyenna.

'Aren't you joining us for lunch?'

'I'd love to, but I have to return to my place of work.'

'I thought your place of work was closed today?

'It is,' said Fyenna, 'but I have just remembered something that I need to do.'

'Will you be back here for this evening's count?'

'Should I? I hadn't planned to come back. There is absolutely no chance that I will be one of the five hundred elected, praise the spirits. I would be bewildered if I garnered a single vote.'

A few of her friends laughed.

'How do you think you were selected for the Corse in the first place?' said a woman. 'You know the procedure for picking new members – we vote on it. You are a war hero and, at forty-seven, you are one of the youngest members of the Corse. I think you might be underestimating your chances, my dear Fyenna.'

'I hope you're joking,' she said. 'I'm far too busy to spend the next five years in the government. Who would look after my... place of work?'

'We all know where it is that you work, Fyenna,' said a man. 'There is no need to obfuscate.'

'I was always told that there are certain things we should never mention,' Fyenna said. 'My place of work is one of them. If any of the pro-Sanctian members of the Corse discovered what I do, they would leak the information to our enemies. I cannot allow that to happen.'

'Yes, you are quite right,' said the man. 'Forgive me.'

'Remember that voting ceases at sunset, Fyenna,' said a woman; 'and the count begins after that. It only takes a couple of hours, and then the results are announced.'

'I will see if I have time,' she said

She inclined her head towards the group, and set off down a corridor. She descended a flight of stairs, and took one of the tunnels that ran under the Corsehall. The nondescript building had no main entrance, and was instead accessed by a multitude of inconspicuous side doors, and via the network of tunnels that led to other locations in the Old City. It was all to keep the location of the Corse headquarters a secret, and Fyenna was sure that almost no one outwith the Corse even knew that an election was taking place that day.

She took the stairs at the end of the tunnel, and emerged into the bathroom of the local library. She closed the door behind her, which had a sign that read *Staff Only*, and made her way through the quiet building, passing the tall bookshelves, and smiling at the librarian on the way out. She glanced up at the sky. It was another beautiful morning in Klef Mordain, with only a few wisps of cloud. The sun felt warm on her skin as she walked along the street towards her place of work. If anything, the location of her workplace was a more heavily guarded secret than that of the Corsehall. People had been executed in the past for saying too much about it, and Fyenna was always careful never to mention any details, not even to her husband. One never knew when a secret police officer might be listening.

She slipped down a narrow alley between two bakeries, and came to a rundown building. She glanced back at the way she had come, then unlocked the door and entered. The interior of the building was far more luxurious than the exterior, and she walked over the thick carpets and into her office on the ground floor. She had barely got through the door when her secretary appeared.

'My lady,' he said, 'a potential new student has been waiting for some time to see you.'

'I know, Rupert,' said Fyenna. 'That is why I am here. When did she arrive?'

'Yesterday morning, my lady,' Rupert said. 'We thought you would be here.'

'I was detained on Corse business.'

'We placed her in temporary accommodation overnight.'

'Where?'

'Upstairs, in one of the spare rooms.'

'Has she interacted in any way with the other students?'

'No, my lady. We have been keeping her isolated.'

Fyenna took off her coat and handed it to her secretary, who hung it from a peg on the wall.

'Make a pot of coffee, Rupert, and then bring her here,' she said.

The secretary bowed his head. 'Yes, my lady.'

Fyenna took her seat as the secretary left her office. She shook her head in annoyance at herself. She had been so taken up with the voting process, that she had forgotten about her new student. And, thanks to what she had heard in the vestibule, she was now aware of the student's identity. She had seen the message left for her by Portia on the previous morning, explaining that she had brought someone from the office of Lord Metrius. Was Fyenna about to interview a real princess?

The door opened again, and Rupert walked in. He set a tray down onto Fyenna's desk, and the aroma of fresh coffee filled the air. Her secretary then gestured towards a young woman, who entered the room. Fyenna frowned at her.

'This can't be right,' she said. 'She's too old.'

'I have been waiting here for over a day,' said the young woman, 'and that's all you have to say to me?'

'Did I give you permission to speak?' said Fyenna. 'If you talk again without being asked a direct question, then I will have you confined to your room for the rest of the day with no food.'

The young woman stared at her.

Fyenna nodded to her secretary. 'Leave us.'

Rupert bowed and left the room, easing the door shut behind him.

'Sit down,' said Fyenna.

The young woman sat.

'Let me make one thing clear, Abigone of Upper Down,' Fyenna went on: 'I don't care if you are a princess. I will not be referring to you by any high-blown title, nor will you be receiving any preferential treatment due to a mere accident of birth. Do you understand?'

'Yes.'

'Wipe that surly expression off your face, girl. I am Lady Fyenna, and you shall refer to me as *ma'am* from now on. I am the Head Maker of this school, which means that, as far as you are concerned, I might as well be your lord and master. I have complete authority over the students, the coursework, and everything else that goes on inside this building. I also have the authority to reject your application to enrol as a student. Give me one good reason why I shouldn't.'

'I... I want to learn, ma'am.'

'What do you want to learn?'

'I want to learn how to become a good Maker.'

'Why?'

'The spirits gave me a gift, ma'am,' she said, 'and it seems wrong to neglect it.'

'You already seem to have been neglecting it. The vast majority of Makers who arrive at this school are fourteen. What age are you?'

'Eighteen, ma'am.'

Fyenna reached over to one of her shelves and picked up a few items. She turned back to Abigone.

'This is your first test,' she said, 'and I will be judging your performance.' She began to place the items onto the surface of her desk. 'We have a block of wood, an ingot of iron, and a piece of charcoal. Summon a simple knife for me. The handle must be of wood, and the blade of steel. Proceed.'

Abigone stared at the three items in front of her.

'What are you waiting for?' said Fyenna.

Abigone's hands started to tremble.

'Either you are a Maker, or you are a liar,' said Fyenna. 'If you are a liar, you will be dead within the hour; is that clear?'

'I will try, ma'am,' said Abigone, her voice a mere whisper. She extended a hand over the items. 'Blessed spirits,' she said, 'with your permission, summon for me a knife.'

There was a rough crackle, and the three items disintegrated. In their place, a misshapen block of wood intermingled with pieces of iron and charcoal appeared a few inches above the desk. It fell, and split apart upon landing.

'That was pathetic,' said Fyenna, 'but at least I know you are not a liar. Tell me; how is it that you are so stupid?'

Abigone looked as though she was about to burst into tears. 'I haven't trained.'

'That is exactly what I mean. I am not calling you stupid because you cannot summon a knife; I am calling you stupid because it is clear that you have neglected your studies for several years. By eighteen, you should be proficient enough to summon a simple tool, even if you had barely scratched the surface of your studies. You know, I have heard of your sister – Kilbride. She made a name for herself during the short time she was in Lesser Down, which, as you should know, is our neighbour to the south. She has a reputation for wisdom and cunning. How was it that she did not oversee your training?'

'I didn't tell her that I was a Maker until the autumn of last year, ma'am. After that, she forced me to read every book in the palace library on the subject. And then she sent me here.'

Fyenna shook her head. 'I pity Kilbride for having a sister as useless as you.'

Anger rolled over Abigone's features. 'It was I who destroyed Prince Valentino's sixty cannon,' she cried. 'I saved Upper Down from the Sanctians. I doubt they would call me useless.'

Fyenna smiled. 'That little outburst will earn you your first punishment, girl. Still, I admit to being a little intrigued by this. How exactly did you deal with the cannon?'

'I went up to the top of the cliff, ma'am,' she said, 'and I asked the spirits to summon as many stone dragons as I was able. They... they didn't look much like dragons, but it was enough to bury the cannon under tons of rock.'

'How many times did you have to repeat this process to bury all sixty?'

'Once was enough.'

Fyenna blinked. 'You little liar. You cannot summon a knife, but you claim to have summoned enough rock to obliterate sixty cannon?'

'That's what happened, ma'am. Kilbride was my witness. I am not a liar.'

Fyenna sat back in her chair. She had heard a few rumours about the rockslide that had ended Valentino's siege of Upper Down, but she refused to believe that Abigone had done it on her own, with only a single summoning. She thought through her options. If she rejected the girl's application, then Portia would come to collect her, and Abigone's body would probably be found floating in the bay within a few days. Her political instincts took over. If she allowed the secret police to murder Kilbride's sister, then the diplomatic ramifications would be unpredictable. Kilbride would soon demand to know what had happened to her younger sibling, and, as usual, the city authorities would deny all knowledge of her. Klef Mordain was already short of allies; was there any need to generate a new enemy?

'What is Upper Down's present attitude towards the Sanctian Empire?' she said.

Abigone frowned. 'We negotiated a treaty with them that guaranteed our independence, ma'am. Prince Valentino was not pleased, but he had no choice but to accept.'

'And what did you have to give away in exchange?'

'We had to open the Kendril Pass to all traffic, ma'am.'

'What else?'

'That was all. Oh, we had to promise not to allow the Westlanders to use our territory as a base to raid the south, but that was fine, as all three regents wanted the Westlanders out. We also had to hand over a hostage – Princess Hygilt – but that was fine, too, as we agreed that my father should never have abducted her in the first place.'

'Are you in favour of Upper Down being annexed into the Sanctian Empire?'

'Of course not. Why would I want that? Sorry. Why would I want that, ma'am?'

'And what about Kilbride? Do you think she would like to see Upper Down join the empire?'

'Absolutely not, ma'am. My sister is determined to keep the realm free for the boy king to inherit, once he is old enough. He might even be a Master. His father was, and so was his grandfather King Alfgang the Great. He was my father, and he made me promise not to tell anyone that I was a Maker. That's why I kept it a secret for so long. He thought it would hurt my marriage prospects, but…'

'Stop talking,' said Fyenna. 'This is not an idle chitchat, girl. I am facing a decision regarding your future – should you live, or should you die – and you are prattling on about all kinds of nonsense.'

Abigone's eyes widened, and she fell silent.

'Can you give me an assurance,' Fyenna went on, 'that you will work hard, apply yourself, and, most importantly, that you will obey every instruction given to you by me, or by the other teacher who works here?'

Abigone nodded. 'Yes, ma'am.'

'Then you may join the school. I will, of course, need to put you into a class that befits your lack of skills and experience. We have two fourteen-year-old sisters starting with us this term – you will be put with them.'

'Might I ask how many students there are in the school, ma'am?'

'Five, including you. We have a sixteen-year-old, who will be beginning her third year here, and a fifteen-year-old, who will be entering her second year. Both are already miles ahead of where you are. The other two are the fourteen-year-olds I mentioned. The majority of the classes are held within this building, and you are not to leave it without my express permission. You will eat here, sleep here, and study here. Around a quarter of the classes are mixed with the boys from the Master school, and...'

'There's a Master school?'

Fyenna narrowed her eyes.

'Sorry, ma'am,' said Abigone.

'That is twice you have interrupted me,' said Fyenna. 'As a punishment, you will be given no food for the rest of the day. You will also be confined to your room, where I expect you to begin reading the textbooks that have been assigned to you. Classes start the day after tomorrow, as soon as breakfast is over. Dismissed.'

Abigone stood. She looked a little surprised.

'Might I speak, ma'am?' she said.

'If it's about the food, then no,' said Fyenna. 'This school is run on discipline, and you will accept your punishments with grace.'

'It wasn't about that,' said Abigone. 'I just wanted to thank you for allowing me to enrol, ma'am.'

Fyenna half-smiled. 'I didn't do it for you, girl. In truth, I don't like you, and I think that you lack the requisite determination to succeed here. However, I do not wish to spark a diplomatic incident with Upper Down. If you must thank anyone, thank your sister.'

Abigone inclined her head, then she left the room.

Fyenna rolled her eyes, then she reached into a drawer for an enrolment form, and began to fill it out.

. . .

The sun had set by the time Fyenna was next interrupted. Her secretary knocked on the door and entered.

'My lady,' Rupert said, 'you have a visitor.'

'Who?' said Fyenna.

'Lady Niscoll of Mordana, ma'am.'

'Show her in.'

Fyenna sorted out her paperwork as she waited for her friend to appear. The door opened again, and Niscoll strode in, a strange light in her eyes.

'I thought you were planning on staying at the count this evening,' said Fyenna, as Niscoll took a seat.

'The count is over,' said Niscoll. 'The five hundred have been selected.'

'That was quick.'

'The counts often are. Lord Metrius has been re-elected, as we had hoped.'

'I had no doubt that he would make it into the five hundred,' said Fyenna. 'How many pro-Sanctians were chosen?'

'At least a hundred and twenty; perhaps more,' said Niscoll.

Fyenna cursed under her breath. 'That's the highest total they have ever managed, as far as I know.'

'Yes, but it remains a way short of a majority. We are assuming that their votes were highly tactical, as they were quite evenly spread among their candidates. Perhaps those idiots in the Second Empire Association actually learnt something from their failure at the last election. Regardless, the five hundred will now move on to the second step – the selection of the thirty members of the government that will rule Klef Mordain for the next five years. An assembly will take place the day after tomorrow, and all five hundred have been ordered to attend.'

'Should you be telling me this?' said Fyenna. 'Aren't these details supposed to be kept secret from all but the five hundred?'

Niscoll smiled. 'You are quite correct.'

Fyenna's eyes widened. 'Were you elected?'

'I was. As were you.'

'No. Is it hot in here, or is it just me?'

Niscoll laughed. 'We received nine votes each, Fyenna. Like it or not, you will be on the five hundred for the next five years. I was dispatched here to bring you the good news.'

Fyenna placed her elbows onto her desk and put her head in her hands.

'This can't be happening,' she said. 'The school term starts in two day's time. I am needed here.'

'No offence, but I doubt that you will be elected onto the government of thirty,' said Niscoll. 'Whatever job you happen to receive, I'm sure you will be able to continue working in the school.'

'Does everyone in the five hundred receive a job?'

'No, not all. Once the thirty have been elected, they hide themselves away, and select another seventy for the junior government roles – tax collectors, secret projects, administrators, and so on. The remaining four hundred then are put through a ballot for a place on one of the auditing committees. There are two hundred and forty chosen that way. That leaves one hundred and sixty with no official role. They remain on stand-by for the entire five year term of government, to fill any role that becomes vacant through death or illness.'

'You were selected to the five hundred once before, yes?'

'That's right; fifteen years ago. I was given a place on the auditing committee overseeing the work done by the secret police. It took up about one day a week. This time, I am hoping for something with a little more responsibility.'

Fyenna smiled. 'Are you angling for my vote?'

'We will both vote as Lord Metrius decides, you know that. He has an excellent chance of making it into the government, and we need him there. No one else in the city can be depended upon to resist the advances of the Sanctians like Lord Metrius.'

'I hope I make it on to the stand-by list.'

'Do you? Why? You are a member of the Corse, and that brings duties as well as privileges, Fyenna. The city needs people like you – people who will fight with the same spirit that you displayed at the Battle of Hader Pull. You are still young – a mere forty-seven – and this will not be the only time you are elected to the five hundred. Accept whatever role you are given with good faith, and do your best.'

'Forgive me; I was thinking of my students. I have five this year, including three with no prior knowledge or experience. They will need a lot of time and attention lavished on them if they are to make progress. What am I allowed to tell my husband?'

'Nothing. You know the rules. The identities of those on the five hundred, and those in the government of thirty must never be disclosed to anyone who is not a member of the Corse. Have you said anything to him about the vote that was held today?'

'No. I didn't mention it.'

'Good. Make sure you keep it that way. Oh, I almost forgot to tell you about the remuneration package. All members of the five hundred are entitled to receive an extra thousand sovereigns a month from the Corse to cover their expenses – even those on stand by.' She smiled. 'Presumably, the thirty get more.' She got to her feet. 'I shall see myself out. Be sure to attend the Corsehall at dawn the day after tomorrow. I will see you there.'

Niscoll strode to the door and left the office. Fyenna stared at the empty chair for a few moments, her thoughts spinning. She had fully expected to have received little or no votes from the five thousand members of the Corse. It was Lord Metrius's doing – there was no other explanation. He wanted her on the five hundred for some reason, but what?

CHAPTER 4
SON AND HEIR

Nether Hall, Klef Mordain – 6th Day of Saluna 108

'Forget not what the Sanctians have done to us, my son,' said the tall, well-built man, his face obscured in the thick shadows of the room. 'They beheaded my father, and forced my brother to kneel before them, before they paraded him in chains through the streets of their cities. My brother died alone, in the dungeons of the Sanctian emperor, his body broken, his proud spirit vanquished. They stole our kingdom – our birthright – and turned it into another province of their criminal empire. Our people strain under their yoke, longing to be free; longing for our family to reclaim the throne that was taken from us.'

'Is that true, Father?' said the young man. 'Do they really yearn for our return? We were an independent realm for only a few decades; before that, Geathan was part of the Elestian Empire.'

'And before that?' his father said, the anger in his tone unmistakable. 'The Kingdom of Geathan has existed ever since people first settled there, thousands of years ago. We were a proud nation, a free nation, subjected to overlordship by the Elestians for centuries, and now the Sanctians are doing the same thing. A governor appointed by Emperor Antonio rules our homeland – of course the people would prefer a native Geathian monarch to the Sanctians. Never doubt that, my son. You are my only child, and you are also the heir to the throne of Geathan. I will never be king. I have made my peace with that; but you, Mor Dennahelm? You are fated for greater things.'

'My grandfather was the last king of that realm.'

'I know that, son.'

'But my other grandfather is Emperor Antonio,' he said. 'My mother, she... she always taught me that I was half-Sanctian, and that the empire was a force for good in the world. She...'

'Speak no more of your mother, boy,' said his father. 'She and I were locked in a loveless marriage for over twenty years. Can you possibly imagine the shame I endured, having to wed the daughter of the Sanctian emperor? For two long decades, I had to pretend that I was happy to be married into the imperial family, as though it were an honour and a privilege, rather than the most abject humiliation. I had to keep my mouth closed, lest I allow my inner feelings to reveal the torment of my heart. I had to watch in silence as you, my only son, were nurtured and educated by Sanctians. The pain I felt seeing you dressed up in imperial uniforms and robes struck me no less than the murder of my father. They were trying to make you one of them. They even tried to rob you of your true name, calling you *Denny*, instead of *Mor Dennahelm*. They were trying to mould you into a good little Sanctian. They failed. You will never be one of them.'

Denny lowered his gaze.

'It may not seem like this to you, my son,' his father went on, 'but what happened is a blessing. It is true that we have wandered the land for a year, homeless and in constant danger of discovery, but I would rather that than have seen you come of age in Sanctos. Instead, you celebrated your eighteenth birthday hundreds of miles from home. And now we are here, in Klef Mordain, where you will be transformed into the man you were destined to be.'

'Do you think the emperor is looking for us?'

'You are one of his grandsons; of course the emperor is looking for you. He will be looking for me, too. He will think that I abducted you from Sanctos against your will; but, my son, they will be looking in the wrong place. They will imagine that I have taken you back to Geathan, to plot an uprising of the people – they will not be searching for us in Klef Mordain. As cold and unfriendly as this city is, it remains free from Sanctian influence. We could hide here for a hundred years without anyone knowing your true identity.'

'Will I ever see my mother again?'

'I cannot answer that. Even if you were to see her at some point in the future, it might be as enemies. If we are successful, and you reclaim the throne of Geathan, then the Sanctians will deem us mortal foes. And, when the emperor finally discovers the truth about you – that you are a Master – his loathing for you will know no bounds. Had he discovered this while you were still on Sanctos, you would have been executed.'

'We don't know that for certain.'

'Don't be so naïve. Antonio keeps his feelings to himself, except in this one regard – he abhors all Masters and Makers, and wishes to see them annihilated from the face of the world. His horror at discovering he has a grandson who is a Master would have sent him into a paroxysm of rage; yet you doubt he would have had you executed? Fleeing was the only choice open to us.'

'I managed to keep my Master abilities a secret for nearly three years,' the young man said. 'If you hadn't found out, then I could have maintained the deception for even longer. And what would my mother have said, had she learned the truth? I do not believe she would have told the emperor.'

'You might be right about your mother,' the man said, 'but that is irrelevant. Had any lowly palace guard or courtier witnessed your abilities, then you and I would be hanging from a gallows.'

'They wouldn't have executed you.'

The man shook his head. 'For all the things they taught you in school, it seems they neglected to instil any wisdom into that head of yours. There are no Masters or Makers anywhere within the imperial bloodline, my son; therefore, your abilities must have passed down through the royal line of Geathan. My grandfather's sister was a Maker;

is that not proof enough? If the emperor had discovered that I could father a Master, he would have done everything in his power to ensure that I fathered no more.'

The man got up from his chair, and walked across the small room to its only window. He peered through the gaps in the closed shutters, his features striped in light and shade.

'Where are they?' he muttered. 'They should have returned by now.'

Denny glanced at his father. He had barely known him while growing up on Sanctos; he had been a distant presence, always there, but remaining in the background. The other younger members of the imperial family had referred to him as the *Reluctant Prince* – a man who acted as though he despised his own rank and station.

'Have you thought of a new name?' his father said.

'No.'

'I have one for you.'

'Can I not go by *Denny*?'

'Denny is a repugnant bastardisation of your actual name, and it is what your Sanctian cousins called you. It would be wise to pretend that you are from somewhere in the Central Provinces – Yearl, perhaps, or Campsie. Even Aubruk would suffice. The name I have thought of is more common in those parts, and your accent is rounded enough for such a deception to be believable.'

Denny smiled. 'Well, Father, are you going to tell me what it is?'

'It is Valiance,' his father said. 'That is the name you will use as soon as you leave this house. Valiance of Campsie. The secret police will no doubt question you before you are allowed to join the school. Tell them nothing but your new name, and refuse to go into any detail. The authorities running Klef Mordain will not care too much about your past – they are greedy for Masters and Makers; but they will take great exception if they uncover your true heritage. Never speak of Sanctos or Geathan in their presence, and never reveal your true name to anyone. This city is cruel and ruthless – they will not hesitate to use you for political means if they discover Antonio's grandson is a Master. Once you have been trained, that is when we can reveal your secret to the world.'

His father smiled as he peered through the window slats. 'Here they come – at last.'

He walked over to the front door of the small house, and unlocked it. He opened the door, and two men walked in, the same two men who had been accompanying them since they had fled from Sanctos the previous year.

'Mor Galthide,' said one, bowing as he entered, 'we have done as you have asked.'

'You have my thanks, Ter Angla,' said Denny's father. 'Do you have the address of the school?'

'No, my lord.'

Mor Galthide closed and relocked the door as soon as both men were in the room. 'Why not?'

'That information is a closely guarded secret, my lord. No amount of gold could persuade our contact to divulge the address. However, we have managed to secure an interview for your son, with the secretary of a member of the Corse.'

'A mere secretary?'

'Yes, my lord. Our contact said that the membership of the Corse is another secret. The most he was prepared to tell us is that there are five thousand citizens of Klef Mordain within the ranks of the Corse, but all government and military roles within are never revealed to outsiders.'

Mor Galthide frowned. 'Then no one knows the name of the ruler of this city?'

'No one but an inner circle within the Corse, my lord. All political business is conducted in secret.'

'We did well to squeeze an interview out of them, my lord,' said the other man. 'The contact asked us all manner of questions that we refused to answer – questions about your noble son, such as his name and place of birth, and his family connections. At one point, I thought he was going to walk away leaving us nothing.'

'He is suspicious,' said Ter Angla, 'as are many in this city, or so it seems. I would expect there to be a secret police presence at the interview. I got the feeling our contact thought we might be spies.'

Denny got to his feet. 'When is the interview?'

'Midnight tonight, my young lord,' said Ter Angla. He removed a slip of paper from a pocket. 'The address is written here.'

Denny took the piece of paper and read the words: *Star Inn, Goodsworth Street, Old City.*

'An inn?' he said.

'The contact insisted upon the meeting being held in a public place, my lord; otherwise, he told us, the secretary would not attend. If you pass the initial tests, then the interview will be moved to a more discreet location.'

'What tests?'

Ter Angla inclined his head. 'That wasn't made clear to us, my lord.'

'Presumably,' said Mor Galthide, 'they wish to make certain that you are a Master, and that you are not a Sanctian spy, my son.'

'On the subject of Sanctian spies, my lord,' said Ter Angla, 'there was an incident over by the Great Northern Highway a few days ago. A man was dragged out from a tavern and executed for espionage. No arrest, no trial. His body is hanging from a lamppost, or so they say.'

'Such is the way of justice in Klef Mordain,' said Mor Galthide. 'This is a city of secret police, where everyone is an informer. What an inauspicious place for a school.'

'My lord,' said Ter Angla, 'your noble son should get ready to depart. We have hired a cart to carry him all the way to the Old City, but the journey across Klef Mordain will take at least two hours. He should set off soon if he is to reach the inn by midnight.'

'A cart? My son is to ride on a cart?'

'A peddler's cart, my lord. He was the only man we could find who was willing to undertake the journey at this hour. The carriage operators refused, as soon as they heard our Geathian accents.'

'This damn city,' said Mor Galthide. 'Ter Angla, you will accompany my son to his interview, and defend him if necessary.'

'It would be an honour, my lord.'

Mor Galthide turned to his son. 'My boy, my sole hope for the future – in you I have placed all my dreams, all my pride in our homeland. With you as the rightful king, Geathan shall once again be free. But first, you must learn how to control and develop your abilities. I wish there was some other way; a way that would not involve us being separated. But, you are a man now, and it is time for you to make your own way in the world. Remember all that I have told you. Stay out of trouble, study hard, and never lose sight of our purpose. Now, pack your things, but take nothing that might link you to Sanctos or Geathan.'

Denny nodded, then he walked into the tiny room where he had a bed. He opened the bag that he had been using since they had left Sanctos, and filled it full of clothes. His father had been over-cautious in his advice – as Denny had nothing remaining from his old life. His clothes were threadbare and cheap, unlike the rich robes he had worn in the imperial palaces of Sanctos, and even his boots were falling apart. His books had all been left behind in the rush to flee the island with his father, and he owned nothing that reminded him of his mother.

He tied the cords on the bag to close it, and then he sat on the bed in the gloom.

He loved his father, but did that mean they wanted the same things? Fleeing Sanctos had seemed like a matter of life and death; but did that translate into a desire to reclaim his grandfather's old throne? Geathan had been notorious as a squalid, backward place between the eras of the Elestian and Sanctian Empires – a poor nation struggling to forge its own path, riddled with bandits that terrorised the countryside, and pirates that preyed upon nearby shipping. The economy had collapsed, and famine, a thing unknown during the long period of the Elestian Empire, had resurfaced, along with rampant disease and soul-crushing poverty. All of that had abated after it had been absorbed into the welcoming bosom of the Sanctian Empire, and the province was once again stable and prosperous. Of course, Denny knew that his version of history had been taken from Sanctian textbooks, but he had been inculcated with a fierce sense that *empire* was a *good thing*, that its blessings benefited the ruled as much as the rulers. Had the short-lived Kingdom of Geathan really been so bad?

His father's opinion was the polar opposite of what the history books had said. Mor Galthide's belief that Geathan was better off alone was not one he ever questioned, yet he had been torn from that nation as a youth of fifteen. His father the king had been executed, and his elder brother, the heir to the throne, had died in a dungeon, leaving Mor Galthide alone in Sanctos. It was imperial policy to integrate the former ruling families of their new provinces into Antonio's bloodline, supplying aristocratic husbands and wives for his many descendants; and, after having first served in the ranks of the imperial army, Mor Galthide had gone to Antonio's youngest daughter. Forced into the army at eighteen, married at twenty-six, and a father at twenty-eight, it had seemed to imperial observers that Antonio's policy had been successful; and yet, beneath the surface, Mor Galthide had wanted nothing more than to revolt against his wife's family. And, in his son, he had found his weapon.

Denny got to his feet and shouldered his bag, then he walked back into the other room.

'I'm ready,' he said.

The three men turned to gaze at him.

'I have given Ter Angla enough gold to pay for your first year at the school,' his father said.

'I thought the school was free to attend.'

'It is, my son, but your food and lodgings must be accounted for. We do not take charity, and the Old City is an expensive place to live. I will remain here, in this humble cottage, and watch your progress from afar. If you need anything, send Ter Angla to me.' He paused, and his eyes softened a little. 'Mor Dennahelm, my only son, know that I love you, and that I am very proud of you. I know you will not let me down.'

He reached out with his strong arms, and they embraced.

'Now be on your way,' Mor Galthide said.

'Farewell, Father,' he said.

They walked to the door, and his father unlocked it. Ter Angla bowed his head, then he led Denny out onto the quiet backstreet, where long rows of cottages stood. The door closed behind them, and Denny heard the key turn in the lock.

'This way, Valiance,' said Ter Angla.

Denny did not respond, his mind on the journey he was about to take.

Ter Angla smiled. 'Valiance?'

Denny blinked. 'Oh, that's me, isn't it?'

'It is the name I shall be calling you from now on. I will also be omitting to call you *my lord*, for which I apologise in advance. Your noble father was very clear about this.'

'Then who are you supposed to be?'

'You can refer to me by my real name, but make out that you hired me as your servant and assistant when you arrived in Klef Mordain. My accent gives away my Geathian roots, and I am too old to change it.'

Denny followed Ter Angla along the alleyway, and they turned left at a main road. A few taverns and shops were open for business, and the street was busy in the lamplight. A small cart harnessed to two ponies was parked in front of a three-storey apartment block, and an old man was watching them from the narrow driver's bench.

'This is the boy I was telling you about,' said Ter Angla, as they approached.

'He looks old enough to be a man,' said the driver.

'I will also be coming,' said Ter Angla.

The driver shrugged. 'Hop up onto the back, and we'll get going.'

Denny and Ter Angla clambered up onto the flat bed of the cart, and gripped the sides. The driver pulled on the reins, and the ponies set off, their iron-shod hooves clattering off the cobbles.

'We'll make for the Great Northern Highway,' said the driver. 'At this time of the evening, it'll be the quickest route to the Old City.'

'I don't care which way you go,' said Ter Angla, 'as long as we reach the *Star Inn* by midnight.'

. . .

They made slow going at first, but their speed increased when they reached the wide, straight Great Northern Highway. The road began hundreds of miles to the south in the old imperial capital of the Elestian Empire, and extended into the far reaches of the sparsely-populated north. Klef Mordain was the only major roadside settlement north of the mountains; and some said it was the only city worthy of the name in the entire Northern Provinces. Tribes of savage Westlanders had tried to conquer the city several times, as they had spread across the north, but Klef Mordain had repelled every assault.

Denny watched as the cart passed countless numbers of side streets, houses and businesses, the scale of the city matching anything on Sanctos. Unlike the cities on Sanctos, however, Klef Mordain had an ungainly, lived-in appearance, as though it were not ashamed to show its rougher edges. Slums stood side-by-side with palatial villas, and armed soldiers were patrolling in far greater quantities than seen on Sanctos. Executed criminals hung from many lampposts, each with a placard hanging over their chests denoting the crime for which they had been found guilty – *Thief*, *Murderer*, *Forger*, *Rapist*, *Arsonist* – the list went on. Some of the bodies had been exposed to the elements for longer than others, and crows pecked at the grisly remains, while rats and flies feasted upon whatever had dripped or trickled onto the cobbles beneath the bodies of the victims. Each criminal had been executed in the same manner, with a vertical slash from their neck to their waist, and their maggot-infested guts were hanging out, adding to the odour that hung over the city like a thick shroud.

'So much death,' Denny muttered.

'It's cheaper than building prisons,' said their driver; 'and it's what the bastards deserve. Everyone knows the rules in Klef Mordain, and everyone can see what happens to those who break the rules.'

The Old City sat upon a small peninsula, and an ancient wall sealed it off from the rest of Klef Mordain. The Great Northern Highway went through a large gatehouse set into the wall, and soldiers were standing guard by the open gates. They glanced at the cart as it approached, but remained at their posts, and the driver steered the ponies through the arched entrance and into the Old City.

Denny sat up and gazed around. The Old City reminded him of any number of Elestian towns. Its streets were wide and clean, and its buildings as impressive as any in the old imperial capital. There were no bodies hanging from lampposts, and the air was noticeably freer of foul odours. The cart left the Great Northern Highway, taking a left and entering a commercial district lined by grand shipping offices and merchants' halls. They stopped in front of an elegant inn, just as the midnight bell tolled.

The driver turned and grinned at them. 'We made it just in time. Here we are – the *Star Inn*. Be aware, this place ain't cheap. It costs more here for a small glass of wine, than it does for an entire meal back in Nether Hall where we started. Also mind that your clothes will mark you out. No offence, but you ain't exactly dressed for this neighbourhood.'

Denny and Ter Angla climbed down to the smooth flag stones. Ter Angla paid the driver, and they entered the inn. The inside was as opulent as the outside was elegant, and the inn was full of well-dressed men and women. Some were drinking at the long mahogany bar, but most were seated round tables, eating a late meal while they conducted business.

'We just need to find our contact,' said Ter Angla, as he gazed around. He smiled. 'I see him. This way.'

They walked towards a comfortable booth, where two men and a woman were sitting. One of the men rose to his feet and met Ter Angla before they could reach the booth.

'I assume this is the lad?' said the man.

'It is,' said Ter Angla. 'His name is Valiance. Valiance of Campsie.'

The man regarded Denny for a few moments. 'Wait here,' he said to Ter Angla. 'We require only the lad for the interview.' He gestured to Denny. 'Come with me.'

Denny followed the man to the booth, leaving Ter Angla standing by the bar. The man sat, and gestured to a chair.

'Sit,' he said.

Denny sat down, and placed his bag onto the polished wooden floor.

The man gestured to the woman. 'This lady works for a member of the Corse,' he said. 'She might be able to help you. Tell us who you are and what you want.'

Denny nodded. 'My name is Valiance, and I come from Campsie. I... I am... Can I say it out loud in here?'

The others said nothing, their gazes upon him.

'I am a Master,' Denny whispered, 'but I don't know how to control my abilities. I heard that there was a school. A school that could help me.'

'Prove your claim,' said the woman.

Denny glanced around at the objects on the table, and the woman pushed a small metal spoon towards him.

'Use that,' she said. 'Spoons go missing in here all the time.'

'Ever-living and blessed spirits,' Denny whispered, 'I call upon your power. Take the iron from this spoon, and in its place put wood.'

There was a soft crackle, and the spoon fell to pieces. Small slivers of a wood-like substance lay entwined with the remaining metal, and some of it had disintegrated into fine dust.

The two men and the women peered closely at the former spoon.

'How old are you?' said the woman.

'Eighteen.'

'Why have you left it so late to begin your training?' she said. 'You should have started years ago.'

'I was ashamed, and I hid my abilities from my family. Then... Then I heard that there might be a school here in Klef Mordain, and so I left Campsie. Can you help me?'

'His accent is too well-educated for Campsie,' said the man sitting next to her; 'and he has a Geathian for a manservant.'

'I am not sure either point is relevant,' said the woman. 'Despite his poor showing with the spoon, now that we know he is a Master, we cannot ignore him.'

'I wasn't suggesting that we ignore him,' said the man. 'There are other... avenues we could explore.'

'The decision of what is to be done lies with me,' said the woman. 'We shall not be dumping this boy's body into the ocean tonight – is that clear?'

The other man smiled. 'I defer to your authority, ma'am. All the same, I counsel caution in this case. He is plainly too old to begin training, and his accent and servant cause me no end of suspicion. There is something else going on here; something that yet eludes us.'

'If that is true, then we will no doubt discover it in due course.' She turned back to Denny. 'We shall move you to a safe house tonight.'

'And then?' he said.

'In the morning,' she went on, 'I shall introduce you to a teacher at the school. If he agrees, then you will start your lessons immediately. Tell me something first, however – what is your opinion of the Sanctian Empire?'

'I... I don't really have an opinion,' he said.

'I suppose that is better than the wrong opinion,' she said. She turned to Ter Angla's contact. 'You did well in arranging this interview. Tie up any loose ends, and come to the safe house in the morning.'

'Yes, ma'am,' the man said.

The woman smiled. 'Well, Valiance; let us see what Klef Mordain can make of you.'

CHAPTER 5
THINGS UNSAID

Old City, Klef Mordain – 6th Day of Saluna 108

Amery stumbled out of bed. He needed to visit the bathroom, but he had no idea where it was. He took a step forward in the darkness, and his shin collided with the edge of a low table. He let out a cry, and began to feel around.

Where was he?

He caught a faint glimmer of light and edged towards it, his hands held out in front of him. His fingers touched the fabric of a set of thick curtains. He pulled them open, and gazed out at the sunset. Had he slept all day? He vaguely remembered going to bed that morning, after working for over thirty-six hours without a break. He had drunk a couple of very large brandies, and had then collapsed onto the soft mattress. He had been so tired that sleep had come instantly, and he had dreamt that he was back in Upper Down.

Amery smiled. No, he was in Klef Mordain; praise the spirits.

He looked out over the rooftops of the city, their tiles glowing a dull red in the last of the daylight. In the distance, he could see the wide estuary as it began to narrow in the west, while, to the south was a large bay, where the commercial harbour was located. That would place the mighty Celestial Bridge somewhere to his right, but Amery had yet to gaze upon the famous architectural marvel of the Elestian age.

He remembered that he needed to pee, and he hurried towards the door. He pulled on a dressing gown and left the bedroom.

'Good evening,' said Annalise, who was arranging a bouquet of flowers on a table by the large bay window. 'Did you sleep well?'

Amery narrowed his eyes. 'Eh, yes. Uh, where is the bathroom?'

'Go up the stairs,' said Annalise. 'The door is on the left when you get to the top.'

'There's an upstairs?'

'And a downstairs,' she said. 'We are on the middle floor. Altogether, this is quite a lovely townhouse; grander than anything in Torrent. Would you like some coffee, or something to eat?'

'Yes. Thank you. Where are the stairs?'

Annalise gestured to her left. 'Down the hallway.'

Amery hurried away. He found the staircase and ran up the steps. A few oil lamps had been lit, and the curtains had all been drawn. Paintings adorned the walls, and soft carpets were on every floor. He entered the room on the left, and found the bathroom. Fragments of memories returned to him as he relieved himself. He had given Lothar and Annalise some money, and told them to rent the best house he could afford; then, while he had been working, Lothar had visited him to let him know that they had found a place, and were moving in. He could even remember the address – Wyburn Avenue, set in the middle of a smart residential district of the Old City, and a ten minute walk from the office of the Second Empire Association.

He washed his hands in the sink, dried them on a fresh towel, and walked back out on to the landing. He gazed up at a few of the huge paintings on the wall to his left. Self-satisfied merchants peered back down at him, their hands resting on accounting books, or, in one case, a large chest full of gold. The painted merchants were uniformly dressed in sumptuous robes, with their hair pulled back from their foreheads in the old Elestian style. Amery descended the stairs, and re-entered the room where he had seen Annalise. The woman had gone, but Lothar had appeared. The Mountain Ranger was sitting on a low couch, and was pulling his boots off.

'That's typical,' said Lothar. 'You're just getting up, while I'm getting home from a day's work.'

'You have a job?' said Amery.

'I told you about it this morning,' Lothar said. 'I'm working in the harbour, shifting crates. I've got a contract to the end of the month, but it'll be extended if I don't fuck it up. The pay is only three hundred a month, but I would bet you a small fortune that I'm the only dockhand living in a place like this.'

Annalise entered with a silver tray. 'Here is the coffee. Fresh and hot.'

She set the tray down onto the large table next to the bouquet of flowers, and filled three cups. She brought one over to Amery.

'Thanks,' he said. 'Do you, eh, work for me now?'

'Isn't that what we agreed?' said Annalise. 'I will look after the house while you boys go out to work. When are you due back at your place of employment, Mister Amery?'

'I'm going to pop into the office this evening,' he said. 'Though I hope I won't be working through the night again. Thirty-six hours without a break. It's no wonder I'm feeling a little groggy.' He sipped the coffee. 'Excellent, but I don't suppose there is any sugar?'

'How many do you take?' said Annalise.

'Three.'

She tapped the side of her head with a finger. 'I'll remember that for next time.'

She took the cup from his hands and went back to the table.

'What were you doing for thirty-six hours?' said Lothar, as he stood and joined Annalise by the table.

'I can't tell you that,' said Amery. 'My new employers insisted that I sign a declaration stating that I would not discuss the nature of my work with anyone. They are a secretive bunch. Did I tell you how much I am getting paid?'

Lothar shook his head, as Annalise stirred in the sugar.

'Three thousand a month,' Amery said.

Annalise smiled as she handed him his cup. 'That's a sizable amount. And here I was worried that we might not be able to afford this place. We should have found something even grander, eh, Lothar?'

'Three thousand?' muttered the Mountain Ranger. 'That's ten times what I am making. Do you want me to contribute some of my wages to the running of the house?'

Amery was about to say *yes*, when he caught a look from Annalise.

'That won't be necessary,' he said. 'How much is the rent?'

'Eight hundred a month,' said Annalise.

'So, if I pay the two drivers a thousand altogether, that should cover their wages, and the upkeep of the horses; and that will still leave me with twelve hundred. Then there's food, water, taxes, clothes and so on. And I will pay you something, Annalise. An allowance. Is three hundred a month all right?'

'That would be acceptable,' said Annalise.

'I'll probably end up with about three hundred a month to spend on myself,' said Amery. 'Still, at least I'll have a nice house and a shiny carriage.'

'And a housekeeper,' said Annalise. 'There are six bedrooms in the townhouse, and there are stables in the back yard. Shall we be inviting the two drivers to live here?'

'I suppose that makes sense. It seems I am the lord of an entire household.'

Lothar snorted.

'I shall send the drivers a message,' said Annalise. 'I know where they have been lodging for the last two nights – a most squalid little tavern in the commercial district. The lads will be delighted to hear the news.'

'I'm sure they will,' said Amery. 'You know, Lothar, when I tell others about this house, I am going to refer to you as my butler; I hope you don't mind. I think it sounds better than saying I have a dockhand as a lodger. Yes – a housekeeper, two drivers and a butler.' He grinned. 'At long last, I have staff. My father would be so proud.'

'Is dinner ready?' said Lothar.

'It is not,' said Annalise. 'I require some help in the kitchen, and I cannot ask Mister Amery for assistance.'

'In other words, you want me to help?' said Lothar.

'I think that would be fair,' said Amery. 'After all, you are paying nothing to live here.'

'Fine,' said Lothar. 'You are lucky I know how to cook.'

'I'll be doing the cooking,' said Annalise. 'You will be taking care of the washing and cleaning. The kitchen is enormous, and I want it spotless each evening before we go to bed. Come on; I will show you where the mops and buckets are kept.'

Lothar grumbled under his breath, then he and Annalise left the sitting room. Amery reclined on the long couch, and sank into the soft cushions as he savoured his coffee. After years of wandering, and working in awful places and for awful employers, it felt as though he had finally established himself. It was true that his new employers had some questionable principles, but he could see beyond that. He pictured himself rising to the top of the legal world of Klef Mordain, and rubbing shoulders with the rich and powerful. Perhaps, one day, he would be able to count himself among their number. It had always been his dream to be fabulously wealthy, and the crime that had seen him exiled from Yearl had crushed his hopes for a while. One ill-timed punch had ruined his reputation, and his prospects in the Central Provinces, but Klef Mordain was another world.

After a pleasant dinner of roast chicken and vegetables, Amery decided to walk to the office of the Second Empire Association. His drivers had yet to bring themselves and their carriage round to Wyburn Avenue, but the evening was warm and balmy, almost as if summer had come early. He smiled at his new neighbours, and took note of the soldiers patrolling the main junctions. Amery wondered if every criminal found in the Old City was taken beyond its walls to be executed, for there were no rotting corpses anywhere to be seen within its bounds. Presumably, the prosperous inhabitants did not wish their streets to be sullied by the sights and smells such displays evoked. A few restaurants and taverns were opening for business as Amery crossed a busy road, then he strode down a familiar backstreet and came to the entrance of the building where his new employers worked.

He frowned. Someone had daubed paint over the outside walls and door.

Death to the Sanctians, it read; and *Klef Mordain free forever*.

Amery glanced at the brushwork. Did this mean that someone knew where the Second Empire Association was based? Fortunately, the graffiti was out of sight from the main road; otherwise, Amery would have been afraid for his safety. He took a key from the pocket of his long black dress coat, and unlocked the door. The burly doorman glanced up at him from where he was sitting, then the man stood.

'Good evening, Mister Amery,' he said, bowing. 'Might I take your coat?'

'Thank you,' said Amery. He slipped it from his shoulders and gave it to the man.

'Lord Tain and Lady Ursula are upstairs, sir,' the doorman went on. 'I suspect both are nursing slight hangovers.'

'What time did they get here?'

'About an hour ago, I'd say, sir.'

Amery went up the stairs to the first floor, and came to an open door. Beyond was the large conference room, where Amery had toiled for many of the thirty six hours he had been working. Tain and Ursula were reclining in deep armchairs, while the long table next to them was covered in a mass of documents and maps of the city.

'The hero returns,' said Tain, a broad grin on his face. 'Sit down, my man. Might I say, Amery, that you are worth every damn penny? One hundred and twenty-seven – can you believe it?'

'Is that the final count, sir?' said Amery, as he sat.

'It is,' said Tain. 'It's easily the highest number of pro-Sanctians ever to be elected on to the five hundred.'

'It was your plan that we followed, sir,' said Amery. 'I was merely carrying out your instructions. Your ideas on how to best spread our votes seem to have paid off handsomely.'

Tain smiled. 'My sister was sceptical, isn't that right, Ursula? Are you prepared to admit that I was correct?'

'Don't speak to me,' croaked Ursula. 'My head feels as though a Master has replaced my blood with lead.'

'Were you celebrating?' said Amery.

'We were,' said Tain, 'and I think we may have over-indulged a little.'

'If my memory serves me well,' said Amery, 'the five hundred will be gathering to vote tomorrow; is that right?'

'Yes,' said Tain. 'They will then select the thirty members of the next government. Are you ready to start work? I have the names and addresses of every pro-Sanction elected to the five hundred.' He smiled at Amery. 'I have also devised a voting method that should maximise how many we are able to place into the thirty.'

'By my calculations, sir,' said Amery, 'sixteen or seventeen votes should suffice to gain a place.'

'Ah,' said Tain, 'but what if we were bolder? Sixteen votes apiece would easily elect seven or eight of our supporters on to the thirty; but I wish to aim higher than that. If we are clever about this, and daring, we may be able to get eleven or twelve pro-Sanctians into the government.'

'That seems a little risky, sir,' said Amery. 'If we lower the votes cast for each candidate, there is a danger that none will be elected.'

'That's what I told him,' croaked Ursula.

'Trust me,' said Tain. 'I have studied the results of the last ten elections, and you might be surprised at how few votes are needed to get someone a seat on the thirty.'

'I am at your service, sir,' said Amery. 'I shall require a list of your top dozen candidates. Once I have that, I will summon the scribes, and we shall write letters to all one hundred and twenty-seven members, instructing them on how to vote.'

'One hundred and twenty-six letters,' said Tain. After all, there is little point in sending a letter to myself.'

Amery narrowed his eyes. 'Were you elected to the five hundred, sir?'

'I was, indeed.'

Amery regained his composure. 'Very well, sir – one hundred and twenty-six letters.'

'I thought your voice would be hoarse by now,' said Ursula; 'considering how many letters you have dictated in the last few days.'

'I am happy to serve, ma'am,' he said.

'Before we start,' said Tain, 'there is a delicate matter we need to discuss first.'

'Can't this wait?' said Ursula.

'I think not, sister,' said Tain. 'I am of the opinion that we should get everything out into the open.'

'To which matter are you referring, sir?' said Amery.

Tain looked into his eyes. 'The death of Lord Denon.'

'Oh.'

'Indeed,' said Tain. 'Why didn't you tell us that you had personally witnessed this outrage?'

'I... didn't think it was relevant, sir.'

'Lord Denon was one of the foremost Sanctians resident in Klef Mordain,' Tain went on. 'He worked at the Sanctian Embassy for over a decade. He leaves on a business trip, and what happens when he returns? The damn secret police point him out to the bloody infantry, who gut him by the side of the Great Northern Highway.'

'I was not aware of the context surrounding this incident, sir.'

'He spoke to you, didn't he?' said Ursula. 'You were in the same tavern, and the infantry's report stated that you were seated at the same table.'

'Yes, we spoke, briefly. Lord Denon was only with us for a few moments before the soldiers charged in. Is it true that he was a spy?'

'He was protected by diplomatic immunity,' said Tain; 'or, he should have been. The Corse had no damn right to have acted like that. More than that, though, he was a good friend, and a most helpful ally for our cause.'

'And what were you doing with a princess, Amery?' said Ursula.

'I was escorting her from Upper Down to Klef Mordain, ma'am,' said Amery. 'Princess Kilbride knew that I was coming here, and she asked me to ensure that her sister reached the city in one piece.'

'Why is a princess of Upper Down in Klef Mordain?' said Tain.

'She is merely visiting, on her way to stay with her other sister in Lesser Down, sir. Princess Nolan is married into the royal family of that realm. Her husband is Prince Wolfgang, the heir to the throne.'

'But did you not pass through Lesser Down on your way here?'

Amery's cheeks flushed. 'Ah, yes. Yes, we did; but Princess Abigone – that is her name – she wished to see the great Klef Mordain, so I led her here.'

'Why didn't she notify the Corse that she was coming?'

'That was an oversight on my part, sir. I made an error of judgement, forgetting that, as one of the regents of Upper Down, Klef Mordain would see Princess Abigone as a sovereign ruler of a foreign realm. She was the junior partner in the regency, if I am being honest, and it slipped my mind. The real power in Upper Down lies with Princess Kilbride and Lord Walter of Ridden. I humbly apologised to Her Highness for my mistake; it was most embarrassing. Perhaps that was why I neglected to mention it. It wasn't my proudest moment.'

'Who else was there?' said Ursula. 'The report stated that there were four in your company.'

Amery's mouth went dry. 'That's right,' he said. 'Princess Abigone had a soldier and a lady-in-waiting to accompany her on her travels.'

'Has she gone yet?' said Ursula. 'Has the princess left the city?'

'I don't know, ma'am.'

'Why not? You escorted her here.'

'That is true, but she had her own plans, while I was searching for a job.'

'There has been no report of her leaving the city,' said Tain. 'The secret police would have recorded such a detail. Is there anything else you wish to tell us about the affair?'

Amery's mind raced. If Tain had access to the records of the secret police, then he would already know where he had taken Abigone.

'I took the princess to the offices of Lord Metrius,' he said. 'As I mentioned to you at my interview, Lord Metrius was one of the few people I knew of in Klef Mordain. Then... well, then, someone from the secret police took the princess away. I don't know why. I suspect the police wished to discover the reason for the princess's visit; but I didn't want to ask. It was none of my business. That's why I have been allowing the soldier and the lady-in-waiting to dwell in my new house. They had no money, and no means to return to Lesser or Upper Down. I am currently employing them as a butler and a housekeeper.'

'It seems as though there is quite a lot you haven't told us, Amery,' said Tain.

'I wonder what they have done with her,' said Ursula. 'They wouldn't execute a princess, would they?'

'Apparently, it was Portia who collected her from outside the offices of Lord Metrius,' said Tain.

'Oh dear,' said Ursula. 'That can't be good. But why would Lord Metrius wish to eliminate a regent from Upper Down?'

'Perhaps the princess misled me, ma'am,' said Amery. 'Perhaps she was coming here to engage in espionage.'

'On whose behalf?'

'I don't know, ma'am.'

'The mystery deepens,' said Tain. 'I will attempt to dig a little deeper. If the Corse has been playing foul with a sovereign ruler of an independent realm, then perhaps we could use that to discredit them. We could print up a few anonymous leaflets, demanding to know what has become of Princess Abigone. How old was she, Amery?'

'Eighteen, sir.'

'We could use that. *Where is the young princess?* we could ask. We could also leak it to the newspapers; create a little scandal.'

'First things first,' said Ursula. 'Amery has a hundred and twenty-six letters to dictate.'

It was long after midnight before Amery was able to stop work for the evening. He, Tain and Ursula had drawn up their shortlist of the dozen candidates they hoped to be elected to the government of thirty, and then Amery had spent hour after hour dictating letters to the association's team of scribes, advising each of the pro-Sanctian members of the five hundred how they should vote to achieve the best result for their cause. As soon as each batch of ten letters had been completed and sealed, a courier would rush off with them, in order to post them through the letterboxes of the recipients. Amery had noted that Lord Tain's name did not appear on the list of the dozen favoured delegates, and he wondered if that signified anything of importance. He now knew that Tain was a member of the Corse, but it appeared that he did not wish to be encumbered with the duties of ruling and administering the city. Perhaps he wanted to keep his hands clean of the taint of compromise with the association's ideological opponents, or perhaps he had no time to spare from the cause.

With his head aching, Amery went up onto the roof of the building to get some fresh air. He stretched and flexed his fingers, and gazed up at the night sky. All three moons were out, but only the Little Red Moon was full. The Big Red Moon was waxing, while the Silver Moon was waning, and each was dominating its area of the sky, blotting out the light from the stars.

He thought back to the conversation about Abigone, and cursed his lack of foresight. He should have been able to predict that Tain or Ursula would discover that he had been in the same tavern as Lord Denon; after all, he had given his correct name to the soldiers who had apprehended the Sanctian diplomat and spy. None of it would have mattered if he had found employment with Lord Metrius, but that ship had long since departed. Being hired by the Second Empire Association had probably made him unemployable among whole sections of polite society, and he doubted that Lord Metrius would ever speak to him again if he found out where he was working.

'It's beautiful, isn't it?' said Lord Tain.

Amery turned. 'Yes, sir.'

'Have you finished the last of the letters?'

'I have, sir.'

'Excellent. Well done.'

'Thank you, sir. However, even if we are wildly successful, will eleven or twelve pro-Sanctians make much difference to the running of the government? The anti-Sanctians will still be able to outvote them.'

'There are several ways to answer that question, Amery. On the face of it, I would tend to agree with you, but the cold hard fact is that no one outwith the government really understands how it is organised. Are ministries distributed evenly, or is every decision brought to a vote? At the last election, we had two pro-Sanctians elected on to the thirty, but the other twenty-eight simply ignored them, and refused to discuss government business with either. We will find out shortly, though. If around ten of our number are successful, the rest of the thirty will not be able to exclude them, and at least one of those we help elect will be able to tell us how the government is organised. Once we know that, I will be better able to answer your question.'

Amery nodded.

'I have been busy,' said Tain. 'Not as busy as you, Amery, but busy nonetheless. I have had my contacts out, trying to unearth more about our missing princess.'

'Is night a useful time for the gathering of intelligence, sir?'

'In some ways, it is the best time. The bars and taverns of the government district are packed with members of the Corse, all speculating about the composition of the five hundred and the thirty. Mix in a few gallons of alcohol, and eavesdropping can become quite profitable. I have a few contacts who work in those taverns, and they listen for me. Tonight, I asked them to listen out for any details about Princess Abigone of Upper Down.'

'And have you learned anything, sir?'

'Nothing. Not a damn word. That, in itself, is suspicious. You would expect there to be some idle gossip about the arrival of a foreign ruler but, instead, there is only silence. I fear the worst, Amery; I fear that Abigone is already dead. Why else would there be nothing to say?'

'I cannot believe it, sir. Why would the secret police murder her? She seemed harmless to me.'

'Perhaps they made a mistake. It wouldn't be the first time. I have some experience of overseeing the activities of the secret police, and they are not as efficient as they would have the native population believe. The Corse's method of administering justice is so swift, that mitigating details are often overlooked. The Sanctians would never tolerate such a system of instant justice. As you know, they put suspected criminals on trial, and determine the evidence before pronouncing a verdict and a sentence. Here? Well, you saw what happened to Lord Denon. Perhaps the secret police believe that Princess Abigone was conspiring with him? Could that be possible? It was a strange coincidence that saw you both in the same tavern at the same time.'

'You might be right, sir.'

'We are not going to be silent about this. I have a plan. I will speak to the newspapers tomorrow, and tell them what I know. I also intend to plaster up hundreds of leaflets, demanding that the Corse release information regarding Abigone's fate. Lastly, I shall be writing to Princess Kilbride and Princess Nolan. They need to know what happened to their sister. We shall stir up a diplomatic incident, and use it to embarrass the Corse. It is time the people of this city realised that their rulers cannot be trusted. The more citizens understand this, the more likely it will be that they accept our annexation by the Sanctian Empire.'

'Do you believe it will ever happen, sir?'

'Believe it? I am certain of it. Nothing can withstand the tide for long. This city will be part of the Sanctian Empire – and its prosperity and glory will only increase. Those who tried to prevent it shall be punished; but those who helped? Well, I would imagine that they will be greatly rewarded. I include you in this, Amery. You have picked the winning side, whether you intended to or not.'

Amery bowed his head to hide the fear in his eyes. 'You do me great honour, sir.'

'Nonsense; you have earned it. Come; let us go downstairs and celebrate. Tomorrow is going to be a good day.'

CHAPTER 6
ONE PASSABLE SPOON

Old City, Klef Mordain – 7th Day of Saluna 108

Abigone sat cross-legged on her bed and sipped from her cup of tea. Her room's only window faced east, and the dawn sunlight was flooding in. She had unloaded her breakfast tray when she had finished eating, and had piled the plates onto her small bedside table, leaving the tray sitting on the folded blankets of her narrow bed. The tray was made of metal, though of which sort Abigone was unsure, and she had already destroyed more than half of it.

She raised her left hand.

'Blessed spirits,' she whispered, 'with your permission, summon for me a spoon.'

Another chunk of the tray disintegrated, and an object appeared a few inches over the blankets. It fell, landing with a soft thud. Abigone picked it up. It was the best spoon she had made so far that morning, but it was still unusable as a utensil. Its handle was crooked, and the bowl at the end was riddled with holes; but at least it almost looked like a spoon, which was a great improvement on some of her earlier efforts.

Where was she going wrong? She was picturing the spoon in her mind – and she had an example of one lying next to her tea cup – and yet whatever she produced bore barely any resemblance to the image in her head. She placed her summoned object next to the others by her pillow. She could see a progression of sorts when she laid them all out side by side, and her latest efforts were clearly better than her first, but she wouldn't have used any to stir her tea. She got up, and placed her bare feet on the warm floorboards. She stretched her legs, then walked over to the window. A bell was ringing somewhere in the Old City of Klef Mordain, the same bell that pealed each morning to gather the spirit-worshippers to prayer in the grand temple. Abigone wondered why there were no temples in Upper Down. The people of her realm also believed in the spirits, but none of them felt inclined to assemble every day at dawn to sing and pray.

Perhaps she should start attending. Maybe a little faith and devotion was what was missing from her summoning. Did she truly believe in the spirit world? She had recited the prayers as a youth, but had she really trusted that the words were true?

A nervous anxiety flitted through her. She was due to attend the first class of spring term that morning, and she felt unprepared. She had spent the previous day skimming through several of the heavy tomes that she had been given, but there hadn't been enough time to digest their contents, and she had found them dry and dull. She thought back to the meeting with Lady Fyenna that had taken place two days before. The older woman had tried to browbeat her, but Abigone didn't care. Lady Fyenna might have believed that she was being intimidating, but the stern lecture was no worse than the many Abigone had received from her sister Kilbride over the years. The one thing that angered her had been the loss of food. Fyenna had been true to her word, and Abigone had been given nothing else to eat for the rest of that day, all because she had possessed the temerity to speak without permission.

She walked back to the bed and sat down. She tried to empty her thoughts, focusing only upon the image of a spoon in her mind, then she raised her hand.

'Blessed spirits,' she said, 'with your permission, summon for me a spoon.'

The tray cracked as another piece of it vanished, then her summoned object fell onto the blankets. Abigone smiled as she picked it up. Its surface was rough and discoloured, but it was recognisably a spoon.

Another bell rang, but that time, it was coming from within the Maker school. It was the signal that the girls were to get washed and dressed, and then make their way downstairs to the classrooms. Abigone had already washed that morning, and all she needed to do was strap her sandals to her feet. She found them under her bed, and fastened the buckles; then she stood and opened the door to her room. Two girls were emerging from another door along the corridor, one of whom was carrying two trays loaded with cups and bowls; and they stopped talking when they saw Abigone.

'You must be the new student,' said the one not holding the trays, who seemed a little older than the other girl. 'Lady Fyenna told us about you. My name is Raewyn, and I will be starting third year. The girl next to me is Stanza, who is about to start her second year here. We heard that you will be with the first years – is that true?'

'Yes,' said Abigone.

'Aren't you a little embarrassed by that?' said Raewyn. 'You will have to sit next to two fourteen-year-olds. And where is your breakfast tray? You are supposed to drop it off in the kitchens each day when you go down to class.'

'I didn't know that,' said Abigone.

'Now you do,' said Raewyn. 'Go and get it.'

'I broke it.'

The two girls glanced at each other.

'You broke it?' said Stanza, who was carrying the two trays.

'Yes,' said Abigone. 'I was using it to practise making spoons.'

'You're going to get into trouble.'

Abigone shrugged. 'It's only a tray.'

'It's school property. If you break something, you are supposed to report it immediately.'

'I want to see your spoons,' said Raewyn. She strode forward, but Abigone closed the door to her room before the girl could peer inside.

'We're going to be late,' said Stanza.

Raewyn shot her a look of contempt. 'Then go. Take the damn trays downstairs, and I will see you in class.'

Stanza lowered her gaze, then she hurried off, almost running towards the stairs.

'Poor old Stanza is rather fond of the rules,' said Raewyn. 'At times, I think she would make an excellent member of the secret police. I should warn you that she will probably tell the kitchen staff what you did. Can I see your spoons now?'

'Why?' said Abigone.

'Because I want to see what you are capable of doing. Lady Fyenna told us that you knew absolutely nothing; that you were a complete beginner. Let me see them. I won't laugh.'

'All right,' said Abigone.

She opened the door, and they both entered. Raewyn gazed around the small room, then Abigone pointed at her pillow, where her various attempts at summoning a spoon lay.

'Oh dear,' said Raewyn, as she picked up a particularly misshapen specimen. She turned to what was left of the tray, and laughed.

'The last one I made wasn't too bad,' said Abigone, gesturing to it.

'It is an improvement,' said Raewyn, 'but I wouldn't want to eat any soup with it. Here; watch how it is done.'

She raised her hand, and a perfectly-formed spoon appeared on the pillow, ripping another chunk from the tray.

Abigone picked it up. 'You didn't move your lips.'

'Of course I didn't. Only first years actually speak out loud; didn't you know that? I will fix this mess for you; it's clear that you need all the help you can get.'

She gathered all of the spoons together, and placed them next to the broken tray. She rolled her shoulders, then raised a hand. There was a crackle, and the mound of broken metal disappeared. A moment later, a pristine tray appeared on the bed.

'There you go,' said Raewyn. 'As good as new. Now, load it up with your dishes, and run down to the kitchens. You might still make it in time for the next bell.'

Raewyn strode from the room, leaving Abigone staring at the tray she had summoned. She was a little aggrieved at the condescending tone Raewyn had adopted, but she was more impressed by what she had done. She stacked her plates, bowl and cup onto the tray, lifted it, and walked back out of the room, just as the second morning bell rang. Abigone picked up her pace, and hurried down the stairs. She entered the large kitchen, where she received a few glances from the three women working there. She set the tray down next to the others, and raced back out into the corridor. She had been shown the classroom the day before, and she made her way there. The door was closed, so she knocked and walked in.

A young woman eyed her from where she was standing at the front of the class.

'Sorry I'm late,' said Abigone.

'Not a good start, Abigone,' said the teacher. 'I am Miss Vesta, and I will be conducting the majority of your classes this year. Please take a seat.'

Abigone turned, and saw two younger girls staring up at her from their desks. One was raven-haired, while the other had long red locks spilling down her shoulders. There were two desks behind the girls, and Abigone walked over to them and sat down next to one. The two girls turned their heads to gaze at her.

'Are you another teacher?' said the one with black hair.

'Silence, Reath,' said Miss Vesta; 'and face the front.'

The black-haired girl frowned.

'Let us begin,' said Vesta. 'We have three first years this term, and I...'

'Is she a first year, miss?' said Reath. 'She's too old.'

'Quiet, Reath; I will get to the introductions in a moment. For now, just listen. As I said, I am in charge of teaching the first years, and I am also responsible for your discipline and behaviour. If you have any problems, come to me, and don't bother Lady Fyenna.'

'What if our problem is with you, miss?' said Reath.

'You will still come to me first. Now, the young lady who has just joined us is called Abigone. Abigone, would you like to tell the class why you are here?'

'All right,' said Abigone. 'I wasn't allowed to tell anyone I was a Maker, so I didn't receive any training. I used my abilities for the first time last year, and my sister decided to send me here to learn more.'

Vesta smiled. 'And who is your sister, Abigone, and what does she do?'

'My sister's name is Kilbride, and she is a regent.'

'What's a regent?' said Reath.

'It means that she is governing a kingdom because the king is too young to rule,' said Vesta. 'Kilbride and Abigone are princesses.'

The red-haired girl's mouth fell open. 'You are a princess?'

'Yes,' said Abigone.

Reath laughed. 'We're in the same class as a damn princess? Do you live in a palace?'

'Not any more,' said Abigone. 'I live here now.'

Reath rolled her eyes. 'Obviously. But you did live in a palace? Did you have lots of servants?'

'That's enough, Reath,' said Vesta. 'Abigone, the two girls in front of you are twin sisters, even though they are not identical. The one on your left is Reath, as I am sure you have gathered, and her sister is called Nyli. Tell us where you both come from, Nyli.'

'Yes, miss,' said the red-haired girl, her voice a bare whisper. 'We come from the Kingdom of Nessos.'

'Nessos?' said Abigone. 'Have you heard of a Prince Henry?'

'Of course we have,' said Reath.

'I was betrothed to him for a while,' said Abigone, 'but the engagement was called off.'

Nyli's eyes widened. 'You were going to marry Prince Henry?'

'That's what she said,' muttered Reath. 'You don't have to repeat everything.'

'Sorry,' said Nyli.

'Why was it called off?' said Reath.

'The Sanctians invaded,' said Abigone. 'They arrived a few weeks before I was due to travel to Nessos. Prince Henry didn't know that I was a Maker – none of them knew. My father said it was the only way I would be able to marry anyone from the royal families of the Central Provinces.'

'Reath and Nyli discovered that they were Makers six months ago,' said Vesta. 'Their family put them on a wagon and sent them here as soon as they found out. They had to cross the entire length of the Central Provinces to get to Klef Mordain, braving the Sanctian authorities on the way.'

'The soldiers weren't interested in two peasant girls,' said Reath.

'You shouldn't call yourself that,' said Vesta.

'Why not? It's true – our whole family are peasants. Fourteen of us lived in a tiny cottage, and we had to work on the farm every day from as soon as we could walk. We didn't go to school, but our mother taught us to read and write, even though our father said it would be a waste of time.'

'Well, it wasn't a waste of time,' said Vesta. 'You both read very well, considering the circumstances. Also, do not forget that the Maker school will also provide you with normal lessons, as well as lessons about being a Maker. Here, you will learn literature, history, arithmetic, and everything else that will help equip you for adulthood. Abigone, am I to assume that you have received a full school education?'

'Yes, miss,' said Abigone. 'The palace had tutors, and I attended classes for ten years.'

'We shall have to consider what to do with you during those lessons,' said Vesta, 'as there is little point in making you endure hours of writing practice. I will speak to Lady Fyenna about this, and we shall come up with a plan.' She smiled. 'Last year, we had three students altogether, but one of them graduated from fourth year, and she has left the school. Have you all met the other two girls?'

'We have,' said Reath.

'I saw them briefly this morning, miss,' said Abigone.

'Raewyn has completed two years of schooling,' said Vesta, 'and Stanza has finished her first year. Stanza is actually a neighbour of yours, Abigone, as she hails from Greater Down; while Raewyn is a native of Klef Mordain.'

Reath whispered something in Nyli's ear, and the red-haired girl laughed.

'What is so amusing, Nyli?' said Vesta.

'Nothing, miss. Sorry.'

'Reath, why don't you tell us what you told your sister?'

The black-haired girl grinned. 'I said that we have a real princess in our class, while Raewyn just thinks she's a princess.'

'Raewyn is a model student,' said Vesta. 'She works hard, and she always listens in class. You would do well to emulate her behaviour, Reath. Now, this morning, as it is your first day, I want to tell you about the school's expectations for you. Have you heard the other girls talk about the *Making*?'

No one responded.

'I will take that as a *No*,' said Vesta. 'The Making is the end-of-year examination that you must all undergo before being permitted to move up into the next year. The first-year Making is comparatively easy, and it gets harder as you make your way through the school years. That is your target; it is what you will be working towards all year. If any of you fail, you will have to re-take first year. However, I am confident that, with some hard work and application, all of you will pass. The Making consists of two parts – a theoretical section, and a practical section. For the theory, you will be required to write a few essays, and we shall practise those as the months unfold. For the practical section, you will each be asked to summon a variety of objects, ranging from the most basic, to something a little more complex. By the end of fourth year, the examination can be quite demanding. Last year, the student who graduated was required to summon a complete set of blacksmith's tools. When I was a student here, I was asked to summon a small-scale replica of the Celestial Bridge, complete with all of the statues that adorn its roadsides. I had to sit by that bridge for weeks, memorising every last detail. I wasn't allowed to look at it during the examination.'

'What did you have to summon in first year?' said Reath.

Vesta narrowed her eyes. 'Let me see if I can remember. It was nine years ago... I think I had to summon a carving knife, a wagon wheel, a velvet glove, and a... what was it? Yes, a simple but working oil lamp. All of the raw materials are provided, of course. The Master school often supplies them for us.'

'When do we get to meet the Masters, miss?' said Nyli.

'I think the first mixed lesson is scheduled to take place in a month or so,' said Vesta. 'Either they come here, or we go to them. Usually, each class is required to demonstrate what they have learned, and then a lecture takes place. On these occasions, Lady Fyenna requires that each girl behaves with modesty and decorum. That means no giggling or pointing, and if any of the boys approach you, you are to remain polite but aloof. Relationships between the students from either school are not permitted.'

Reath grimaced. 'If any of the boys try to approach me, I'll punch him in the face.'

'I doubt Lady Fyenna would look kindly upon you if you did that, Reath,' said Vesta. 'If I can give you all one piece of advice, it is this – do not get on Lady Fyenna's wrong side. She is a war hero, decorated for valour at the Battle of Hader Pull, and she has earned the respect of everyone in Klef Mordain. She can be strict at times, but there is a very good reason for that. It is well known that the classes for Makers and Masters differ considerably, and I wouldn't be lying if I said that the boys have a far easier time of it. Being a Master does not require the intense levels of research and study compared to being a Maker – that is a sad and unfair fact of life, and you will have to get used to it. To be a successful Maker, you will have to dedicate many long hours to your studies.' She glanced at Abigone. 'Take, for instance, a simple object such as a spoon. It is not enough to merely visualise the shape of the spoon in your mind; a true Maker must also have an understanding of the exact materials that go into the spoon. Is it made of steel, for example; or pewter, or iron, or even tin? Each is utterly different – pewter is an alloy, and steel contains more than just metal. A Maker must also comprehend every last detail about how the spoon was made in the first place – was it forged, or was it stamped out by a pressing machine? These differences matter. Experienced Makers are like walking encyclopaedias; their minds are full of obscure information about all manner of artefacts. The very best Makers could even summon living creatures – can you imagine the complexity of that?'

'Why did you say *could*?' said Reath. 'Can't they do it now?'

'There has been no record of any Maker being able to successfully summon a live animal for well over a century,' said Vesta, 'not since the massacres that signalled the end of the Elestian Empire. Even Lady Fyenna, for all her undoubted skill and knowledge, cannot accomplish such a feat. Perhaps no one will ever be able to do so again. The golden age of Masters and Makers is over, and it might never return. Nyli, why don't you tell the class what you have been able to summon?'

The red-haired girl's cheeks flushed. 'I... uh...'

'Talk a little louder, Nyli, so that we can all hear you.'

'I made a wooden clog once,' the girl said, 'because I lost one of my own. That was... that was how I discovered I was a Maker, miss.'

'Well done,' said Vesta, 'that was a good start; it shows promise. Did the clog fit?'

'Yes, miss.'

'And who made the original clog?'

'My father did.'

'Did you see him make it?'

'Yes, miss.'

'And did you know from which type of tree the wood belonged?'

'It was carved from beech wood, miss.'

'There you have it. Nyli knew the type of wood, and how the clog had been carved, without having been explicitly taught any of this information, and so she was able to successfully summon a replacement. It is your turn, Reath – what have you summoned?'

'Lots of things,' said the black-haired girl, 'but they were all crap.'

'Please don't use that word in my class, Reath. Give us an example.'

'I tried to make a new plough, because the stupid oxen went too close to a ditch, and our old one broke. The thing I summoned was a mess. It didn't even look like a plough. I also tried to make a doll for our younger sister, but it was the most evil-looking doll you've ever seen in your life. It looked like a demon. Our sister cried when she saw it, and our mother threw it onto the fire.'

'Do you all see the problems Reath was facing? Unlike Nyli and the clog, Reath had no way of understanding how a plough or a doll was made in the first place. A plough might look simple, but it is the product of generations of constant development and improvement; while a doll might consist of a dozen different materials. All the same, Reath, I applaud your ambition; it will stand you in good stead for the future. Your turn, Abigone. Tell us what you have managed to summon.'

'Can I speak freely in here?' said Abigone.

'Of course. We have all taken the same oath of secrecy.'

'All right. I have summoned dragons a few times. Once from wood, and twice from stone. They didn't look anything like dragons, though.'

'That would make sense,' said Vesta, 'as dragons are legendary creatures with no basis in reality.'

'They still did what I wanted them to do,' said Abigone. 'The shape didn't matter.'

'And what did you do with them?'

'I destroyed sixty of the Sanctian Empire's cannon.'

Reath burst out laughing, and Nyli turned in her seat to stare at Abigone.

'Quiet, Reath,' said Vesta. 'Lady Fyenna mentioned that you might bring this up, Abigone.'

'She thinks I'm lying about it, miss,' said Abigone.

'I am aware of that,' said Vesta.

'It isn't a lie. The Sanctians were besieging the Kendril Wall, and they were blowing it to pieces. My sister forced me to go with her up to the top of a cliff, from where we could see the cannon, then she ordered me to create a landslide. I didn't really know what I was doing, but it worked. Tons of rock fell down into the bottom of the valley, and the cannon were buried. My stone dragons saved Upper Down.'

The classroom fell into silence.

'I believe you,' said Nyli.

'How many people did you kill?' said Reath.

'I'm not sure,' said Abigone. 'My sister pulled me back from the cliff's edge because it was starting to collapse, so I didn't see how many died. Maybe a few dozen? Kilbride was very pleased. She knew that the Sanctians would be forced to negotiate. She didn't care that I felt guilty about killing so many people.'

'Do you regret your actions?' said Vesta.

'How can I? If I hadn't done it, the Sanctians would have conquered Upper Down, and the kingdom would have been abolished. I would probably be a prisoner in Sanctos right now, instead of being here.'

'That is highly unlikely, Abigone,' said Vesta.

'I knew you wouldn't believe me.'

'That's not what I meant,' said Vesta. 'If you had been captured by the Sanctians, then you would be dead right now. They don't put Makers into prison – they execute them.'

Vesta walked to her desk, and picked up three slim books. She placed one onto each desk.

'Open your books at page one,' she said. 'Today, we are going to start to learn about the properties of wood.'

Abigone glanced down at the book. The words were in large print, and the book was filled with child-like illustrations. The first picture showed a smiling man with an axe standing next to a tree.

Reath groaned aloud.

Vesta smiled. 'Why don't you read for us, Reath?' She sat down at her desk as Reath began to read from the book. Vesta glanced over at Abigone, and they made eye contact, before the teacher looked away.

Abigone lowered her gaze, and followed along with the words.

CHAPTER 7
CORSE BUSINESS

Old City, Klef Mordain – 7th Day of Saluna 108

'What are you thinking, Fyenna?' said Niscoll.

Fyenna turned to her old friend. 'I was wondering what was happening at my place of work. I haven't missed the first day of term in twelve years.'

'I am sure you left the place in capable hands.'

'I'm not worried about that. I had a little tradition, where I would visit everyone on the first day, to see how they were doing. I suppose I can always do it tomorrow, if we ever get out of here.'

'The vote will take place soon,' said Niscoll. 'There is always a long period of time beforehand, while those who wish to get themselves elected on to the thirty try to garner support.'

Fyenna glanced around the large voting chamber, deep within the heart of the Corsehall. The pro-Sanctians had gathered in one corner, and were whispering among themselves, while Lord Metrius was holding court in another corner, speaking to those who opposed any union with the Sanctians. In the middle of the hall, those not aligned to either side stood in small groups around the voting hall.

'One hundred and twenty-seven,' Fyenna muttered. 'What a damn disgrace. Do you see them all whispering? And look at the smug expressions on their faces.'

'The pro-Sanctians have every right to feel smug, Fyenna. They succeeded beyond anyone's wildest expectations. Let us see if they can pull off the same trick twice.'

An older man approached them. 'Greetings, ladies,' he said. 'Lord Metrius would like a quick word with you both.'

Fyenna and Niscoll got up from their chairs and walked over to where Metrius was surrounded by a group of his supporters.

'Lady Niscoll and Lady Fyenna,' he said, beaming; 'thank you for coming over to speak to me, and congratulations upon your election to the five hundred.'

'Thank you,' said Niscoll, inclining her head.

'Yes, thank you,' said Fyenna.

'It appears that the pro-Sanctians are rather more organised than they were at the last elections five years ago,' Metrius went on. 'I have it on good authority that each one of them received a letter last night, instructing them on how to vote today. If we aren't careful, they may get as many as six or seven elected into the government of thirty. Do I need to remind you that this would be a catastrophe for the city? There were only two pro-Sanctians in the last government, and the others were able to successfully sideline them, but that would be impossible with six or seven. They will have to be given ministerial positions – can you imagine? Of course, the most important roles will be reserved for patriots, but even so, the pro-Sanctians could do a lot of damage. They will have access to all kinds of secret information that could easily undermine the city's security, especially if that information was leaked to the Sanctian Embassy. In any case, this is the reason why I am going ask you both not to vote for me in today's election.'

'We are *not* to vote for you?' said Fyenna.

'That is correct,' said Metrius. 'I already have enough support to get elected – any extra votes would, in effect, be wasted. Lady Niscoll, how would you feel about being in the thirty for the next five years?'

'Me, my lord?' said Niscoll.

Metrius smiled. 'Yes. I can arrange for you to receive enough votes to see you elected. Vote for yourself; and Lady Fyenna, please also vote for Lady Niscoll.'

'But, my lord,' said Niscoll, 'I hadn't planned to be elected. I don't know how the thirty works in practice.'

'Of course you don't, as you have never been elected to the thirty before. Worry not about that – I will ensure you are given the information you require. The city would be lucky to have a patriot of your calibre serving in the government. As for you, Lady Fyenna, I am sure your time will come.'

'I will do as you bid,' said Fyenna; 'providing Lady Niscoll agrees.'

'Well, Lady Niscoll?' said Metrius.

Niscoll inclined her head again. 'It would be an honour to serve, my lord.'

'Excellent,' said Metrius. He turned to a colleague. 'Please inform the clerk that we are ready for the vote to take place.'

'Yes, my lord,' said the man.

'Now,' said Metrius, 'we shall see if the pro-Sanctians are also ready. If they are, then that will confirm my suspicions that they already know how they are going to vote.'

They watched as Metrius's colleague walked through the hall, passing the large upturned bell in the centre of the floor. He stopped next to a group of robed men and women, and they spoke for a few moments. One of the robed women nodded, then she walked over to where the bell sat.

'Ladies and gentlemen,' she cried, her voice raised. The hall stilled. 'Thank you,' the clerk went on. 'Is there anyone present who is not ready to cast their ballot for the membership of the new government?'

No one spoke.

'I will ask once again,' said the clerk; 'does anyone need more time to come to a decision?' She gazed around the hall, but no one uttered a word. 'Very well,' she went on. 'There are ten voting booths, and when I clap my hands, I would ask that you form ten queues. Each of you will be given one ballot paper before you enter the booths. Write the name of your chosen candidate on the paper, fold it in half, and drop it into the bell. Once you have done so, please make your way from the voting hall. The count will take place as soon as all five hundred votes have been cast. Remain in the building until the results are ready to be announced. All voting slips will be available for viewing, to enable you to confirm that the vote was carried out in a fair and honest manner.'

She clapped her hands, and ten junior clerks walked into the hall, each armed with a pile of blank voting slips. They took up position next to the ten booths, and the five hundred members of the Corse began to form up in lines. Fyenna and Niscoll went to the end of one line, and waited. Niscoll looked anxious, as though the last thing she wanted was to be elected into the government.

'It will be over soon,' Fyenna whispered.

'Five years isn't soon enough,' Niscoll whispered back.

The first slips were issued to those at the head of each queue, and the lines began to slowly edge forward. Fyenna and Niscoll drew closer to the bell, then moved past it, as more delegates voted. Soldiers were standing round the bell, their hands resting on the hilts of their ceremonial swords, and their eyes on those returning from the booths to place their slips into the cavernous bell. When Fyenna reached the front of her queue, a clerk handed her a voting slip. She walked into the booth, and picked up a pencil.

She hesitated for a second, then wrote *Lady Niscoll* on the piece of paper, just under where the official seal of the Corse had been stamped. She folded the paper, then she strode towards the bell, and dropped it in. She walked from the chamber, leaving by one of its main doorways, and headed towards a bar. It was packed with members of the five hundred when she arrived, and waiters were mingling through the crowds, offering glasses of white wine. Fyenna took one, and retired to a quiet corner. She could see Metrius standing in a deep alcove, surrounded by his supporters; then she saw Lord Tain, a notable pro-Sanctian, walking across the floor with a large smile on his face. He slapped a couple of his colleagues on the back, then shook their hands. Fyenna cursed under her breath at the sight. How anyone in Klef

Mordain could think that joining the Sanctian Empire was a good idea was beyond her. She was tempted to walk up to them, but she remembered her students, and the importance of secrecy. Niscoll entered the bar, took a glass of wine from a waiter, and walked over to where Fyenna was standing.

'I feel nothing but dread,' said Niscoll. 'Whoever suggested to Lord Metrius that I would be a suitable candidate?'

'I think you would do very well,' said Fyenna. 'You love this city, and I would trust you with a powerful position.'

'It's all the secrecy,' said Niscoll. 'It's bad enough just being in the Corse, but if I am elected, then I will soon be burdened with a thousand more secrets. And I won't be able to tell my husband or children the slightest thing about any of it. I had hoped that retirement would herald a time of peace and quiet – and now this?'

A clerk walked into the bar.

'Voting has now closed,' he shouted. 'The voting chamber will be sealed until the votes are counted.'

He inclined his head at the crowd, then turned and strode away.

'I wonder how one becomes a clerk,' said Fyenna. 'They are trusted as much as any members of the Corse.'

'There is presumably some arcane and overly-complicated procedure for hiring them,' said Niscoll. She smiled. 'Perhaps they are never permitted to leave the Corsehall.'

'You've been through this before,' Fyenna said. 'How long did this stage take last time?'

'A few minutes. It doesn't take too long to count five hundred ballots. The vast majority of the delegates will have received no votes whatsoever. The number of votes needed to gain entry into the thirty depends upon how many delegates wasted their ballots by voting for themselves or their friends, when they have no hope of being elected. Another avenue of wasted votes comes from delegates trying to impress their leader, by giving them far more ballots than they actually need. It's a tricky calculation, and it requires a steady nerve. In many ways, the result will come down to how much discipline Lord Metrius was able to exert over his coalition of anti-Sanctians.'

'And whether the pro-Sanctians were more disciplined?'

'Exactly. There are a hundred and twenty-seven pro-Sanctians, and if Lord Metrius was correct, and they all received letters last night instructing them on how to vote, then, in theory, they could surprise us all. Five years ago, the pro-Sanctians split their votes too widely, and only two of their number made it onto the thirty. I think they will do a little better this time.'

'What is the cause of this newfound organisation of the pro-Sanctians?'

Niscoll nodded towards Lord Tain. 'Do you see that tall gentleman with the red scarf over his shoulders?'

'Lord Tain?'

'Yes. It is rumoured that he is behind it all. Have you heard of the Second Empire Association?'

'I've heard of it.'

'It is said that Lord Tain runs it with his sister Lady Ursula. She is also a member of the Corse, but she didn't receive enough votes to make the five hundred.'

'Why didn't the old government shut them down?'

'The secret police have been watching them closely,' said Niscoll, 'but unless they do something illegal, there are no grounds to take action. This is where our system of justice fails us. If Lord Denon had been arrested and thoroughly interrogated, then he might have provided evidence of illegal activity on the part of Lord Tain and his associates. Instead, they gutted him by the side of the Great Northern Highway.'

Several clerks appeared by the entrance.

'The votes have been counted,' one cried, 'and the results are on display within the voting hall.'

The crowd inside the bar stirred, and most began to follow the clerks as they strode away. Fyenna and Niscoll joined the others, and they made their way back to the voting hall. On the left-hand side of the chamber, all five hundred ballot papers had been pinned to the wall, sorted by name. A line of soldiers was standing close by, to prevent anyone from tampering with the votes, and the crowd surged forward, with each delegate eager to get a good view.

The chief clerk clapped her hands for attention, and the crowd stilled.

'The member with the most votes was Lord Metrius,' she cried, 'with eighteen.'

There was some polite applause, but a wave of fury passed over Metrius's face at the news.

'Five members received twelve votes,' the clerk went on. She began to read the names from a document held out in front of her, and Fyenna listened. All five members were well-known anti-Sanctians.

Niscoll shook her head. 'Oh dear. That's a lot of wasted votes.'

'Twenty-three members received ten votes apiece,' the clerk said. Again, she began to read out from a list of names, and the hall fell into silence. Many of the names were only known vaguely to Fyenna, and she watched the reactions of the faces of the others. With every name that was read out, she could see Lord Metrius's features fall further; while Lord Tain and his colleagues began to cheer and grin. Near the end of the list, Lady Niscoll's name was read out, and the old woman groaned quietly, and shook her head.

'You made it,' Fyenna whispered.

'May the spirits preserve me,' Niscoll whispered back.

'Finally,' said the clerk, 'four members each received nine votes. As there is but one seat upon the thirty remaining, a random ballot will now take place, to decide which of the four shall be accepted.'

The four delegates were called forward, and a clerk held out a velvet bag in front of them. Each delegate placed their hand into the bag and withdrew a token. The victorious candidate held his marked token aloft, to the sound of another cheer from the pro-Sanctians.

'Silence, please,' said the chief clerk. 'No other member received sufficient votes to be eligible for entry into the thirty. The successful candidates are now required to withdraw from the voting hall in order to form the government that shall rule Klef Mordain for the coming five years. All other delegates must remain in the Corsehall, to await the selection of the seventy by the thirty. Thank you.'

The crowd broke out into loud chatter, as the thirty elected delegates shook their colleagues' hands, and began to move towards one of the doorways, where soldiers and clerks were waiting to escort them from the hall.

'The next time we bump into each other,' Niscoll said to Fyenna, 'we will each have to pretend that none of this happened.'

'Such is the way of it,' said Fyenna. 'Good luck.'

'And good luck to you, Fyenna. You're not out of this yet.'

Fyenna stood back as she watched the thirty successful delegates be led from the hall. When the last of them had been escorted out, the door was closed, and two soldiers took up positions by it, sealing it off from the others. Fyenna glanced around at those left behind. As a relatively new member of the Corse, she had few close friends among them. She saw Lord Tain standing on her right, an expression of pure jubilation on his face as he talked to his colleagues, while a few from Lord Metrius's camp were almost in tears. Lord Tain glanced in her direction, and she looked away, but not before he had seen her staring at him.

He broke away from his colleagues and approached.

'Lady Fyenna, is it? I don't believe we have ever met.'

'Why would we have met, Lord Tain? I imagine we sit at opposite ends of the political spectrum.'

'Ah, I didn't know that. I was under the impression that you might be one of the unaligned members of the Corse. What did you think of the result?'

'I confess that I am not entirely sure what has just transpired. Many of the names were unfamiliar to me.'

'I see. Perhaps I should clarify things for you.' He smiled at her. 'Those in favour of a union with the Sanctian Empire got eleven delegates elected to the thirty.'

Fyenna's eyes widened. 'Eleven?'

'Indeed. A most spectacular result, wouldn't you say? Did you see Lord Metrius's face? He was furious with some of his own supporters for throwing their votes away on hopeless candidates, while our side behaved with impeccable discipline. Might I ask you a question in good faith?'

Fyenna said nothing.

'What would it take,' Tain went on, 'for you to come round to our point of view? Can you not see the enormous economic and cultural benefits that would arise from our union with the Sanctian Empire? At a stroke, all trade tariffs with the south would be abolished, and we would come under the protection of the mighty Sanctian army and navy. The city would be more prosperous than ever, and we would never again have to fear an attack from the Westlanders.'

Fyenna narrowed her eyes. 'It seems that you don't actually know who I am. I have a little experience of fighting Westlanders.'

'I remember that about you. You were at the Battle of Hader Pull, were you not?'

'I was. Do you recall what I did upon that battlefield?'

Tain narrowed his eyes, then he smiled. 'Ah. Yes. I see.'

'Then it must be clear to you why I could never support our annexation by the Sanctian Empire.'

'Let me say this to you – I am not in favour of the empire's policy towards Masters and Makers. I feel it is unnecessarily draconian.'

'And yet you would be willing to sacrifice them to further your aims.'

'Klef Mordain would have leverage in any negotiations with the Sanctians,' said Tain. 'We could stipulate, as a necessary precondition for us joining the empire, that no Masters and Makers within the city would be harmed.'

'Do you honestly believe Emperor Antonio would agree to that? And, if he did agree, how long do you think it would take before he went back upon his word? Once we are in the empire, we will have to obey their laws. There will be no going back.'

'All the same, my lady, our future lies with the Sanctians; it is inevitable. The longer we try to hold back the tide, the more difficult our position becomes. If you were to change your allegiance and join us, then you could assist in the negotiations. Together, we could force the Sanctians into accepting the presence of Masters and Makers in Klef Mordain.'

Fyenna laughed. 'Are you delusional, Lord Tain? The Sanctians' first demand will be that we hand over all of our Masters and Makers.'

'But how many of them actually live in the city? There is you, but I know of no other.'

Fyenna smiled. 'Come now, Lord Tain; even if I knew the answer to that question, do you think I would tell you? You are, with all due respect, nothing but a tool of the Sanctians. You do their bidding, and you place their interests above those of the city you profess to love.'

'What nonsense. The best interests of the city lie with joining the Sanctians. I can be true to both.'

'Does saying that help you sleep at night?'

'Let me assure you, my lady; I have no problems sleeping. My conscience is clear.'

'If that is the case, and you would be happy to see the Sanctians burn me at a stake, then perhaps you have no conscience.'

Lord Tain inclined his head. 'It has been a pleasure speaking with you.'

'And you, my lord.'

Tain turned, and strode away. Fyenna watched him walk up to a group of unaligned delegates, and engage them in conversation, then she lowered her gaze.

She hadn't realised it before, but with the success of the pro-Sanctians, she was probably destined to become one of their greatest enemies. She was the only member of the Corse that was widely known to be a Maker; even the peasants of the Arnos Bank knew what she had done at the Battle of Hader Pull. As such, it was inevitable that the Sanctians would be aware of her existence. Would they suspect that she knew the identities of every Master and Maker in Klef Mordain? A ripple of fear ran down her back. The strict secrecy of the Corse had served her well, but that secrecy was without any value once the pro-Sanctians had infiltrated the innermost circles of government. How long would it take them to suspect that Fyenna knew about the two schools? Perhaps they already suspected the truth, and Lord Tain had merely been rubbing her face in it.

Fyenna turned, then she walked back to the bar, which was starting to fill up again. She took a glass of white wine from a waiter's tray, and settled down to wait.

Four hours had passed before the clerks summoned everyone back to the voting hall.

The chief clerk strode into the centre of the large chamber, and clapped her hands.

'The thirty have selected the seventy,' she cried. 'The names of the seventy selected delegates have been pinned to the wall behind me. If you see your name upon the list, you will exit the hall by the right-hand door. If you do not see your name, you shall remain here. The random ballot to select those appointed to the auditing committees will take place as soon as all seventy have left the hall.'

She clapped her hands again, and the delegates rushed forward. Fyenna joined the press of men and women, as they peered up at the seven large sheets of paper that that been nailed to the back wall. Each sheet contained ten names, written in large, bold letters. A trickle of delegates began to leave the voting hall by the guarded right-hand entrance, while others returned to the centre of the chamber. Fyenna reached the front of the crowd, and began to scan the names. It was upon the second sheet that she recognised her own name. She staggered back a step.

She had been picked for something, but what? Her knowledge of the inner workings of the government was hazy at best, but she knew that the seventy tended to be appointed to junior roles – assisting members of the thirty, or taking charge of some smaller department.

Fyenna extricated herself from the crowd. She knew her duty, but a mixture of dread and disbelief made her legs feel as though they were frozen to the floor. A clerk noticed her.

'This way, ma'am,' he said, gesturing to the right-hand doorway.

Fyenna walked as though in a daze. A soldier checked her name at the entrance, and then she was allowed through. She followed a long corridor, and came to a chamber where the other members of the seventy were sitting in silence.

'What now?' she said to a clerk.

'Now, ma'am,' he said, 'you wait until your name is called out.'

More hours passed. Every ten minutes or so, a clerk would read out two or three names, and the chosen delegates would be escorted from the room. There was almost no talking in the windowless chamber, as each delegate pondered their fate.

When there were only a dozen left in the room, Fyenna's name was called out by a clerk. She got to her feet, and the clerk led her down another corridor. They ascended a flight of stairs, and the clerk knocked upon a door.

'Enter,' said a voice from within.

The clerk opened the door, and gestured for Fyenna to go inside. She strode through the entrance, and the clerk closed the door behind her.

'This is my new office,' said Lord Metrius from behind a grand desk. 'Do you like it, Fyenna?'

She glanced at the opulent furnishings, and the elegant tapestries on the walls.

'Yes, my lord,' she said.

'Take a seat.'

Fyenna walked forwards, and sat down in a comfortable armchair.

'This day has been an unmitigated disaster,' Metrius said. 'The government of Klef Mordain is now riddled with those who would sell us to the Sanctians for a sniff of glory. Yet, all is not lost. I have been selected to take on the role as Minister for Defence and Foreign Affairs.

I had wanted the financial ministry, but the gains made by the pro-Sanctians have warranted a shift in our strategy. Therefore, it has become imperative that we prevent the pro-Sanctians from being placed in charge of the city's defences. It was I who selected you for the seventy, Fyenna. I have a task of the utmost importance under my remit, and, quite frankly, you are the best woman for the job.'

'To what position have I been assigned, my lord?'

'I am placing you in charge of the city's Masters and Makers programme, Fyenna. You will be responsible for mobilising them in times of crisis. You must prepare all Master and Makers in the city, even your younger students, to be ready to repel an invasion by the Sanctians.'

Fyenna stared at the older man.

'If we are fortunate,' Metrius went on, 'there will be no such invasion. However, we cannot afford to be complacent. I am also appointing you to the rank of major in our armed forces. This will be a discreet appointment, but it will allow you to deal with the army and navy as an equal within the chain of command. You will, of course, be taking your orders directly from me. You will have to notify Head Master Drummond regarding these changes, as you will be responsible for both schools from now on. You will introduce the concepts of patriotism and duty into the hearts of each young Master and Maker, to instil within them the courage and fortitude they will require if the Sanctians decide to act. For your efforts, you will be entitled to a stipend of two thousand sovereigns a month, on top of your existing wages. You will contact me via my usual office, and it is from there that I will issue you with orders. We shall have our first strategy meeting three days from now, so I expect to see you at dawn that day. Train the students well, Fyenna, and organise the adult Masters and Makers into a coherent fighting unit. They will listen to you – after all, have you not once already saved this city? Your feats at the Battle of Hader Pull have earned you this commission, and I know that you will not let me down. Do you have any questions?'

'I'm sorry, my lord,' she said, 'but are you asking me to prepare children to fight for the city? Some of them are as young as fourteen.'

'Over the last few decades,' Metrius said, 'Klef Mordain has spent a considerable amount of money on our two secret schools; while hosting Masters and Makers within our city has also made us a target in the eyes of Emperor Antonio. Are we not entitled to call upon them in our hour of need? Were you aware that some of my fellow anti-Sanctians deem the schools to be a waste of money? They ask to see the reward for all of the risk and expense we have incurred on behalf of a small group of students. The reason the schools have not been closed is due to the great respect in which you are held, not because of any benefit we have received. Prepare them for a war that we hope never comes, Fyenna. By doing so, I will be able to assuage the doubts of my colleagues.' He nodded to her. 'Dismissed.'

Fyenna rose to her feet. She inclined her head towards Lord Metrius, and left the room. The clerk had been waiting outside in the corridor, and he glanced in her direction.

'What happens now?' she said.

'You are free to leave the Corsehall, ma'am.'

She gazed up and down the corridor. 'Which way is it? I am unfamiliar with this part of the building.'

'Go to your right, ma'am, and descend the stairs. At the bottom, carry on straight ahead, and you will find yourself in the main vestibule.'

'Thank you,' she said.

The clerk bowed. 'It is an honour to serve, ma'am.'

Fyenna slid the key into the lock, and opened the front door of her home in the residential district of the Old City. A solitary lamp had been left burning for her, and she locked the door as she entered the small hallway. She hung up her coat, unhooked the lamp from the wall, and crept over the floorboards.

Her husband appeared from a room to her left.

'There you are,' he said, kissing her on the cheek.

'You didn't have to wait up for me,' she said.

'I was worried. You are never usually back this late. The midnight bell pealed some time ago.'

'I was busy. Coming home late might be a more common occurrence from now on.'

'Shall I put the kettle on?' he said.

'I want to go straight to bed. It's been a long day.'

'This might be a silly question,' he said, 'but can you tell me anything about what you've been doing?'

She smiled at him. 'No.'

'Corse business?'

She nodded.

Her husband took the lamp from her hand. 'Then bed it is.'

He held up the lamp to illuminate their way, and led her up the stairs.

CHAPTER 8
THE SHARED ENEMY

Old City, Klef Mordain – 8th Day of Saluna 108

If Denny stood on the room's only chair, then he could just see out of the small window. The view was of the rooftops, domes and towers of the Old City, and, if he squinted to the left, he could see the tall arches of the Celestial Bridge crossing the estuary to the north. For two nights, he had been confined to the locked room in the attic of the safe house, with nothing to do but read one of the several books that had been left for him. With only one small lamp, the hours in which he could read were limited, and boredom was starting to creep through his mind. He got down from the chair and paced the room. The sun was rising, and he would soon be able to read again. Of more interest to him, he knew his breakfast would be on its way, sent upstairs from the kitchen he had passed when he had first arrived. It was always the same two men who brought him his food, and one would always be watching Denny, in case he tried to escape.

He stared at the door as his stomach rumbled. Breakfast was his favourite time of the day, as it signalled the end of another long night. He heard footsteps on the stairs outside, and smiled. A key turned in the lock, and the door opened.

Denny's smile disappeared. Instead of the usual two men with his tray, two different men were standing in the doorway.

'Good morning, Valiance,' said one, 'and apologies for keeping you here for longer than expected. You happen to have arrived in the midst of a very busy period for the Corse, and I am grateful for your patience. Might I come in?'

'Feel free,' said Denny, 'but there is only one seat.'

The man nodded to his colleague, who disappeared back down the stairs. The other man entered. He was middle aged, perhaps in his mid-forties, and he glanced at the pile of books sitting on the floor next to the mattress.

'Have you been reading?' he said.

'Whenever the light allows,' said Denny.

His colleague appeared with another chair. He set it down in the small room, then he inclined his head to the older man, and stepped outside. Denny and the older man sat.

'I have a few questions,' the man said. 'First, though – my name is Drummond, and you will refer to me as *sir*. I was told that you hail from Campsie. Which part?'

'I would rather not say, sir,' said Denny.

'Why not?'

'My family would be... embarrassed if they found out that I was here, sir. They don't know that I am a Master.'

'We pride ourselves on our discretion, Valiance,' said Drummond. 'Anything you say to me will go no further.'

'All the same, sir,' said Denny, 'I will not answer any questions about my past, my family, or where I was brought up. I don't know you. You could have been sent here to do me harm.'

Drummond frowned.

'Your caution is admirable,' he said, 'but unnecessary. I work for the Corse, and you are under my protection.'

'Isn't that exactly what an enemy would say?'

'Do you have enemies, Valiance?'

'Yes. They will be looking for me but, as far as I know, they won't be searching in Klef Mordain.'

'Are you trying to convince me to reject your application?' said Drummond. 'Do you know what happens if I refuse to accept you into the school for Masters?'

Denny hesitated. 'No.'

'You will be killed. It's really as simple as that. The city will not tolerate the presence of a rogue eighteen-year-old Master. Two agents from the secret police are currently waiting downstairs; the same two agents who have been bringing you food for the past few days. If I descend to tell them that I have decided not to enrol you, they will have you executed. Shall we begin again, Valiance? Where were you born?'

'Campsie.'

'Where in Campsie?'

Denny closed his mouth and looked away.

'You do not sound as though you come from Campsie,' Drummond went on.

Denny said nothing.

'Do you want to know from where I believe your accent originates?' said Drummond. 'To my ears, it is a little further south than Campsie. Only people from Subnestia or Sanctos enunciate their words as you do. Am I getting closer?'

Denny kept his expression unmoved. If he told Drummond the truth about who he was, then he had no doubt that the secret police would take him into custody. His father would be shamed, and the Sanctians outraged; and Klef Mordain would have gained a useful bargaining chip in their negotiations with the empire.

'I apologise, sir,' he said, 'but I will not reveal any more to you than I already have. If that is not good enough for you, then so be it.'

Drummond chuckled. 'It seems I have a stubborn little bastard on my hands. I sense more than a little arrogance in you. Perhaps you are unteachable.'

'Perhaps I am, sir.'

'All the same,' Drummond went on, 'I can remember how insufferable I was as an eighteen-year-old, and it is my job to guide the young

Masters who come to us into adulthood. Let us try a different tack. Why do you want to join the school, Valiance?'

'To learn how to be a Master, sir.'

'Yes, but why?'

'I have potential, sir. I don't want to waste it.'

'Then why did you not come here when you were fourteen? That is the customary age for new admissions.'

'I didn't know the school existed when I was fourteen, sir.'

'I am going to tell you something about one of the other students under my authority,' said Drummond. 'I shouldn't, but I will. He is fifteen, and he is due to start lessons this coming term. A year later than usual, but he has good reason to be late. He comes from Subnestia, which, as I am sure you know, is a subjugated province of the famed Sanctian Empire. His uncle was a Master, and he discovered the lad's secret, and began training him. Unfortunately, they were betrayed by their fellow Subnestians, and handed over to the Sanctians. His uncle was put to death in a public square, and the boy fled, on his own and penniless. He is safe now, for I will ensure that no harm comes to him. Tell me, Valiance – is your story any worse than that? If the Sanctians find out that we are harbouring one of their young fugitives, they will kick up a fuss. Do you know what? I don't care. To me, his well-being comes first. I look after my students, and I will protect them unto death. The entire school system for Masters and Makers is shrouded in secrecy, and I trust every single member of staff who works there. I also trust my students. The problem here is you, Valiance. If you cannot bring yourself to trust me, than we shall have nothing else to say to each other.'

'So much for discretion, sir,' said Denny. 'You just revealed that boy's secrets to me.'

'Yes. Does it matter? If I refuse your application, the secret will die with you; and if I accept it, you will be meeting this boy later today.'

'I want to tell you my past, but I can't. It's not about trust, sir; it's about...'

'Yes?'

'I will say no more, sir. If you accept me into the school, then I will do my best. I know that I will need to catch up. I know that I... that my past situation prevented me from training or studying. I cannot change that, nor am I able to change the fact that I have been forbidden from divulging any personal details to you.'

'Now we are getting somewhere,' said Drummond. 'You were *forbidden* from speaking. By whom, I wonder?' He got to his feet and opened the door, where his colleague was standing guard. 'Do we have any information about the man who brought Valiance to the *Star Inn*?'

The man whispered something into Drummond's ear.

'I see,' said Drummond. 'That is unfortunate. Once again, the secret police have acted prematurely, and now we have no way to trace the people who escorted Valiance to Klef Mordain.'

He closed the door and re-took his seat.

'What were you talking about, sir?' said Denny. 'Did something happen to Ter Angla?'

'Was that the man who led you to the *Star Inn*?'

'Yes.'

'The secret police slit his throat and dumped his body into the harbour, just minutes after you were separated from him.'

Denny's mouth opened. 'They killed him?'

'He was a loose end,' said Drummond, 'and the secret police don't like loose ends. He knew the name and face of an agent with contacts in the Corse; therefore, the police could not allow him to live. Was this man close to you?'

'He was my servant.'

'And how did you come to employ a servant with a name that clearly marks him out as being from Geathan?'

Denny said nothing.

'You are certainly not from Geathan,' said Drummond. 'At least, you were not born and brought up there. Do you have relatives from Geathan?'

'I am saying nothing.'

'A large sum of gold was retrieved from your... servant,' Drummond said; 'gold that I assume was meant to pay for your board and lodgings at the school. How did you come by such an amount?'

Denny clamped his mouth shut.

'You are giving me no choice,' said Drummond. 'Unless you are prepared to say something that will change my mind, I will refuse to allow you to enrol in the school.'

Denny gazed at the bare wooden floor of the room, his thoughts on what had happened to Ter Angla. The man had accompanied him and his father for hundreds of miles across the Central Provinces after they had fled from Sanctos, only to die at the hands of suspicious agents in Klef Mordain. The injustice of it rankled. Ter Angla had done nothing to deserve his fate; nothing but be loyal to Denny's father.

'The enemies who are looking for me,' he said.

'Yes?'

'They are from the Sanctian Empire.'

'And why are they looking for you?'

'Because I ran away.'

'Why did you run?

'Why do you think, sir? If they had discovered that I am a Master, they would have executed me. I managed to hide my abilities for nearly four years.'

'Are your parents alive?'

'Yes, as far as I know, sir.'

'Did one of them send you here?'

'Yes, sir. That's where I got the gold.'

Drummond got to his feet.

'I will be back soon, Valiance,' he said. 'I need to discuss your case with a few others.'

Denny remained where he was as the man left the room. He heard the door being locked, and then his stomach rumbled again. He wondered what his father was doing, and if he knew what had happened to Ter Angla; then he wondered why he wasn't afraid. He should be, he reasoned. If Drummond refused to enrol him, then agents from the city's secret police would ascend the stairs to kill him, and yet Denny felt calm. He would fight back, but he would not give them the satisfaction of seeing him scared.

The key sounded in the lock, and Denny prepared himself. The door opened, and Drummond appeared in the entrance.

'Come with me, Valiance,' he said. 'We have decided to let you join the school.'

After two hours of sitting blindfolded in the back of a wagon, Denny was led down onto the ground. He felt the cobbles beneath his feet, then an arm guided him forward. He ascended a few steps, and then entered a building. The door was closed behind him, and the blindfold was removed.

'Welcome to the School for Masters, Valiance,' said Drummond. 'Its location is a strict secret, and you are not permitted to leave on your own.'

Denny gazed around at the interior of the hallway.

'I live here,' Drummond went on, 'and my apartment is on the ground floor, along with the kitchen and laundry room. Above are the classrooms, and then the students' accommodation is on the top floor. We only had two students last year, and both will be continuing with their studies. With four new boys starting this year, the students will have to share rooms, but, due to your age, you will be getting a room of your own. As you have probably gathered, I am the Head Master, the governor of this school. The other boys will be sitting down to lunch – should we join them?'

'Can I ask – what made you accept me, sir? I thought you were going to reject my application.'

'You came very close to being rejected. What swung it, I think, was that you and Klef Mordain share the same enemy – the Sanctian Empire. You did very well to point that out to me. The Sanctians have many spies in this city, and they are aware that we are secretly training both Masters and Makers. However, they don't know where the two schools are located, and they don't know the identities of any of the staff who work in either of them.'

'Does that mean the girls are in a different building, sir?'

Drummond smiled. 'Yes, Valiance. We come together for a few shared classes, but the Makers live elsewhere. Try not to be disappointed, and remember that the majority of the Maker students are a little too young for you.'

Denny nodded. 'Yes, sir.'

'Come on; follow me.'

Drummond started to lead Denny along a corridor.

'My rooms are on the left, while the offices, kitchen and laundrette are on the right,' Drummond said. 'You are responsible for washing your own clothes and bedding, but meals will be prepared for you. If you have any problems, speak to your teacher first, and then come to me if you feel that you're not getting anywhere. The gold that was on your servant was more than enough to cover the expenses for the whole of your first year, and so, to prove that we are not crooks, we will issue you with a small allowance for the remainder – fifteen sovereigns a week. One of the staff can go shopping for you; just hand them a list and the money. We are going to allow you to buy a little wine or beer with your allowance, but you must not give any to the younger students.'

They ascended a flight of stairs, and passed a series of empty classrooms.

'Will I be in with the first years for every class, sir?' Denny said.

'For most of them. When classes are held with the Makers, we put you all in together. Those lessons are more theoretical, and cover the history of Masters and Makers, as well as your general studies and so on.'

They ascended again, and came to a wood-lined dining room with two long tables. As soon as they entered, five boys glanced up from the lower table.

'Good morning,' said Drummond, 'or has the noon bell rung already? I lose track. Anyway, boys, I'd like to introduce our newest student, who has arrived here just in time to start the spring term. This is Valiance of Campsie. He is eighteen, which makes him the oldest student here, but he is untrained, and so will be joining the first year classes.' He pointed at the oldest boy. 'Valiance, this is Constans, our only fourth year student. He will be eighteen next winter, and has three years of study under his belt. He has had a room of his own for three years but, this year, he will be sharing with two first years – Salus, who is his younger cousin, and Ignatius. Both are fourteen.'

Constans frowned.

'As you can see, Valiance,' said Drummond, 'Constans is delighted with this arrangement. On Constan's left is Aplin, who will be starting second year, and next to him is Marlow. They are both fifteen, but Marlow will be beginning first year, along with you. They are also sharing a room. Sit down, Valiance, and get something to eat while I check to see if your room is ready.'

Drummond walked from the dining room, and Denny strode towards the table.

'Hello,' he said. 'I have already forgotten your names, but I guess I will learn them all soon enough.'

He sat, and began to pile food onto a spare plate.

Constans eyed him. 'You are eighteen, and untrained?'

'That's right.'

'I could kill you with a flick of my hand.'

Denny shrugged. 'What's stopping you?'

'Why have you not been trained?' said Salus.

Denny glanced at him. 'Are you the younger cousin?'

'Yes. Constans is my father's nephew. Both of our fathers are members of the Corse.'

Denny began to eat. 'That means nothing to me.'

Marlow laughed.

'Do you think that was funny, you little prick?' said Constans.

'Yes, I do,' said Marlow. 'You and your cousin are stuck-up arseholes.'

'Is that a Subnestian accent?' said Denny, remembering what

Drummond had told him about the student who had run away after his uncle's execution.

'Yeah,' said Marlow. 'Is that a problem?'

'Not at all,' said Denny. 'I have nothing against Subnestians.'

'Well,' said Constans, 'you are from Campsie, so that doesn't surprise me. The people down there are hardly renowned for their sophistication. *The peasants of that ilk...*'

'*Doth lie with ignorance*,' said Denny. 'You are not the only one here who can quote Tydian the Great, Constans. I may not have trained as a Master, but that doesn't mean I didn't receive an education.'

'Who's Tydian the Great?' said Ignatius.

'Poor Ignatius can barely read,' said Salus. 'Head Master Drummond almost rejected his application on grounds of illiteracy.'

'Tydian was a poet from the Elestian Empire,' said Denny. 'If you need any help with your reading and writing, Ignatius, I'd be happy to lend a hand. Where are you from?'

'The Arnos Bank.'

'I haven't heard of it.'

'It's a vast slum on the northern outskirts of Klef Mordain,' said Salus. 'My father says that we built it there, so that if the Westlanders ever attack us again, they will have to pass through miles of shanty-dwellings before they reach the civilised parts of the city.'

'Are the Westlanders likely to attack again?' said Denny.

'Not since we kicked their arses at the Battle of Hader Pull,' said Salus. 'Our army killed over twenty thousand of the savages that day.'

'Fuck you,' spat Aplin. 'What have I told you about calling Westlanders savages?'

'Well, they are,' said Salus.

Aplin clenched his fists.

'What's the problem?' said Denny.

'My mother was a Westlander,' said Aplin. 'She was captured in the retreat from Hader Pull.'

'They got what they deserved,' said Constans. 'They were trying to conquer our city. What's the matter, Aplin – does the truth hurt? Are you going to go off crying to your moon gods again?'

'Leave him be,' said Denny. 'None of us choose our parents. We can, however, choose when to be civil, and when to be an arsehole.'

Constans and Salus glared at him.

'Why didn't you get any training?' said Ignatius.

'Where I come from,' Denny said, 'being a Master would get you killed. I had never heard of this school, so I kept my mouth closed and told no one what I could do – which isn't much. I had no one around who could show me how to do anything, and I couldn't bring it up, in case I was arrested.'

'I know the feeling,' said Marlow. 'I had my uncle, though. He showed me a few things.'

'You will still have to go through first year,' said Constans. 'Your uncle didn't show you that much; just a few parlour tricks.'

Marlow glanced at Denny. 'Do you see what I mean about them being stuck up? I've been here for three weeks, waiting for term to begin, and all I've heard from Constans and Salus is how wonderful they think they are.' He smiled at Constans. 'You aren't the oldest any more.'

'Do you think I care?' said Constans. 'I know far more about being a Master than Valiance. I will be graduating from this school while he finishes first year, if he makes it that far. He might be too old to learn anything.'

'You might be right,' said Denny. 'I'll be starting at the beginning. There's no shame in that; everyone has to start somewhere.'

'Can you do anything?' said Ignatius.

'I can probably do less than the others joining first year,' he said. 'That's why I'm here – to learn. We can help each other, so that we can all be the best Masters we are capable of becoming. I'm serious. Competition is good, but only if it spurs us on; there's no point in squabbling and fighting like children, not when we're all on the same side.'

Constans laughed. 'Are we on the same side? When I graduate, I intend to dedicate my career to the defence of Klef Mordain. What are you going to do, Valiance?'

'I will probably fight the Sanctian Empire,' said Denny. 'I guess that's the real reason I'm here. Emperor Antonio has made a terrible mistake in his campaign to wipe out all Masters and Makers. I think he's frightened of us.'

'What would you know about Emperor Antonio?' said Salus.

'The same as everyone else,' said Denny. 'He hates us, and wants to kill us. I don't need to know any more.' He pushed his plate away. 'That feels better. Is the food here always this good?'

Ignatius nodded. 'Yes. Mealtimes are the best parts of each day.'

Aplin laughed. 'Just wait until you have your first lessons with the Makers. That's the best thing about being here. It's the only time we get to see any girls.'

'Just keep your hands off Raewyn,' said Constans.

'How many Makers are in their school?' said Marlow.

'There were three last year,' said Aplin, 'but one of them was in fourth year, and she graduated at the end of last term. There might be some new first years, though. Whatever you do, don't piss off the Head Maker. Lady Fyenna is a lot stricter than Head Master Drummond. If you speak in her class without permission, she's liable to send you to your room without any dinner.'

'Does she teach the mixed classes?' said Denny.

'Some of them,' said Aplin. 'She fought at Hader Pull, so I don't think she likes me much.'

'Master Drummond was also at Hader Pull,' said Constans, 'but he was only twenty-two at the time. Maker Fyenna was a few years older than him, so she was his superior officer.'

'That's quite right,' said Drummond.

They turned, and saw the Head Master standing by the entrance to the dining room.

He stepped forward. 'I played my role in the battle,' he said, 'but it was Maker Fyenna who turned the tide. She summoned a wall of timber spikes just as the Westlander cavalry were charging towards our foot soldiers. I have never seen anything like it.'

'But you used your powers, sir, to make the wood she needed,' said Constans.

'Yes, I did. I transformed tons of soil and rock into timber for her, but she had to stand out in full view of the charging horsemen in order to summon the spikes. She had them appear a yard in front of her – a yard! It takes nerves of steel to do such a thing, and you will all accord her the respect she is due. Now, Valiance, if you would please come with me? Your room is ready.'

Denny got to his feet and followed Drummond out of the dining room. They ascended another flight of stairs, and came to a corridor with several doors on either side.

'What do you think of your fellow students?' said Drummond.

'I like them, sir,' said Denny, 'but I don't like the way that Constans and Salus belittle the others.'

'Their upbringing was quite different from the rest of the students. So, you have read Tydian the Great, have you?'

Denny shook his head. 'You were listening to us, sir, weren't you?'

'Of course I was. I wanted to see how the others would react to your presence, and I wanted to see how you would react to them. I liked your little speech about helping each other.'

'I meant it, sir.'

'Did you?'

'Yes, sir.'

They stopped at a door. 'That's good to hear,' said Drummond, 'because, as of this moment, I am placing you partly responsible for Ignatius's lessons on reading and writing. I heard you offer to help him, and I think it's a good idea. You won't be doing it alone, of course, but I would like you to spend an hour or two each evening working with him. He is the youngest, and you are the oldest, so it makes sense. Don't you agree?'

'Yes, sir.'

Drummond opened the door to a tiny room, with a single narrow window. Sitting on the low bed was Denny's pack, along with the pile of books he had been reading in the safe house.

'This used to be a storage cupboard,' Drummond said, 'and it is now your room. It's small, but you have it all to yourself. I know for a fact that Constans would bite my hand off to obtain this room, instead of having to share with Salus and Ignatius.'

'The size is fine, sir. I don't have many possessions.'

'The bell will ring when it's dinnertime,' said Drummond. 'Your teacher will be there, so make sure you are on time.'

Drummond walked away, and Denny entered his room. He strode over to the window and gazed out at a view of the bay. To his right he could see the Celestial Bridge, while, before him, the commercial harbour stretched away, its long piers filled with ships of all sizes and types. The sun was overhead, and the waters of the bay were sparkling in its light.

Denny smiled, then he sat down on the bed, picked up a book, and began to read.

CHAPTER 9
THINGS UNWRITTEN

Old City, Klef Mordain – 18th Day of Saluna 108

'Lift your feet while I am trying to sweep,' said Annalise, 'and put your glass onto a coaster; it's going to leave a mark on the table.'

Lothar rolled his eyes, and raised his feet off the floor.

'This is so typical,' Annalise said, as she swept under him. 'I'm doing all the work, while you sit there and get drunk.'

'I have one day off every fortnight,' said Lothar. 'The last time I had a drink was fourteen days ago.'

'I would have thought you'd have known better,' she said.

Lothar narrowed his eyes. 'What is that supposed to mean?'

'It's no secret that Duke Hector was paying you to keep poor Walter drunk all the time. Have you no shame?'

'Believe me; I have plenty of shame, but that doesn't mean I'm planning on remaining sober for the rest of my life.'

Amery opened his eyes. He had been lying on a couch near the window, trying to get some sleep, and the sound of Lothar and Annalise arguing had pulled him from a pleasant dream.

He sat up. 'Stop bickering, you two. I have a headache.'

Lothar's eyes widened. 'I didn't even know you were there.'

'Such are the perils of daytime drinking,' said Annalise. 'Mister Amery has been sleeping on that couch for hours.'

Lothar staggered to his feet. He swayed, and almost fell into Annalise.

'Watch where you're going, you big oaf,' she cried.

Lothar reached into a pocket, and took out a crumpled piece of paper. He stumbled over to Amery, and threw it at him.

'What do you make of that?' he shouted.

Amery blinked, then he peered down at the paper lying in his lap. 'I don't know. What is it?'

'Read it,' Lothar said.

Amery picked up the piece of paper and smoothed it out. As soon as he had done so, he recognised it.

'Ah.'

'Well? Is it true? Is Abigone missing? The lads I work with are all convinced the secret police have murdered her. Half of them are keeping one eye on the docks, to see if her body appears in the water.'

'My employer is merely trying to discredit the Corse; it's nothing to worry about.'

Lothar's expression darkened. 'Your employer is responsible for these leaflets? They've been posted up all over town.'

'Please don't shout,' said Amery. 'I am feeling a little fragile. Look; everything is fine. My employers have no idea that a secret school for Makers even exists. All they know about Abigone is that she arrived in the city, and that she hasn't been seen since. And I can hardly tell them the truth, now, can I? I have to pretend that I also have no clue as to her whereabouts.'

'Are you certain that there is nothing more to it than that?'

'Quite certain, Lothar.'

'I want to see the princess. I need to confirm that she is all right with my own eyes.'

'I'm afraid that is out of the question.'

'Why?'

'Because I don't know the location of the school. Like everything else in this city, it's a secret.'

'I'm going to visit Lord Metrius. I remember where his office is. I shall demand to gain access to Princess Abigone, and I won't be taking no for an answer.'

'If you do that, Lothar, then the body your colleagues find bobbing up and down in the bay will be yours.'

Lothar snorted. 'I'm not frightened of a few secret police officers. Fuck them.'

'Do you have any relatives living in Upper Down?'

'Why?'

'So I shall know who to write to in the event of your untimely death.'

'Listen to Mister Amery, Lothar,' said Annalise. 'I am also worried about the princess, but marching around the city demanding answers will do more harm than good. Just think – you were one of the last people seen with Abigone; you might be arrested as a suspect.'

Lothar narrowed his eyes.

'Furthermore,' said Amery, 'you know about the existence of the secret school. That would give the Corse a very good reason to have you strangled and flung into the bay.'

Lothar sat down on the couch. 'Lord Walter gave me one job,' he said: 'to look after Princess Abigone.'

'Lord Walter did not understand the complexity of the situation,' said Amery. 'It is not your fault that you have been unable to fulfil his request. No one could have.'

'Then what do we do?'

'Nothing. We sit tight, and wait for the school year to end.'

'That's months away. Perhaps I should write a letter to Walter, explaining things.'

'Any letter would be opened and read by the secret police. You would have to find a trusted courier to memorise your message, and then bear it to Upper Down in person. Even then, there are risks. What if the courier is interrogated when they are trying to leave the city?

Would they keep your secrets if threatened with torture? Besides, letters have already been sent.'

'What letters?'

'My employers are concerned about Abigone's well-being, and so they have dispatched agents to deliver letters to Princess Nolan in Lesser Down, and to Princess Kilbride in Upper Down, informing them that Abigone is missing, presumed dead.'

'Wouldn't those letters also be stopped and read by the police?'

'No. My employers are both... em... Let's just say that they are now able to act without too much interference from the Corse.'

'Why? Are they members of the Corse?'

'I didn't say that.'

'You didn't have to. It's fucking obvious.'

'Watch your language, Lothar,' said Annalise.

'Who else could afford to pay Amery so much money?' said Lothar. 'And all the long hours, working through the night, the secrecy...'

'You mustn't speak of it,' said Amery.

'Why not? There's no one here but us.'

'No, but you are drunk, Lothar, and alcohol is hardly renowned for its ability to help one keep a secret.'

'Why do you think I get drunk in the house, instead of going out to a tavern? I am well aware of what too much alcohol can do. My colleagues down at the docks think I don't like them, because I never go out drinking with them.' He leaned back against the cushions. 'I am sick of lying to everyone. I can't talk about Abigone, or the real reason I'm in Klef Mordain, or about who I know in Upper Down. I've told so many lies I'm starting to forget them.'

'For all our sakes,' said Amery, 'let us hope your memory improves.'

'Why are you worried? You aren't in any danger.'

'I am in more danger than you,' said Amery. 'My employers do not know that it was I who told Lord Metrius that Abigone was a Maker. Were they to discover this, I would be lucky to preserve my life, never mind my job.'

'Why would they care? If they are members of the Corse, then aren't they supporters of the secret school?'

'The politics of Klef Mordain have radically changed in recent days, and more change is to come. All I can say for now is that certain divisions may have opened up within the Corse, with some favouring one policy, and others favouring another. Secrets are being wrapped within secrets, and I doubt that any single member of the Corse knows all that is happening. It is a dangerous time, when one wrong word to the wrong person is all it would take for blood to be spilled.'

'Were we wrong to come here?' said Annalise.

'Not at all,' said Amery. 'We did exactly as the regents of Upper Down requested. All we need to do is keep our composure, and bide our time.' He stood. 'Has the water been heated?'

'It has.'

'Then I think I shall have a bath, and get ready for work.'

'Are you working again tonight?' said Annalise.

'I am. Could you ask the drivers to have the carriage ready to leave one hour from now?'

'Of course,' she said. 'Shall I make you some dinner before you go?'

'There is no need,' he said. 'I will be eating elsewhere this evening.'

Amery had the carriage halt along a main street, and he walked the last hundred yards to the offices of the Second Empire Association. He kept his gaze lowered, and wondered if any members of the secret police were watching him. Those opposed to his employers' cause would no doubt be aware that Amery was working for the association, and he had often imagined that he was being followed. He strode down the alleyway towards the front door of the building. Two armed men were standing guard by the entrance, and no more graffiti had been daubed on the walls. The two men nodded to Amery as he opened the door and passed into the interior. Inside, the ground floor was a hive of activity, with staff rushing from room to room. Over a dozen new men and women had been hired by the Second Empire Association since the election – secretaries, scribes, guards, and even a cook had been recruited; and the building never fell silent.

Amery ascended the stairs as Lord Tain was descending them, and they met halfway.

'Good evening, Amery,' said Tain. 'Did you bring your carriage?'

'I did, sir. It is parked on the main road.'

'Then it shall take us to this evening's destination. My sister has already gone ahead, along with a few other members of the association. I will tell you where we are going on the way.'

'Very good, sir.'

Amery turned, and they began walking down the stairs.

'Can your drivers be trusted?' Tain said.

'Yes, sir. They are both loyal to me.'

'And how did you come by their loyalty?'

'I pay them, feed them, and allow them to live in my townhouse, sir. They are strangers in Klef Mordain and, frankly, they depend upon me.'

A few of the staff bowed their heads as Tain and Amery passed them in the hallway, then they left the building.

'We are going out for the evening,' Tain said to the two guards in the alleyway.

'Do you require an escort, sir?' said one.

'That won't be necessary,' said Tain. 'We shall be perfectly safe.'

They walked to the end of the alleyway, and turned right at the main road.

Amery glanced at the crowds on the pavement. 'Do you think we are being watched, sir?'

'I would be disappointed with the secret police if we weren't. How far is your carriage?'

Amery pointed. 'It's just up ahead, sir.'

The two drivers were sitting by the rear of the carriage, and they got to their feet as Amery and Tain approached.

'I require your services again already,' said Amery.

'No problem, sir,' said one of the drivers. 'Where are we going?'

Amery glanced at Tain.

'Take us to Cornmarket Road,' said Tain. 'Park there, and await our return.'

The drivers bowed. 'Yes, sir.'

One opened the side door, and Amery gestured for Tain to climb aboard. Amery followed him into the carriage, and the door was closed. Amery sat down opposite Tain, and the two men waited for the carriage to set off. Its wheels began to move over the cobbles, and Tain glanced out at the street.

'We are going to the Sanctian Embassy,' he said. 'We have a meeting with the ambassador, and you will be present.'

'It would be an honour, sir,' said Amery.

'We shall be walking in through the front door,' Tain went on, 'in the clear knowledge that our enemies will have agents watching us as we do so. There are always agents outside the Sanctian Embassy; it is one of the certainties of life. In this case, however, I want them to see us enter the building. It amuses me to picture the panic and confusion our presence there will inspire in our enemies.'

'Is there anything I need to know before we get there, sir?'

'I don't think so. No, wait; you should probably know that word arrived this morning from the Central Provinces. It seems that, about a month ago, Yearl officially joined the Sanctian Empire, after years of being an associate member. As it is your homeland, I thought you should probably know.'

'Thank you for telling me, sir.'

'It means, of course, that the old capital of the Elestian Empire is now a major city of the Sanctian Empire. I suspect that Campsie and Jallin will follow soon, and then, in time, Lesser and Greater Down. The Central Provinces are being reunited. Does this news please you or upset you?'

'Neither, if I am honest, sir. Yearl has been a member of the Sanctian Empire in all but name for many long years. It was only a matter of time before they formalised the relationship. Do you know what happened to the King of Yearl and his family?'

'The king was forced to abdicate but, beyond that, I have no news of his fate. If I had to speculate, I would imagine that he has been placed onto a remote country estate, and is living off a large pension. The Sanctians wouldn't have made a martyr of him; it's not their way. He'll be safe enough, as long as he makes no attempt to reclaim his throne. Anyway; enough about Yearl. You have only been working for us for two weeks, but I think it would be a good idea to let you into a few secrets. The first is one that I am sure that you will have already guessed. Both Lady Ursula and I are indeed members of the Corse. I have twice been elected into the ranks of the five hundred. The first time it happened, I was selected to sit on the auditing committee that oversees the activities of the secret police – again, you might have already guessed this from some of the things I have told you. I gained a firsthand insight into how the secret police operate, and I witnessed their successes, and their failures. In truth, they are not as competent as most people believe, and they are subject to the same biases and mistakes that afflict everyone else. They have a few extremely proficient operatives, but they mostly rely upon ordinary citizens coming forward with information. Of course, I lost my seat on that committee when the previous government dissolved itself. With the latest round of elections, I found myself placed on to the stand-by list, and I now have no official role to play. Part of me cannot help but wonder if this was intentional. My political enemies know about my leadership of the Second Empire Association, and it would not surprise me if they had conspired to ensure that I was given no position of power.'

'That might be true, sir.'

'At today's meeting,' Tain went on, 'you will be introduced to the ambassador and his staff, and you will also be seeing a few other members of the Corse – members that your hard work helped elect into the ranks of the thirty. One of them, a Lord Harrow, is likely to...'

'I beg you not to say any more, sir,' said Amery. 'With that last statement, you have just broken article seventeen of the Klef Mordain criminal code of law. As my employer, you are entitled to confide in me that you are a member of the Corse, but you are not permitted to speak about the membership of the thirty.'

Tain gazed at Amery, his thoughts unreadable.

'Forgive me, sir,' said Amery. 'You hired me to dispense legal advice, and so I feel it is my duty to help you avoid straying into criminality.'

Tain smiled. 'Perhaps you should look at it in a different way. All pro-Sanctian members of the five hundred, and of the thirty, are affiliates of the Second Empire Association. One could even say that they are fellow employees; in which case I was merely sharing relevant information among the employees of the organisation I head. Does that assuage your concerns?'

It didn't, but Amery nodded.

'During the meeting,' Tain went on, 'I want you to sit next to the scribe who will be recording the minutes. There is a... slim chance that some things will be said that, perhaps, may wander a little over the line between legality and illegality. If that occurs, you are to ensure that the scribe's notes can never be used against us in any investigation or prosecution. Is that clear?'

'You wish me to excise or amend any criminal remarks, sir?'

'Indeed. If necessary, you will re-write the scribe's notes in their entirety.'

'Perhaps it would be better if no minutes were taken, sir.'

'Oh, we can't have that. The Second Empire Association prides itself on honesty and transparency, in stark contrast to the secrecy and lies propounded by the Corse. The minutes are a vital part of that, and they shall be stored in the association's archives. That way, the next time the secret police decide to raid the premises, they will be able to confirm that no criminal activity has taken place. Of course, now that we have eleven pro-Sanctians elected to the thirty, the likelihood of a raid has diminished somewhat, but there is no harm in taking sensible precautions.'

The carriage came to halt, and one of the drivers stepped down to the roadside. He opened the side door.

'My lords,' he said, 'we have arrived on Cornmarket Road.'

'Thank you, my good man,' said Tain.

Amery and Tain descended from the carriage. They were still in the government district of the Old City, and the street was bustling with smartly-attired men and women of the Klef Mordain elite. Amery glanced up at the building in front of them. From outward appearances, it looked like a fortress, with narrow slit windows, and battlements on the upper storeys. Its main entrance was a heavily-guarded door set into a deep archway, and the blue and white flag of the Sanctian Empire was fluttering from a pole positioned a yard above it.

Tain gestured to Amery, and the two men made their way to the entrance. The guards seemed to recognise Lord Tain, and they moved aside, while one held the door open for them. Amery and Tain passed through into a large entrance hall, where several courtiers and officials were waiting.

'My lord,' said one, bowing before Tain, 'welcome back to the Sanctian Embassy. His Eminence the ambassador awaits your presence in the reception hall. Might I take your guest's name for our records?'

'This is Mister Amery of Yearl, my lawyer,' said Tain. 'He is a citizen of the Sanctian Empire.'

'Thank you, my lord,' said the official. 'Please come with me.'

The official led Amery and Tain through the large building. They ascended an ornate staircase flanked with paintings of the emperor and his family, and Amery gazed up at the stern visage of Antonio. In another painting he saw Antonio standing next to his two siblings, and Amery recognised Prince Valentino from the siege of Upper Down. The woman next to them was their sister Princess Carla, the mother of Count Sebastian's wife.

They entered a great hall at the top of the stairs, where a small crowd was gathered. Lady Ursula was there, talking to several people unknown to Amery. Tain made straight for a man dressed in a fine suit, who was speaking to a few members of the Corse that Amery recognised from their visits to the Second Empire Association.

'Your Eminence,' said Tain, bowing.

'Lord Tain,' said the man; 'so good of you to come.'

'Lord Ambassador,' Tain went on, 'might I introduce Mister Amery of Yearl to you? He is a lawyer by profession, and he was instrumental in our recent success at the elections.'

'How nice to meet you, Mister Amery,' said the ambassador.

'The honour is mine, Your Eminence,' said Amery, bowing. 'Lord Tain is, of course, exaggerating somewhat. The electoral plan was the fruit of his genius alone, and I am merely his humble servant.'

The ambassador laughed. 'A modest lawyer, eh? Wherever did you find him, Tain? Shall we sit? I think everyone is present.'

The crowd moved toward a long table. The ambassador and his staff took their places down one side, while Tain, Ursula and the others from Klef Mordain sat down opposite them. Amery ensured he was sitting next to Petros, a scribe from the Second Empire Association, who was carrying paper, quills and an ink pot.

The ambassador remained standing.

'Welcome all,' he said. 'For those of you who do not know me, I am Ambassador Tertius of Sanctos, the representative of the Sanctian Empire in the city of Klef Mordain. It has been my pleasure to serve the blessed emperor in this capacity for seven years and, if His Imperial Majesty is willing, then I look forward to serving for many more years.' He smiled. 'Not too many, though. It is the will of the blessed emperor that all former peoples and nations of the old Elestian Empire will one day see fit to join the Sanctian Empire. Klef Mordain was once the premier port city of that first empire, and I hope that, in the near future, it can ascend to a similar role in the second. Before we begin, I would like to offer my sincere and heartfelt congratulations to the Second Empire Association upon the results of the recent election.'

Amery's hand crept out to block the scribe from writing any more. Petros shot him a glance, and Amery shook his head.

'With eleven pro-Sanctians now securely embedded within the government of this city,' the ambassador went on, 'I cannot help but feel that change is coming to Klef Mordain. Our political opponents have taken the ministries of defence, foreign affairs, and justice, among others; but that has left several other ministries under the control of those who long for Klef Mordain to join the Sanctian Empire. The purpose of this meeting is to begin a new conversation – a conversation that examines what we should do with this tremendous opportunity.' He smiled again. 'Sitting before me are two newly-elected members of the thirty – Lord Harrow and Lord Penny, and I now invite them to speak to us all.'

Amery groaned quietly as the ambassador took his seat. More than half of what he had said had included information that someone in his position shouldn't know; secret information reserved to the innermost circles of the Corse.

Lord Harrow stood. 'Thank you, Your Eminence. I have been given the ministry of education, a position unknown within the government of the Sanctian Empire. With this ministry, the previous governments of Klef Mordain have fed the children of this city a diet of unadulterated propaganda. Textbooks were censored, and history rewritten, in order to present the Sanctian Empire in the worst possible light. That will end. Even as I speak, teaching materials are being removed from the schools of Klef Mordain, and teachers have been issued with fresh instructions. New books are being printed, books that will offer a more positive impression of the Sanctian Empire.'

There was a smattering of applause.

'Thank you,' he said. 'There are, however, two schools in the city that remain outwith my control.'

The large room fell into complete silence.

'I refer, of course,' Lord Harrow went on, 'to the School for Makers, and the School for Masters. Officially, these schools do not exist, and when I made enquiries about them, I was told in no uncertain terms by Lord Metrius to mind my own business. These schools are a breeding ground for hatred against the Sanctian Empire, and it is imperative that we uncover the truth about their locations, and the staff who work there. For many long years, we have been kept in ignorance regarding these details, but we now have reason to suspect that a certain Lady Fyenna of Liliacos might be involved. As the city's highest-profile Maker – indeed, as the only known Maker within the bounds of the city – she was elected onto the five hundred, and then selected onto the seventy. Now, the roles of the seventy are open knowledge among the thirty, as it was we who selected them in the first place. Lord Metrius himself picked Lady Fyenna, but he has refused to reveal the position given to her. Would it not make sense that it pertains in some way to the running of these secret schools? I propose that a team of dedicated agents is commissioned to keep a close watch over Lady Fyenna and, if necessary, to eliminate her.'

'Come now,' said Lady Ursula. 'Lady Fyenna is a war hero, and she is much beloved by the ordinary citizens of Klef Mordain. We cannot simply *eliminate* her, as you put it. Would it not be better to catch her in the midst of a revolutionary plot, in order to discredit her first? I agree that agents should be commissioned, but they should record everything she says and does, in order to find a means by which we could open a formal investigation into her activities. There are so many laws in this city, that it is almost impossible to exist without breaking a few. Let us find out which ones Lady Fyenna is breaking, and let justice take its course.'

'I have a suggestion as to how we could do that,' said Lord Tain, as Lord Harrow took his seat. 'I happen to know a little about Lady Fyenna's domestic situation. In fact, I have it on good authority that her husband is a pro-Sanctian sympathiser. He is a successful businessman, with significant stakes in several large shipping companies. On the one hand, he can see the obvious economic advantages that would accrue from our entry into the empire, but, on the other, he is naturally protective of his wife. He knows the Sanctians' policy regarding Makers. However, he may have a weakness. We suspect that one of his companies is involved in the illegal import of goods from the Central Provinces, goods that are shipped into the city covertly, in order to avoid paying taxes upon them. Could we not investigate this further? If any crimes have been committed, then the secret police could threaten to have him gutted on some back street in Nether Hall, unless he was willing to assist us in the case against his wife.'

Lord Penny got to his feet. 'I may be able to assist Lord Tain's endeavours, as I have been appointed as Minister of Trade. The harbour and customs authorities are now under my jurisdiction, and I could easily arrange a raid upon the ships belonging to the husband of Lady Fyenna.'

'Say no more,' said the ambassador. 'Do what you feel you must do to further our cause, Lords Tain and Penny. If we can threaten the tranquillity of Lady Fyenna's household, then she might disclose the locations of the schools in order to save her husband's life.'

Lord Penny bowed his head. 'Lord Tain, I will speak to you about this in more detail later.' He sat down again.

'Now,' said the ambassador, 'I wish to speak of another matter, one that is out of my hands. I have been notified by my superiors on Sanctos that the blessed emperor has decided to make a demonstration of his power to the ordinary citizens of Klef Mordain. To this end, he has ordered the entire northern fleet of the Sanctian Empire to sail to the shores of this city. Ostensibly, they shall be coming here as friends, on a mission to rid the ocean coasts of piracy, but it will be an opportunity for the common folk to witness at first hand the might of the Sanctian Navy. The emotion we wish to evoke is awe, rather than fear; though I shall not be concerned if our political enemies feel a certain frisson of terror at the sight. The fleet shall be here for a few days only; long enough to take on supplies of fresh water, and, as ambassador, I shall be sailing out into the bay to pay them a visit. Keep this news to yourselves, for I wish Lord Metrius to be taken by surprise.'

He paused as waiters and waitresses entered the hall bearing silver trays.

'The refreshments have arrived,' said the ambassador. 'Let us halt our business for a few moments while we take some food and drink.'

The table descended into several separate conversations, as glasses and plates were set down in front of those seated.

Petros leaned over towards Amery. 'When can I start writing again, sir?'

'When I tell you,' whispered Amery, 'and not a moment before.'

'But all I have is the ambassador's opening address.'

'That is irrelevant.'

The scribe lowered his gaze, and nodded.

Amery frowned as he looked at the distinguished dignitaries around the table. While they were all resting in their beds that coming night, Amery would still be up, working to fill in the gaps in the official minutes of the meeting. Was he crossing a line? He had done some unsavoury things for Duke Hector in Upper Down, and he had sworn to himself that his next job would be one that allowed him to behave within the law at all times. And yet, there he was again, helping the unscrupulous to cover their tracks.

'Wine, sir?' said a waitress.

Amery put on his best smile. 'Thank you, that would be wonderful.'

CHAPTER 10
TALES FROM THE GOLDEN AGE

Old City, Klef Mordain – 25th Day of Saluna 108

'What are you doing up here, Abigone?' said Stanza. 'First years aren't allowed onto the roof on their own.'

Abigone turned. 'Miss Vesta said it was all right.'

'That's not fair. I had to wait until I was in second year before I could come up here. The rules should apply to everyone.'

Abigone decided not to engage in an argument with the girl. She had awoken feeling miserable that morning, and the last thing she wanted was another row with Stanza.

'I'm going to tell Lady Fyenna,' said Stanza.

'I'm not stopping you,' said Abigone.

Stanza squinted at Abigone's face. 'Have you been crying?'

'It's none of your business.'

'What's wrong?'

'Nothing; just feeling a little homesick.'

'Oh. I got that last year. It wasn't nice. Do you miss Upper Down?'

'Yes. I miss my sister, and Walter, and I miss Tulip.'

'What about your fancy palaces; do you miss them, too?'

'I miss my privacy more than I miss living in a palace. You can't do anything in this school without everyone finding out about it. You can't even go up onto the roof without someone threatening to tell the Head Maker.'

Stanza shrugged. 'I'm still going to tell her. I don't think you should be allowed to break the rules just because you're eighteen.' She pointed. 'Do you see those mountains in the distance? Greater Down is on the other side of them; well, after you get past Lesser Down. Lesser Down is so backward in comparison to Greater Down. What's Upper Down like? All I know about it is that your father used to let the Westlanders live there. Those savages would raid the towns and villages where I was brought up, and everyone I knew hated Upper Down. We got scared whenever we heard horses approach. One time, my mother locked me and my sisters in the cellar, because we had been told that the Westlanders were kidnapping all the local girls. They would kill the men and the old women, and take the young women back with them to Upper Down. Why did your father let that happen?'

'Money,' said Abigone. 'The Westlanders made my father very rich. It's over now; my father is dead, and the Westlanders have been thrown out of Upper Down.'

'Are you going to pay compensation to all of the bereaved families? That would be fair. It wasn't just your father who got rich. I bet that the entire realm grew wealthy because of the Westlanders. You should pay it all back.'

'I lost any say in the running of Upper Down the moment I set foot in Klef Mordain. My opinion doesn't matter any more.'

Raewyn appeared on the roof by the stairs. 'I thought you would be up here,' she said. 'Didn't you hear the bell?'

'No,' said Abigone. 'Lessons are over for the morning; why did the bell ring?'

'Lady Fyenna wants all of the students to gather in the lecture hall,' said Raewyn.

'Abigone shouldn't be up here,' said Stanza. 'She's only a first year, and the rules say that no first years are allowed on the roof on their own.'

Raewyn smiled. 'But she isn't on her own, is she? You were up here with her, you idiot.'

'But...'

'Oh, be quiet,' said Raewyn. 'And if you even think about informing Lady Fyenna about this, I will make your life sheer misery.'

Stanza closed her mouth and looked away.

'Listen,' said Raewyn; 'I heard some gossip about why we are all supposed to meet in the lecture hall. Apparently, the boys from the Masters' school are coming here for a shared lesson.'

'But I look a mess,' said Stanza. 'I need to brush my hair.'

'You always look a mess, Stanza,' said Raewyn; 'I doubt any of the boys will notice.' She smiled. 'Constans will be there. I haven't seen him in months. I wonder if he's changed.'

'Who is Constans?' said Abigone.

'He's seventeen,' said Raewyn. 'A fourth year.' She eyed Abigone. 'Don't be getting any ideas about him. In fact, if he speaks to you, act like a bitch towards him.'

'I'm not your competition, Raewyn,' said Abigone. 'I have no interest in seventeen-year-old boys.'

'We'd better go,' said Stanza. 'We shouldn't be late.'

They walked towards the stairs, and descended into the building until they reached the floor where the lecture hall was situated. Despite its grand name, the lecture hall was a small chamber with barely two dozen seats, separated by a central aisle. Reath and Nyli were already there, whispering to each other, while Miss Vesta was standing on the low platform at the far end of the room.

'There you are, girls,' Vesta said. 'Please sit on the left-hand side of the hall.'

Raewyn smiled. 'Why, miss? Why can't I sit on the right-hand side today?'

Vesta eyed her. 'I suspect you might already know the answer to that question, Raewyn.'

Raewyn turned to Abigone. 'Told you,' she whispered.

'Miss Vesta,' said Stanza, as Raewyn and Abigone took their seats in the row behind Reath and Nyli.

'Yes, Stanza?' said the teacher.

'Miss, Abigone was up on the roof on her own, and that is against the rules.'

'I have made an exception in her case, Stanza.'

'Why, miss? That isn't fair.'

'The rule is there to stop young first years from falling to their deaths, Stanza. Abigone is old enough to be trusted.'

'But...'

'Please take your seat, Stanza.'

'Little telltale,' Reath called out, as Stanza walked over to the left-hand side of the hall.

'Shut up,' Stanza muttered.

Fury swept over Reath's face. 'Don't you dare tell me to shut up!' she cried, getting to her feet, her fists clenched. 'I will break your nose, you ugly cow.'

Nyli shrank backwards, as Stanza stared open-mouthed at Reath.

'Everyone,' said Vesta; 'sit down and be quiet. Reath, that's enough.'

'She threatened me, miss,' said Stanza.

'Sit, Stanza,' said Raewyn, her eyes tight.

Stanza bowed her head and sat down next to Raewyn and Abigone.

'You're making a fool of yourself,' Raewyn went on.

'But Reath...'

'Ignore that little witch,' said Raewyn. 'Reath is nothing but a loud-mouthed peasant girl. She enjoys provoking you.'

'I heard that,' said Reath, turning her head. 'Don't think for a minute that I won't kick the shit out of you as well, Raewyn.'

'Girls!' Vesta cried. 'The next one of you to speak out of turn will be immediately sent to your room for the rest of the day. If Lady Fyenna were to walk in and hear the things you have just said, then none of you would be getting any dinner.'

Nyli raised her hand.

'Yes?' said Vesta.

'Abigone and I didn't say anything.'

'I know, Nyli.'

Reath gave her sister a look of disgust, and Nyli gazed down at her desk, her shoulders sagging.

'That's better,' said Vesta. 'All right; in a few short moments, we shall be receiving some visitors, and I would like you all to at least pretend that you are well-behaved, courteous young ladies. Ah, here they come.'

All five students turned to see Lady Fyenna stride into the hall. A man a little younger than her was by her side, and they were leading the boys from the Masters' school. Abigone's gaze went over them quickly. There were five boys, and four looked around fourteen or fifteen, while the boy at the front seemed a little older. That must be Constans, she reasoned. At the rear was a young man, whom Abigone assumed was a teacher, like Vesta. Raewyn smiled at Constans, and they locked gazes for a brief moment, before Lady Fyenna showed the boys where to sit – on the other side of the aisle from the girls. The older man remained by Fyenna's side, then, to Abigone's surprise, the one she had assumed was a teacher sat down next to the other boys.

'Girls,' said Fyenna, as she faced the hall, 'the time has come for this year's first mixed class. Raewyn and Stanza will know the identity of the man standing to my right, but I shall introduce him for the benefit of the others. This is Head Master Drummond, who runs the Master school.'

The man smiled. 'Hello, everyone. It is good to be back here with the young Makers. The Master school received four new first years this term, so let me quickly introduce them before Lady Fyenna begins today's lecture. Sitting in the front row are Ignatius, Salus and Marlow. Behind them, some of you girls will recognise Aplin and Constans from last year. And, in the third row, is the last of our new first years: Valiance.'

'He's a student?' whispered Raewyn.

'Thank you, Master Drummond,' said Fyenna. 'For the benefit of the boys, the girls in the first row are Nyli and Reath; while the second row contains Raewyn, Abigone and Stanza. Now, when I look at you all, my heart is filled with pride – eleven young Masters and Makers; the largest set of students we have had since the school was founded twenty years ago. The subject of today's lecture will be... Aplin, stop whispering. If you have something to say, then tell us all.'

Aplin's face flushed. 'Sorry, ma'am. It's just that I don't remember Abigone from last year, ma'am.'

'That's right,' said Fyenna. 'Just as the Masters have received an older boy in first year, the Makers have received Abigone. Like Valiance, she is eighteen, and has no prior experience or training.'

Abigone glanced over at Valiance, but he was keeping his gaze lowered.

'I shall continue,' said Fyenna. 'Today, Head Master Drummond and I would like to discuss the golden age of Masters and Makers with you all. None of us were alive during this period, and so it can be hard to imagine what it was like. Schools for Masters and Makers were spread all over the Elestian Empire. They had no need to be kept secret and hidden, because there was no danger attached to being a Master or a Maker; in fact, the opposite was true. Throughout the long era of the Elestian Empire, Masters and Makers ascended to the very summit of authority, privilege and power. They were the elite of the empire, and they lived like kings and queens. Lamentine the Sixteenth, the last emperor, was himself a Master, as were his forebears. The entire imperial family was full of Masters and Makers, and the emperors employed them as advisors and military leaders, and sent them out to govern the provinces.'

Fyenna glanced at Abigone. 'Here is a little example of what I mean,' she said. 'Three hundred years ago, Emperor Clement the Third sent a trusted friend and ally to take control of one of the passes through the mountains that connects the Central Provinces to what were the Northern Provinces, as there had been an outbreak of trouble there. He was a Master, and his name was Shiel. At the fall of the Elestian Empire, that man's family was still ruling the mountain pass, and one of his descendants was crowned as Alfgang, the first king of Upper Down – Abigone's great grandfather.'

Every eye in the room turned towards Abigone.

'As it turns out,' Fyenna went on, 'House Shiel was an exception. The vast majority of the Masters and Makers who had helped govern the Elestian Empire were massacred when that empire fell. Upper Down was too remote to be affected by the upheaval, and so the line continued, as it does to this day. Abigone's father was a Master, and she has inherited that ancient bloodline. In some ways, Abigone is a link to a past that no longer exists; a time when Masters and Makers were revered and lauded, rather than feared and hunted down. Klef Mordain is one of the few refuges where Masters and Makers are protected, and even here, thanks to our enemies, we have to hide you away, as though you were criminals or renegades. You might wonder to which enemy I am referring, but to some of you, the answer will be obvious. Raewyn – who is the enemy I speak of?'

'The Sanctian Empire, ma'am.'

Fyenna smiled. 'Correct. Can anyone tell me why the Sanctian Empire is the enemy of Masters and Makers? Aplin?'

'Because they want to kill us all, ma'am?'

'Yes. Emperor Antonio of Sanctos issued a proclamation at the start of his reign, condemning every Master and Maker to death for insurrection and treason. For forty years, his soldiers have combed the lands under the sway of the Sanctian Empire, searching for Masters and Makers to arrest and execute.'

Marlow raised his hand.

'Yes?' said Fyenna.

'My uncle was arrested by Sanctian soldiers, ma'am. He was a Master. They killed him.'

'I am very sorry to hear that, Marlow,' said Fyenna. 'Truly, this is a tragedy; a vile crime perpetrated by Emperor Antonio. Would that we could return to the old days, when we didn't have to hide our powers in the darkness, always fearful for our lives. That is one reason why it would be a dreadful error to condemn Valiance for having neglected his training. He is from Campsie, which is not technically a part of the Sanctian Empire, but Antonio's policies and military might have greatly influenced the affairs of that realm. Had Valiance openly flouted his abilities, then he would have suffered the same fate as Marlow's poor uncle.'

Abigone squirmed in her seat, painfully aware that Fyenna had seen fit to include Valiance in her description, but not her.

'But let me go back in time to the very beginnings of the Elestian Empire,' Fyenna went on. 'It was founded by a king and a queen of Yearl – the heart of the old empire. And yes, before you ask – the king was a Master, and his queen a Maker. Between them, they were able to conquer Jallin and Campsie. They founded Subnestia, and then they spread south to the Isle of Sanctos, north to the old County of Down, and west beyond the Great Forest to the open plains of Mylos and Anster. Almost all of that was achieved in their lifetime. Their descendants added to the empire, incorporating the Northern Provinces, and, in time, the lands of Geathan in the far south-west. At this stage, I do not wish to open a discussion about the various faults of certain emperors and empresses, and I will not cover the many wars the empire fought against the Westlanders, or their attempts to set up colonies in the land by the Thousand Lakes. All of these topics will be covered when Head Master Drummond speaks later. Instead, I want to focus solely on what it meant to be a Master or a Maker in those times. Detailed records were once kept in the city of Elestia, where the name of every known Master and Maker was recorded for posterity. As time went on, the Masters and Makers became the elite class of the empire, and some old records state that almost the entire imperial aristocracy was composed of them and their families. What is less well known is what happened if a Master or a Maker was born to poor parents. Perhaps they were farmers, or peasants, or one of the many living in poverty in one of the empire's great cities – it mattered not. Once their abilities were discovered, the empire would lavish riches upon them, sending their children to the best schools, and elevating their families to the very pinnacle of society. Imperial agents used to comb the countryside, visiting tiny villages and remote mountain communities, looking for young Masters and Makers. In some ways, this is happening again now, only the Sanctian agents have a different purpose in mind. Where the Elestian agents wished to honour and revere any Masters and Makers they found on their travels, the Sanctians wish to kill them.'

Reath held up her hand.

'Yes?' said Fyenna.

'Everyone knows that the Sanctians want to kill us; but why? Why does Emperor Antonio hate us so much?'

Miss Vesta glared at the girl.

'Sorry,' said Reath. 'I forgot to say *ma'am*.'

'That is a good question, Reath,' said Fyenna. 'Why, indeed? Officially, the Sanctian Empire states that Masters and Makers are a danger to society, and that, if left to their own devices, they will exploit those who do not posses the same abilities, and set themselves up as tyrants to rule over others.'

Abigone raised her hand.

'Yes?'

'When I was in Upper Down, ma'am,' Abigone said, 'I spent some time with one of Prince Valentino's granddaughters, a princess by the name of Hygilt. I asked her why they hated Master and Makers, and she told me it was because of religious reasons. She said that the Sanctians believe Masters and Makers twist the power of the spirits. She said it was sacrilegious, and she told me the spirits hate us.'

Irritation passed over Fyenna's face. 'Well, Princess Hygilt is very young, so I am not sure how much stock we should place in her answers. I would prefer to rely upon the word of the Sanctians themselves, rather than the opinion of a little girl.'

Valiance raised his head, as though he was about to speak, then he lowered his gaze again.

'Regardless,' Fyenna went on, 'there is some truth in the accusations of the Sanctians. It pains me to say it, but many Masters and Makers did act as tyrants, especially in the last years of the Elestian Empire. If they had behaved with a little more restraint, then the empire might not have collapsed. Some Masters and Makers grew obscenely wealthy, and they used their abilities to increase their hold on power. Some forgot their responsibilities to the people they governed. Sanctos, in particular, was very badly ruled for a period of time; so perhaps it should not come as a surprise to learn that they were the first to successfully rebel against their imperial overlords. As an island, they were able to slaughter the Elestian Masters and Makers stationed there before the empire could send reinforcements. By the time those reinforcements arrived, it was too late, and the Sanctians were able to repel them. This one little stone led to a tremendous landslide and, within the next decade, multiple revolts broke out all over the Central Provinces, accompanied by the slaughter of any Masters and Makers the mobs could get their hands on. The greatest and most terrible massacre took place in the capital city of Elestia itself. An enormous crowd of disgruntled citizens stormed the imperial palaces, and set them alight. Over two hundred Masters and Makers, including most of the imperial family, perished in the flames, and more were slain in the days that followed. This was the signal for the rest of the provinces to declare themselves independent. Chaos and anarchy ensued. During this time, Klef Mordain was a little oasis of calm. There was no rebellion here, and very little civil unrest. Why, you might ask? The most likely reason is that the people of Klef Mordain were devoted to the Elestian Empire; after all, the city was founded by them five centuries ago. The original colonists hailed from the towns and countryside of Yearl, and so the citizens did not feel as though a foreign power had conquered them, nor did it seem as though they were being oppressed. They belonged to Elestia in a way that, say, Geathan or Mylos, didn't. When it became apparent that the Elestian Empire was gone for good, Klef Mordain declared its own independence, but it was with reluctance and a heavy heart. For this reason, the city where you all now dwell never fostered the same level of contempt, fear and hatred towards Masters and Makers as did other places. There were certainly no massacres here. As for the rest of the old empire, you all know what happened next. The Westlanders swarmed over the undefended Northern Provinces, conquering as they went. Were it not for the resistance of Klef Mordain, they would have reached the ocean by now. The Central Provinces splintered into dozens of small realms, duchies and principalities, while Geathan reverted to its old, backward customs. Then, a few decades ago, the so-called second empire arose. This time, it was based on Sanctos. In a series of highly aggressive manoeuvres, they began to conquer the divided lands of the Central Provinces, and now their influence stretches far and wide; indeed, even to the doorstep of Klef Mordain. To our south lies the realm of Lesser Down, an impoverished kingdom that was hived off from the original County of Down. Through a combination of threats and bribes, the Sanctians practically control that realm now, and with it, the entire length of the Great Northern Highway, from Elestia to the frontier of Klef Mordain.'

Fyenna fell silent for a moment, as she gazed at each of the students in turn.

'If the Sanctians have their way,' she said, 'they will annex this city, and they will execute you all. They will also execute Miss Vesta, Head Master Drummond, and every other member of staff who works in the secret schools. And, of course, they will execute me. This city has taken on a great risk by sheltering you here, and by providing you with an education. One day, the Sanctians might even decide to invade. They have cannon, and we do not. Their warships could destroy our entire fleet in a matter of minutes, and their army would annihilate our brigades of archers and infantry. The sole advantage we possess is you. Think on that, my young Masters and Makers, and ponder what you would do if the worst happened. Ask yourself how you would react, if Sanctian soldiers and sailors tried to take our freedom and our lives.'

The hall fell into complete silence for a few moments, then Fyenna smiled.

'I think it's time for a short break,' she said. 'The dining room has been prepared with refreshments for you; make your way there, and return here when the mid-afternoon bell rings.'

Fyenna turned away from the students, and began to speak in a low tone to Drummond and Vesta. The students got to their feet, and made their way out of the lecture hall without a word being spoken. The girls led the boys to the dining hall, and they all sat down at the lower table. Jugs of water and freshly-pressed apple juice had been set out, along with bowls of olives and bread. Constans tried to start up a conversation with Raewyn, but he stopped as soon as he noticed that she was staring at Valiance, who was keeping to himself at the end of the table.

Abigone sat down at the far end of the table from Valiance, and Reath turned to her.

'If any Sanctians come here,' Reath said, 'we'll kick their arses for them. You're the only one of us who has actually fought the Sanctians; what do you think?'

'I don't know,' said Abigone. 'When I faced them before, I was standing at the top of a cliff.'

Constans smiled at her. 'So, you are a real princess? That's what Lady Fyenna said.'

Abigone nodded.

'She's proper Elestian royalty,' said Reath.

'I can tell,' said Constans. 'She looks like a princess.'

Raewyn pulled her gaze from Valiance. 'It's good to see you again,' she said.

'Yes?' said Constans. 'You seem more interested in our eighteen-year-old first year.'

'And you seem more interested in ours,' said Raewyn.

Reath laughed. 'Are you two in love?'

'Relationships between Masters and Makers at the schools are forbidden,' said Stanza.

'Stop telling us what we can't do,' said Reath. 'You are a pain in the arse at times, Stanza. The next time you open your mouth to give anyone a telling off, I'm going to slap it shut.'

A few of the younger boys laughed.

Stanza's cheeks flushed, and she stared at the surface of the table.

'Leave her alone,' said Raewyn.

'Me?' said Reath. 'You bully Stanza more than anyone else in this damn school. You're always ordering her around, as if she was your servant or something; and Stanza's too timid to ever say no. *Carry my dishes, Stanza. Get me a glass of water, Stanza.* If you ever speak to me the way you speak to her, then you'll soon find out what happens next.'

'Where are you from, Reath?' said Ignatius.

'None of your damn business.'

'Isn't she delightful?' said Raewyn. 'You boys are lucky that you only have to put up with Reath for one afternoon; we have to endure her every day.'

'It was so much quieter last year,' said Aplin, 'when it was just three girls and two boys.'

'I miss those days,' said Stanza.

Reath smirked at her. 'You would. Well, it's tough; I'm here now, and you're just going to have to deal with it.'

Valiance shook his head and got to his feet, then he strode from the dining hall.

Reath laughed. 'Was it something I said?'

Abigone glanced at the doorway. 'I'll find out if he's all right,' she said, standing.

'Be sure that's all you do,' said Reath.

Abigone left the hall. She saw Valiance standing by himself at the end of the corridor, took a breath, and approached him.

'Hello,' she said.

He eyed her.

'It's a bit strange, isn't it?' she went on. 'We're older than everyone else, and yet we're still in first year.'

'I suppose so.'

'How have you been settling in?'

'Fine.'

Abigone nodded. 'Have you been assigned a lot of work to do? I have a mountain of books to read, and every day it seems as though I am packing in as much information as my head can take. I never knew there was so much to learn about wood.'

He glanced away. 'I have been meditating.'

'Meditating?'

'That's the key to being a Master, apparently. You have to clear your mind and think of nothing.'

'Being a Maker is the opposite,' said Abigone. 'You have to understand every last detail about what you are trying to summon. I'm exhausted all the time. Do you have any brothers or sisters?'

He shrugged.

'I have two sisters,' she went on. 'I also had a brother, but he died. What was it like growing up in Campsie? I don't know all that much about it, to be honest.'

Valiance exhaled. 'Look, Abigone; I'm sure you're a very nice person, but I'm not looking to make any friends here. It might be best if you leave me alone.'

Abigone stared at him. 'Oh. Well, I'm dreadfully sorry to have bothered you. Goodbye.'

She hurried away, as a sickly sense of humiliation washed over her. Not once in her life had a boy ever spoken to her like that; they had usually clamoured for her attention. She paused by the entrance to the dining hall, and looked inside. The rest of the students were chatting, and Reath was needling Stanza and Raewyn again, while Aplin and Constans were laughing. Abigone turned away. She felt tears come to her eyes, and knew it was from the homesickness, not from Valiance's rude behaviour. She would never waste tears on a boy like that.

She straightened her back and composed herself, then she walked back to the lecture hall.

CHAPTER 11
THE SALUTE

Old City, Klef Mordain – 10th Day of Ara 108

'Are you listening to me, Selanius?' said Fyenna.

Her husband looked at her from over the top of his newspaper. 'You were talking about the price of food in the market.'

'It would be nice to receive the occasional acknowledgment,' she said. 'Even a grunt now and again would do. Sometimes, I feel as though I am talking to myself. Anyway, I asked the woman at the stall why her prices have almost doubled in the last few months, and she tried to give me some excuse about rising costs.'

'She is right,' said her husband. 'The Central Provinces have increased their trade tariffs again. Everything that crosses the frontier has an extra charge placed on it. There's an article about it in today's paper.'

'In other words, it's the fault of the Sanctians? Who else could force the realms of the Central Provinces to raise their prices like that? And, I assume that it's only Klef Mordain that's being affected. It's economic blackmail, pure and simple. They are punishing us for refusing to enter into negotiations about annexation.'

'Maybe,' he said.

'Surely you can see it,' she said. 'Their diplomatic efforts have failed, and so they are trying to impoverish us. What's next – war?'

Selanius placed the newspaper onto the table, and refilled his cup with coffee from a small pot.

'You know my feelings on this,' he said. 'Do I think Klef Mordain would benefit economically from a union with the empire? Yes. Does that mean I am in favour of such a union? No. I will oppose the Sanctians for as long as they insist upon retaining their barbarous policy against Masters and Makers. However, you should know that these latest tariffs will persuade more of the city's businessmen and women that a union would be preferable to bankruptcy and poverty. Take the cotton merchants as an example. All cotton is grown in the Central Provinces, and these tariffs will result in cotton garments produced here in the city becoming too expensive for the ordinary citizens to afford. If nothing changes soon, then many merchants are going to go out of business. That will lead to further shortages of manufactured clothing.'

'I know how it works,' said Fyenna, 'but are you saying that these merchants would prefer the city to be occupied and governed by a foreign empire? What about freedom?'

'Whose freedom?' he said. 'The lower classes of Klef Mordain would arguably have a far better quality of life under the Sanctians than they do at present. The Corse has served us well, but why do they have to be so secretive? Every decision they make is taken behind closed doors. Most normal realms at least know the identity of their rulers. Here, we are left in absolute ignorance. Do you think I like the fact that you are not permitted to tell me what it is that you do each day at work? Aren't marriages supposed to be built upon a foundation of trust and honesty?'

Fyenna lowered her gaze. 'I wish I could tell you what I do. Some days, I long to be able to speak to you about something that happened at my place of work, just to have someone to share it with. But, I can't.'

'What if I were to guess it?' he said. 'I think I know enough about you to be able to guess what it is that you do all day. Would you confirm or deny the truth of it? You wouldn't have to say anything – a mere nod or shake of the head would suffice.'

'Are you serious?' she said. 'I beg you not to put me in that position. I love you, but I cannot break my oaths. There are other people's lives at stake.'

'Yes, I know,' he said. 'You have your duty, and your oaths, and I understood the rules when we got married. You mentioned having a one-sided conversation – that sums up what it has felt like for me these past decades. I could sit here and tell you all about the cargos I have sent sailing across the seas, some across the ocean, others bound for Subnestia and Geathan; but I would feel as though I was talking to myself.'

Fyenna took a sip from her coffee cup. 'Has something sparked this line of thought? You haven't brought this up in a long time.'

Selanius caught her glance, then he looked away. 'Perhaps the silence of the house has reminded me of the silence at the heart of our marriage. When our son was still alive, his voice would fill this kitchen each morning. I miss him.'

'I miss him, too,' she said. 'It's been eight years since he was lost at sea, but that time hasn't lessened the pain.'

A strange look passed over her husband's face, and for a moment she thought she saw his eyes well a little. She took his hand.

'One day,' she said, 'when we are old and grey, I will tell you what I have been doing all these years. Until then, you shall have to trust me.' She got to her feet. 'I should go. I don't want to be late.'

Selanius said nothing, and Fyenna walked out of the kitchen. She descended the stairs to the ground floor, and took her jacket from a peg by the front door. She slipped out of the house, checking both ways to see if anyone was watching her building. She had a habit of varying her walk to the school each day, often utilising the sprawling network of tunnels that lay under the Old City, but she began her walk that morning by keeping to the main roads. She came to the Great Northern Highway, which split the city in two, and crossed into the commercial district. She thought about her husband's strange mood as she walked.

It had been ten years, at least, since he had last mentioned the secrecy that barred Fyenna from speaking about her place of work. She was sure that, had he tried to guess her occupation, he would have been correct. Selanius knew she was a Maker. It had never been a secret between them, and she had sometimes talked of what she had done at the Battle of Hader Pull. To go from that to concluding that she was involved in the secret schools was no great leap.

She passed a row of magnificent buildings, each housing one of the great companies that owned the city's vast trading fleet. Her husband had a share in more than one of them, and he also held the papers for several ships in his own name, ships that ploughed the seas along the eastern coast of the continent. The ships had made them rich, but Fyenna understood how fragile the entire enterprise could be. A storm, pirates, hidden rocks – any of those hazards could lead to the loss of a vessel. Three such mishaps would see Selanius go from wealthy to bankrupt in the blink of an eye, and yet the profits on offer from the ships that made it home safely could blind even the most sensible person to the risks.

Fyenna took a right turn at a junction, and entered a small store selling crafted leather goods. The old man behind the counter glanced up at her, then, without a word being exchanged, he unlocked a door at the side of the shop. He didn't know her name or occupation, but she had used his shop dozens of times to enter the maze of caverns, cisterns and tunnels that ran beneath the streets of the Old City. Fyenna passed through the entrance, and descended a set of steep stairs into the gloom of a tunnel. She heard the door being locked above her, and picked up a small lamp. She lit the short wick with a match, and the light from the flames flickered off the walls. The air underground was humid, and condensation was dripping from the smooth limestone ceiling. Fyenna set off. If she had been followed, her pursuers would know that she had entered the tunnels, but they would have no idea where she would emerge. She came to a large crossroads, from where each of the four quarters of the Old City could be reached, and selected the tunnel that led towards the commercial docks. A few minutes later, she took a side branch that ran north. She ascended a spiral stone-cut staircase, and came into a cellar beneath a tavern. She extinguished the lamp and set it down by the steps, then she ascended another flight of stairs, and appeared in a storeroom behind the kitchens. Two chefs were preparing food by a long counter, and they eyed Fyenna as she strode past them. She walked out onto the street, and breathed in the fresh air. In front of her, the wide estuary turned into the bay where the commercial harbour lay, and several merchant vessels were anchored a hundred yards from the rocky shore.

Trees lined the road, and a multitude of cafés and inns stretched along the esplanade. The sun came out from behind a cloud, and the waters of the estuary glistened in the soft light. A few cats were lingering by the tables sitting out under the shade of the trees, and a smattering of citizens were drinking coffee as they sat and gazed at the view.

Fyenna found the café she had been looking for. She nodded at Drummond, who was already sitting by a table, a cup of coffee in his right hand. A silver pot had been placed in front of him, along with a plate of delicate pastries. He got to his feet when he saw her approach.

'My lady,' he said; 'what a beautiful morning.'

'Indeed it is,' she said. 'It feels as though summer is upon us.'

They shook hands, then took their seats. Drummond filled a cup with coffee, and slid it towards Fyenna.

'You have chosen a good location for our meeting this morning,' she said.

'Was it wise to arrange such a meeting in full view of the public?'

'Let us hide in plain sight,' she said. 'I trust you used tunnels to get here?'

'Of course. Though, out of the two of us, it is more likely that you were followed. Far fewer people in this city know of my abilities; whereas you are a renowned war hero.'

'Even so, my face is unknown to most. How goes it at your place of work?'

'Tobold is teaching the first years, and he's making steady progress with them,' he said. 'We had expected some trouble with our eighteen-year-old, but he has taken to his lessons well, and he has been helping one of the younger students with his reading and writing.'

'I wish I could say the same about my eighteen-year-old,' Fyenna said. 'The books we have given her to study are aimed at younger children, and that has been a cause of some frustration. I don't think that girl has ever had to work hard in her life. She seems to think the knowledge she requires will come easily, and then she gets angry when she realises her mistake.'

'Perhaps you are being a little hard on her? She probably feels embarrassed that she has to sit with children far younger than she is.'

'And yet your eighteen-year-old has settled in well.'

'You cannot compare the two. Your students spend their time cramming as much information into their heads as possible; while my students have to learn how to empty their minds. Of the two, I know which is the easier task.'

'All the same, I am glad I am not teaching the first years this term. It isn't just the eighteen-year-old who is causing problems; you have met our young girl Reath. She possesses a most disagreeable manner, and she seems to delight in riling up the others. She is driving Miss Vesta to despair. Anyway, enough talk of the first years. One of the reasons I called this meeting is to discuss our more advanced students. I need to know if any are capable of taking on more onerous duties.'

Drummond's eyes tightened slightly. 'What kind of duties?'

'Of the military sort.'

'I see, or, rather, I do not. Is it remotely likely that our students will be called upon to fight?'

Fyenna glanced out over the waters of the estuary. 'I don't know, but I have been ordered to ensure that we are prepared for anything. I need to know the exact extent of our capabilities in the event of a crisis. Of the girls, there is only one I would deem able to cope with the pressure of armed conflict, and even she is far too young.'

'You are speaking of Raewyn?'

'I am. She is certainly skilled enough, but she is only sixteen.'

'Of the boys, there is Constans,' said Drummond, 'but I would hate to see him involved in warfare.'

'Is he timid?'

'He claims to be the opposite. He says he would be eager to help the city if war broke out; eager, and rash. Are you aware that he is very fond of your Raewyn?'

'How could I not be aware? Stanza is forever giving away the secrets of the other girls, and she has reported her concerns to me on multiple occasions.' She smiled. 'She would make a good member of the secret police.' She sipped her coffee. 'That gives us four Makers – me, Vesta, Eshia and Raewyn; and three Masters – you, Tobold and Constans. Is it enough?'

'For what?'

'To save the city if the Sanctians declare war?'

'Are there no former students upon whom we could call?'

'None that remain in the city,' she said. 'Tobold, Vesta and Eshia are the only graduates we have.'

'And to think how many students have passed through our schools in the last twenty years. Perhaps we should have insisted that they remained in Klef Mordain.'

'If we made that a condition of attendance, we would receive no fresh students. No one would want to come here if they knew they wouldn't be allowed to leave.'

'Then you and I will have to suffice,' he said. 'We need not involve the younger generation. Tobold and Vesta are in their early twenties, and the other three are teenagers. I would be loath to ask any of them to kill, and perhaps die, on behalf of the city.'

'That is not your choice to make,' said Fyenna; 'nor is it mine. I have my orders.'

'Should I mention anything to Constans about this?'

'Not yet. Instead, we shall start to place more emphasis in our lessons on the martial aspects of our abilities. How to attack; how to defend; and how to work together – Masters and Makers combined.'

'Just as we two combined at Hader Pull?'

'Precisely. This will involve bringing the two schools closer together for a time. An outdoor location would be ideal – somewhere that could mimic a battlefield.'

'But any battle would probably take place in the streets of Klef Mordain.'

'True, but we cannot hold any military exercises there. Perhaps the countryside south of Cliephus could be made to work. All students should attend, not just Raewyn and Constans, so we can judge who can remain calm under intense pressure. Tobold, Vesta and Eshia should also be there.'

'I don't like this. The students are children, not soldiers.'

'I don't like it, either, Drummond, but think of it this way – if the Sanctians try to invade, then their first targets will be our students. Don't we have a responsibility to teach them how to protect themselves?'

'Be honest,' he said. 'I know you are not permitted to reveal everything to me, but if the Sanctians are planning an invasion of Klef Mordain, then I would rather know about it.'

'The situation within the Corse is very... delicate at the moment. Those in favour of our annexation into the Sanctian Empire have achieved some political gains, and they hold more power than at any time in the past. The future of the city hangs in the balance. You are right to be concerned.'

'Then, though it pains me, I shall do whatever it takes to prepare our students for the worst.'

'As shall I.'

Drummond frowned as he gazed at the water of the bay. 'Damn the Sanctians. Their ancient grudge against Masters and Makers is the cause of our troubles. Why can't they just let us live in peace?'

'They fear us.'

'We are not the cruel tyrants who ruled in the last days of the Elestian Empire; their crimes are not ours.'

'And yet the Sanctians believe us capable of doing what our predecessors did.'

'Sometimes, I look at the great ships that sail across the ocean, and wonder if we would have a better life in the lands far to the east.' He withdrew a few coins from his pocket and placed them onto the table. 'I'm tired of hiding, tired of taking tunnels every day, and tired of being taken for granted by a city that refuses to reveal its secrets.' He got to his feet. 'Farewell, my lady; I will see you at the next joint lesson.'

Fyenna watched as Drummond strode away from the café, then she turned back to the view of the estuary, and finished her coffee.

Ten minutes later, Fyenna was walking along the esplanade with the coast to her left. The sun was rising in the sky to the east, and she savoured the warmth on her face. The Maker school was located in the dense network of streets on her right, close to the city's cluster of theatres, but she decided that she would walk round the headland that morning, and approach the school from the north. She followed the esplanade as it curved to the right, and the enormous Celestial Bridge came into sight, its high arches spanning the Arnos Estuary at its narrowest point. At either end of the bridge stood a colossal statue. The one to the north, on the far shore, was of a Master, his right hand raised; while the other, which stood by the edge of the city, was of a Maker. For five hundred years, the two statues had stood sentinel, watching over Klef Mordain. Fyenna was about to turn away from the coast when she saw a line of eight ships anchored on the eastern side of the bridge. A small crowd of civilians had gathered by the shore to take a look at the vessels, and Fyenna joined them.

Her gaze went over the high masts, looking for a flag, then her attention went to a series of hatches running down the flank of each ship.

'When did they get here?' said a man.

'About an hour ago,' said someone else.

The wind picked up a little, and a blue and white flag coiled out in the breeze from one of the masts. Fyenna gasped. Sanctians. The eight vessels were Sanctian warships.

'The hatches are opening,' said a woman, her hand raised to point at the ships.

Fyenna raised her own hand, to shield her eyes from the sun. Along the port side of each ship, two dozen hatches were being swung open, revealing dark holes that led into their hulls.

'Cannon,' whispered an old man. 'Every ship has two dozen of them down each side.'

A roar of noise louder than anything Fyenna had experienced exploded over the estuary as every cannon fired at the same time, and the crowd panicked. Smoke rose from the sides of the eight ships, as hundreds of birds ascended into the sky over the city. Fyenna was pushed back as the terrified citizens started to run for cover. Fyenna's eyes went to the buildings along the shore, but she saw no sign of any damage.

'It was nothing but a salute,' said one of the few to have remained calm. 'The bastards aren't firing at the city.'

A few members of the crowd began to drift back to the shore.

'They're just trying to scare us,' said a man.

'That's near two hundred cannon pointing at us,' said someone else. 'If they wanted to, they could turn Klef Mordain into a smoking heap of rubble. What can our longbows do against that?'

A small ship's launch was lowered from the side of one of the vessels. It splashed into the water, and a dozen oars began to push the craft towards the shore.

'Here they come,' said a man. 'With any luck, we might find out what they want.'

'Are you dreaming?' said another. 'Do you think the Corse will tell us what's happening?'

'This is for Lord Denon,' said a woman. 'The Sanctians have come for revenge.'

Fyenna slipped away from the crowd, her ears still ringing from the sound of the cannon. She took a side street, barely able to concentrate on where she was going, her heart racing from the demonstration of power exhibited by the eight warships. Until that moment, she had never seen cannon used before; she had heard all about the Sanctians' great and terrible new weapon, and how it had been employed to first destroy the navies of the Central Provinces, and then to conquer those same lands, but none had ever been brought as far north as Klef Mordain. She remembered Abigone talking about the cannon that had breached the famous Kendril Wall, and her heart sank into despair.

Bells began to toll all over the Old City, and civilians were running here and there with terror on their faces. Fyenna reached the school, and entered through a hidden side door. She hurried up the stairs to the classrooms, and walked into the chamber where Vesta was with the three first years. All four of them were standing by a window, gazing north.

'I assume you heard that noise from here,' said Fyenna.

Vesta glanced at her. 'What caused it, ma'am? Abigone said she thinks the sound came from cannon fire.'

'Abigone is correct,' said Fyenna, as the three students turned their gazes towards her. 'Eight Sanctian warships are anchored next to the Celestial Bridge; but don't panic – there was smoke and noise, but nothing else. It was a salute, or so someone said.'

'No cannon balls?' said Abigone.

Fyenna narrowed her eyes.

'Sorry, ma'am,' said Abigone. 'Were there no cannon balls fired into the city?'

'There were none,' said Fyenna. 'It was a demonstration, presumably meant to intimidate us. Miss Vesta, please bring Raewyn and Stanza here; I wish to address the students together.'

Vesta hurried from the classroom, and Fyenna walked up to the window. The view of the estuary was obscured by the building opposite the school, and the eight warships were out of sight; but a pall of smoke could be seen rising over the rooftops.

'Why are the Sanctians here, ma'am?' said Nyli, her voice a whisper.

'Why do you think?' said Reath. 'They've come to kill us.'

'Let us not jump to any rash conclusions,' said Fyenna. 'I watched as a small launch was being rowed from the ships towards the shore. The

Sanctians clearly wish to talk. Had they so desired to attack the city, much of Klef Mordain would already be reduced to ruins.'

Vesta appeared by the door with Raewyn and Stanza.

'Sit, girls,' said Fyenna.

'What was that noise, ma'am?' said Stanza. 'I thought the world was ending.'

'Sit down, and I will explain,' said Fyenna.

She waited until all of the students had taken a seat.

'At this moment,' Fyenna went on, 'there are eight Sanctian warships anchored next to the Celestial Bridge. That noise was their way of letting us know that they are here. They wish to talk. The Sanctian Navy contains dozens of such vessels, and they have sent a mere squadron. If they wished to do us harm, they would have sent more. They would have sent troopships. We are not in any imminent danger, so please remain calm.'

The students glanced at each other.

'Nevertheless,' Fyenna said, 'we must take sensible precautions. Head Master Drummond and I have decided to make a few changes to this term's syllabus. Starting today, the students from both schools will be learning how to fight.' She smiled. 'Do not be alarmed by this prospect. The chances of a war breaking out between Klef Mordain and the Sanctian Empire remain slight; however, it would be prudent to act as though it is a real possibility. Abigone, please come up here and stand next to me.'

Abigone rose from her chair and walked to the front of the class.

'Abigone is the only student with experience of cannon,' Fyenna said. 'She knows what they are capable of doing, and she knows their weaknesses. On her own, she destroyed sixty such weapons, and I want you all to listen carefully to what she has to say. Abigone, please relate all that you know about cannon to your fellow students.'

'Yes, ma'am,' said Abigone.

Fyenna took a seat next to Vesta, as Abigone began to speak. The class fell into utter silence as they listened to Abigone's words, and Fyenna saw the fear in each student's eyes. It was there on Vesta's face, too. Fyenna steeled her heart. Despite the raw terror in the pit of her stomach, she had to appear calm and confident for the sake of the others. She was a decorated and respected war hero, partly responsible for inflicting the greatest defeat on the Westlanders in the previous century.

She clasped her hands to stop them trembling, and kept a smile firmly fixed to her face.

CHAPTER 12
SALT AND WATER

Old City, Klef Mordain – 13th Day of Ara 108

'Focus on your breathing, and nothing else,' said Tobold in a low voice. 'In... out. In... out. Ensure that you are relaxed, and that none of your muscles are tensed.'

Denny sat on the floor of the classroom with his eyes closed. He was getting better at quelling the thoughts in his head but, after receiving intensive and repeated lessons on meditation for the month he had been at the school, that was no surprise. Every morning, before any lecture or practical assignment had taken place, the first years would spend an hour in silent contemplation, freeing their minds to allow their Master abilities to come easier.

'In... out. In... out,' Tobold said again, his voice a mere whisper. 'Feel the presence of the spirits wash over you like a warm breeze. In... out.'

They had been meditating three days previously when the sound of the cannon had ripped through the air. Denny had recognised the noise immediately. A moment after it had passed, he had realised that it had been nothing but a salute; if cannon balls had been fired, then the sound of buildings being struck would have followed, yet there had been nothing.

'Now open your eyes,' said Tobold. 'Stretch your arms, and get to your feet.'

Denny opened his eyes. On his left was Marlow, while Salus and Ignatius were sitting to his right. They stood, and Ignatius swayed, as though he had been close to falling asleep. At the front of the classroom, Tobold was sitting on the edge of his desk, and he gestured for the first years to come forward.

'Today,' he said, 'we are going to be examining water. Can anyone tell me how it might be useful to transform water into another substance?'

None of the boys spoke.

'Salus,' said Tobold, 'what do you think?'

'I'm finding it hard to concentrate, sir,' said the boy. 'All I can think about are the eight Sanctian warships sitting in the estuary.'

'This is exactly why we try to clear our minds,' said Tobold. 'The correct use of Master powers depends upon the tranquillity of the man's thoughts. One stray idea is enough to mar a transformation. In battle, a Master needs to disregard the arrows flying by his head, and the shouts and screams of the dying. If he does not, then his abilities are almost worthless.'

Salus hung his head. 'Sorry, sir.'

'There is no need to apologise,' said Tobold. 'This is not something that comes easily, which is why we practise it so often. Eventually, you should be able to move your mind into a tranquil state of being without a second thought, but none of you are at that stage yet. Let's think back to the water. Does anyone have any suggestions as to why it might be a useful substance to transform?'

Denny raised a hand.

'Yes?'

'To kill people, sir.'

'Please explain that for the rest of the class, Valiance.'

'Yes, sir,' said Denny. 'The human body contains a lot of water. If it is transformed into something else, the host will die.'

'Correct, Valiance,' said Tobold. 'Transforming the water in the body of an enemy is, in fact, the most efficient way for a Master to kill someone. For simplicity's sake, the most common target substances would be salt, or iron – each would bring about instantaneous death. Nothing fancier than that is required. It is worth noting that Makers have no such easy recourse to killing. They could summon a sword or a knife, but they would still have to use such a weapon; or, perhaps, if they were feeling brave, they could attempt to summon a living animal. They would fail, naturally, as no Maker has been able to successfully summon a living animal for a very long time, but the effect would be to strip flesh, bone and blood from whomever is standing nearby. A most indiscriminate and bloody way to kill someone. Compared to that, a good Master can kill with ease.'

'Have you ever killed anyone, sir?' said Marlow.

'No,' said Tobold, 'and I hope that will always be the case. However, as you know, I have been asked by the Head Master to instruct you on this subject. If the Sanctians come, then you will need to know how to defend yourselves.'

'But the Sanctians have come,' said Marlow.

'I think you know what I meant,' said Tobold. 'If they invade, or if they attack the city, then the Masters and Makers dwelling here will be pressed into the service of Klef Mordain. If you would walk to the work benches by the windows, you will see four glass tanks of water. Select one each.'

The first years turned away from the teacher and walked over to the narrow, shuttered windows. Denny picked the tank on the left, and gazed at its clear contents. The other boys stood by the rest of the tanks, and Tobold joined them.

'By each tank,' Tobold said, 'you will also see a block of wood. We shall practise on that first, before attempting to transform the water. Now, raise your right hand and repeat after me: *Ever-living and blessed spirits, I call upon your power. Take the wood from this block, and in its place put iron.*'

Denny and the three younger boys lifted their hands, and chanted the words in unison. There was a soft rustling sound, and Denny frowned. Not one of them had managed to complete the task successfully. Salus's block of wood seemed almost unchanged, with just its colour having greyed a little, while the block in front of Ignatius had crumbled into powder. Marlow's block had traces of iron running through it, while Denny's looked like petrified wood.

'Don't be disheartened,' said Tobold. 'We all know that these things take time and practice. The reason I asked you to try the wood first is so that you can compare how different water feels. Up until now, we have only tried out your abilities upon solid objects – wood, metals, and so on. Liquids are not the same. They require a different level of concentration to transform. Are you ready to try? All right; raise your right hand again and repeat after me: *Ever-living and blessed spirits, I call upon your power. Take the water from this tank, and in its place put salt.*'

The students lifted their hands, and recited the words. By Denny's right, Marlow's water froze, and his tank cracked from the pressure of the ice. The contents of the other three tanks looked unaltered.

'Sorry, sir,' said Marlow.

'That's quite all right, Marlow,' said Tobold, as he stepped forward; 'we can easily fix the tank later. I must say, I have never seen water freeze during this experiment before. For the other three boys, I would like you to place a finger into your tanks and taste the water.'

Denny put his index finger into the water, then he pressed it to his tongue. He grimaced.

'Well?' said Tobold. 'Valiance, could you taste the salt?'

'Yes, sir. It's disgusting, like seawater.'

'Very good. Salus?'

The boy shook his head. 'Just water, sir.

'Ignatius?'

'Mine is a tiny bit salty, sir.'

'And did it feel different?'

'Yes, sir.'

Tobold examined the four tanks. 'Two of you have transformed enough water to kill a man. Had you done that to an enemy, Valiance and Ignatius, they would now be dead. Marlow, I feel that your victim would also be dead, though not quite in the manner that I had intended. Salus, better luck next time.'

'It's the Sanctians, sir,' said Salus. 'I can't get them out of my mind.'

'The only cure for that is more meditation,' said Tobold.

'How long did it take you to get it right, sir?' said Marlow.

'I was in second year before I could empty my mind correctly,' said Tobold. 'There was a very attractive girl in the Maker school, and I spent most of first year day-dreaming about her. Don't tell anyone, but her name is Miss Vesta.'

Ignatius and Marlow laughed.

'You were in love with a teacher, sir?' said Salus.

'Miss Vesta is the same age as me,' said Tobold, 'and we joined our respective schools at the same time. And no, I wasn't in love with her – it was more of a teenage infatuation.' He smiled. 'She knows about it, of course; I was only joking about not telling anyone. I now count her as one of my best friends.'

'Why aren't we allowed to court girls from the Maker's school, sir?' said Marlow.

'It's because we teachers don't want you getting too distracted,' said Tobold. 'Masters need to keep their minds empty and clear; while the poor Makers have to digest and understand a whole library's-worth of knowledge. And we have your parents to think about. The adults of several realms like to arrange the marriages for their children, and we wouldn't want to interfere with that. You are all at an age when heads can easily be turned, but there is no harm in encouraging friendships between Masters and Makers. In the Battle of Hader Pull, Head Master Drummond combined magnificently with Head Maker Fyenna, and that was partly due to their pre-existing friendship.'

'Indeed it was,' said Drummond.

Tobold and the students turned, as Drummond strode into the room.

'Water into salt, I see,' said Drummond, as he approached. 'And ice, so it appears.'

'Yes, Head Master,' said Tobold. 'Three deaths out of four.'

Drummond frowned. 'We should not be glorifying that aspect, Mister Tobold,' he said. 'The taking of another's life is a terrible thing.'

'Yes, Head Master. I did not mean to make it seem otherwise.'

'Forgive me, Tobold. It is with great regret that I agreed to the necessity of teaching our students how to kill. It does not sit well with me.' He glanced at the four students. 'The sun is shining, and I have decided to take you all out for an excursion.'

'We are going outside, sir?' said Marlow, his eyes lighting up.

'Indeed, we are,' said Drummond. 'Constans and Aplin are waiting for us downstairs. Mister Tobold will also be accompanying us. Follow me.'

Drummond strode from the room, then Tobold and the four students followed him. They descended to a hall on the ground floor, where Constans and Aplin were standing by the front door of the building.

Drummond faced the students. 'We have left the school before,' he said, 'to visit the Makers, but this time will be different, as we shall be entering a public space. Therefore, I would like to issue a few rules. Firstly, on no account will you tell anyone who you are or which school you attend. I am taking a risk by allowing you to leave the premises, and anyone who breaks this rule will be severely dealt with. Secondly, you will follow my instructions to the letter, without question, and without hesitation. Thirdly, you will not use your Master abilities without my express permission. Think of this as a trial. If you behave appropriately, then we shall schedule more excursions in the future.' He smiled at them. 'Also, we shall not be leaving by the front door. Come with me.'

Drummond led them to the rear of the building, and they entered a small storeroom. Drummond withdrew a key from a pocket, and unlocked a small door that came up to Denny's waist, then he swung the door open, and crouched by the entrance.

'Prepare a few lamps, Mister Tobold,' he said. 'It will be rather dark where we are going.'

'Are we entering the tunnels, sir?' said Constans.

'Ah, so at least one of you is aware that tunnels exist beneath the Old City of Klef Mordain.'

'My father mentioned them to me as well, sir,' said Salus.

'They were originally dug to provide cisterns for the citizens,' said Drummond, as Tobold filled three lamps with oil. 'This was before the aqueduct was built, at a time when the Old City was in dire need of fresh water. Some of those cisterns are still in use, while others have been converted into other uses. Burials, for example, often take place underground. There are also tunnels – many miles of tunnels – that link the four districts of the Old City. If you ever wondered how the secret police seem to appear from thin air, this is your answer. I should also tell you that this is a great privilege, as not many people living in Klef Mordain are allowed to access these tunnels; in fact, outwith the Old City, few know of their existence.'

Tobold lit the three lamps. He handed one to Drummond, then he eyed the students, and handed the other to Denny.

'Constans,' said Drummond, 'you will follow directly behind me; then Marlow, Ignatius and Salus will come after. Mister Tobold and Valiance will remain at the rear. And boys, please do not stray from the path. I would hate to have to inform your parents that I had lost one of you down there.'

Drummond held his lamp out, and climbed through the doorway.

'Stay close to me, Valiance,' said Tobold, 'and keep an eye on the younger ones.'

Denny watched as the other boys began to follow Drummond into the entrance. 'Did you know we were going to leave the school today, sir?'

'I did not,' said Tobold. 'Master Drummond certainly likes to spring his surprises. To be honest, apart from our trips to visit the Makers, I wasn't allowed to leave this school for the entire four years I studied here.' He gestured to the entrance. 'Your turn.'

Denny crouched, and passed through the doorway. He lifted his lamp, and saw a flight of stone-cut stairs descending in front of him. He went down after the others, and they came to a level tunnel, where Drummond had stopped.

'Is everyone here?' the Head Master said. 'Good. Mister Tobold, did you close the hatch?'

'Yes, sir.'

'Then we shall proceed.'

Drummond set off, his lamp bobbing through the humid air of the tunnel. He led them on for what seemed to Denny to be around fifteen minutes, passing several junctions where other tunnels branched off, and an assortment of barred and locked doors. The Head Master came to a halt at the foot of a spiral staircase burrowing upwards through the soft rock.

'Up there is a wine cellar,' Drummond said. 'The cellar belongs to a friend of mine, and he won't mind us passing through; but don't touch anything.'

Drummond climbed the steps, and the others went after him. The Head Master pushed at a flat door in the ceiling of the stairs, and it opened. One by one, the teachers and students clambered out from the stairs, and into the musty wine cellar. Wooden racks of dust-coated bottles ran along three walls, while light was coming in from a series of street-level apertures next to the ceiling. The lamps were extinguished, and Drummond placed them onto the first step of the spiral staircase, then he closed the hatch. They went through a doorway, and ascended a flight of stairs, entering the ground floor of a house. Drummond opened the front door, and they stepped out into the bright sunshine, the waters of the estuary gleaming before them.

A couple of the boys gasped. Directly in front of them were the eight Sanctian warships, anchored just off the eastern flank of the Celestial Bridge.

'There they are,' said Drummond, as the students gathered around him. 'For three days, they have sat anchored within our waters, sending their messages back and forth to the Corse. Don't ask me what they have been discussing, because I don't know. Now, it is time to let you into another little secret. We will be joined today by the girls from the other school; so, I want you all on your best behaviour. Lady Fyenna will be also waiting for us, and be assured that she will be watching for any signs of impropriety.'

He set off again, striding along the esplanade towards the Celestial Bridge.

'What does *impropriety* mean, Valiance?' Ignatius whispered.

'Acting inappropriately,' said Denny. 'In other words, no flirting with the girls.'

They reached the southern end of the bridge, and Denny gazed up at the colossal statue that stood beside the road.

'That's the Great Maker,' said Tobold. 'The Great Master is at the other end. When both statues, and the bridge itself, were built, Masters and Makers helped with the construction.'

'Does the bridge carry the Great Northern Road?' said Denny.

'Yes, but Klef Mordain is the northernmost city on the route. The road goes up to the farms and settlements in the north; or it did. The area is depopulated now, thanks to the raids of the Westlanders, and the bridge is quieter than it was in the old days.'

'Why is it so high?' said Marlow.

'The bridge?'

'Yes.'

'The shipyards and commercial docks are further along the estuary,' said Tobold, 'and the arches of the bridge need to be tall enough for even the largest ship to pass underneath.'

They walked up the pavement on the right-hand side of the road. Carved stone railings edged the walkway, and the eight anchored Sanctian warships were clearly visible. Denny glanced back at the city as they ascended the bridge towards its apex. The densely-packed yellow sandstone buildings of the Old City were gleaming in the morning sunlight, a tight jumble of towers, steeples and domes. The city had no defensive wall running along the shore of the estuary, and Denny could see how vulnerable it was, when faced with the dozens of Sanctian ship-borne cannon.

A set of stairs descended into the stonework of the bridge near its apex, and a man and a woman were standing by the top of the steps. Denny narrowed his eyes at the woman – it was the same one who had been present at his interview in the *Star Inn*, the woman Denny suspected had ordered the elimination of Ter Angla. Drummond stopped by the top of the stairs, and talked to the man and the woman in hushed tones for a few moments.

'Who is she?' Denny said to Tobold.

The teacher shrugged his shoulders.

'Is she secret police?' Denny went on.

'This is Klef Mordain,' said Tobold; 'it would be wise to assume that every stranger is a member of the secret police.'

Drummond shook hands with the man and the woman, and then the Head Master gestured for the students to descend the stairs. Denny kept his gaze on the woman as he strode towards the steps, but she did not return his glance. They went down the flight of stairs, and emerged into a square chamber cut into the interior of the bridge. On the right was a circular opening that looked out over the approaches to the estuary, and the Sanctian warships were visible through it. Fyenna, Vesta, and the students from the Maker school were already in the chamber, and they turned to watch as the young Masters joined them. Drummond walked up to Fyenna, and they spoke for a few moments, as both sets of students eyed each other. Denny shared a quick glance with Abigone, then both looked away. It had been several weeks since he had seen any of the Makers, and he remembered brushing off Abigone's attempts at conversation. It was nothing personal, he told himself; it was more that there was little point in making friends with someone to whom he would never be able to reveal his true identity. He would be lying every time they spoke together, so any friendship would be little more than a sham.

'Students,' said Fyenna; 'gather round.'

The Masters and Makers turned to gaze at Fyenna and Drummond.

'This outing has been arranged for a specific purpose,' Fyenna said. A ship's whistle sounded, and she smiled. 'Right on cue,' she said. 'Turn your attention to the eight Sanctians ships, if you would.'

The students walked over to the circular aperture and gazed down at the warships. The sails were being hoisted, and dozens of sailors were scrambling over the rigging. Anchors were raised, and the eight ships began to move off in the wind, heading east, away from the city.

'Our friends from the Sanctian Empire are leaving,' Fyenna said; 'but they shall be returning. I received word yesterday evening regarding this. The Sanctians have requested permission to hunt pirates in our waters along the coast, and the Corse have negotiated an agreement to allow them to do so. Squadrons of warships will be coming and going, and Klef Mordain shall, for a price, supply those ships with food and fresh water. No sailors will be allowed to disembark from their vessels, so we shall not be meeting any Sanctian sailors in the streets. Head Master Drummond and I decided to make this bridge the first location for a series of outside lessons, so that you could see the Sanctians depart. We should all be able to sleep a little more easily from now on, as, it seems, the Sanctians do not intend to take any hostile action against us. However, there is no room for complacency, and the lessons on defence will continue. To this end, we have decided to split you all up into pairs. Each pair shall have one Master, and one Maker.'

The students glanced at each other.

'There is a very good reason for this,' Drummond said. 'In the Battle of Hader Pull, Head Maker Fyenna and I combined our abilities to thwart the Westlanders. We all know that Masters and Makers can work perfectly well on their own, but when the two are linked together in combination, the sum proves greater than the parts. Head Maker Fyenna and I have thought long and hard about the suitable pairings, and we have decided to group you by age and ability. As an example, and as a model for you to emulate, Mister Tobold and Miss Vesta will also pair up for the duration of these special lessons. I will now read out the pairings. Once your name had been called, please separate off with your pair, and await further instructions. All right. The first pairing shall be Constans and Raewyn, the two most experienced of our students.'

Constans and Raewyn smiled at each other, and walked off to the side of the chamber together.

'Next,' said Drummond, 'Aplin shall pair with Stanza, as both are second year students. For the first years, Marlow shall pair with Reath; while Salus and Ignatius shall share the pairing with Nyli, as there are more boys than girls. Lastly, it makes sense to pair our two oldest students, Valiance and Abigone.'

The boys and girls sorted themselves into their pairings. Denny walked up next to Abigone, but they avoided eye contract.

'The rest of the lesson is simple,' said Fyenna. 'We would like you all to spend some time with your partner. Learn each other's abilities, and get to know each other. In the heat of battle, a Master and Maker team need to be able to trust each other implicitly; they need to be able to anticipate their partner's thoughts and needs, and understand their skills, and their limitations. Find out if you can work well together, and relax. This is not a test.' She glanced at Constans and Raewyn. 'For the avoidance of doubt, must I add that this is not a marriage service, either? The partnerships we are seeking are not of the romantic variety. Is that clear?'

Constans and Raewyn glanced away, their cheeks flushing, while Reath cackled with laughter.

The four teachers withdrew to the edge of the chamber, leaving the students in their pairings.

Denny tried to smile. 'Where do you want to start, Abigone?'

'I don't know,' she said. 'You have already made it quite obvious that you desire neither my friendship nor my company. What more needs to be said?'

'I didn't mean my words to be cruel or hurtful,' he said. 'I'm sorry if you took it that way.'

'It is of no concern to me.'

'For the sake of the lesson, shouldn't we try to get along?'

'Oh, it's for the lesson?'

'Yes. That's what we've been asked to do. Why don't I begin by telling you what I know about you, and you can correct me if I make any mistakes?'

Abigone folded her arms across her chest and said nothing.

'I know that you are a princess of Upper Down,' he said. 'You have two sisters, and you once had a brother.'

'I remember telling you that,' she said. 'Do you recall what happened next? I asked if you had any siblings, and you refused to answer.'

'I remember. I don't talk about my past, and I don't talk about my family. It's not you; I don't talk about these matters with anyone.'

'Then what exactly are we supposed to discuss?'

'We could talk about you.'

'This isn't going to work.'

'Why don't we talk about what we can do? I mean, our abilities as a Master and a Maker?'

'I doubt that would take very long. I can do almost nothing. I have attempted to summon over a hundred spoons, and I haven't yet managed a single one properly. Wooden spoons, metal spoons... it doesn't really matter; I'm hopeless.'

'Head Master Drummond is always telling us that the Makers have a far harder time of it. You spend your days studying, while we spend ours meditating.'

'So, it's easy for you?'

'That part is easy, but I'm still no good at actually transforming things. I did manage to make some water turn a little salty earlier today, but I still can't change wood into metal.'

Miss Vesta walked over. 'How are you two getting on?'

Abigone smiled. 'Fine, ma'am.'

'Very good,' said Vesta, then she moved on to another pair.

'Why did you lie?' said Denny.

Abigone shrugged her shoulders. 'As silly as it may sound, I would rather be paired with you than with one of the younger boys. This is humiliating, but it could be worse.'

Denny laughed.

'I am glad you find me amusing,' she said.

'No, I agree with every word you said. Look at Constans and Raewyn, trying to pretend that they are nothing but friends; and look at the expression on Marlow's face as Reath is being rude to him.' He smiled. 'Stanza and Aplin are united by their dislike for each other, and poor Nyli has two awkward boys to contend with. I'm a lot safer with you, Abigone.'

'Answer me this,' she said. 'Why won't you talk about yourself?'

'The answer to that is exactly what I am trying to avoid saying. I'm sorry, but that's the way it is. I swore an oath.'

'An oath?'

'To my father. I don't break oaths, Abigone.'

'Then how are we ever supposed to trust one another? Isn't that the point of this exercise?'

'Did you have many suitors in court?'

'Why would you ask that?'

'I was curious. You are a princess. Upper Down is a small kingdom, but I'm sure you must have a royal court there. And a palace?'

'Yes, there is a palace.'

'Why haven't you been married off?'

'Why do you think?'

'Because you are a Maker?'

'I was once engaged, but my prospective husband did not know that I was a Maker. And then the Sanctian army arrived, so the point was moot.'

'Was he a prince?'

'He still is, or so I believe.'

'Was he angry that the engagement was broken off?'

'I have no idea. This feels a little like an interrogation. Why aren't you married?'

Denny glanced away.

'Valiance is a strange name,' Abigone said. 'Were you called that after your father?'

Denny remained silent.

'Yes, I thought so,' she said. 'I am not attracted by the prospect of a one-way conversation, especially as you are clearly only pretending to be interested in me. Let us not upset our teachers by arguing; instead, let us both pretend to be interested in each other. But be under no illusions; you and I shall never be friends.'

Denny smiled. 'At least we can agree on something.'

CHAPTER 13
AN ADMIRAL CALLS

Old City, Klef Mordain – 4th Day of Considera 108

'Tell me a little about your background,' said Amery.

The young woman sitting opposite him smiled. 'I graduated as a qualified notary from the Consideral a few months ago,' she said.

'The *Consideral*?' said Amery.

'Haven't you heard of it?' said the woman. 'The Consideral College of Law. It's where every lawyer and notary in Klef Mordain is trained. It was named after Emperor Considera the Third, just as the month was; the month we are currently in.'

'Oh. I didn't know the college was called that. And your name?'

'Loryn of Cliephus.'

'And why do you want to work for the Second Empire Association?'

'I want to be able to use the skills I learned,' she said. 'The politics of the association do not sway me one way or another.'

'Would this be your first job?'

'I have had several jobs over the years, but this would be the first in the legal profession. I am qualified to draft and review contracts, summonses, affidavits and the like, and I have also studied Sanctian law, as well as the old Elestian codes.'

Amery pretended to write a few notes in his journal. His headache was getting worse, and he could feel himself perspiring. Worse, the job applicant sitting opposite him was distractingly beautiful, and he was having to concentrate so that his gaze didn't stray too far from her face.

'So, you have no actual work experience?' he said.

'Not as a notary. That is indeed what I said.'

'What other jobs have you done?'

'Is that relevant? I have worked in various taverns and cafés, so that I could earn some money while attending the Consideral. I can pour a decent pint of ale, and I know the difference between Subnestian and Campsian wines. Is that helpful? How many people work here?'

'What? Oh, eh, around three dozen or so? I lose track. There are only four of us in the legal department, if you can call it a department. There's myself, two scribes, and a notary.'

'Is it a good place to work?'

'The hours are long, and it can be demanding at times; which is why I have been authorised to recruit another notary.'

She narrowed her eyes slightly. 'I'm sorry; are you ill?'

'No, not ill,' he said. 'It was rather a late night last night. I may have had too much wine.'

'Are you conducting this interview while hungover? Mister Amery, you are not persuading me that the Second Empire Association is a particularly professional place of business. Do your employers not mind you coming to work in this condition?'

Amery tried to smile. 'They would mind if they found out. Happily, my work speaks for itself, and my employers have had no reason to complain about my standards. Now, as for your work, I have taken a look at the various documents you drafted and amended prior to the start of this interview. I am pleased to say that I found no errors or misinterpretations of the law.'

'Might I make a suggestion? Those documents hardly presented much of a challenge. Most first years at the Consideral would have managed the tasks you set me. Perhaps you should make it more difficult. Add in some complications, for example. The leasing agreement was far too straightforward, and I find that real life is a little more complex. Now, I took the liberty of perusing some of the other documents that were left in the office where I carried out the tasks, and I noticed a mistake in the minutes of a meeting with the Sanctian ambassador that was held a few weeks ago. There was a mix up in the chronology of events that made no sense. Mister Amery, if your intention was to re-write history, then I feel that you could perhaps have done a better job of covering your tracks.'

Amery peered at her.

'Have I gone too far?' she said. 'I have a very precise mind, and I can sometimes cause upset by pointing out the errors of others. Are you offended?'

'No, but I would like you to show me the mistake you referred to.'

'I shall. You really shouldn't be leaving sensitive documents like that lying around your office, especially minutes that show evidence of being tampered with.'

'And do the, uh, ethical issues raised by that cause you any concerns?'

'Were you instructed by your employer to re-draft the minutes? If so, then I would claim that this falls under the remit of your position. It is not our place to question the motives or morality of our employers. They make the decisions, and we see that they are presented in a manner that does not constitute a breach of the law.'

'Good answer. Do you have any more questions, Loryn?'

'Yes. Are you going to offer me the job?'

'I might need to take some time to think it over.'

'Why? I am fully qualified, and I understand that many graduates in my position would refuse to work for the Second Empire Association. The fact that you are interviewing graduates at all tells me that you have endured problems finding experienced notaries. Furthermore, I am ready to start work immediately; today, if needs be.'

'You would be on call day and night.'

'I would expect nothing less.'

'My employers can be quite demanding.'

'I relish a challenge.'

Amery scratched his head. The position had been advertised in every tavern in the Old City where members of the legal profession socialised, and Loryn was the sole applicant. Two things worried him about her – that her levels of professionalism and diligence would show up his own work, and that she would distract him merely by her presence. It occurred to him that neither reason made any rational sense, but his headache was pounding.

'I would like to offer you the job,' he said.

Loryn smiled. 'Thank you. I accept. When do I start?'

'You haven't asked about the salary.'

'I felt it might be impolite to ask. I trust that an organisation such as this would not allow its qualified employees to be paid less than the market rate. Am I wrong?'

'It's twelve hundred sovereigns a month,' he said.

'That will be adequate.'

'I will fill in the papers, and you can start tomorrow.'

'Might I start now? You don't need to pay me for today, but I would like to immerse myself into the affairs of the association as soon as possible. Do you have much on today?'

Amery rifled through a drawer in his desk, and withdrew a document printed on one side. He placed it onto the desk in front of Loryn.

'This is a confidentiality agreement. You would have to sign it before I could include you in anything we do.'

Loryn picked it up, and Amery savoured the quiet as she took a moment to read it. He blamed Lothar for his hangover. He had been intending to have a relaxing evening, but it had coincided with one of Lothar's rare days off from working in the commercial harbour, and the Mountain Ranger had insisted that Amery join him in drinking a few bottles of wine.

Loryn took a quill from the desk, dipped it into an ink pot, and signed her name at the bottom of the document.

Amery smiled. 'Welcome to the Second Empire Association.'

They stood, and Loryn extended her arm. Amery wiped his palm on his trousers, then shook her hand.

'What shall we do first, sir?' she said.

'You're calling me *sir* now?'

'It wasn't appropriate prior to my employment, but you are now my supervisor. Would you prefer me to call you Mister Amery?'

He pulled his gaze away from her. 'I'll think about it. Are you aware that a few Sanctian warships returned to Klef Mordain yesterday evening?'

'I think the entire city is aware of it, sir.'

'One of the vessels is an admiral's flagship, the *Bitter Respite*. Lord Tain and Lady Ursula are expecting... Sorry, do you know those names?'

'Yes, sir. I studied the publicly available records of the association before attending the interview. I am familiar with its leadership.'

'All right. Well, the lord and lady are expecting a summons to the Sanctian Embassy. The assumption is that someone from the flagship will wish to speak to the ambassador, and the association will most likely be a part of those talks. Before we go any further, do you understand the aims of the association?'

'I do, sir.'

'And that doesn't bother you in any way?'

'Why would it bother me, sir?'

'Do you agree with those aims?'

'Do you, sir?'

'That is none of your business, Loryn.'

'Exactly. We are professionals, sir, and our private political desires should not interfere with our jobs. The Consideral was very clear on this topic.'

The door opened and Ursula walked into the office. 'There you are, Amery. Get your things; we're leaving. Is your carriage handy? We...' She trailed off as she noticed Loryn by the desk.

'This is my new notary, ma'am,' said Amery. 'Her name is Loryn of Cliephus, and she has just started working for the association.'

'Has she signed the confidentiality agreement?'

'The ink of her signature is still wet, ma'am. Loryn, this is Lady Ursula.'

Loryn curtsied. 'It is an honour to meet you, ma'am.'

'I'm sure,' said Ursula.

'I was thinking of bringing Loryn along with us today, ma'am,' said Amery.

'What you do with your notaries is of no concern to me, Amery,' said Ursula. 'Be warned though; she will not be permitted to sit in on any meetings with the ambassador. Her credentials will need to be verified by the embassy first.'

'A most wise precaution, ma'am,' said Loryn. 'I shall register my credentials with the relevant embassy staff upon arrival.'

'Take this, and visit the reception here,' said Amery, as he wrote a short note. 'They will furnish you with a pass to get in and out of the building; then I shall meet you by the main entrance.'

He handed Loryn the note, then she inclined her head and strode from the office.

Ursula glanced at Amery. 'I hope you haven't just hired the first attractive young woman to walk through the door.'

'I hired the sole applicant for the position, ma'am,' he said. 'She has excellent qualifications.'

'I'm sure she does. My brother has already left for the embassy, so I will join you and... Loryn in your carriage, if it is available.'

'I always keep it close by, ma'am. I will have it brought round to the entrance of the alleyway.'

'Then I will see you in ten minutes.'

Lady Ursula left the room, and Amery collapsed into his chair.

'Just get me through today, blessed spirits,' he mumbled, 'and then I promise I will never drink again.'

Forty minutes later, Amery's carriage pulled up on Cornmarket Road next to the Sanctian Embassy.

'Before we exit the carriage,' Amery said, 'you should know, Loryn, that agents from the secret police will notice your presence with myself and Lady Ursula. They are always watching the Sanctian Embassy.'

'We are doing nothing illegal, sir,' said Loryn.

Amery opened the side door of the carriage and stepped down to the cobbles. He lifted a hand to assist Lady Ursula to descend, then he did the same for Loryn. The driver closed the door, and Lady Ursula led Amery and Loryn into the embassy. It had been a quiet journey, and Amery suspected that Ursula had not wished to say too much in front of a new employee.

Several embassy courtiers approached them as they crossed through the entrance hall. To their left, a group of marines from the Sanctian Navy were waiting by the base of the staircase, their steel breastplates gleaming from the sunlight coming in through the tall windows.

'Greetings, Lady Ursula,' said one of the courtiers. 'Your noble brother is upstairs, awaiting the ambassador. Shall I take you to him?'

'Thank you, yes,' said Ursula.

The courtier glanced at Amery, then his gaze fell upon Loryn.

'I do not recognise this woman, my lady,' he said.

'She's new,' said Ursula.

'Her name is Loryn,' said Amery.

Loryn withdrew a thick envelope from her clothes. 'I have here the necessary credentials for your inspection – my certificate of birth, my diploma from the Consideral College of Law, and several references.'

The courtier inclined his head, then he took the envelope from her hands. 'You shall have to remain downstairs while these are being checked, ma'am.'

'Of course,' she said. 'It is an honour and a privilege to be inside the Sanctian Embassy.'

The courtier gave her a cold smile, then he gestured to a colleague. 'Please accompany Miss Loryn to the reception office,' he said, handing him the envelope.

The other courtier bowed, then he led Loryn away. The first courtier gestured to the stairs, and Amery followed him and Ursula up to the next storey. The courtier took them to a tapestry-filled room, where Lord Tain was pacing the floor, accompanied by a handful of his assistants.

'Ah, sister,' he said. 'Prepare yourself; we might be in for a long wait.'

Ursula strode into the chamber, with Amery a pace behind. 'I assume the ambassador is meeting with someone from the flagship?' she said.

'Yes. A full admiral. They've been locked up in the audience hall for quite a while now. And no, I haven't the slightest notion what they are discussing.' He glanced at Amery. 'How goes it with our intrepid lawyer?'

'He hired a new notary this morning,' said Ursula. 'You'll like her. She's your type.'

'I am sure she will do well, sir,' said Amery. 'She has very fine credentials.'

'From where does she hail?'

'Klef Mordain, sir. Cliephus, to be precise.'

'Is she from the Consideral?'

'She is, yes.'

'And she sees no difficulties in working for us? Is her heart with the cause?'

'She is a professional, sir.'

'I thought the graduates from the Consideral were boycotting the association. Has she been vetted?'

'The embassy staff are examining her credentials as we speak, sir.'

Tain nodded, then he went back to pacing the floor.

'You are making my head spin, brother,' said Ursula.

'Then sit down and pour yourself a cup of coffee,' said Tain. 'Pour me one, too.'

'You look as though you have consumed quite enough coffee for one morning, brother.'

'Stop fussing, and let me pace. Two sugars, if you will.'

Ursula frowned. 'See to it, Amery.'

Amery suppressed his headache and smiled. 'Yes, ma'am.'

. . .

Two hours passed before the doors to the audience hall opened. Several courtiers emerged first, followed by the ambassador and a tall man wearing the uniform of a senior officer in the Sanctian Navy. Tain stopped pacing, and Ursula got to her feet. The ambassador gestured towards the siblings, and pointed them out to the naval officer.

'This is Admiral Assanio,' said the ambassador. 'Admiral, this is Lord Tain and Lady Ursula.'

'How nice to meet you,' said the admiral. 'The ambassador has told me much about the great work you have been doing here in Klef Mordain. The Sanctian Empire owes you its gratitude.'

'Thank you,' said Tain, inclining his head. 'It is an honour to work towards our city's integration into the empire.'

'Yes, well, keep it up, old chap. I have to return to my ship now, but I am sure I will be hearing more about your efforts in due course.'

'My staff shall escort you to the front door, Admiral,' said the ambassador.

The two men shook hands, then the admiral was led away by several courtiers.

Ambassador Tertius gestured towards the entrance of the audience chamber. 'Now it is time for a little discussion.'

'Thank you, Your Eminence,' said Lady Ursula.

Amery followed the ambassador and the two siblings into the hall, and a courtier closed the door. They walked over to a meeting table, and the ambassador took his place at its head.

'Sit,' he said.

Tain, Ursula and Amery took their seats a few places down from the ambassador. Amery removed a quill, ink pot, sand-shaker and a sheaf of blank paper from his robes. He dipped the quill into the ink, and readied himself.

'Naturally,' said the ambassador, as Amery recorded his words, 'I am not at liberty to disclose all that passed between myself and the noble admiral, but there are a few matters I would like to bring to your attention. Firstly, the anti-piracy patrols have been fairly successful, with three unlicensed vessels being confiscated from the local coastal waters near Klef Mordain. Please ensure that this news reaches the ears of the general public; they need to know the good work that is being carried out by our friends in the Sanctian Navy.' He eyed his guests. 'That is the official reason for the admiral's visit – to bring us this news. Everything else I say, with one significant exception, will be confidential.'

Tain glanced at Amery. 'Take no minutes beyond this point.'

Amery put down his quill. 'Yes, sir.'

'It is the will of the Most Exalted Emperor Antonio,' said the ambassador, 'that more pressure is brought to bear upon the government of this city, in order to force them to come to their senses. You will already know of the recent increases in the trade tariffs – these are to be doubled again, effective immediately.'

'Doubled, Your Eminence?' said Tain. 'That will lead to a string of bankruptcies among the merchant class, and some may decide to blame the Sanctian Empire for their losses.'

'It is the job of the Second Empire Association to ensure that this does not happen,' said the ambassador. 'You will present this increase to the public as the fault of the intransigent Corse. After all, the tariffs will be dropped as soon as Klef Mordain agrees to enter negotiations regarding the annexation of this territory into the warm embrace of the empire. However, the pressure does not end with mere tariffs. The blessed emperor has also authorised the Sanctian Navy to begin harassing the merchant fleet of this city, under the guise of searching for spies, pirates, and those attempting to avoid paying the new tariffs. It will all happen out of sight of Klef Mordain, but you should expect to hear news of ship's cargoes being confiscated without compensation.'

'That will be harder to justify to the public, Your Eminence,' said Lady Ursula.

'I understand, but orders are orders, my lady. Have you had any luck investigating the business affairs of the husband of Lady Fyenna?'

'Not yet, Your Eminence,' said Tain. 'It appears that the earlier information regarding Selanius may have been exaggerated, as he seems to have kept strictly to the law. It may be necessary to fabricate some evidence.'

'Say no more,' said Tertius. 'I do not require to hear the details. Do what you must. The admiral was keen to relay to me the vital importance the exalted emperor places upon finding the location of the secret school for Masters and Makers. His Imperial Majesty wishes to make it plain that he regards the sheltering of Masters and Makers within this city as a shameful and grievous crime, and he is greatly angered that the students have not yet been found and expelled from Klef Mordain.' He paused for a moment. 'You should also know that twenty thousand soldiers are to be boarded upon the navy's fleet of transport vessels. They are being moved up as far as Lesser Down, to await further orders. The monarchy of that realm will no doubt complain, but there is nothing they can do to prevent the fleet from docking in their harbours. Lesser Down will most likely send a secret message to their friends in the Corse, informing them of the troops' movements. If questioned about it, you will say that the soldiers are there to ensure that the trade routes remain open along the coastal highways of the Central Provinces. You are not to imply in any way that they might be diverted to Klef Mordain in the event of a crisis.

'Lastly,' he went on, 'I would like to dictate a letter for the attention of the Corse. It falls to you to deliver this letter into the correct hands. It must be read out to the government of thirty at the earliest opportunity.'

Amery picked up the quill, and prepared a fresh sheet of paper. 'Please proceed, Your Eminence.'

The ambassador got to his feet.

'Begin thus, Mister Amery,' he said. 'From His Eminence Lord Tertius, Imperial Ambassador of the court of the throne of the Most Exalted Emperor Antonio of the Sanctian Empire, to the government of Klef Mordain. Greetings. The Sanctian Empire wishes to bestow its heartfelt gratitude upon your fair city, for allowing the ships of the Sanctian Navy safe harbour in order to pursue and eliminate all criminals from the waters of Klef Mordain. The cooperation you have shown in this matter shall not be forgotten, and it is my personal wish that this will lead to more cooperation in the future. One area where the Corse can provide assistance to the Sanctian Empire would be the opening of a public, formal investigation into the political assassination of Lord Denon, a diplomat from the Sanctian Empire who was so cruelly slain without due process some two months ago. Under the authority of the Most Exalted Emperor, I hereby admonish the government of Klef Mordain, and make a formal protest regarding their lack of action in this matter. The Corse would do well to remember that all diplomats are sacrosanct, and they should acknowledge that a grievous crime was committed when Lord Denon was butchered on the streets of their city. The Sanctian Empire demands that those responsible for this crime be swiftly brought to justice.'

Amery reached for another blank sheet, and the ambassador paused for a moment until he was ready to continue writing.

'A second area where cooperation might prove fruitful,' Tertius went on, 'is assistance in the locating of a certain Princess Abigone, regent of Upper Down. As an ally of the Sanctian Empire, Upper Down falls under the protection of the Most Exalted Emperor, and it is with great distress that we have learned of the disappearance of Her Highness Princess Abigone within the bounds of Klef Mordain. If the Corse has any knowledge of her whereabouts, they must publish that information immediately. If it is discovered that the Corse has withheld any relevant details regarding the missing princess, then Klef Mordain will find itself in breach of its international obligations, and stern measures may be taken by the Sanctian Empire and its allies to remedy this fault. I eagerly await your response on these matters; Yours, et cetera.'

The ambassador smiled. 'Did you get all that, Mister Amery?'

'I did, Your Eminence. The letter is ready for your signature.'

Tertius walked over to where Amery sat. He scanned the two pages of the letter, then he appended his signature to the bottom of both sheets. Amery folded the sheets together and prepared a piece of red wax, as the ambassador held his signet ring over the low flame of an oil lamp. When it was hot enough, he pressed the ring into the wax, and the seal of the embassy was affixed to the paper.

Tain held out his hand, and Amery passed him the letter.

'I shall deliver this at once to Lord Penny,' Tain said.

'Thank you,' said Tertius.

Tain, Ursula and Amery got to their feet. All three inclined their heads, then they left the audience hall. No words were exchanged between them as they were led down the stairs by a few embassy courtiers, and they found Loryn waiting for them by the main entrance.

Tain turned to his sister. 'I shall take the letter to Lord Penny's home.'

'We need to discuss its contents,' said Ursula.

'Let me make sure it gets into Penny's hands first,' said Tain, 'and we can talk about it back at the association later.' He glanced at Loryn. 'You must be the new notary.'

Loryn curtsied. 'Yes, my lord.'

'Have the embassy staff finished checking your credentials?'

'Not yet, my lord. They say it may take a day or two.'

'Fine,' he said. 'I will see you all back at the association.'

He strode away, and disappeared through the front door.

'Shall we board my carriage, ma'am?' said Amery.

Ursula nodded, her features an expressionless mask. They walked outside into the bright sunshine, and the driver held open the carriage door for them. Ursula's composure cracked as soon as the door had been closed.

'This is too much,' she said. 'Tariffs being doubled, again; twenty thousand soldiers being posted to Lesser Down, merchant ships to be harassed... Where does it end, Amery? Does the Emperor think that this city will take these insults kindly? Are we not supposed to be trying to persuade the people of the benefits the Sanctians bring? These measures will not achieve that; they merely bring war one step closer.'

'Indeed, ma'am,' said Amery.

'And that letter?' Ursula went on. 'What was meant by *stern measures*? It was nothing but a naked threat, for the ambassador must know that the Corse will never reveal what they have done with Princess Abigone. That girl is as good as dead.' She stared out of the side window. 'Our jobs become more difficult with each passing day. Find yourself a bodyguard; that's my advice, Amery. The Second Empire Association is about to feel the wrath of the masses.'

They sat in silence for the rest of the short journey, as Ursula simmered with rage. When they arrived at the association building, Ursula hurried into the interior without another word, leaving Amery and Loryn alone in the carriage.

'I want you to forget everything you heard come from the lips of Lady Ursula,' Amery said, as they stepped down onto the cobbles.

'Was it all true, sir?' said Loryn. 'Are we close to war?'

'I don't know, Loryn. Let's just say that pressure is being applied upon Klef Mordain, and, if the Corse continues to remain obdurate, then things might escalate.' He eyed her. 'Are you regretting taking the position here?'

'Not at all, sir.' She smiled. 'All in all, I feel it has been a most profitable and rewarding first day. Shall I see you in the office at dawn?'

Amery nodded.

'Then I shall bid you farewell until then,' she said.

Amery watched her stride along the alleyway, then he shook his head, rubbed his face, and walked into the building.

CHAPTER 14
HOMESICK

Old City, Klef Mordain – 6th Day of Considera 108

'Marlow is a repulsive boy,' said Reath, 'and he smells funny.'

'You're lucky having Marlow as a partner,' said Nyli in her quiet voice. 'I have two boys.'

Reath laughed. 'Yes. One of them can barely read, and the other is a snob from the gentry.'

'Salus is Constans's little cousin,' said Abigone. 'They are both members of the Klef Mordain aristocracy.'

'Then you should have been put with one of them,' said Reath. 'You know, being royalty.'

'What's Valiance like?' said Nyli. 'Is he nice?'

'He's quiet,' said Abigone. 'He refuses to answer the simplest questions. He wouldn't even tell me if he has any brothers or sisters.'

Nyli gasped. 'I wonder why he would do that. Is he hiding a dark secret?'

Reath made vomiting noises. 'The way you idolise him turns my stomach,' she said. 'You're a disgrace to the family name, Nyli. Besides, Valiance is much too old for you. He wouldn't be interested in a fourteen-year-old.'

Nyli's face went red.

'Can we stop talking about the boys from the Master school?' said Abigone. She pointed at the thick textbooks laid out in front of them. 'We are supposed to be learning about tree formation.'

'But it's so boring,' said Reath. 'Who cares about stupid trees and how they grow?'

'I couldn't agree more,' said Abigone, 'but we'll never be able to summon wooden objects properly if we don't study. We're supposed to be reading chapter seven of the book today.'

'You're one to talk,' said Reath. 'You hate studying more than any of us. You never stop complaining about it.'

'Don't exaggerate.'

'I'm not. You're always tired and grumpy, and you're always complaining. *Valiance won't speak to me. Why do we have to read so many books? Lady Fyenna doesn't like me.* Wah, wah; like a baby. I wish Marlow wouldn't speak to me, then we might get on better. In fact, I would like him a whole lot more if he stood several yards away, so that I wouldn't have to smell his weirdness.'

'I think it's the soap he uses,' said Nyli. 'It has a strange odour.'

'That's assuming he washes at all,' said Reath. 'He's from Subnestia, remember?'

Abigone sighed. 'At least be quiet while I read.'

'I will not,' said Reath. 'I'm going to keep talking, just to annoy you. Upper Down is quite a backward place, isn't it? Do the men wash there, or do they all smell as bad as Marlow?'

Abigone ignored her, and her gaze went to the text of the book.

'Are you a virgin?' said Reath.

Abigone's eyes narrowed. 'That is not an appropriate question.'

'So? Do you think I care about what's appropriate? Let's think it through. You're a princess, so your father probably had armed guards posted by your bedroom door every night. But, on the other hand, you are eighteen, nearly nineteen. Hmm. I think I'm going to pick *Yes* – you are a virgin. A frustrated virgin. Is that why you're always bad-tempered? Were you hoping that Valiance might steal your flower?'

Nyli grimaced. 'Don't call it that.'

'I was being polite,' said Reath. 'I could be far more vulgar, if you like.'

'I know you could,' said Nyli. 'Please don't.'

'I am waiting until I am married,' said Abigone. 'It's what civilised women do.'

Reath cackled. 'Which idiot told you that? Am I annoying you yet?'

'You have annoyed me since the moment I arrived at this school.'

'That's what I like to hear, Abigone. I take pride in my work.'

'Why must you provoke me?' Abigone cried. 'Asking stupid questions, and constantly prattling on... Do you realise how close you are to getting a slap in the face?'

'Try it,' said Reath. 'I would knock your teeth right down your throat. You aren't strong; you look as though a breeze could push you over. Have you ever punched anyone? I have. It's quite satisfying.'

'I once rammed a knife into the eye of a duke,' said Abigone; 'and I was scared of him. I'm not scared of you.'

Reath and Nyli glanced at each other.

'Reath was always getting into fights in our village,' said Nyli.

'Half of them were to get you out of trouble,' said Reath. 'You let bullies walk all over you, sister. Out of everyone in the school, I would love to punch Stanza the most. That would teach the little bitch to tell tales. Then I would shove the school rulebook up her fat...'

Miss Vesta walked into the classroom, and Reath pretended to be reading the book.

'Good afternoon, class,' Vesta said. 'How are you getting on with chapter seven?'

Reath smiled. 'Nearly finished, ma'am.'

'I shall give you a few more minutes to complete the chapter,' Vesta said, 'and then we shall try a summoning.'

Abigone's eyes went back to the text. For two months, she had read everything that had been given to her, and her mind was spinning with information. She had learned how to identify several dozen different types of trees from simply looking at a leaf or a block of wood – elm, oak, birch, beech, the list went on and on. She had studied how each blossomed in spring, bore fruit in summer, and shed their leaves in autumn. She knew their lifecycles, from the first shoots, to their eventual collapse and death – was there anything she didn't know about wood?

'Time's up,' said Vesta. 'Close your books and come to the front of the class.'

Abigone, Reath and Nyli got up from their seats and gathered next to Vesta. The teacher gestured to a workbench, where three blocks of wood were sitting.

'Can anyone identify the tree used to produce these blocks?' said Vesta.

'Pine, ma'am,' said Abigone.

'Be more specific.'

Abigone narrowed her eyes. 'Mylian fir, ma'am?'

'Very good, Abigone. I want you all to hold that in your mind as you each attempt to summon a wooden spoon.'

'Not a spoon again, ma'am?' said Reath. 'Why is it always spoons?'

'They are one of the simplest wooden objects to summon, Reath. We will not be moving on until each of you is capable of this task. So far, none of you have managed it successfully. When you do so, there will be no more spoons. I promise.' She placed a long-handled wooden spoon onto the desk. 'Use this as your template. On you go. You know the words; you don't need me to say them for you.'

Abigone raised her hand. 'Blessed spirits,' she whispered, 'with your permission, summon for me a wooden spoon.'

The air rustled, then a perfectly-formed wooden spoon appeared a few inches above the desk. It fell onto the flat surface, and Abigone stared at it, ignoring the disappointed complaints coming from Reath and Nyli.

'You're getting better, Reath,' said Vesta.

'Am I? Look at that pathetic specimen. I'm terrible at this.'

'You, too, Nyli,' Vesta went on; 'a vast improvement.' She turned to glance at Abigone's spoon, and her eyes widened. 'You did it, Abigone.'

Reath snorted. 'What? Let me see.'

Abigone remained where she was, her gaze fixed upon what she had summoned. Vesta was right – it was perfect; identical to the template that had been placed close by.

'Well done!' said Vesta. She picked up Abigone's spoon. 'I am very proud of you.'

Abigone started to cry.

'No; don't cry,' said Vesta. 'This is fabulous; there's no need for tears.'

Reath laughed. 'I think she's weeping with relief, ma'am. She never has to make another spoon again.'

Abigone put a hand to her face.

'Perhaps you should leave the classroom for a moment or two,' said Vesta, 'so that you can regain your composure. And really, Abigone – that was well done. I wasn't able to summon a wooden spoon until half way through first year. Come back when you're ready.'

Abigone nodded, then she walked from the room. She felt like an idiot. She should have been celebrating, not crying like a child. Perhaps Reath had been right – maybe it was the sheer relief of having finally succeeded at something. She wandered along the corridor, as tears continued to stream down her cheeks. A yearning for home raced through her mind. She missed the comfortable familiarity of her rooms in the palace in Torrent but, more than that, she missed her sister Kilbride, as well as Walter and Tulip. A year before, she had imagined that her life was unfolding as expected. She had her father the king, and her brother, and she was betrothed to a prince. Everything had seemed perfect. She had barely thought about being a Maker, and her sheltered lifestyle had allowed her to turn a blind eye to the evil being committed by her father. And now she had no father, no brother, and no prince to whom she was betrothed. Instead, she was confined to a school building with Vesta, Reath and Nyli, and burdened with more work than she had ever known in her life.

She found herself descending the stairs to the ground floor of the school building. She would speak to Lady Fyenna, she decided. Despite her wariness of the woman, she needed an adult to talk to, someone who might be able to reassure her; someone who would see things sensibly, as Kilbride had always done.

When she reached the entrance to Fyenna's office, the door was slightly open. Abigone raised her hand to knock, then she heard voices coming from the interior.

'I'll admit that I didn't know him very well,' Fyenna was saying. 'Was it a long illness?'

'He was poorly for a few years,' said the voice of another woman. 'That would probably explain why you didn't see too much of him, but he passed over to the spirits in his sleep; which is about as much as any of us could ask for. The funeral will be tomorrow, at mid-morning. It will take place in the usual location.'

'I don't wish to seem ungrateful,' said Fyenna, 'but why have I been invited to the funeral?'

'I suspect Lord Metrius wishes to address a few close allies,' said the other woman, 'but you didn't hear that from me. Before I go, I wanted to ask you something. You don't seem yourself this afternoon, my old friend. Is everything all right?'

'Yes. Fine.'

'Are you sure?'

'It's nothing. Just a personal matter.'

'Is it anything I can help you with?'

'Thank you, but no. It's Selanius. He... well, he has been behaving rather strangely recently, and I don't know what to make of it. He barely spoke to me at breakfast this morning.'

'Perhaps he has worries concerning his shipping business. It might not be anything that you have done.'

'I can't help but feel that it might be related to the secrets I am obliged to keep from him. It has taken a toll on our marriage, but, if I'm honest, Selanius has usually been able to brush it off. It can be hard at times, not being able to say the slightest thing about what I do or where I work.'

'We who lead this city all have our sacrifices to make, Fyenna.'

'I know. I understand that, but... I wish... Oh, what's the use? I know my duty. Anyway, thank you for coming here to let me know about tomorrow, Niscoll. I will be there.'

'It was a pleasure to see you again.'

The sound of chair legs scraping against floorboards reached Abigone, and she backed away a few paces, so that it wouldn't seem as though she had been eavesdropping.

The door opened more fully, and Fyenna emerged from her office with an older woman. Fyenna noticed Abigone, and her smile faded.

'What are you doing out of class, girl?' she said. 'You shouldn't be down here.'

'Miss Vesta gave me permission to leave, ma'am,' said Abigone.

Fyenna narrowed her eyes. 'Why are you crying? Hold on a moment.' She turned to the other woman. 'I had best deal with this.'

The older woman smiled. 'That's fine; I know the way out. I shall see you tomorrow.'

The older woman walked away, and Fyenna gestured towards the office door. 'In you come, Abigone.'

Abigone and Fyenna walked into the office.

'Take a seat,' said Fyenna; 'close the door first.'

Abigone shut the door, then she sat down opposite Fyenna, who took her chair behind the wide desk.

'Well?' said Fyenna. 'Is there a problem I need to know about? Has Reath finally made your patience snap?'

'It's not Reath, ma'am,' said Abigone.

Fyenna passed her a handkerchief. 'Wipe your eyes, girl.'

'Today, ma'am,' Abigone said, as she dabbed at her face, 'I managed to summon a wooden spoon.'

Fyenna nodded. 'Yes, and?'

'I've been here two months, and that's all I've been able to do.'

'Two months isn't all that bad. Some first years struggle to summon anything whatsoever. Wait – is that why you're crying? Dear spirits, I thought it was something serious.'

Abigone wiped her eyes. 'I miss my home and my family.'

'Aren't you a little old to be homesick?'

'I feel so out of place here, ma'am. The girls in my class are four years younger than me, and I don't have anyone my own age to talk to. Even Valiance from the boys' school hardly speaks to me. We're supposed to be a pair, but he won't tell me anything about himself.'

Fyenna laughed. 'You are not alone in that. Valiance has refused to utter a word about his past to Head Master Drummond, or to anyone else, for that matter. He is a very secretive young man; try not to take it personally. Look, Abigone; we all knew that it would be difficult for you here. At your age, you should be in fourth year; but we are doing all we can to help you improve your Maker abilities. Are you studying every evening?'

'Yes, ma'am.'

'I know you find some of the books a little childish, but all you can do is persist with them.' She paused for a moment. 'Let me ask you something unrelated to being a Maker. When you were in Upper Down, did you happen to see any of the fighting? I understand that the siege was quite short; did you witness any of it?'

'Yes, ma'am. I saw some fighting, and I saw... men die around me.' She lowered her gaze. 'I killed some of them myself.'

'You? You killed people?'

'Westlanders. One of their chiefs wanted to marry me, and there was a battle. I... I was stuck in the middle of it. Walter, the King's Champion, was leading the resistance against the invading Sanctians, but he was also fighting the Westlanders, who were holding me captive. I crushed a few with my stone dragons. That's where my sister got the idea for destroying the cannon.'

'Let me understand this for a moment – you were personally responsible for killing several Westlander warriors?'

'Is that bad, ma'am?'

'How did those deaths make you feel?'

'I thought they deserved it, ma'am. They were going to hurt me. I didn't want to marry their chief.'

'And yet you cry over a little homesickness?'

'Some of the tears might have been from relief. I have tried to summon hundreds of spoons since I got here. Seeing one that actually came out right set me off. And now I'm a little embarrassed.'

'Answer me this – if it came to it, would you be prepared to kill again? I mean, if your life, or the lives of those you care about were in danger?'

'Yes, ma'am. Does that make me an evil person?'

'Not in the slightest, girl. Defending your home and loved ones is an honourable profession. What you did in Upper Down has shown me that you can perform under the pressures of the battlefield.'

'But you don't believe that I destroyed sixty cannon with a single summoning?'

'Now, Abigone – let's not bring up that old argument. For an untrained Maker to have achieved such a remarkable feat stretches the bounds of credulity. You would have to be... well, you would have to be one of the most naturally gifted Makers of the last century to have accomplished that.'

'But how could I do it, ma'am, when it took me two months to learn how to summon a simple spoon?'

'You are confusing raw talent with precision, Abigone. You have already admitted to me that your stone dragons were nothing more than shapeless lumps of rock. Shapeless lumps are all untrained Makers are capable of summoning. To craft something with detail and accuracy – now that needs years of study. And, if I am being frank, two months isn't a very long time for a spoon. Did Reath or Nyli also manage to complete this task?'

'No, ma'am.'

'You know, I cannot fix your homesickness, but I may be able to provide you with books aimed more at your age.' She stood, and turned her gaze to the volumes stacked on her shelves.

'Am I ready for fourth-year Maker textbooks, ma'am?'

'No, you are not, but you might be ready for this.' She withdrew a hefty tome from a shelf, then she sat down and placed it onto the table. 'This is a book on battle tactics. It was written during the era of the

Elestian Empire, and so it contains a few chapters on how Masters and Makers can best be integrated into an army. It covers siege operations, and both offensive and defensive manoeuvres. Head Master Drummond and I studied it intensively before the Battle of Hader Pull. Prior to that, neither of us had any experience of fighting. Of course, the actual battle was very different from reading a book, but it should give you a few ideas.'

'Thank you, ma'am.'

'Take it to your room, and don't tell the other girls about it,' said Fyenna. 'Raewyn might get envious, and Stanza would most likely complain. After you have deposited it in your room, go back to your class.'

Abigone picked up the book and got to her feet.

'You are doing well,' said Fyenna, 'but you are at the beginning of a very long path. I had my doubts about your work ethic, and your feelings of entitlement; but perhaps you are starting to prove me wrong. Keep it up.'

'Yes, ma'am.'

Abigone walked out of the office and closed the door. She took a breath. The tears had gone, and she thought about what Fyenna had said. It was true – she had killed people in Upper Down, so why had she got so upset about a wooden spoon? She clutched the heavy book to her chest and ascended the flight of stairs to the first floor. She could hear the sound of Reath's voice coming from the classroom, then she saw Miss Vesta leaning over Nyli's desk as they looked at a textbook.

'Are you feeling any better, Abigone?' said Vesta, as she glanced up.

'Yes, miss. Thank you.'

Vesta's eyes went to the book that Abigone was carrying, then she lifted her gaze again. 'The kitchen staff were just here, and I'm afraid I have some rather disturbing news to break to you,' she said. 'Apparently, a large rat was seen in the kitchens a couple of days ago.'

'Thank you for letting me know, miss,' said Abigone. 'Rats don't particularly bother me; I am not scared of them.'

'What about cats?' said Miss Vesta. 'Are you scared of them?'

Abigone narrowed her eyes.

'I ask, because the kitchen has just procured one as a rat-catcher,' said Vesta, 'and they are looking for someone to take responsibility for feeding it.'

'Cats are a nuisance,' said Reath.

'Has anyone volunteered, miss?' said Abigone.

'I don't think so,' said Vesta. 'If you are interested, let the kitchen staff know.'

'I need to put this book in my room,' said Abigone. 'Can I go to the kitchen after that, miss? I won't be long.'

'Of course,' said Vesta. 'I will see you here in a few minutes.'

Abigone ascended another flight of stairs to the level where the students' rooms lay, and she walked along the corridor until she reached her door. She opened it and entered her small room. She set down her new book on the bedside table and glanced at its cover. Something in Fyenna's eyes had changed when Abigone had mentioned that she had killed a few Westlanders in Upper Down; and now the Head Maker wanted her to read a book about military tactics. It was clear what Fyenna had in mind – she wanted to exploit any advantage that the schools could provide. Abigone might lack the ability to summon a carriage or a clock, but what did that matter if she could drop tons of rock onto the heads of an enemy?

She left her room, and went down two flights of stairs to the kitchen. Inside, the three women who worked there were busy chopping vegetables and heating large pans of water.

Abigone smiled. 'I heard that we have a new cat?'

'Interested in looking after it, are you?' said one of the women.

'Yes, please. I had a cat in Upper Down, but I had to leave him there when I left to travel to Klef Mordain.'

The woman pointed at a cupboard. 'It's hiding under there. The wretched creature is too scared to come out.'

'I doubt it'll be catching any rats,' said another woman. 'We'll have to get ourselves some poison.'

Abigone crouched down, and peered under the cupboard. Almost hidden in the shadows, she saw the small grey cat's blue eyes staring at her.

'Is it a boy or a girl?' she said.

One of the women shrugged. 'A girl, we think.'

'What's her name?'

The kitchen women laughed.

'Why would we give it a name?' said one. 'Should we give the rat a name, too?'

Abigone stood. She glanced around, then she picked up a small slice of pork from a chopping board. She crouched down again, and held the meat out. Slowly, the grey cat began to edge forward, but she remained out of Abigone's reach. Abigone placed the meat onto the floor, and backed away a step. The cat advanced a little more, then she snatched up the meat, and ate it. Abigone held out a hand. She kept it still, and the cat approached, rubbing the side of her head against Abigone's knuckles. Abigone attempted to stroke her. At first, the cat backed away, then she came forward again, and allowed Abigone to rub behind her ears.

'I'll call her Meg,' said Abigone.

'Call it whatever you like, dear,' said one of the women. 'It'll need to be fed morning and night, and you can clean up any mess it makes.'

'All right,' she said. She stroked the grey fur of the cat, and Meg began to purr. 'I will see you later, little Meg; I'm going to look after you. I will fetch you a blanket, and make a bed for you, but you can come up to my room and keep me company while I'm studying.'

One of the women shook her head. 'It's as though the girl thinks that creature can understand what she's saying.'

Abigone stood, and Meg rubbed her flanks against her ankles.

'I'll see you after classes,' she said. 'Be a good girl.'

The kitchen staff laughed, but Abigone didn't care. She walked out into the hallway, and then she hurried up the stairs and entered the classroom.

'Come in and sit down,' said Vesta. 'The other girls have moved on to chapter eight of the book.'

Abigone took her seat, and opened the textbook to the correct page.

'Did you see the cat?' whispered Nyli.

Abigone smiled. 'Yes.'

'What about the rat?' said Reath. 'Did you see that, too?'

Abigone shook her head.

'If I ever see it,' Reath went on, 'it'll be its last day alive. Be careful when you go to sleep. Rats climb up onto beds in the middle of the night and eat the face of whoever's sleeping there.'

'Quiet, Reath,' said Vesta; 'and that simply isn't true.'

'It is true, ma'am,' said Reath. 'It happened to a boy in our village. He woke up with a bloody hole where his nose had been.'

'And did you see the boy after this happened?'

'His parents sent him away before we could get a good look. They didn't want a boy with no nose.'

Vesta rolled her eyes. 'Back to reading, girls.'

Abigone smiled again as she began to read. It would be after dinner before she would be able to return to the kitchen, and she would make sure she would have the choicest samples for Meg to feast upon. She imagined the grey cat cuddling into her each evening while she was studying, and, suddenly, her life seemed a little bit brighter.

CHAPTER 15
THE FUNERAL GUESTS

Old City, Klef Mordain – 7th Day of Considera 108

Wearing a simple black dress that came down to her ankles, Fyenna walked along the quiet alleyway. A café was setting up for the day, and a waiter was placing cutlery onto the small tables that sat under the branches of a cypress tree. He glanced at Fyenna as she walked by, but she kept her gaze lowered. The left-hand side of the alley backed on to the high walls of the Temple of the Blessed Spirits, and its ancient stonework was starting to crumble in places. The stone used to build the Old City of Klef Mordain was soft, which meant that many of the older buildings were in a slightly dilapidated state, fraying at the edges like clothes that had been worn too many times. The softness had another attribute – it was easy to tunnel through. The stone that had gone into the construction of the temple had been delved out from beneath the streets the citizens walked over every day, though few knew it.

Fyenna came to a small door in the side of the temple, and knocked. A grille opened, and a set of eyes peered out at her. The man behind the grille nodded, and the door was opened.

'Do you know your way round the catacombs, ma'am?' he said, as

Fyenna entered a dimly-lit chamber containing a set of stairs that went down into the darkness.

'I have been in them once or twice before,' she said, 'but I don't know the location of today's funeral.'

The man lit an oil lamp and passed it to her. 'Down the stairs,' he said; 'second left, left again, then third on the right. You should see the flames from the other lamps by that point.'

Fyenna smiled. 'Thank you. Does anyone ever get lost down there?'

The man stared at her. 'Yes.'

'Well, I, uh, will try my best not to,' she said.

With the lamp held high, she pulled up the hem of her dress, and descended the worn stone-cut steps. The air grew humid as she passed down into the depths under the city. Alcoves and small shrines to the spirits had been cut from the rock on either side of the stairs, and she saw monstrous carved faces, and images of ships and anchors. A few arcane symbols that she didn't recognise were also etched into the face of the rock, their significance lost to the ages. At the bottom of the stairs, a long passageway stretched out in front of her. On either side, lead and stone coffins sat upon shelves cut from the rock, and several rows of disembodied human skulls stared vacantly at her as she made her way through the shadows and flickering light. As a member of the Corse, she had the right to be interred within the sprawling catacombs when her last breath had been taken; and a small sum was deducted from her salary every year to pay for the expense. She followed the directions given to her by the man, and saw how easy it would be to take a wrong turn and find yourself in the midst of a vast maze. Burial chambers both large and small pocked the sides of every passageway, while narrow side tunnels opened out into family vaults. She took the last turn, and heard voices before she saw the flicker of light. She ducked her head through a low opening, and emerged into a large cavern, its walls lined with shelves for bodies. Around half of the shelves were empty, and a brand new coffin sat festooned with flowers and candles in an alcove on the right. In the centre of the cavern, a long table had been cut from the rock, and nearly two dozen people were sitting on cushions around it, eating and drinking.

Lord Metrius glanced up from a cushion. 'Ah, Lady Fyenna; so good of you to come. Sitting on my right is the renowned Lady Mabda, the widow of the late Lord Erno, whose funeral we are attending this day.'

Fyenna approached the old lady, and bowed her head. 'My commiserations for your loss, Lady Mabda.'

'All friends of Lord Metrius are welcome here, Lady Fyenna,' the woman said. 'Please sit, and partake of the food and drink on offer.'

'Is there to be a service?' said Fyenna, as she sat down next to Lady Niscoll.

'The feast is the service,' said Lady Mabda. 'By eating and drinking with us, you will be celebrating the life of my dear Erno, may the spirits watch over his soul. Would you like to say a few words, Metrius, my old friend?'

'I would be honoured, my lady,' said Metrius. 'Everyone, fill your glasses.'

Niscoll poured some dark red wine into a glass and passed it to Fyenna.

'This is one of those rare occasions,' Lord Metrius went on, 'when all can speak freely. I know every person who has gathered here for Lord Erno's sake; all are trusted friends. Lord Erno dedicated his life to the service of this great city, and he was already an experienced member of the Corse when I first joined all those years ago. Such was his love for Klef Mordain, I have no doubt that he would approve of us meeting like this to celebrate his life; I also would guess that he would bless our discussions, and urge us onwards to success.' He raised a glass. 'To the eternal spirit of Lord Erno, a stalwart of the city, a model citizen and patriot, a gold coin amid a mountain of counterfeits. If any of us here can emulate even half of his achievements, then we would be fortunate indeed.'

The others raised their glasses and drank.

'One of the happy results of us all assembling like this,' Metrius said, 'is that I am able to speak frankly to you, without having to mask my words or speak in riddles. However, the news I bear is not so happy. I have received information from a trusted source I have recently embedded into the disgraceful Second Empire Association. Three days ago, an admiral from the Sanctian Navy attended a private meeting with the Sanctian ambassador. The embassy has released an official statement regarding this meeting, which I am sure you will have heard. It relates to the seizure of a few vessels allegedly dabbling in piracy off our coastal waters; but I know the truth of the matter. The meeting, in fact, was to pave the way for a full invasion by the forces of the Sanctian Empire.'

The cavern hushed.

'This is not merely hyperbole,' said Metrius; 'the trouble we feared is coming, and coming fast. Let me list the ways the Sanctians mean to provoke us – they have doubled the trade tariffs, again; they are intending to harass our merchant fleet, under the pretence that they are hunting for pirates – what nonsense! Cargoes will be confiscated, our sailors imprisoned, and our merchants reduced to penury. But this is not all. As I speak these words to you, twenty thousand Sanctian soldiers are being placed onto ships. They are being sent to Lesser Down, our neighbour upon the southern frontier; but do not doubt for a single moment their true, hidden destination. They are coming for us.'

He pulled a letter from his robes, and flourished it in the humid, smoky air of the cavern.

'Those among you who are members of the thirty will already know the contents of this letter,' Metrius went on, 'as it was read out by the perfidious Lord Penny at a meeting of the government yesterday morning. For those who are not members of the thirty, I will now pick out the salient points of this missive. It was authored by His Eminence Ambassador Tertius and, naturally, it is couched in diplomatic language, but the threat it represents is real. He makes two demands of us – demands! As though we were but the slaves of the Sanctians. His first demand is that we investigate the judicious execution of the spy Lord Denon, who was brought to justice for his crimes against Klef Mordain. His second demand is more troubling – he wishes us to reveal the fate of Princess Abigone of Upper Down, and advises that *stern measures* – his words – will be taken against us if we do not comply. Presumably, his stern measures amount to the twenty thousand soldiers sailing north towards our shores. Alas, the thirty is crippled with indecision, poisoned as it is by the eleven pro-Sanctian traitors who sit on that hallowed body. It is known as a bald truth that these eleven routinely relate the doings of the thirty to their friends in the Sanctian Empire; nothing discussed there can any longer be kept a secret from our enemy, an enemy who means to swallow us whole. Hence, I decided that this group should gather here, for we must plot out our course in secret, far from the eyes and ears of the traitors who would betray us.'

One of the older men raised a hand. 'But, Lord Metrius, as dire as this sounds, I know nothing of the whereabouts of any Princess Abigone. I am not completely ignorant; I know that she entered the city some two months ago, and that she has apparently disappeared. However, I do not understand why the Sanctians believe that we are responsible for her fate.'

Metrius nodded. 'It is time for all here to know the truth about the matter of the missing princess. Lady Fyenna, would you be so good as to elaborate for these ladies and gentlemen?'

Fyenna blinked. 'But...'

'There are no secrets within this chamber,' said Metrius. 'As I have already stated, every person here is a trusted friend and patriot. All must have a grasp of the facts if we are to devise a suitable response to the Sanctians.'

'Yes, my lord,' she said. 'This is hard for me to say, as I have been watching my words for so many years that I find it difficult to express myself honestly.'

'Nevertheless,' said Metrius, 'I order you to proceed.'

Fyenna glanced at the cavern floor. 'Princess Abigone is currently attending the school for Makers.'

A few of those gathered round the table showed surprise on their faces, while many others remained expressionless.

'She is safe and well,' Fyenna went on, 'and progressing with her studies.'

'Thank you,' said Metrius. 'I hope everyone is now able to grasp why we cannot simply announce this to the Sanctians. This information is none of their business, and we all know what the Sanctians would like to do to every Master and Maker still alive upon this world. We are protecting the princess, but we are unable to admit it publically. If the Sanctians invade, the Masters and Makers currently dwelling in Klef Mordain will become a vital part of our defence. Fyenna, please give us some details regarding our current disposition.'

'Yes, my lord. At the present moment, we have three adult Makers and two adult Masters in Klef Mordain. That number includes myself.'

'There was a Master who assisted you at the Battle of Hader Pull,' said an old woman. 'His name has been stricken from the history books, so I do not know his identity. Does he still live, Lady Fyenna?'

'He does, ma'am. Aside from that man and myself, none of the other adults have any experience of fighting. Ironically enough, Princess Abigone has a good deal of experience in such matters, and she would be willing to help in the defence Klef Mordain if called upon to do so.'

'Are you seriously entertaining the idea that children would fight on our behalf?'

'The princess is eighteen years old, my lady,' said Fyenna; 'no younger than many of the recruits in the army.'

'But she cannot fight for us – she is the sovereign leader of a foreign realm.'

'Not so,' said Lord Metrius. 'It happens that the city has recently received two further letters, and I am in receipt of both.' He withdrew two envelopes from his robes. 'It appears that these are replies to letters sent out by someone within Klef Mordain. My suspicion is that the original letters were written and dispatched by the Second Empire Association, in order to stir up trouble. The first letter is from Princess Nolan of Lesser Down. In it, she politely enquires after the health of her sister, Princess Abigone. Why would she have sent this, had she not first been contacted by a telltale within our city? The second letter is more subtle. It comes from Princess Kilbride of Upper Down. The noble princess does not enquire after Abigone's health. Instead, she merely notes that she has received a letter, from whom she does not say, and she points out that Princess Abigone's status as regent has been temporarily revoked for the duration of her stay within Klef Mordain.'

'What does that mean?' said an old man.

'It means, my friend,' said Metrius, 'that Princess Kilbride has deep levels of cunning. Imagine you were she, and that you received a letter from the Second Empire Association stating that your sister was missing within Klef Mordain. Imagine also that Kilbride understands fine well the reason for her sister being here. While Princess Nolan, who almost certainly received the same letter, enquires after her sister's health; Kilbride merely states that Abigone is not to be treated as the leader of a foreign nation. In other words, Kilbride is removing a weapon from the hands of our enemies. If Princess Abigone is not a regent, then the diplomatic crisis is immediately dampened.'

'I can confirm this,' said Fyenna. 'I have it from the mouth of Abigone that she was sent to this city by Princess Kilbride. It stands to reason that Kilbride is well aware of her sister's latent abilities as a Maker.'

'But Upper Down is an ally of the Sanctian Empire,' said the old man.

'Yes,' said Metrius, 'but are they willing allies? The authorities of Upper Down signed a peace treaty while thousands of Sanctian soldiers were camped outside its ruined defences. I perceive that Princess Kilbride is sending a message to those with the wit to read it. I would also guess that Princess Nolan is unaware that Abigone is a Maker.'

'That is all very well,' said the old man, 'but how do we respond to the accusations of the Sanctians? We cannot admit the truth to them. Do we merely state that we do not know the present location of the princess?'

'That is all we can say, my friend,' said Metrius. 'Any official response would have to be channelled through the thirty, and I am not prepared to reveal the full truth within that chamber. Lord Penny would run to the Sanctian ambassador with the news. I am prepared, however, to send a secret communication to Princess Kilbride, thanking her for her letter, and noting that her sister will no longer be deemed a sovereign leader of Upper Down. If Kilbride is as deft as I believe her to be, she will glean the hidden message that Abigone is alive and well.'

'This means we are free to use Abigone's talents to defend this city,' said the older woman. 'Should we order a full mobilisation of our reserves? If twenty thousand Sanctian soldiers are on their way here, we need to be prepared.'

'I would like to question Lord Metrius's source for this information,' said a younger man. 'Can we be sure that we are not being fed lies to mislead us? If we mobilise, no amount of secrecy will hide our actions from the Sanctian embassy.'

'I cannot give you the exact details,' said Metrius, 'as this could endanger my agent's life. All I shall say is that I have placed said agent into the Second Empire Association as an employee. I was careful to erase any link to me in the agent's credentials, so the association should suspect nothing.'

'Is it Amery?' said an old man.

'It is not,' said Metrius. 'Mister Amery of Yearl is, I believe, a conscientious employee of the association. I now regret not having offered him a job in my own office, as his skills assisted the association in the recent election. However, in time, I anticipate that Amery will come round to our cause. I happen to know a few things regarding his past actions that would bring him into disrepute with his employers. I will use this information at a suitable moment to turn him.'

A woman raised her hand, and Fyenna recognised Portia sitting by the table.

'Yes?' said Metrius.

'I have Mister Amery's name on a list of possible assassinations to be carried out in the event of an invasion. Should it be removed, my lord?'

'Yes, Portia,' said Metrius. 'Do not target anyone working within the legal department of the association.'

'Understood, my lord.'

'Perhaps you should enlighten everyone here as to the true state of the secret police, Portia.'

'Yes, my lord. Regrettably, the secret police have been compromised.'

There were a few gasps from those seated around the table.

'We have begun to receive conflicting orders from the thirty,' Portia went on. 'Some come from the anti-Sanctian wing, others from the pro-Sanctians. We are ordered to arrest a certain person, then those orders are overturned. We are ordered to follow certain citizens, then told that those citizens should be free to go about their business. Consequently, some members of my profession have become disillusioned and confused as to their ultimate loyalties. A state of inertia is taking hold of the secret police. If it comes to war, I advise you not to place too much faith in their abilities to thwart the Sanctians.'

'This is an outrage!' cried an old man.

'It is what happens when eleven pro-Sanctians are voted on to the thirty, my friend,' said Metrius. 'Their presence has paralysed the organs of government, and the secret police is no exception.'

'We should kill them all!' the older man went on. 'They are traitors, and should be exterminated before they bring the city to ruin. And not just the eleven, but every pro-Sanctian member of the Corse should feel a knife at their throats. As for the damned Second Empire Association, it should be burned to the ground! Lord Tain and Lady Ursula's gutted corpses should be hanging from a lamppost in the Nether Town!'

'Tell me, my friend,' said Metrius; 'what do you think the Sanctians would do if Klef Mordain descended into civil conflict? A wave of killings as widespread as you recommend would ignite the flames that already smoulder about us.'

'Then we are doomed,' said the older man. 'The city shall fall, and the Sanctian vultures will pick at the remains.'

Metrius smiled. 'I did not say that we should rule out assassinations entirely, only that we should target them with precision. Lord Tain and Lady Ursula's lives I hereby declare to be forfeit, along with Lord Penny, Lord Asquith and Lord Harrow of the thirty. Their deaths should be made to look accidental. Portia, I deliver this weighty task into your hands; do you have sufficient forces loyal to you for this?'

'I do, my lord,' said Portia. 'Your will shall be done.'

'You have my thanks. The rest of us should be aware of the likely consequences of these assassinations. It is probable that they will provoke the pro-Sanctians into responding in a similar manner. All of you should look to your personal protection, and take every reasonable precaution. As the names of our enemies are known to us, we are known to them. As the minister responsible for the defence of Klef Mordain, I will authorise a full mobilisation of our reserve forces. This is necessary but, again, it may provoke the Sanctians into responding. I will say the mobilisation is merely for exercises, but I doubt anyone will be fooled. I will also order our armament manufacturers to increase production of arrows, bows, armour and the like. Lady Fyenna, I command you to bring the Masters and Makers of this city to a state of full readiness, and that includes Abigone, and any other student old enough and capable enough of aiding our defence.'

'I will make it so, my lord,' said Fyenna.

Metrius sat back, and his shoulders slumped a little. 'These are dire days, the worst seen since the collapse of the Elestian Empire over one hundred years ago. I cannot stress enough that we are entering a conflict in which we are by far the weaker party. The cannon borne by the warships of the Sanctians could level the coastal areas of the city in a matter of hours, bringing untold suffering and destruction to our people. Moreover, our merchant fleet is extremely vulnerable from those same cannon.'

'Why haven't we developed our own cannon?' said an old woman. 'Surely it is not beyond our wit?'

'My dear friend,' said Metrius, 'if only you knew how hard we have tried to emulate the weapons of our enemies, then you would not say such a thing. It is true that our forges and foundries can cast the metal tubes necessary to launch a ball of stone or iron, but the mysteries of the black powder have continued to elude us. The Sanctians manufacture it within secret and hidden facilities upon their home island, and they guard the truth as keenly as the Corse guards its own secrets.'

'The cannon are not invulnerable,' said Fyenna. 'Princess Abigone personally destroyed sixty of them before the gates of Upper Down. That was the sole reason the empire was forced to reach an agreement with that realm. If there is a way for the Masters and Makers to nullify this seaborne threat, we shall not rest until we find it.'

'She destroyed sixty cannon?' said a man. 'I am glad indeed that she is willing to fight for us, and I am grateful to Kilbride for sending her here in our time of need.'

'We may, in time,' said Metrius, 'all have cause to thank Princess Kilbride for her foresight and acumen. I will be sure to express my gratitude to her in the secret letter I intend to dispatch to Upper Down. Now, let us depart from this place below the ground. Lady Mabda, I praise your hospitality, and I honour the memory of Lord Erno. If we are successful in our endeavours, then each of us present here today will remember the occasion upon which our resolve hardened into action.'

'Thank you, Metrius, my friend,' said Mabda; 'and thank you all for coming. May my husband's memory and achievements light your way through this uncertain future.'

The funeral guests began to rise from the cushions. Each bowed low before Lady Mabda, then they filed out of the rock-hewn chamber.

'Lady Fyenna, a moment, if you please,' said Metrius. 'Come aside with me, as I wish to talk privately.'

Fyenna followed Metrius into the shadows of a deep alcove, its walls lined with coffins upon shelves.

'Lady Niscoll mentioned that she visited you yesterday,' Metrius said.

'Yes, my lord. She came to inform me about today's arrangements.'

'She also told me of your concerns regarding your husband, the good Selanius.'

Fyenna frowned.

'I have looked into the matter,' Metrius went on, 'and it seems that your concerns are not without warrant. Lord Penny, in his capacity as minister for trade, has opened an investigation into your husband's business concerns. Agents at the commercial harbour have been inspecting every transaction your husband has made, spanning back years, in a search for any wrong-doing.'

'But why? Why would they target my husband?'

'Come now; you are an intelligent woman. Surely you can perceive the reason?'

'It's because of me? Does that mean they know about the school?'

'We do not know exactly what they know,' said Metrius; 'but, you are the only prominent Maker within Klef Mordain, and you are known for your deeds at the Battle of Hader Pull. It may be that this is all they know, and they have deduced that you may be connected to the school. If this is the case, then presumably they intend to use your husband as leverage. Has Selanius asked you for any information regarding your place of work?'

Fyenna flushed in the darkness. 'No, my lord.'

'And, to the best of your knowledge, has he committed any breaches of the law with regard to his business interests? Will Penny's agents find anything to use against him?'

'No, my lord.'

'Are you certain?'

'Quite certain, my lord.'

'I hope you are right. The penalty for smuggling goods into Klef Mordain is death, as I am sure you are aware. A man with that kind of threat hanging over him may be inspired to commit acts of desperation. No matter what occurs, Fyenna, you must reveal nothing to your husband; not even to save his life. Do you understand?'

'Yes, my lord.'

'I would do anything to protect this city; anything. I would slay my own children rather than see Klef Mordain brought low; I would even sacrifice my beloved wife to preserve the secrets essential to our survival. Think on that.'

'I will, my lord.'

'I know you will, Fyenna; you have ever had the best interests of this city close to your heart. Good day.'

Metrius turned and strode away, leaving Fyenna alone in the shadows of the alcove. The air felt thick, hot and heavy, and she wiped some perspiration from her forehead. She thought back to her husband's recent behaviour. He had seemed restless, and anxious, and he had indeed questioned her about her place of work. A wave of nausea passed through her.

'Oh, Selanius,' she whispered; 'what have you done?'

CHAPTER 16
INSTINCTIVE

Old City, Klef Mordain – 15th Day of Considera 108

Denny and the other boys from the Master school ascended the rock-cut stairs rising from the underground tunnel, and emerged into the back room of a bakery, where ovens were blasting out waves of heat. Head Master Drummond was waiting by the top of the steps, and Mister Tobold was at the rear of the column.

Drummond eyed the students. 'No one get lost down there? Good. Our carriages should be waiting outside for us.'

'Where are we going, sir?' said Marlow.

'That will be revealed soon,' said Drummond. 'Follow me.'

They left the building by a back door, and found two carriages lined up in the narrow alleyway.

'Climb aboard,' said Drummond. 'Mister Tobold, take the rear carriage; I shall travel in the lead.'

'First years with me,' said Tobold; 'except for Salus; he can ride with his cousin.'

Denny, Ignatius and Marlow climbed into the rear carriage, then Tobold boarded, and closed the door behind him.

'Keep the curtains closed,' said Tobold. 'The journey should take around an hour, so I would like you all to practice meditating until we reach our destination.'

'Will the girls be there, sir?' said Marlow.

Tobold smiled. 'Yes. Does that please you?'

Marlow frowned. 'No, sir. Reath does nothing but insult and berate me. Why did I have to be paired with her?'

'Because you are a year older than her, Marlow. I fear Reath would have eaten Salus or Ignatius for breakfast.'

Denny laughed.

'It's not fair,' said Marlow. 'You've got Abigone, and she seems nice, and she's... well, you know?'

'What?' said Denny.

Marlow's cheeks flushed. 'Do I have to say it? It's pretty obvious.'

'It's not obvious to me.'

'Well, she's beautiful, isn't she? And she's a princess. You get her, and I get bloody Reath.'

'Watch your language,' said Tobold. 'And remember, you are supposed to be meditating.'

Denny closed his eyes, and leaned back against the comfortable bench. Abigone was indeed beautiful, but it was clear that she didn't much care for Denny's company, not when he refused to tell her anything about his past life. He wondered what she would think if she knew the truth, that he was a grandson of Emperor Antonio, and the son of a rebel leader of Geathan. As a princess, she might be one of the few people in Klef Mordain who would understand his position, but that didn't mean he would break his vow of silence. The carriage moved off, and Denny drifted into sleep.

He awoke when Tobold tapped him on the shoulder.

'Are we there?' said Denny.

'We are. Did you enjoy your meditation, Valiance?'

'Uh, yes.'

'You were snoring,' said Ignatius. 'I couldn't concentrate for the noise.'

Tobold smiled. 'Well, I hope you are refreshed for today's activities; they may prove to be a little more strenuous than usual.'

He opened the side door, and jumped down onto a sward of grass. Denny glanced at their surroundings as he stepped down. A forest was bordering them on three sides, while fields, meadows and low hills lay to the east. A few yards away, three other carriages were parked by the side of the track. One of them contained Drummond and the other boys, who were climbing down to the ground; while the young Makers were standing next to the others, along with Lady Fyenna, Miss Vesta, and another woman Denny didn't recognise.

Drummond and Fyenna shook hands and talked for a moment, then the two groups assembled together.

'Good morning, Masters,' said Fyenna. 'Before we get started, I would like to introduce Miss Eshia to you.' She gestured to the other woman, who smiled. 'Eshia was a student in the Maker school until last year, when she graduated. Gathered here today is every Master and Maker in Klef Mordain. We represent not only the hope for the future, but the last line of defence for our beloved city. Today, we shall be practising battlefield manoeuvres and tactics.'

Reath raised her hand. 'Where are we, ma'am?'

'We are several miles north of the city,' said Fyenna, 'on the far bank of the estuary.'

Reath nudged Nyli. 'I told you. I knew we crossed the Celestial Bridge. I felt us go up and then down again.'

'No one lives out here,' said Fyenna, 'so we should not be interrupted. Our first lesson shall be on preparing defences. A normal army would employ its soldiers to dig ditches and raise earthen ramparts. If they have time, they would also construct a wooden palisade to crown the rampart. The nearby trees would have to be chopped down to prepare such a palisade. All of this takes time and a considerable amount of effort. If Masters and Makers combine together effectively, they can save the army this labour, freeing them to perform other duties.'

'Is that what you did at Hader Pull, ma'am?' said Reath.

Fyenna's brow crinkled slightly.

'Not quite,' said Drummond. 'We did something slightly different at Hader Pull. I transformed earth into wood; that was the first stage. The effect of this was to create a long ditch in the ground, behind which our longbows sheltered. Head Maker Fyenna then stood out in front of the ditch to await the charge of the Westlanders. At the last possible moment, she used the wood I had transformed to summon hundreds of wooden spikes, upon which the Westlanders dashed themselves to pieces. The longbows then loosed everything they had, and the invaders were slaughtered.'

'You missed out the part about having to rescue me from the bottom of the ditch,' said Fyenna.

Drummond smiled.

'We won't be trying anything quite so ambitious today,' Fyenna went on. 'Split off into your pairs and move to a position where you will be able to work in peace. I want each Master to transform earth into wood, creating a ditch, and then I want each Maker to summon beams from that wood, preferably sharpened at both ends. Get to it. We shall be watching.'

Denny walked up to Abigone. 'Where do you want to go?'

Abigone shrugged. 'Anywhere will be fine.'

'Let's go to the edge of the woods,' he said.

'Why?'

'So the students who are younger and better than us won't see how bad we are at it.'

Abigone said nothing, and they began to walk away from the others. They neared one flank of the forest, and Denny glanced at the ground.

'Earth into wood. Shit.'

'Can you manage it?' said Abigone.

'I'll give it a try.' He raised one hand, and tried to clear his thoughts.

'Nyli thinks you're hiding a dark secret,' she said.

'Are you trying to distract me?' he said. 'I'm supposed to empty my head.'

'I think she has a crush on you.'

'And Marlow has a crush on you. So what? To them, we probably seem like adults.'

'We are adults.'

'You know, I sometimes forget that. It's probably to do with sitting with first years every day. Now, can I ask you to be quiet for a moment? I didn't want that to sound rude, but I need to concentrate.'

Abigone rolled her eyes.

'Ever-living and blessed spirits,' Denny said, 'I call upon your power. Take the earth from the ground, and in its place put wood.'

The grass a yard in front of Denny withered, and the level of the ground sank a few inches.

'Is that it?' said Abigone. 'Where's the wood?'

Denny knelt by the grass, and felt through the soil. He plucked out a small sliver of wood and showed it to Abigone.

'I'm not sure I'll be able to summon a palisade wall out of that,' she said. She turned towards the forest. 'Now, wood – wood I know. Blessed spirits,' she said, 'with your permission, summon for me the beams for a palisade.'

The air rustled, and Denny stared as wood was stripped from the nearest trees. Branches snapped, and bark was ripped off, then two trees fell with a thunderous crack. An instant later, a dozen straight beams of wood materialised in front of them, neatly stacked up on the ground.

Abigone smiled.

'By all the spirits, Abigone,' said Denny; 'that was amazing. I thought you were as hopeless as me.'

'Not when it comes to wood,' she said. 'Don't ask me to summon anything else, though, and don't request anything complicated, like a wagon, or even a wagon wheel. Wooden beams, I can do. Does Marlow really have a crush on me?'

'What? Oh, yes. He said you were beautiful on the way here.'

'Perhaps he was just being polite.'

'Are you saying I'm not?'

'I know nothing about you, Valiance,' she said. 'I wouldn't dare to hazard a guess as to whether or not you are a gentleman.'

Tobold strode over to them. 'How are you getting on?' he said. 'I must say, that's a fine-looking stack of wood, but where is the ditch?'

'Do you see that small patch of withered grass, sir?' said Denny. 'That's my ditch.'

Tobold frowned. 'I see. So, where did the wood come from?'

'Abigone ripped it from the forest, sir.'

Tobold glanced over, then his eyes widened at the sight of the collapsed and damaged trees.

'That is very impressive, Abigone,' he said.

'Thank you, sir,' she said. 'I can only do wood.'

'But it was rock that crushed the Sanctian cannon.'

'How do you know about that, sir?' said Abigone.

'Teachers do tend to talk among themselves, Abigone,' Tobold said.

'Well, my rock was misshapen. I can summon it, I suppose, but I cannot control what it looks like.'

'Your raw talent is considerable,' he said. 'Perhaps you should be paired with another Master.'

'Can I keep Valiance, sir?' she said. 'The other Masters are a little young, and I like being with someone my own age.'

'I wasn't talking about pairing you with a student, Abigone. I was thinking of pairing you with myself.'

'But you have Miss Vesta and Miss Eshia, sir.'

'I know. I was being mildly facetious; think nothing of it. Valiance, you shall need to improve, and quickly, if you are to keep up with Abigone.'

'Thank you, sir,' said Denny.

Tobold strode away.

'What an odd man,' said Abigone.

'He often says things that you shouldn't take too seriously,' said

Denny. 'Sometimes, it's hard to tell if he's joking or not. Anyway, I'm touched that you want to remain as my partner.'

'Are you joking now?'

'No. But I do need to improve.'

'Do you want to meditate for a while?'

'That might help, I suppose.'

'Then do so. I will wait.'

'All right.'

Denny sat down on the soft grass with his legs crossed under him, and closed his eyes. He focussed on his breathing and began to clear his mind of stray thoughts. Somehow, the mere fact that he knew Abigone was standing close to his right shoulder was enough to put him off. She was quite beautiful, come to think of it; Marlow wasn't wrong about that. And the way she had effortlessly summoned a large pile of wooden beams had made him think differently of her. She had told Tobold that she wanted to keep him as her partner; was there any significance to that?

He opened his eyes. 'It's no good. I can't empty my head of thoughts.'

'What is it that you are thinking about?' she said.

'Oh, nothing in particular. What do you think about when you summon things?'

Abigone sat down on the grass a yard in front of him. 'I think about the thing I am trying to summon,' she said. 'That has to be the sole object of my thoughts, and the more I know about that thing, whatever it is, the more easily I can summon it. Hence, study will help me to become a better Maker. Well, that's the theory.'

'You seem a lot more confident than the last time we met. I wish I felt the same.'

'How are you supposed to empty your mind?' she said.

'We focus on our breathing; and we have to be relaxed. Breathe in, breathe out. No distractions, just concentrate on breathing. The problem is that I have too many thoughts flying around inside my head. As soon as I push one out, another one appears.'

A cheer sounded from another corner of the clearing, and Denny turned to see Constans and Raewyn being congratulated by Fyenna and Drummond.

'The golden couple,' said Denny.

'They have had years of practice,' said Abigone.

'I wish I had started when I was fourteen.'

'Why didn't you?'

Denny gazed at her, wondering if there was a way he could tell her without breaking his oath.

'I knew that I was a Maker,' said Abigone, 'but I didn't tell anyone, apart from my father. He told me to keep it a secret. He said that if I didn't, no one would want to marry me.'

'That seems a little harsh.'

'He was right, though. My pool of eligible men was restricted to the aristocracy and royalty of the Central Provinces – and none of them would knowingly marry a Maker, not when the Sanctian Empire is so opposed to us.'

'My situation was... different,' he said.

Abigone looked into his eyes, waiting for him to continue.

'I didn't tell a single other person for three years,' he went on. 'Part of my family would have been disappointed... No. That word doesn't cover it – they would have been outraged. The other part of my family would have tried to take advantage of my abilities. The two sides don't really get along.'

'And you were trapped between them?' she said.

'Something like that. And here I am, having to hide my real name. You know, I am sorry for pretending to be someone I'm not. I want to be open with you.'

'When we first talked, you said that you didn't want to make any friends.'

'That seems a long time ago.'

'It was only a few months.'

'In a strange way, I feel more at home here in Klef Mordain than I did in... my old house. The only thing preventing me from being truly accepted is my damn oath. It's like a wall, keeping me on the outside, and I want to smash it down. But, I can't. Everything would change if Drummond and Fyenna discovered my real name, and not for the better. So, I continue as I am, neither completely in, nor completely out.'

Abigone said nothing, and they both glanced away.

Another cry came from the opposite corner of the clearing, a cry of alarm. Denny and Abigone turned their heads, and Denny jumped to his feet. Four horsemen were charging out from the woods towards the group where Constans, Raewyn and the teachers were standing. Swords were drawn, and Raewyn screamed.

'Westlanders,' said Abigone.

Drummond raised a hand, but was knocked down by one of the horses. More cries broke out from the younger students, and a few of them began to panic, running for the shelter of the woods. Another four horsemen burst out from the trees fifty yards to Denny's right. They made for the fleeing group containing Ignatius, Nyli, Aplin and Salus. Salus was struck by a boot, and fell to the grass as the Westlanders charged into the group's midst, then another horseman leaned over and scooped up Nyli. He pulled her onto the saddle across his knees, then the horsemen began to turn. They raced back to where Abigone and Denny were standing, aiming for the trees. Three of them veered off towards the edge of the forest, but the fourth charged directly at Denny and Abigone.

Denny's trained instincts took over his movements. He pushed Abigone to the side as the horseman approached, then he sprang up at the Westlander. A fist lashed out, and Denny ducked as he grabbed at the horseman, his momentum dragging the man backwards off the saddle as the horse reared. They landed together on the grass, and Denny slammed his elbow into the Westlander's face, breaking his nose. He got to his feet, caught hold of the reins of the riderless horse, and leapt up into the saddle. He brought the horse under control, then dug his heels in. The horse set off at a gallop, chasing after the men who had taken Nyli. They entered the woods, and Denny kept his head low as he weaved the horse between the trees. He caught up with the Westlanders as they reached a small glade. The three men were looking back to see what had happened to their colleague, and Denny charged into their midst. Two of the horses panicked, and Denny saw Nyli being held down against a saddle as the third Westlander tried to bring his mount under control. Denny lifted himself up in the stirrups, and launched himself through the air. He collided with the Westlander, and Nyli fell to the ground. The rider of the horse punched Denny, the blow striking his shoulder, and Denny also fell, hitting the earth by the roots of a tree. The horse reared above him, and Denny rolled to get out of the way of the hooves. He reached Nyli, grabbed her hand, and pulled her back, as the Westlanders circled in the gloom of the forest.

'Do not leave my side,' Denny hissed to Nyli, who was staring at him with terror in her eyes. 'Run.'

Denny dragged her along, and they sprinted through the undergrowth. A horseman burst through the cover in front of them, and they veered to the right, dodging the wild swing of a sword. Thorns ripped at Denny's legs as he and Nyli fled. They came to a hidden slope in the woods, and tumbled down it. At the bottom, they fell into Aplin and Ignatius, who were hiding among some boulders. Denny and Nyli joined them, and Denny glanced back up the side of the low hill.

'We can't stay here,' Denny said, as he saw two of the Westlanders staring down the slope.

'You have blood on your shoulder,' said Ignatius.

'Shut up and do exactly as I say,' Denny whispered. 'When I signal, run back towards the clearing.'

'Which way is it?' said Aplin.

Denny glanced up, and caught the rough position of the sun. He pointed to their left. 'That way. Now wait for my signal.'

'I'm not going anywhere without you,' said Nyli.

'Don't worry; I will be by your side all the way. I'll be back in a moment.' He turned to the horsemen, then he crawled along the ground between the boulders, circling to the north of them. Halfway up the slope, he paused by the trunk of a pine tree.

'Over here!' he called out in the language of the Westlanders. 'The girl is fleeing north! Over here!'

Three of the horsemen began urging their horses in his direction, and he scampered back down the slope.

'Run,' he hissed at the other students. 'Aplin, you are in the lead. And don't look back.'

He pulled Nyli and Ignatius to their feet, and pushed them onwards as they raced to the south. Denny remained at the rear so that he could see the three younger students. He heard horses behind him. The Westlanders had not been fooled for long by his distraction, but he kept the others running.

'Keep going!' he cried, as the sound of the hooves increased.

They burst out of the forest and onto the grass of the clearing, with the three horsemen only yards to their rear. Ahead of them, Drummond was standing, his eyes wide at the sight of Denny and the others.

'Get down!' Drummond shouted.

Denny pulled Nyli and Ignatius to the ground, as Aplin dove for cover. Drummond lifted his hand, and the three horsemen screamed. Their mounts reared up, then collapsed, sending their dead riders falling to the grass, as silence enveloped the clearing.

Denny raised his head. The three Westlanders had salt encrusting their eyes and issuing from their mouths, and their horses were the same.

'Is everyone all right?' cried Fyenna, as she and Drummond ran forward.

The other teachers and students approached, keeping together in a single group.

'Where are the other Westlanders?' said Denny.

'Head Master Drummond has taken care of them,' said Fyenna. 'On your feet, Valiance.'

Denny pulled himself up. He saw Abigone staring at him, then he realised that all eyes were upon him.

'Just what did you think you were doing, young man?' said Fyenna.

Denny straightened his back. 'I was doing my duty, ma'am. I was protecting the younger students.'

'He saved me,' said Nyli, her voice barely rising above a whisper. 'The Westlanders were carrying me away.'

'And then he saved us, too,' said Aplin. 'He spoke in the Westlander tongue to confuse them.'

'He spoke Westlander?' said Drummond.

'I heard him do it, sir,' said Aplin.

'What happened to the Westlander I brought down in the clearing?' said Denny. 'I think I broke his nose.'

Drummond shook his head. 'You broke his neck, Valiance. He was the sole Westlander I didn't need to kill.'

Denny stared at the Head Master, as a wave of nausea and disbelief washed over him.

'I killed someone?' he said. He swayed, and Drummond took hold of his arm.

The older man glanced at Denny's shoulder. 'You're bleeding.'

'One of the Westlanders punched me, sir.'

'He stabbed you, more like,' said Drummond. 'Did you not feel it?'

'I sense it now, sir, but I was too busy to feel it before.'

'Let us all take a moment,' said Fyenna. 'We should return to the carriages and get back to Klef Mordain, as there may be other Westlander raiders in this area. But first, I want to thank you, Valiance. You were reckless, and you acted without orders, but, by doing so, you saved Nyli, Ignatius and Aplin from the Westlanders.'

'I was just lucky, ma'am,' said Denny.

'That wasn't luck,' said Drummond. 'No one is that lucky. You have been trained, haven't you? Someone has taken great care to prepare you for this sort of thing.' He ripped the fabric from Denny's shoulder and examined it closely. 'The wound isn't too deep, but it will need to be cleaned and dressed.'

'Everyone, back to the carriages,' said Fyenna.

Denny staggered as the others began to walk across the clearing, and Drummond put his arm round him to support him. Reath was holding onto her sister's hand, and she pulled Nyli over to Denny.

'You saved my sister,' Reath said. 'You're all right, Valiance.'

'Anyone would have done the same,' said Denny.

'But they didn't. You did.'

'He surely did,' said Drummond. 'Get into your carriage, girls.'

The students began to step up into the four carriages, while the teachers clustered round Drummond and Denny.

'Does he need to see a doctor?' said Fyenna.

'I can deal with his stab wound,' said Drummond. 'I have everything I need at the Master school.'

'The girls are going to talk about nothing else,' said Fyenna. She glanced at Denny. 'What should I tell them, young man? How did you know what to do?'

'I... I did it without thinking, ma'am.'

'And where did you learn how to do it?'

Denny glanced at the ground, as the pain in his shoulder grew worse.

'Head Master Drummond was right,' Fyenna went on; 'only someone who has been thoroughly trained could have acted as you did. And you speak the tongue of the Westlanders? I doubt many in Campsie have that particular ability.'

'He was magnificent,' said Vesta. 'When he knocked that man off his horse, it was as though I was watching a gymnast perform a show at the theatre.'

'Is Abigone all right?' said Denny.

Vesta gestured, and Denny saw Abigone standing behind her.

'I'm sorry,' said Denny; 'sorry for leaving you like that.'

'I was fine,' said Abigone. 'You killed the rider who was charging at us.' She smiled. 'You know, before you charged off into the forest, unarmed, to rescue Nyli.'

'Honestly, it was just good luck.'

'You are fooling no one,' said Fyenna.

Denny swayed again, as the pain in his shoulder flared. 'I didn't mean to kill anyone.'

'It doesn't matter,' said Drummond. 'You did what you had to do. I'm proud of you, lad. Now, climb aboard, and keep your hand firmly pressed against the wound in your shoulder.'

Drummond helped Denny step up into the carriage, then the teachers retired for a few moments, their heads together as they talked about what had happened. Denny saw Abigone standing alone as the others conversed, and their gazes met.

'Who are you?' she mouthed.

'No one,' he mouthed back.

She gave him a disbelieving smile, then she strode off towards her carriage.

Denny turned towards Ignatius and Marlow, who were sitting opposite him.

'Are you a soldier?' said Marlow.

Denny shook his head.

'Constans and Raewyn froze,' Marlow went on. 'They just stood there, looking terrified; that's why Drummond and the other teachers couldn't get to Nyli at first. They had to save the others before they could go after you.'

Drummond boarded the carriage, and closed the side door.

'I will be riding back with you, while Mister Tobold takes the other carriage,' he said. 'I want to keep an eye on your shoulder, Valiance.'

'It's not too bad, sir,' Denny said, as the carriages set off. 'How many Westlanders did you kill?'

'Seven,' said Drummond. 'It is not something I am proud of. I took their lives to save the students. Try not to feel bad about what you did, Valiance. That horseman was trying to ride both you and Abigone down.'

'I thought I only broke his nose.'

'He was most likely already dead by that point, lad. It was the fall that killed him. How do you feel?'

'Dizzy, sir. Tired and sick.'

'That's normal. You'll be fine in a few days, though your shoulder will take a little longer to fully heal.' He eyed him. 'Miss Vesta echoed my own thoughts earlier – you were like a gymnast, the way you sprang through the air to knock that rider down. Tell me this one thing – you have practised that before, haven't you?'

Denny stared at the carriage floor. 'Yes, sir. At least a hundred times. That was... that was the first time I have had to do it in real life.'

Drummond glanced at Aplin and Ignatius. 'I will require you both to tell me everything you saw, boys,' he said. 'There is one thing I want to say to you all; what occurred today will never happen again. We will not be going anywhere else without adequate protection. I want to apologise to you. As Head Master, I am responsible for your safety, and were it not for Valiance's actions, I would have failed in my duties. Valiance, I am in your debt; and Lady Fyenna feels the same way. You might not be able to make a ditch, but by all the spirits, you were exactly what we needed. And who knows – perhaps you are exactly what Klef Mordain needs. Is there anything you want or require?'

'I just want to be treated the same as everyone else, sir.'

Drummond smiled. 'Good lad. Let's go home.'

CHAPTER 17
BITTER RESPITE

Old City, Klef Mordain – 22nd Day of Tempora 108

A sailor reached down, and pulled Amery up onto the deck of the Sanctian flag ship.

'Thank you,' said Amery.

'No problem, sir,' said the sailor. 'Could you please move aside so that I can help the others board?'

Amery nodded, then he walked forward a few paces, and stood next to Lord Tain and Lady Ursula, as the sailor reached down and pulled Loryn up from the ship's launch. A few yards to their right, Ambassador Tertius was standing on the wide deck with Lords Penny and Harrow from the government of thirty. Several naval officers were close by, dressed in their immaculate Sanctian uniforms. Amery basked in the sun for a few moments. Summer had arrived in Klef Mordain, and the sky was a deep blue overhead. In the distance, Amery could see the waterfront of the city spread out, and the high arches of the Celestial Bridge lay just a little to the west of where the flag ship was anchored.

'This is my first time on a boat,' Amery said.

'Your first time?' said Tain.

'I'm not one for the ocean,' Amery went on. 'I prefer dry land.'

'I was on my first merchant galley at thirteen,' said Tain. 'I remember it well – we sailed down to Subnestia to sell coffee and spices, and I was shown how to climb the rigging.'

'I wasn't allowed to go until I was sixteen,' said Ursula, 'but my father insisted I wear a dress, so I certainly wasn't climbing any rigging. Not that I wanted to, if I'm honest.'

Loryn inclined her head as she approached.

'Have you been on many ships?' said Amery.

'Several dozen, sir,' said Loryn. 'It's in your blood if you hail from Klef Mordain.'

'Isn't that a fact?' said Tain. 'We are a city of sailors at heart.'

A lieutenant strode down the deck towards them. 'Gentlemen, ladies,' he said, 'the admiral requests your presence in the wardroom. If you would please follow me?'

'Lead on, my good man,' said Tain.

They joined the ambassador's group and, together, they walked to a large hatch in the central area of the deck. They descended into a lower deck, and Amery saw the dozens of cannon lined up down either side, their muzzles pointing towards a series of closed hatches. Piles of iron balls were stacked up by each cannon, with nets over them to stop them from rolling, and sailors were busy cleaning the deck. The lieutenant led them towards the front of the ship, and then he knocked on a door. Another officer opened it, and the guests were shown into a large cabin with a bolted-down table running down the centre. Flags and standards covered one end of the cabin, and the table had been laid out with plates, bowls, and jugs of wine, water and brandy. At one end, the admiral was sitting with a few senior officers, and they rose to their feet when the delegation from Klef Mordain entered.

'Good morning, Admiral,' said the ambassador.

'And to you, Tertius, Your Eminence,' said the admiral.

'Please allow me to make a few introductions,' the ambassador went on. 'These two distinguished gentlemen on my right are Lord Penny and Lord Harrow, members of the Corse's most inner circle, and our trusted friends.'

The two politicians bowed.

'It is an honour to meet you,' said the admiral.

'And this is Lord Tain and Lady Ursula of the Second Empire Association,' the ambassador went on.

'I recall meeting them when I last disembarked,' said the admiral.

'The others are members of the association's legal staff,' said Tertius; 'a Mister Amery and a Miss Loryn. They shall be keeping the minutes and offering any necessary legal advice.'

'Well met, all of you,' said the admiral, 'and welcome to the flag ship, the *Bitter Respite*. Please, be seated.'

The guests took their places round the long table, and sat.

'We shall be keeping the lower ranks out of the cabin for the duration of this meeting,' the admiral went on, 'so everyone shall please help themselves to the refreshments on offer.'

Several of the officers and guests poured wine or placed some food onto their plates, and Amery and Loryn set out their parchment, ink pots and quills.

'It would be advisable if not every word we utter today is committed to paper,' said the admiral.

'Mister Amery is an old hand at this, Admiral,' said Lady Ursula. 'The minutes will contain nothing that will bring anyone into disrepute.'

'If I may,' said the ambassador, 'I shall begin by summarising our current position. As we all know, the twenty thousand soldiers from Sanctos arrived in Lesser Down without incident. At present, they are patrolling the Great Northern Highway right up to the border with Klef Mordain. The authorities of Lesser Down have lodged a protest with the local embassy there, but nothing will come of it. With the road effectively blockaded, no goods are able to enter Klef Mordain from the south by land. If we consider also the recent activities of the fleet, the city is being slowly throttled.'

'I can confirm that,' said the admiral. 'While we have not been able to prevent every single merchant ship from passing through our lines, we estimate that we are stopping and diverting over three quarters of the ship-borne traffic attempting to enter or leave Klef Mordain. Requisitioned ships, along with their confiscated cargoes, as well as their crews, are being held in the ports of Lesser Down. At the last report, we had over three thousand sailors locked up down there. The cargoes are being sold at auction to cover the expenses of the army and the fleet. How is the Corse reacting to these events?'

'Lord Metrius is beside himself with impotent rage, Admiral,' said Lord Penny. 'His allies cannot debate the situation openly among the thirty, and the shortages are beginning to bite. Klef Mordain imports almost half of its foodstuffs from abroad, and some of the poorer classes among the populace are starting to go hungry.'

'And who are they blaming for their misfortunes?' said the admiral.

'Public opinion is split,' said Tain. 'The Second Empire Association is engaged in a propaganda battle with those opposed to Sanctian rule. Local agitators from both sides have been going into the poorer districts, drumming up support. Some of these occasions have been marred with violence, but I am not detecting the hand of the secret police.'

'You are correct,' said Lord Harrow. 'The secret police are hopelessly divided. Every order they receive from Metrius is countermanded by the pro-Sanctians. They have been reduced to the position of bystanders.'

'How are the city's military preparations unfolding?' said the admiral.

'The reservists were called up over a month ago,' said Lord Penny, 'and I sent them home again. Metrius issued further orders for mobilisation, but only half of the required regiments turned up at the mustering stations. We have been using our positions in the thirty to sow confusion and discord, paralysing many of the city's institutions.'

The ambassador smiled. 'And so the secrecy of the Corse shall be its downfall. Without clear leadership, the city's population knows not which way to turn. Conflicting orders and contrary guidance have provoked apathy and inertia. The time is fast becoming ripe, Admiral.'

'So it seems. It is the aim of the Most Exalted Emperor Antonio that when this city is welcomed into the empire, it shall be whole and undamaged. Klef Mordain will be of little use if it is smouldering in ruins. What we need to achieve is quite simple – the elimination of the leadership without hurting the body politic; and the transfer of power from the Corse to an appointed board of governors. The first act of these governors will be to invite the Sanctians to help administer this territory, and then all trade restrictions will be immediately lifted. With any luck, the masses will barely notice the difference – all they will know is that food is available in the markets again.'

'With all due respect, Admiral,' said Tain, 'we might be overlooking one small point – the Masters and Makers. As far as we know, they remain wedded to the cause of Metrius; and for good reason. The policy of the Sanctian Empire is to arrest and execute all Masters and Makers found within their lands, and so it is natural that they will oppose any change to the status of Klef Mordain. It would take but a handful of them to disrupt our preparations.'

'And what is the Second Empire Association doing to prevent this outcome?'

'Our main objective is still to locate the secret school, or schools, as there may be two – one for Makers, and one for Masters. We are convinced of their existence, but the staff belong to Metrius, and no one is talking.' He smiled. 'Well, perhaps not no one. The association is bringing severe pressure to bear upon the husband of Lady Fyenna, whom we suspect of being involved.'

'Why don't you simply have Lady Fyenna followed?'

'Alas, she is an expert on using the tunnels beneath the city, Admiral. We could have her assassinated, as we know where she lives, but that would bring us no closer to finding the schools.'

'Could we not arrest and interrogate her?'

'We could, Admiral,' said Tain, 'but we haven't, for two reasons – one, she would most likely die before revealing anything to us; and two, she is a renowned war hero, and her torture might persuade many of the city's inhabitants to oppose our cause. However, her husband is starting to crack.'

'This is true,' said Lord Penny. 'My agents in the commercial harbour have been investigating every detail of his business transactions. So far, we have found nothing that would lead to a conviction for smuggling, but we have found several discrepancies in his accounts. These discrepancies are not enough to threaten him with execution, but the fines involved would bankrupt him, and the poor man is desperate to save his wealth. From what he has already told Lord Tain, it is clear that he knows nothing about the locations of the schools, but he might be willing to give us information about some of the other staff who work there.'

'Would he know such things? Has his wife told him anything?'

'They were married prior to the Battle of Hader Pull,' said Tain.

'How is that relevant?'

'Well, Admiral,' said Tain; 'it was spoken of at the time that Lady Fyenna had a young Master companion, who aided her in that battle. However, the official records reveal no such Master, and so we assume that his identity was erased. We can also assume that this Master, if he lives, would also be involved in the secret schools. We believe that Fyenna's husband would remember this Master, from the days of the battle. If we can find him, we can find the schools.'

'It would be wise to continue upon this course,' said the admiral. 'The taint of these Masters and Makers has hung over Klef Mordain for too long, staining its reputation. It is the will of the Most Exalted Emperor that none remain in Klef Mordain when this city is joined to the empire. Could not some citizens lose their lives in a way that would look as though some rebel Masters and Makers had done it? If the people turn on them, there will be nowhere left to hide.'

'We can spread false rumours, Admiral,' said Ursula, 'but it would be difficult to recreate a scene that bears the hallmarks of Masters and Makers.'

'Find Fyenna's Master from the battle,' said Penny. 'Once you have his identity, I will deploy trusted agents to do the rest.'

'We are doing what we can, my lord,' said Tain.

'Then do it faster.'

'Hold, Lord Penny,' said the admiral. 'Is there any cause for haste? A considered approach may reap more rewards.'

Penny and Harrow glanced at each other.

'There is something you don't yet know, Admiral,' said the ambassador. 'An unfortunate... accident befell a certain Lord Asquith last week.'

The admiral frowned. 'Asquith?'

'He was a member of the thirty,' the ambassador went on, 'and he was found drowned in his bath by his housekeeper. He was an ally of the pro-Sanctian cause, and our friends here are concerned that it may have been a deliberate assassination.'

'Is there any proof of that?'

'None,' said Lord Harrow. 'To any observer, his death appeared to be a tragic accident. However, we know that a small band of secret police agents remains loyal to Lord Metrius, and they are more than capable of carrying out such a heinous act.'

The admiral shook his head. 'I was just told that the secret police are impotent. Are they powerless, or are they still able to kill our allies?'

'Both can be true at the same time,' said Lord Penny. 'They are in disarray, but small elements remain dangerous. But this works both ways, Admiral. If Tain can find the Master who aided Fyenna in the Battle of Hader Pull, then I will turn to my own loyal forces within the secret police to carry out the arrest and interrogation.'

'It seems our hands are tied until we can resolve this issue,' said the admiral. 'I am wary of ordering the takeover of Klef Mordain until the threat from the Masters and Makers has been neutralised. If we cannot find the school, then we shall do the next best thing, and eliminate Fyenna. Without their leader, the others may panic. It will be the job of the Second Empire Association to ensure that any blame falls upon Metrius's head. Concoct a disagreement between them before carrying out the assassination; but do this only if you are unable to locate the Master.'

Tain and Ursula bowed their heads.

'Admiral,' said the ambassador, 'for how long is the Most Exulted

Emperor prepared to wait for Klef Mordain to be absorbed into the empire? These investigations may take time.'

'We have until the onset of winter, Your Eminence,' said the admiral. 'His Imperial Majesty will remain patient with our efforts until then, but the city must be ours before the end of autumn; otherwise, the fleet will have to withdraw to safer climes, and the army in Lesser Down shall have to be transferred back to their winter garrisons in Subnestia. This must not happen. I swear it now that if the school is not found, then I shall order the takeover of Klef Mordain by the end of autumn, along with the assassinations of Fyenna, Metrius, and every other leader of the loyalists that we can get our hands on. It will be bloody, and potentially ruinous, but it is better than the alternative. I was commissioned to deliver this city to the empire, and I refuse to return home empty-handed.'

'Portions of the city will begin to starve before then, Admiral,' said Harrow. 'It is possible that the people will rise up and overthrow the Corse of their own accord.'

'If that happens, jump immediately into action,' said the admiral. 'I can have the twenty thousand based in Lesser Down marched here within ten days of any official request for aid. For the moment, pour all of our resources into locating those damn schools. Use whatever means necessary, for all will be forgiven when this city is enfolded into the imperial embrace.' He snapped his fingers at one of his senior officers, who produced several thin sheets of paper. 'These are copies of a draft constitution for the new government that will replace the Corse,' the admiral said. 'It embodies Sanctian law, and prepares the way for full annexation.'

'May I?' said Amery.

'Certainly,' said admiral. 'Take a copy, and study it.'

The officer slid a copy of the document over the table, and Amery placed it with his other papers.

'Enact the constitution the moment the Corse falls from power,' said the admiral. 'Call for our aid, and then we shall do the rest. Dismissed.'

The guests rose to their feet, and then each inclined their head towards the admiral. A lieutenant opened the door, and the guests filed back out into the lower deck.

'Let me see what you wrote,' Amery said to Loryn, as they were led back to the stairs.

Loryn passed him her minutes, and Amery scanned them quickly.

'You've barely recorded anything,' he said.

'There was little I was able to write, sir.'

'We'll pad them out when we get back to the office.'

The lieutenant showed them up onto the main deck. The small launch was bobbing up and down in the waters of the estuary alongside the flag ship, and the sailors assisted the guests to descend into the vessel. Harrow, Penny, Tain and Ursula joined the ambassador at the rear, while Amery and Loryn sat close to the bow, taking their seats on a bench to get out of the way of the sailors.

'May I read the proposed constitution, sir?' said Loryn.

Amery passed her the document as he began scribbling notes over her neat minutes.

'This describes a military-style government, sir,' Loryn said, as she read.

'It was written by an admiral,' said Amery, 'so that shouldn't surprise you.'

'The Sanctians are going to exceptional ends to present their annexation as legal; when they could invade any time they liked.'

'It's the narrative they want to tell everyone. It looks much better if the Central Provinces believe Klef Mordain joined the empire of its own free will. Also, as the admiral said, they don't want to inherit a pile of rubble.'

A faint look of disgust passed over Loryn's features.

'You should be safe, no matter what happens,' Amery said. 'The Sanctians won't forget who aided them, and who opposed them.'

'I am not concerned with my personal safety, sir.'

'Then what's bothering you?'

'Nothing, sir.

'Come on; I saw the look on your face a moment ago. You don't approve of the Sanctians' methods, do you?'

'That is none of my business, sir.'

'I get it, Loryn. Klef Mordain is your city, and the admiral was talking about it as if he was referring to a slave in the marketplace. You are entitled to your opinion, even if you need to keep that opinion to yourself.'

'And you, sir? Do you have an opinion that you have to keep hidden from our employers?'

Amery glanced around to make sure no one was in earshot. 'Perhaps I do. I like my life here, and yet I am working for people who would turn that upside down.'

'So, it is your wealth and mansion that you are worried about, sir; not the welfare of the city's inhabitants?'

'I'm just trying to do my job, Loryn.'

'As am I, sir.'

Amery stared out at the approaching coastline. He was starting to feel a little queasy, and decided that he didn't enjoy travelling by boat. It was either that, or his conscience was finally beginning to trouble him. In some ways, working for the Second Empire Association was worse than working for Duke Hector. True, he lived like a king, with more money than he had ever earned before, but the price was that he had to listen to talk of conspiracies, assassinations, blockades and outright treachery. He looked down at the minutes he had been falsifying, and a tremor of guilt and self-loathing passed through him. Was that why he had trained to be a lawyer – to lie and cover up the crimes of his employers? It occurred to him that if he was arrested by agents loyal to Metrius, he would be executed for treason. He was complicit, and it was too late to pretend otherwise.

'I need a drink,' he muttered.

'Again, sir? You had two bottles of wine yesterday evening.'

'Are you keeping count?'

'Is drinking a sign that you wish to distance yourself from your obligations to the association, sir?'

'I don't know what you're talking about, Loryn.'

The notary passed him the constitution. 'You, too, are entitled to your opinion, sir.'

They fell into silence as the launch crossed the estuary and docked at the waterfront of Klef Mordain's Old City. Several carriages were waiting for them, and the area had been cleared by harbour officials working for Lord Penny. They stepped off the launch and onto the stone quayside, and separated into groups for their journeys, with half going to the embassy, and the other half intending to travel to the association. The ambassador shared a few last words with Tain and Ursula, then they boarded the carriages. Amery sat down next to Loryn, with Tain and Ursula opposite them, and the carriage set off across the cobbles, drawing them into the city.

Tain stared out of the window, as Ursula maintained a sullen silence.

'I will have the revised minutes ready for your perusal later today, my lord and lady,' said Amery.

'Do what you like, Amery,' said Ursula. 'I've had just about as much as I can take.'

'Grow up, sister,' said Tain. 'You knew what the likely outcome would be when we set up the association.'

'Did I?' said Ursula. 'I thought we formed the association to promote the benefits of joining the Sanctian Empire, not to bring in a wave of killings, disorder and famine. The city is under blockade; have you visited a market recently? The Sanctians are starving the citizens; our people.'

'It's only temporary,' said Tain. 'The restrictions will be lifted as soon as the Corse falls from power.'

'And when will that be? When we are wading in their blood? Did you hear the admiral – he wants us to assassinate Fyenna – a war hero! She saved this city from the Westlanders, but to them she is nothing but an obstacle to be eliminated.'

'But what can we do?' said Tain. 'The Sanctians hate Masters and

Makers; we knew that. The emperor will never accept us if we don't remove them from the city.'

'By *remove*, you mean murder? If the price of joining the empire is that we have to murder those who defended this city from the Westlanders, then I'm not sure I want to be a part of it any more.'

'But you hate the Corse. How many times have you complained to me about how badly this city is governed?'

'Many times, brother. I loathe the secret police, and the secrecy. But this? There must be a better way; a peaceful way.'

'Metrius will never allow that to happen. We have tried to persuade the Corse to open negotiations, but they have defied us at every turn. Blood will be spilled – there is no alternative. Think of things as they will be a few years hence, when everything has calmed down, and Klef Mordain is a part of the empire. It will all be worth it; I promise.'

'I wish I could believe you, brother.'

Amery narrowed his eyes. 'Why are we stopping? We are not at the association yet.'

The others quietened, then Tain glanced through the little window that led to the driver's bench.

'There is an obstruction,' he said. 'An overturned cart. We'll be going again in a few minutes.'

They sat still as the carriage came to a complete stop. Outside, the streets were busy with citizens going about their business, then Amery saw a small hooded group run to the side of the carriage. Then he saw the crossbows in their hands.

'Get down!' Amery yelled. He pushed Loryn to the floor of the carriage as the side door was pulled open.

Three men pointed their crossbows into the interior of the carriage and loosed. One bolt struck Tain's left arm, one passed through the opposite window, and the third hit Ursula in the stomach. Arms reached in and pulled the wounded Ursula out of the carriage. She was dragged down to the cobbles, then one of the men crouched and drove a knife into the back of her neck. He released the hilt, and the three men raced off, barging their way through the crowds and disappearing down an alleyway.

Tain staggered out of the carriage, his left arm streaming blood, and he fell to his knees next to his sister. The two drivers jumped down to help, but Ursula was already dead.

Amery and Loryn stepped down to the cobbles. Amery glanced up and down the street, his heart racing. A crowd had gathered by the side of the road, all staring at Tain by his slain sister's side. Tain sobbed aloud, his right hand clutching Ursula's.

'We need to move, sir,' said one of the drivers. 'There might be more assassins in the vicinity.'

'Get your hands off me!' Tain cried. 'Can't you see what they've done? Sister, my sister; I will avenge you!' He raised his eyes to the blue sky. 'Metrius, I curse you. I swear it by all the spirits; I shall have your blood for this.'

CHAPTER 18
THE RUSTING PROCESS

Old City, Klef Mordain – 2nd Day of Desira 108

'Blessed spirits,' said Abigone, 'with your permission, summon for me a wooden stool.'

The air rustled, and the blocks of wood on the table vanished. In their place, a fully-formed, three-legged stool appeared three feet above the floor. It fell, and Miss Vesta caught it.

'Well done, Abigone,' said Vesta. 'One of these days, I'm going to start teaching you how to make the object appear in different places. There's no point in summoning a crystal vase, for instance, if it's going to break when it hits the floor.'

'I would like to learn that, ma'am.'

Vesta glanced over at Reath and Nyli, who were still struggling to summon spoons. 'I will teach you if I have the time, Abigone. For now, just know that it involves picturing the summoned object in its new place. It's quite tricky to master at first, but that's the general technique.' She set the stool down and walked over to Reath. 'How was your latest attempt?'

'Terrible!' Reath cried. 'I will never be able to make a stupid spoon. Why did I bother leaving the village?'

Abigone sat down and waited as Vesta examined Reath's crooked piece of cutlery.

'What about you, Nyli?'

The girl flushed and shook her head.

'Oh dear,' said Vesta, as she picked up Nyli's attempt. 'For some reason, Nyli, you seem to be getting worse at this. Not to worry, though, I'm sure you will both pick it up in time.'

'I'm going to fail the Making,' Nyli whispered.

'Don't say that. The Making is many months away, and you have plenty of time to improve.' She glanced at Nyli. 'Are you still thinking about what happened in the forest?'

Nyli nodded.

'Are you still having nightmares about it?'

The girl nodded again.

'Can you blame her, ma'am?' said Reath. 'A Westlander picked her up and carried her away.'

'Of course I don't blame her, Reath,' said Vesta. 'I partly blame myself. I was busy with the other adults congratulating Raewyn and Constans on their ditch and palisade, and we weren't keeping a close eye on what was happening at the other side of the clearing.'

'Is that why we haven't had any more outings since then?' said Reath.

'Yes. We looked into employing soldiers or secret police to guard the students, but Lady Fyenna felt that too many people would know about the schools if we did that. One of our main responsibilities is keeping you all safe and hidden away, so, until we find a solution, there will be no more excursions.'

'But we haven't seen the boys in over a month.'

Vesta smiled. 'But I thought you didn't like Marlow, Reath?'

'I don't, but Nyli is pining for Valiance.'

'I'm not,' said Nyli.

Reath laughed. 'I would pine for him, too, sister, if he had rescued me from the filthy Westlanders. Anyway, it was worth it just to see Raewyn humbled. She screeched and wet her pants when the Westlanders appeared; and Constans wasn't much better. Even Stanza was braver; she pushed me behind her – can you believe that?'

'I saw her do it,' said Vesta. 'Marlow also kept his nerve, but that boy has been through a lot. He had to flee through Sanctian territory on his own to reach Klef Mordain.'

'Really?' said Reath. 'Oh.'

'A lot of the children here have had a difficult time.'

'Abigone hasn't,' said Reath. 'She lived in a palace before coming here.'

'Yes, but Abigone destroyed...'

I know,' said Reath. 'She destroyed sixty cannon, but she was standing at the top of a cliff at the time. She wasn't actually in danger.'

Abigone sighed. She seemed to be spending most of her classes doing little while Reath and Nyli tried to catch up.

'Is that true, Abigone?' said Nyli.

'No, it's not true. Like you, Nyli, I was also once carried off by Westlanders.'

'What?' said Reath. 'You didn't tell us that.'

'I'm telling you now. They abducted me and another princess, and fled north. One of their chiefs wanted to marry me.'

'How did you escape?' said Vesta.

'I summoned wooden dragons, and we ran away in the confusion.'

'You used your Maker powers? Well done. More importantly, you kept your nerve.'

'I don't know about that, ma'am. I was terrified. Then, the King's Champion arrived, and he helped us get back to town.'

Reath frowned. 'You're not normal. You had no skills, and no training, and yet you managed to escape the Westlanders *and* destroy the cannon. How could she do it, ma'am?'

Vesta chewed her lip for a moment. 'Abigone seems to have been blessed with a prodigious amount of natural talent. She is quite unlike any other trainee Maker I have taught. Her potential... is considerable. All right – Reath and Nyli, I want you to re-read chapters six to ten of your book on the formation of wood, and the lifecycle of a tree.'

Both girls groaned.

'It's the only way to make sure the knowledge sticks in your brain,' said Vesta. 'Repetition. Read it again and again until you know it backwards. Sit down and begin. Abigone, please come with me.'

Vesta led Abigone from the classroom. They walked along the corridor until they reached Vesta's small office, and they went inside.

'Sit,' said Vesta.

Abigone took a seat, while Vesta went to stand by the narrow, open window.

'I know you're bored,' said Vesta. 'I can see it in your eyes, though you have the good grace to pretend otherwise. This can happen, when one student starts to pull ahead of the others. If we had more staff, then I would probably put you into a separate class for a while, to allow you to move at your own speed.'

'What does Miss Eshia do for a living, ma'am?'

Vesta narrowed her eyes.

'Maybe we could ask her if she would be interested in helping out?' Abigone went on.

'Eshia isn't a qualified teacher, Abigone. And she's only a year older than you.'

'It was only an idea.'

'Yes, but damn it, it was a good one.' Vesta began to pace the room. 'Even one day a week would help.'

'Where does she currently work, ma'am?'

'She helps out in her uncle's forge. She's very talented at summoning metal implements from raw ore. I will need to speak to Lady Fyenna first, though. If she agrees, then it would mean you beginning on metals before we had finished with wood. Would you be happy with that?'

'Yes, ma'am; very happy.'

Vesta pulled a book from a shelf and passed it to Abigone. 'Start reading that while I talk to Lady Fyenna. I shouldn't be more than ten minutes.'

Vesta left the room, and Abigone opened the book. It was a beginner's introduction to forging metal, written specifically for young Makers, and Abigone quickly scanned the text. She was getting better at absorbing information, and she had almost completed the first chapter when Vesta arrived, with Lady Fyenna by her side. The two women entered the room, and Vesta closed the door.

Abigone closed the book and placed it onto the desk. She got to her feet and inclined her head.

'Sit down,' said Fyenna. 'Miss Vesta has gone over your suggestion, but I am afraid it is not quite as simple as that.'

Abigone nodded as she sat, but said nothing.

'There is a complication,' Fyenna went on. 'I made a promise to Miss Eshia's father and uncle not to involve her in school matters without their express permission and, after the events in the forest clearing, both are understandably reluctant to allow Eshia to be drawn into anything that might risk her safety. She will be available if the Sanctians invade, naturally, but her relatives wish to keep her exposure to a minimum. I will have to ask them if it is all right, before moving ahead.'

'I understand, ma'am,' said Abigone.

'Do her relatives understand the seriousness of the situation, ma'am?' said Vesta.

A trace of a wry smile flitted over Fyenna's features. 'They most certainly do, Miss Vesta. This is what we shall do – I will make a personal visit to the girl's father, and see what he has to say. Abigone, you may go to your room and continue to read the new book Miss Vesta has loaned you. I will let you know when I have returned.'

'Yes, ma'am.' Abigone walked to the door, then she paused. 'Would it be all right if I took Meg up to my room, ma'am?'

'Who? Oh, you mean the school cat?' said Fyenna. 'Why?'

'I like having her there while I am reading, ma'am.'

'Hmm. Very well. Visit the kitchen on your way upstairs.'

'Thank you, ma'am.'

. . .

Ten minutes later, Abigone opened the door to her room and strode in. She released the grey cat from her arms, and Meg jumped down onto the bed.

Abigone sat down, and Meg trotted towards her. She stroked her head and scratched behind her ears, then she set her new book down next to her and reached into a pocket. She hand-fed Meg the cheese and morsels of fish and meat she had taken from the kitchen, and the grey cat ate it all. When Meg had finished, she jumped onto Abigone's lap, circled twice, then settled down. Abigone opened the book again. She skipped forward to the illustrations, and glanced at the various drawings of metal tools and objects. The first to be depicted was, predictably enough, a spoon, but then there were pages of knives, axes and sword blades, and then a page of spear heads and arrow heads. She passed over the pictures of horseshoes and farming implements, and saw a few drawings on the last pages of objects that used both wood and metal. The last illustration was of a large cart, with wood for the boards and wheels, and iron for the nails that held it together, and the axles that ran underneath. She moved back to the front of the book, and began reading.

It was close to lunchtime when Lady Fyenna knocked on her door. Abigone placed Meg back onto the bed, and opened the door a crack.

'Are you ready to leave?' said Fyenna.

'Uh, yes, ma'am.'

She set Meg down onto the floor, and the cat ran from the room. Abigone and Fyenna went into the corridor, and Abigone closed the door.

'Where are we going, ma'am?'

'To the forge where Miss Eshia works,' said Fyenna. 'A carriage is waiting to take us there.'

'Are we both going?'

'We are. I am not about to send you off through the city on your own, girl. The pro-Sanctians would tear you to pieces if they got their hands on you. Miss Vesta shall continue teaching the other first years in your absence. If this works out well, we can make it a regular arrangement. Come.'

They descended the stairs, and Abigone's stomach rumbled as they passed the kitchen.

'Hungry again already?' said Fyenna. 'I heard that you had taken food from the kitchen, and so I had assumed we could skip lunch.'

'Yes, ma'am,' said Abigone, suppressing her appetite.

They reached the ground floor and left the school via a back door. A carriage was parked in the narrow alleyway next to the rear of a theatre, and Fyenna and Abigone boarded. Fyenna tapped on the access window, and the driver set the horses in motion.

'Is there any news about the Sanctians, ma'am?' said Abigone.

'Nothing good,' said Fyenna. 'The city is entering its second month of being blockaded by land and sea; though, of course, the Sanctians call it *patrolling for pirates* or *apprehending smugglers*; anything but the truth. Some of the markets in the poorer parts of town have completely run out of bread, along with fresh fruit and vegetables. Four men were killed yesterday in a riot in Nether Hall that was provoked when a merchant ran out of flour. The Sanctians mean to starve us into submission; that much seems clear.'

'But we always have plenty to eat in the school, ma'am.'

'Klef Mordain looks after its young Masters and Makers, Abigone. The schools' allowance is protected by ordinance. Even if prices quadruple, we will still have enough to feed you.'

'That makes me feel terrible, ma'am. Are people suffering?'

'They are. The fools among them are clamouring for the Corse to seek entry into the Sanctian Empire. They would rather eat than be free. Can't they see that this is the emperor's doing? Antonio is the cause of their hunger, not the Corse, and so he should be the target of their ire.' She eyed Abigone. 'I have my doubts about moving you on to metals so soon, but Miss Vesta has assured me that you are ready.'

'Is Miss Eshia willing to teach me, ma'am?'

'She is. Miss Eshia is still only nineteen, however, and she has not been trained as a teacher. It is likely that she will ask you to watch her at work before allowing you to summon anything from metal. There is something else you need to know about her; something I am telling you with great reluctance. Not even Miss Vesta knows the truth, so you must promise me here and now that you will not reveal this to anyone. Do I have your solemn word?'

'Yes, ma'am.'

'Very well. Miss Eshia is Head Master Drummond's only child. Eshia's mother died in childbirth, and the only relatives who know she is a Maker are her father and her uncle, who owns the forge. This is why I had to seek special permission before taking you to see her today. I am placing a lot of trust in you, Abigone. If you let me down, my wrath will be implacable.'

'I'm not sure I understand, ma'am.'

'What don't you understand?'

'Well, ma'am; you have made it plain since I arrived at the school that you do not particularly care for me. You have called me entitled, spoiled, arrogant, lazy, and a few other epithets I'd rather not repeat. If that is the case, then why would you decide to trust me with this?'

Fyenna gazed out of the window. 'Because, girl, despite it all, I cannot deny that you are a very rare talent. I saw the beams you summoned in the clearing. You have battle experience. You have destroyed Sanctian cannon. The unvarnished truth is this – this city needs you if it is to prevail against the Sanctians. That is more important than my personal feelings towards you.'

'I see, ma'am. Then you still harbour those feelings?'

'I will admit that you are not quite as useless as I heretofore assumed. Perhaps if you weren't of royal stock, then I would see you in a different light. I abhor monarchy. I detest the idea that power is inherited from one generation to the next, regardless of the individual's virtue, or lack thereof. You are a princess merely because you happened to be born of a royal father. These credentials do not impress me. You were handed wealth and opportunity without having to work for it;

thus, you epitomise unearned privilege. In some ways, there is little difference between you and Emperor Antonio.'

'But being a princess has also brought me pain,' Abigone said. 'I was almost forcibly married to a Westlander chief, who wouldn't have been remotely interested in me had I not been a member of the royal family. Even in my home town, I cannot walk the streets without courtiers, ladies-in-waiting, and soldiers to escort me. I have no privacy, and I am not free to marry whomever I wish. I have to dress up for public holidays, and put myself on display for everyone to gawk at. Everyone is judging me, all the time – what I wear, what I say, and even the expression on my face. I have no real friends, because I have learned to mistrust the motives of others.'

'Then tell me this, Abigone – would you renounce your royal blood, and live like a commoner, if you could?'

Abigone frowned. 'I don't know. I've never thought about it. My sister Kilbride would laugh at the notion, but she is a born leader. She would have risen to the top even if she wasn't a princess.'

'Princess Kilbride is different – she has earned the respect of others by her actions.'

'But she hadn't done anything by the time she was eighteen, ma'am.'

'You might be right.' She looked out of the window. 'We are nearly at our destination. Be on your best behaviour. One other thing – we decided that it would be prudent not to use your full name while we are here, as too many people in the city have heard of Princess Abigone. We shall instead refer to you as Abbie. Is that all right?'

'Yes, ma'am. It's what Kilbride calls me.'

The carriage ground to a halt on a busy street of workshops, smithies and taverns. Their driver opened the side door for them, and Fyenna stepped down to the uneven cobbles, followed by Abigone. They had stopped in front of a house with a forge attached to its side. The forge was open on two sides, and its chimney rose above the roof of the house. Drummond and Eshia were standing amid the shadows next to the furnace, along with another man, who was wearing a stained apron. Fyenna raised her hand in greeting, then she led Abigone under the sloping roof of the forge.

'Good morning, my lady,' said Drummond. 'You know my brother Heston; Heston, this is the girl we talked about.'

'Abbie, was it?' said the other man. He took a step forward and eyed Abigone, who curtsied.

'Thank you for agreeing to meet her, Heston,' said Fyenna. 'As you can see, she is a little older than is usual for students of her experience.'

'Do you know anything about metalwork, Abbie?' said Heston.

'Nothing, sir,' she said.

Heston nodded. 'Well, then, my first piece of advice is not to touch anything unless Eshia or I tell you to. Stand back and watch at first, until you learn where everything goes. And you'll need an apron.'

'I can get her one, Uncle,' said Eshia.

'Take her indoors and find her a spare pair of boots while you're at it,' said Heston. 'And gloves. And make sure she ties her hair back.'

'Yes, Uncle,' said Eshia. She gestured towards Abigone, and they walked to a side door that led into the adjoining house. Eshia opened the door, and they entered a storeroom that was lined with shelves.

'This is where we keep everything we need,' Eshia said. 'Spare tools, buckets, aprons and the like.'

Abigone picked up an apron and placed it over her shoulders. 'Thank you for this,' she said. 'How long have you worked here?'

'Since I was twelve.'

'Before you knew you were a Maker?'

'Remember not to say that part out loud when we're outside, Abbie; but yes. And then, when I attended the school, I was given permission to keep working here one day a week. I specialise in metals, so they thought it would be a good idea. I hear that you've progressed past the other first years?'

'Only a little, and only with wood.'

Eshia smiled. 'I was never very skilled with wood. Metal, though, I understand.' She reached up to a shelf and took down a pair of boots. 'See if these fit you.'

Abigone placed them on the floor, and crouched down. She removed her sandals, and slipped her feet into the heavy, iron-capped boots.

'They aren't exactly dainty, but they'll stop your toes from getting crushed,' said Eshia. 'Wear thick socks the next time you come, and they'll be more comfortable.'

Abigone laced up the boots, and stood, then Eshia passed her a pair of leather-coated gloves. Abigone tried them on, and nodded.

'Turn round,' said Eshia, 'and I'll tie your hair into a bun.'

'I have a question,' Abigone said, as Eshia reached up and began twisting her hair. 'Are you able to use your skills while wearing gloves?'

'Yes,' said Eshia. 'Can you?'

'I have never tried.'

'It's all in the mind. You don't actually need to raise your hand, or even say the words. Everything flows outwards from your thoughts. The school doesn't teach that until third year, though, so you should do whatever works for you.'

'Is it the same for Masters?'

'I think so. My father always raises his hand, but that's for the benefit of the students, so that they can see what he's doing. Miss Vesta is your teacher, isn't she? She was in fourth year when I joined the school.'

'Yes, she's my teacher.'

'And I had Raewyn and Stanza below me when I graduated.'

'I don't see too much of them. I'm with Nyli and Reath.'

Eshia laughed. 'That Reath can be a handful. She's fortunate that Lady Fyenna isn't very strict.'

'Are you joking? She has been quite strict with me.'

'That's because you're older. She has a kind heart, but she needs to assert her authority, and that's harder to do with eighteen-year-olds compared to fourteen-year-olds. You'll win her round if you work hard and show her some respect. To be honest, she must like you if she's agreed to let you come here once a week.'

'Was that the agreement – once a week?'

'I think so. There; your hair is out of the way. You don't want it getting singed. I sometimes wear a leather skullcap if we're busy and the embers are flying around.'

Abigone turned. 'Thanks. What kinds of things do you summon here?'

'Whatever my uncle needs – tools, mostly. It saves him a lot of time and money, but I can't do too much; otherwise, the other smithies on the street would start to get suspicious. If I wanted to, I could double his work rate, but then everyone would guess that he had a Maker working for him. Have you eaten anything for lunch?'

'Not yet.'

'Then I'll take you to *The Quenching Bucket* later. It's the best tavern on the street.'

Drummond appeared by the door. 'I'm not sure that's a good idea, Eshia,' he said. 'Let's keep Abbie to ourselves for now, at least until the other smiths are used to seeing her here.' He glanced at Abigone. 'Well, you look the part.'

Fyenna joined him. 'The agreement is in place, Abbie. Heston will keep you here for the afternoon, and I will send a carriage along later to collect you.'

'Are you leaving now, ma'am?'

'Yes. I will go back to my place of work. Mister Drummond has kindly agreed to remain here today to supervise you. Once you've settled in, it will be just you, Heston and Eshia. Behave yourself, Abbie, and I will see you later.'

Abigone inclined her head, and Fyenna strode away.

'Right,' said Drummond; 'let's get started. Do you have any questions, Abbie?'

'Just one, sir,' she said. 'Is Valiance all right? Has his stab wound healed?'

'His shoulder is a bit stiff and sore, but yes, the wound has closed up and is healing well. There's no infection. Would you like me to pass on a message?'

'Uh... Well, perhaps. If you could just tell him that I hope he's feeling better, and that I hope his meditation lessons are going well.'

'I can do that,' said Drummond. He gestured towards the door, and Abigone walked back outside, followed by Eshia. Heston was leaning over the forge, and he turned his head.

'I've placed a stool by the large tub for you, Abbie,' he said. 'Sit there for now, and watch.'

Abigone bowed her head, then she walked over to the stool and sat down. Eshia joined her uncle by the forge, and Drummond came over to where Abigone was sitting, and leaned against the tub.

'There won't be much for you to do today,' Drummond said. 'Just watch what they do, and ask me any questions that come into your head. Do you have a book to read in the evenings on metals?'

'Miss Vesta gave me one, sir.'

'Good. Make sure you read some every night. Now, the most common metal worked here is iron, and I want you to focus on that for now. We can leave bronze, pewter and other alloys until later, and don't concern yourself with steel at this stage. Iron is one of the most utilised metals, but it has a major drawback – it rusts when left out in the open air, or when it comes into contact with water. Understanding why it rusts is vital for summoning iron. Are you with me?'

'Yes, sir.'

Drummond smiled, then he began talking about the rusting process, and Abigone remained silent as she listened.

The afternoon drew on, and Abigone still hadn't eaten anything for lunch. Heston and Eshia remained hard at work, repairing a large plough that a farmer had brought in the previous day. Drummond remained by Abigone's side, providing a running commentary to explain what they were doing, and pausing to see if she had any questions.

The mid-afternoon bell had rung in the distance when a covered wagon drew up next to the forge. Five men stepped down to the cobbles and approached, while another man remained on the driver's bench. One of the men was carrying a broken sword, and he entered the forge while the others hung back.

'Is this Heston's forge?' said the man.

Heston glanced up from a large tub of water. 'And who is asking?'

'Are you Heston? Can you repair this sword for me? I need it for the mustering of the reserves.'

Heston wiped his hands on a towel and peered at the sword. 'I could take a look at it tomorrow.'

'I need it fixed by the end of the day.'

'Then I suggest you try another smith; there are plenty on the street. I'm busy with this plough today.'

'I can pay you extra.'

'Sorry, friend,' said Heston, 'but I have already promised to repair the plough.'

Abigone glanced at the other men, who were slowly walking round to the other side of the forge. Drummond noticed them too, and his eyes narrowed a little.

'All right,' said the man with the sword. 'I'll try somewhere else.'

He turned as if to leave, then he picked up a hammer from a workbench and swung it at Heston's head. The blacksmith ducked, but not far enough, and the hammer struck his right temple. Eshia cried out as her uncle fell to the ground, then the four other men rushed at Drummond. Two men gripped hold of his arms, as Abigone was shoved to the ground by another man, who placed a boot on her back to keep her pinned down. Drummond struggled in the men's grasp, then the man with the hammer swung it into Drummond's face. Several teeth went flying, and Drummond went limp.

'Get them into the wagon,' hissed the man with the hammer.

Two of the men started to drag Heston away by his arms, and Eshia ran at them, her fists clenched. The man with the hammer grabbed her by the throat, and pushed her down to her knees. He struck her across the face with the back of his hand, and she fell. Abigone tried to pull herself up, as Drummond was carried over to the wagon, but the boot was fixing her to the ground.

'Stay where you are, girl,' said the man standing on her. 'This doesn't concern you.'

Drummond and Heston were carried into the back of the wagon, and the other men climbed aboard. The man with his boot on Abigone's back ran over to the wagon as it started to move off, and Abigone pushed herself up to her knees. The driver whipped the horses, and the carriage sped away as Abigone ran out from the forge. She raised her hand, but could think of nothing that she could summon that would help. Three men from another forge raced over the road, as the carriage disappeared around a corner.

'What happened, girl?' said one of the men.

'Men were here,' Abigone said. 'They took Heston and Drummond.'

An older man hurried into the forge and helped Eshia get to her feet.

'Look at me, girl,' a man said to Abigone. 'They took Heston, you say? Why?'

'I don't know,' said Abigone. 'They were arguing over a broken sword.'

Eshia limped out from the forge, as blood trickled down from her nose.

'My father,' she sobbed. 'My uncle.'

Eshia sat down by the side of the road, and wept into her hands.

'I'll fetch the local militia,' said one of the men, running off.

Abigone crouched down by Eshia. 'We should go. The militia will want to question us, and... We should go.'

Eshia stared at her.

'We can't be here when the militia arrive,' Abigone whispered. 'We have to go back to Fyenna. I don't know the address, but you do. We can hail a carriage.'

Eshia nodded and Abigone helped her stand.

'Where are you two off to?' said a man.

'I'm taking her to see a doctor,' said Abigone. 'We'll be back in a few minutes.'

'Make sure you're here when the militia arrive.'

'Yes, sir,' said Abigone, as she helped Eshia walk. Abigone led Eshia to the left, and the men watched them leave. Abigone noticed that her hands were shaking, and she felt as though she was about to throw up in the street. They turned the corner, and Abigone picked up her speed, desperate to be as far away from the forge as possible.

Drummond was gone. It was Drummond the men had been after; Heston had been an afterthought, and the two young women had meant nothing to them. Someone had discovered that he was a Master; it was the only explanation.

Abigone saw an empty carriage, and raised her arm to hail the driver, who was standing leaning against a wheel.

'Where to, ladies?' he said, then his eyes widened at the blood on Eshia's face.

'The theatre district,' said Abigone, 'and quickly.'

The driver helped Abigone and Eshia board the carriage, then he closed the door and climbed up onto the bench. He gripped the reins, and the carriage began to trundle over the cobbles.

Abigone put her arm round Eshia's shoulder.

'Everything will be all right,' Abigone whispered. 'Lady Fyenna will know what to do.'

CHAPTER 19
GIVING NOTHING AWAY

Old City, Klef Mordain – 26th Day of Desira 108

Fyenna stared into space as her husband read the morning newspaper.

'Has there been any news?' he said.

'News about what?'

'About your missing friend.'

Fyenna said nothing.

'You told me a while ago that a friend of yours had gone missing,' her husband went on. 'I was just wondering if you had heard any news about him or her.'

Fyenna glanced up, but the newspaper was blocking her husband's face. 'It's been twenty-two days since he was abducted in broad daylight from the streets of the city. Any news at this stage would only be bad.'

'What a terrible business.'

Fyenna glanced away.

'There's been nothing in the paper about it,' he said. 'I check every day for you.'

'How can you check for him,' she said, 'when you don't know his name? Up until a few moments ago, you didn't even know my friend was a man.'

'I look for any mention of a missing person.'

'You've been in a better mood recently,' she said.

He folded the paper and placed it onto the breakfast table. 'You noticed, did you? I have had some good news. The harbour authorities have dropped their investigation against me.'

Fyenna frowned. 'Why would they do that?'

'Because I had nothing to hide. All that worry I've gone through, it was for nothing in the end.'

'I thought there were some discrepancies in your accounts.'

'There were a few, but it wasn't enough to prove anything.'

'Does this mean you can go back to work?'

'My office is still unusable,' he said, 'after it was thoroughly ransacked by the investigators, but I can sit here at home and go over the paperwork. I'm not sure there's much point, though, seeing as how the city is under blockade. When is the Corse going to see sense? They cannot win against the might of the entire Sanctian Empire.'

'Are you suggesting that we capitulate?'

'No, I am suggesting that we negotiate. There must be a civilised agreement that can be reached between us. What's the alternative – starvation?'

'And what about me? Don't you care what happens to me?'

'Of course I care. The Sanctians would never harm a war hero.'

'I can't believe you just said that. Are you delusional?'

'Fyenna,' he said, 'has it ever occurred to you that you might be putting your own interests above the million inhabitants of Klef Mordain? Thousands are going without food, and more businesses close with each day that passes. How many need to die before you are prepared to speak to the Sanctians? Shouldn't we hear what they have to offer before condemning them out of hand?'

Fyenna shook her head in disgust. 'You would sacrifice me, would you? You think I am the selfish one?'

'You are twisting my words. You need to understand that the common people, and the merchant classes, just want this to be over. The stubborn bloody-mindedness of the Corse is dragging us down to ruin. Nothing in this city seems to work any more. The courts have ground to a halt, criminals are going unpunished, and people are fighting over scraps of food. Law and order could collapse at any moment, and then the Old City will be inundated with the hungry masses. The Corse should resign, and allow someone else the opportunity to rule the city. Their obsession with secrecy has brought them low.'

'And who else should rule?'

Selanius pointed at an article on the front page of the newspaper. 'The Second Empire Association has published a draft of a temporary constitution – one that would be open and transparent. Officials would be elected by all property owners, and the secret police disbanded for good.'

'What does it say about Masters and Makers?'

'Uh, nothing. It doesn't mention them.'

'Why do you think that is? It doesn't mention Masters and Makers because they don't want the common people to know what the Sanctians intend to do to us.'

'You are being paranoid,' he snapped. 'You see threats where there are none.'

'How dare you?' she cried.

'Why are you losing your temper? I am getting sick of hearing how persecuted you are, when it isn't you who is suffering any consequences of the blockade.'

'We would be hunted down if the Second Empire Association gets into power.'

'The only thing threatening your safety is your damnable intransigence, Fyenna. Look what happened to Drummond...'

Fyenna stared at her husband.

'I... uh, well...' Selanius stammered.

'How did you know his name?' said Fyenna. Her blood chilled. 'Dear spirits; it was you.'

'What was me? I don't know what you're talking about.'

Fyenna got to her feet. 'It was you. You told them about Drummond. Is that why they dropped the case?'

'You've got it wrong,' he said. 'I didn't tell anyone anything.'

'You bastard,' she cried. 'You sold out a Master to the pro-Sanctians. Are you going to sell me out, too?'

'No! I was trying to protect you; you have to believe me.'

Fyenna clenched her fists as Selanius stared at her, then she turned and hurried from the room, as tears streamed down her cheeks. She raced down the stairs, grabbed her coat, and rushed out of the house. She took a breath, conscious that her enemies were probably watching her. She pulled on her coat, and tried to walk as though nothing was wrong, but she felt sick, and stunned. Metrius had warned her about her husband, but she had ignored his advice.

She glanced up and down the street, wondering which of the many citizens were spying on her, then she made for the nearest entrance to the tunnel network.

Thirty minutes later, she was standing in a subterranean chamber with Lord Metrius.

'I'm sorry, my lord,' she said.

'So am I, Fyenna; so am I,' said Metrius. 'The question is – what should I do about it? If Selanius were not married to you, I would already be sending agents to your home to kill him.'

'I know.'

'What else does he have? What other nuggets of information might Selanius share with our enemies?'

'Nothing that I know of, sir.'

'Were you aware that he might have remembered Drummond's name?'

'It was a long time ago.'

'But you suspected that he might know?'

'Drummond once came round to the house where Selanius and I lived at the time, right after the Battle of Hader Pull. We didn't think anything of it back then. I have been faithful to my oath. I haven't uttered a word to my husband since I started work at the Maker school.'

'You should have told me about this. I cannot express how disappointed I am to hear how your indiscretions have cost us so dearly. Drummond is bad enough, but we were very close to losing Miss Eshia and Princess Abigone at the same time. Can you imagine what would occur if the Sanctians got their hands on Abigone? As for Drummond... Perhaps you should come with me.'

Metrius turned away, and Fyenna followed him through a doorway and into a small room, which was equipped with a long table. Upon the table, a body was lying covered with a blanket. Fyenna put a hand to her face as Metrius pulled the cover away.

'His body was recovered from the harbour two days ago,' Metrius said.

Fyenna broke down in tears. 'Dear spirits,' she gasped.

'Yes, it's not a pretty sight, is it? I had a coroner examine the body. The bruising around his face is relatively old, probably from the time of his abduction. He also shows signs of malnourishment, so we can assume that he was given very little food during his captivity. And then there are the signs of torture – the missing fingers and toes, the pulled-out fingernails, the cuts, and so on. The fatal wound was inflicted by a dagger-like blade thrust into his heart. The coroner estimates that this occurred just before the body was dumped into the harbour. So, Drummond was first beaten, and then he was starved, probably until he was too weak to call upon his abilities as a Master. After that, he was grievously tortured, before his interrogators dispatched him. The wanton cruelty of some of the acts of torture tells me something else – that Drummond did not part willingly with his secrets. You don't need to inflict such wounds if your prisoner is telling you what you need to know. If I had to hazard a guess, I would say that the final wounds show signs of desperation on the part of his interrogators. Perhaps Drummond gave them nothing, and so they lashed out in anger. It is but a small hope, but I will cling on to it nevertheless.'

Fyenna bowed her head, unable to look upon the mutilated body of her friend.

'Your husband did this, Fyenna,' said Metrius. 'Drummond's name was all he had, and so he gave it to our enemies to save himself. Can you give me a reason to spare his life?'

Fyenna hesitated. 'He was my son's father,' she said.

'Drummond was also a father. At the very least, I want to bring Selanius in for questioning. If he reveals the names of those to whom he spoke, then we might still have a chance of locating Heston, who is still missing. Now, Fyenna, think very carefully before you answer this – does Heston know anything about the schools?'

'He knows that his niece attended the Maker school, and he also knows that Abigone is a student there. Apart from that, I don't think so.'

'That is quite enough. Might Drummond or Eshia have confided more in him?'

'I can ask Eshia; she is living in the Maker school at the moment.'

'Do so, if you please. One thing that puzzles me – how did the men who abducted them know that Drummond would be at his brother's forge that day?'

'I presume they must have followed him from his home that morning, sir.'

Metrius shook his head. 'Then you also came within a hair's width of being captured. We are losing, Fyenna; we are losing this war before it has even begun.' He pulled the cover over Drummond's body. 'I don't think we should allow Eshia to see her father like this; do you agree?'

'Yes, sir.'

'I will have the body cremated, and then I shall send her the ashes in an urn. Have you appointed Mister Tobold as Head Master?'

'I have, though it was an interim position.'

'You had better make it permanent.'

'I will, my lord.'

Metrius sighed as he gazed at her. 'What a damnable mess. We are left in a state of uncertainty, not knowing what, if anything, Drummond told them, while knowing that Heston probably remains in their hands.'

'I do not believe that Drummond would have given them our secrets, my lord. He was a good man; a brave and honourable man.'

'He was, indeed; one of the best, in fact. I am inclined to believe that you are right, but we still have Heston to worry about. If he tells them that Abigone is a student at the Maker school, then the Sanctians will use that against us. They will claim to their allies and subjects in the Central Provinces that we are holding the princess against her will, in order to garner more support for their actions in Klef Mordain. We will lose whatever sympathy we had left. Even Lesser Down will cease their complaints and fall into line. Is Heston also honourable and brave? Would he be willing to undergo torture to keep our secrets?'

'I don't know, my lord.'

'You should never have taken Abigone to his forge, Fyenna. It was another mistake on your part.'

'I was trying to do the best for my students, my lord. Abigone has immense reservoirs of untapped talent. I was trying to develop her abilities.'

'Secrecy is far more important than that; you of all people should know this. No more outings from now on – is that understood? The students must remain within the school buildings at all times. I also want you to examine your evacuation plans, in the event that we are wrong about Drummond. He knew everything there is to know about both schools. You must be ready to flee into the catacombs at a moment's notice.'

'We are prepared for that eventuality, my lord.'

'Even in your absence? What if traitorous members of the secret police are raiding the buildings as we speak?'

'Miss Vesta and Head Master Tobold have each been trained on this situation, my lord. I trust them to know what to do.'

'That puts my mind at ease, a little,' he said. 'And now we have another matter at hand to deal with. Are you ready for your second shock of the day, Fyenna?'

'Has someone else died?'

'It's nothing like that. It's more of a rebirth than a death. Perhaps you can give me some advice on how best we should deal with it. Follow me.'

They left the chamber, then Metrius led her through more tunnels, a lamp in his right hand to light the way. They descended to a deeper level, and Metrius lit a few wall lamps when they reached a long cavern hewn from the rock. A man's voice called out as soon as the lamps were lit, and Fyenna saw a face appear at a barred window.

'You do wrong to keep me imprisoned in here!' the man cried. 'I have breached no laws of this unfriendly city. I demand to be released.'

'Hush, hush,' said Metrius. He glanced at Fyenna. 'I would be very impressed at this juncture if you were able to guess this man's identity.'

'I have no idea who it is, my lord.'

'Question him, but tell him not your name. I want to see your reaction to his claims.'

'They are not claims, you dog,' cried the man in the cell. 'I have told you naught but the truth.'

Fyenna approached the cell door and peered through the bars of the small opening. The man standing in the cell was far larger than she had previously appreciated – broad-shouldered, and so tall that he had to stoop to see out of the window set into the cell door.

'What is your name?' she said.

'And who are you, woman? Are you a member of this city's accursed secret police?'

'Your name, if you please, sir.'

'My name is Mor Galthide, and by that name I shall curse you if you do not release me from this confinement.'

Fyenna turned to Metrius. 'His name means nothing to me.'

'One of my agents arrested him this morning,' Metrius said. 'He was demanding entrance into my private offices. He has a most interesting tale to tell.'

'But who is he?'

'It seems that you have not been keeping track of court politics in

Sanctos, my dear friend. Mor Galthide is married to one of Emperor Antonio's daughters.'

Fyenna's eyes widened. 'We have a member of the imperial family in custody? But... Are you planning to use him to barter for concessions? Why is he in Klef Mordain?'

Metrius raised his palms. 'One question at a time. Unfortunately for the city, Mor Galthide is no longer beloved by the emperor. His Imperial Majesty would likely invite us to hang him rather than concede to any of our demands. He is of very little use to us in that way.'

'Cease prattling about me while I stand before you,' said Mor Galthide. 'I curse Emperor Antonio, the devourer of my homeland, and I curse his family, and the rotten empire over which he presides. You know what I want, Metrius, so why are you denying me my rights?'

'What does he want?' said Fyenna.

'Address me when you speak, woman!' Mor Galthide cried.

Fyenna turned back to face the cell door. 'All right. What do you want?'

'I want this city to return my son into my hands,' said Mor Galthide. 'Klef Mordain is doomed, and I must have my son in order to flee before the Sanctians dance on the ruins of this city. Where is he, Metrius? Where is my son?'

'Who is your son?' said Fyenna.

'His name is Mor Dennahelm, woman.'

'I don't know anyone by that name.'

Metrius chuckled, but it was a bitter sound. 'Prepare yourself, my friend. Mor Galthide, why don't you tell my companion the pseudonym you bestowed upon your son?'

Mor Galthide lowered his stern gaze. 'I instructed my boy to go by the name of Valiance.'

Fyenna staggered back a step. 'What? Valiance is the grandson of Emperor Antonio? No. It can't be.'

'Do you now see our quandary?' said Metrius. 'Not only do we have a princess of Upper Down in our care, but we also have a prince of the Sanctian Empire.'

'Is my son your student, woman?' said Mor Galthide.

'Stop calling me that,' said Fyenna. 'And no, he is not my student, but I am responsible for his welfare. Why did you bring him here? Why did you bring your son to Klef Mordain?'

'So he could be trained as a Master,' said Mor Galthide. 'He is the rightful king of Geathan and, through him, we shall recover our lost homeland.'

'This is the nature of Mor Galthide's disagreement with Emperor Antonio,' said Metrius. 'The father does not approve of the way his son's upbringing has been corrupted by the Sanctians. In fact, I would say that he hates the Sanctian Empire with as much passion as you or I. He stole his son away from the imperial court last year...'

'I stole him not,' said Mor Galthide. 'A father cannot steal his own son. I saved him from Sanctos. Had that cur Antonio discovered that my boy was a Master, he would have had him executed. Was I to remain quiet and allow that to happen? He is my only son, the sole heir to the realm of Geathan. And yes, I loathe the Sanctian Empire with all my being; and yet you continue to hold me here against my will.'

'Why don't you stay here and help us fight the Sanctians, if you hate them so much?' said Metrius.

Mor Galthide shook his head. 'This city is a lost cause. To the south, twenty thousand Sanctian soldiers are preparing to march upon Klef Mordain, while their damn gunboats sit in the estuary, pointing their cannon at the Old City. The markets are empty, and the people are restless, and angry with their government. One spark would ignite an inferno that would raze this city to the ground. I will not cast away the life of my son in vain. In time, you will capitulate to the Sanctians; that is as clear as daylight to me. You have no choice. Your people will not rally to your aid. It is over, yet you have not realised this. You will, soon enough.'

Fyenna looked away.

'Tell me,' Mor Galthide went on; 'is my son well? Does he thrive? How have his lessons been progressing? I had a servant who was to keep me informed, but I have not seen him for months.'

'Valiance is doing very well,' said Fyenna. 'He is brave, resourceful, and calm in a crisis. He does you credit.'

'I thank you for those words. When can I collect him?'

'That is out of the question,' said Metrius. 'Your son is an enrolled student in one of the city's institutions. He will not be leaving that institution until we say he can.'

'It is you who has stolen my son,' Mor Galthide said. 'You faithless dog.'

'Let us agree upon something,' said Metrius. 'All three of us here abhor the Sanctian Empire, yes? All three of us scorn that hated order to hunt down and kill Masters and Makers, yes? Right now, Mor Galthide, Sanctian agents are scouring the city, searching for any clue that will lead them to the schools where we train the young Masters and Makers who come to us. Any breach of secrecy will imperil us all.'

'That is all the more reason to deliver my son into my hands. I do not need to see these schools, nor do I need to know anything about their locations, or who works there. You can keep your secrets, but give me my son!'

'We need him,' said Fyenna.

'To what end? To become a martyr for your hopeless cause? I will not have it. Mor Dennahelm is destined to rule Geathan as king; he will not die for nothing in this pestilent city.'

'This city is nurturing your son's abilities.'

'That is a state of affairs that will not last the season. You may have done him some good in the past, and for that I am grateful, but forcing him to remain here while the Sanctians knock upon the door will lead to nothing but his death. You must let him go. I beg you, good woman; let my son go before it is too late. I beseech you humbly. You are a mother, are you not? Do you know what it is to have children? If you do, then you will understand the pain in my heart. I would die, gladly and willingly, to save my son from the swords of the Sanctians.'

Fyenna bowed her head and said nothing.

'If truly you cared for the students of your schools,' Mor Galthide went on; 'you would send them all to safety. Alas – you care more about sacrificing them to defend the indefensible.'

'Hush,' said Metrius. 'The Masters and Makers in this city are pledged to our cause. We shall need their abilities if we are to prevail.'

Mor Galthide hung his head, as anger twisted his features.

'Would the Sanctians slay a grandson of the emperor?' said Fyenna.

'They will not see that,' said Mor Galthide; 'they will only see that he is a Master. His grandfather has disowned him.'

'That is not true,' said Metrius. 'The emperor has disowned you, Mor Galthide, and he now calls you traitor; but he has not disowned your son.'

'That is only because Antonio does not know that my son is a Master. But he will, if he remains here. And, as soon as he does, all grandfatherly feelings of compassion will evaporate. Would Antonio kill his grandson, if he knew his grandson to be a Master? You each know the answer to that in your hearts. You know he would.'

'I feel that this conversation is over,' said Metrius. He turned to Fyenna. 'Shall we?'

They turned for the cavern entrance and Mor Galthide gripped the bars of his cell door.

'Come back, you dogs!' he shouted. 'Leave me not to rot in the darkness.'

Metrius extinguished all lamps but one, which he picked up as they left the cavern. Metrius closed the heavy door, blocking out the sounds of Mor Galthide's cries. They travelled along a few tunnels, until they came to a set of stairs going up that Fyenna recognised.

'Well, Fyenna,' Metrius said; 'what should we do with Mor Galthide, the runaway prince of Sanctos?'

'I don't know, my lord.'

'I also confess to being at a loss. We could slit his throat and burn the body, but that seems a little heartless. After all, he has done nothing wrong. Desiring the safety of your son is not a crime. All the same, knowing what he knows, we cannot allow him to walk the streets. So, for now, we shall keep him here. I will have a trusted agent bring him food and water each day.'

'We should tell Valiance, my lord.'

'What would that achieve?'

'Doesn't the boy have a right to know?'

'Perhaps; perhaps not.'

'If Valiance would tell his father to his face that he doesn't want to leave the city, then maybe Mor Galthide would be satisfied with that.'

'And then what? Would we allow Mor Galthide to depart in peace? He would never agree to it, Fyenna. And are you altogether sure that Valiance would refuse his father's request? Has the boy ever mentioned anything to you about his connections, or about the extinct realm of Geathan?'

'Never, no. He knows how to keep a secret, and he has kept his well. We should also bear in mind that he is eighteen. If he is old enough to fight for us, then he is old enough to be told the truth.'

Metrius raised an eyebrow. 'A most curious chain of logic, and not one that I can agree with. With Drummond's death, and the uncertainty that this has brought us, is this the right time to be burdening young Valiance with such matters? Would it not be better that he is kept in a state of blissful ignorance? I hope that you are not thinking of making another mistake, Fyenna. Your last one cost us dearly.'

'I will do as you command, my lord.'

'Then I command you to say nothing to the boy. Now, go back to your home, and tell your husband that if he does not hand himself in to my office before the day is out, I shall dispatch agents to drag him there. I am telling you this as a courtesy. Make sure he understands what he has to do.'

'Yes, my lord.' Fyenna said. She inclined her head, and then she ascended the stairs, leaving Metrius and the lamp behind.

Forty minutes later, Fyenna crossed the threshold of her home. She hung up her coat in silence, and walked up the stairs to the main living area. She looked into the sitting room, where her husband usually worked when he was at home, but he wasn't there.

'Selanius!' she called.

She walked into the kitchen, and saw that the breakfast dishes were still on the dining table. She frowned; couldn't he at least tidy up after himself? She went into the bedroom, and noticed that Selanius's wardrobe was open. She glanced inside – it was empty. She hurried over to the bed and looked under it – his travelling trunk was gone.

'Selanius!' she shouted into the silence of the house. She searched for a note or a letter, but there was nothing. She opened a drawer, where she kept a purse of money for emergencies. It had been taken.

Fyenna sat down on a chair in the bedroom. Her husband had fled. He had guessed that she would tell Metrius, and he had left rather than face the consequences of his actions.

So be it, she thought. If there was no one else in the house, then there was no one to lie to anymore.

CHAPTER 20
TWELFTH IN LINE

Old City, Klef Mordain – 2nd Day of Lamenta 108

Denny tried to clear his mind, but an image of Drummond seemed stamped upon his brain. It had been eight days since Mister Tobold had told the student Masters that the body of Drummond had been found in the harbour. He had been murdered, that much was clear, but Tobold had been sparing with the details.

Denny focussed on his breathing. He shifted his legs before cramp could set in, and tried to get comfortable in his new position.

The other students had been distraught upon hearing the news. Aplin had wept, and Ignatius's face had paled until he appeared almost ghost-like. Constans had grown more irritable than usual, and had been snapping at the other boys. Salus, in particular, had often borne the brunt of his older cousin's ire. Only Marlow and Denny had not broken down in front of the others, but Denny suspected that he and the other boy were just better at hiding their feelings.

Drummond had always told them that secrecy was paramount; that a single indiscretion would bring assassins to the front doors of the two schools. The obvious conclusion was that someone in the city had betrayed Drummond's secret, but Tobold had insisted that they were all safe, that there was nothing to worry about.

'Concentrate on your breathing, boys,' said Tobold, but his voice sounded dispirited.

Denny's brow furrowed in frustration. He had been in the school for months, and yet he still seemed incapable of finding peace within his mind. Without that, even the simplest transformations turned out wrong. Young Salus was starting to progress ahead of him, much to Constans's smug delight; and even Ignatius, who could barely spell his own name, was doing no worse than Denny.

'In... Out...,' said Tobold.

Denny made a conscious decision to think about Abigone's face. She often wore a slightly surly expression, as though she doubted the veracity of whatever was being said. It was an expression he had seen on the faces of some of his cousins in the palaces of Sanctos; an expression that bespoke of the haughty arrogance of authority. And yet, Abigone was rarely arrogant. She used the expression to keep her distance, as though she didn't want anyone getting too close to her. She seldom smiled, but when she did, her whole face lit up in a way that Denny couldn't help but like. He remembered her smile from when he had last seen her, just as they were about to board their carriages after the incident with the Westlanders. He had felt ashamed for having left her alone while chasing off after Nyli. He had presumed that the man he had brought down was still alive, even though he had already been dead when Denny had slammed his elbow into his face. The thought sickened him, and he went back to thinking about Abigone. Focus on her, he told himself, not on the act of breathing.

Abigone, he murmured silently, and his mind began to clear. For the first time in months, he felt at peace, his mind holding nothing but the image of Abigone's face. He forgot all about his breathing, and relaxed. He opened his eyes, got to his feet, and walked over to a workbench, which was filled with a variety of objects.

He concentrated on Abigone's eyes, and glanced at a block of wood.

'Ever-living and blessed spirits,' he whispered, 'I call upon your power. Take the wood from the block on the table, and in its place put iron.'

The air rustled, and the block of wood shrunk, and its colour changed to that of rust. Denny stared at it. It wasn't perfect, but it was the best he had managed in five months.

Marlow got up to take a look, as Denny prodded the small block of rusted iron.

'Not bad, Valiance,' said the younger boy. 'Pity about the rust, though.'

Denny smiled.

'My, that is a decent effort,' said Tobold, as he walked over to the bench. 'Well done, Valiance.'

'Why is it so rusty, sir?' he said.

'Iron can be tricky for precisely that reason,' said Tobold, as he picked up the small block of corroded metal. 'That's why we usually start with wood and earth. Next time, pick a metal that doesn't rust; or try stone – but select your variety first. Sandstone, granite and the like. Don't be vague; the spirits prefer us Masters to be specific. I assume your breathing exercises are finally paying off?'

'Yes, sir.'

'I don't know how you are able to clear your mind,' said Constans, who was sitting close by. 'How can anyone focus properly after what happened?'

'Please don't talk about Master Drummond,' said Salus. 'I can't concentrate when you do.'

'Oh, shut up,' said Constans. 'Who cares about your feeble powers, Salus? The city is hardly relying upon you to save it.'

'That's enough,' said Tobold. 'If you can't focus now, when things seem dire, then how will you ever be able to focus in the heat of battle?'

'We already know how Constans reacts in a battle, sir,' said Marlow. 'We all heard him screech like a baby when the Westlanders appeared.'

Constans leapt to his feet, his fists clenched, and Tobold stepped between him and Marlow.

'Say that to my face, Marlow, you coward,' Constans cried.

'I just did,' said Marlow. 'I'll say it again, if you like.'

Aplin pointed at Denny. 'We should be talking about him,' he said.

'It's normal for teenage boys to be frightened when armed horsemen charge at them. What Valiance did wasn't normal. I want to know how he learned what to do. I want to be able to do the same if we're ever attacked again.'

'Aplin makes a good point,' said Mister Tobold. 'Only two boys didn't panic – Marlow and Valiance. You others have nothing to be ashamed of; you reacted in a way that merely tells me that you have never come face to face with mortal danger before. Now, Marlow kept his nerve, which is commendable, but what Valiance did was extraordinary. Perhaps you could give the other boys some advice, Valiance? I wouldn't mind hearing it myself.'

Denny puffed out his cheeks. 'I don't really know how I did it.'

'Come now,' said Tobold. 'Don't be modest.'

'I'm not being modest, sir. I didn't think about what I was doing; I just did it.'

'That sounds to my ears like the product of training. Where were you trained, Valiance?'

'I will not say, sir.'

'Can you train us?' said Aplin. 'You rode a horse better than me, and I practised for years when I was younger. And how do you know the language of the Westlanders? My mother taught me; who taught you?'

'My upbringing was very... disciplined,' Denny said. 'It wasn't much fun.'

'But look at how it moulded you,' said Marlow, as the boys gathered round. 'I stayed calm when the Westlanders appeared, because I was chased by Sanctian soldiers all over the Central Provinces on my way here; but I didn't know what to do.'

'Can you speak any other languages?' said Salus.

Denny shrugged.

'That means yes,' said Aplin.

'And he knows Elestian poetry,' said Salus. 'I remember him quoting Tydian the Great. What kind of school taught him all that?'

'Why won't you tell us, Valiance?' said Aplin.

'You know why. I swore an oath.'

'Your stupid oath might get us all killed,' said Constans. 'You should share what you know.'

'Bring me a horse, and I will teach you how to ride it properly.'

'What else can you do?' said Salus.

'I can cook, and I can sew my own clothes.'

Constans laughed. 'Women's work.'

'It's called self-sufficiency,' said Denny. 'Why mock the skills that keep you fed and dressed? Anyway, I don't wish to speak about myself any longer. We're supposed to be meditating.'

'Quite right,' said Tobold.

An old woman appeared at the classroom door, and Denny recognised her from working in the kitchen of the Maker school.

'Mister Tobold, sir?' she said.

Tobold turned his head. 'Yes?'

'Might I have a quiet word, sir?'

Tobold walked over to the door, and then he and the woman talked in hushed tones for a few moments.

Tobold nodded, then he glanced back at the students. 'Valiance, would you come over here, please?'

Denny went to the door.

'This lady is here to take you to the Maker school, Valiance,' Tobold said.

'I have a carriage waiting outside,' said the woman.

'All right,' said Denny.

'Pass on my regards to Miss Eshia if you see her,' said Tobold. 'Let her know that everyone in the Master school commiserates with her loss.'

'I will, sir.'

The woman led Denny out of the room, and they descended the stairs to the ground floor of the school. The doorman escorted them to a back door, and they left the building.

. . .

Half an hour later, Denny was sitting in Lady Fyenna's office in the Maker school. He had been waiting for Fyenna to say something for several minutes but, instead, she had sat across the desk from him in silence.

'How are you getting along, Valiance?' she said, finally.

'Well, ma'am. I had a little breakthrough this morning, and managed to transform wood into iron.'

Fyenna nodded. 'Well done.'

'It was covered in a thick layer of rust, ma'am.'

'That's quite normal, at your stage. Iron has a natural tendency towards its own corrosion, and both Masters and Makers have to struggle against that. It is almost as though iron wishes to betray itself.' She gave him a wry smile. 'I think I know how it feels.'

Denny said nothing.

'I am not supposed to be doing what I am about to do,' Fyenna went on. 'However, after much thought, I have decided to do it anyway. You are an adult, after all, and I think you deserve to hear the truth.'

'What truth, ma'am?'

'How ironic it is,' she said; 'you came to a city renowned for its secrecy while carrying your own secret with you. Isn't that so, Valiance, or should I call you Mor Dennahelm, Prince of Sanctos?'

He stared at her.

'Well, I see that had the desired effect,' she said. 'I admit that I had never heard of you until a few days ago, but I was never all that familiar with the various members of the imperial family. There are so many of them, for a start – Antonio and his siblings have been remarkably fecund. So, I did some research, and found that you had indeed vanished from Sanctos last year, reputedly in the presence of your father. The emperor is looking for you both, as you probably know. Your father he wishes to execute, while, as for you? That is a more complicated matter. It seems that Emperor Antonio is unaware that you are a Master. He thinks that your father forced you into leaving Sanctos, as part of a doomed attempt to reinvigorate the old realm of Geathan.

That is where he has sent soldiers to look for you. Are you going to deny any of this?'

Denny remained silent.

'Well, Mor Dennahelm?'

'Please don't call me that, ma'am. Only my father calls me by my full name.'

'I see. What do you prefer?'

'Denny, ma'am. It's what my cousins called me.'

'Denny. All right. And how many cousins do you have, exactly?'

'Fifteen, ma'am.'

'The emperor has sixteen grandchildren?'

'No, ma'am. The emperor has seven grandchildren. I was including my second cousins – the grandchildren of Prince Valentino and Princess Carla, the emperor's two siblings.'

'And where do you sit in relation to the throne? I presume you aren't next in line?'

'I am twelfth in line to the throne, ma'am.'

'Ah. Then it is unlikely we will be seeing a Master take over as emperor?'

'Very unlikely, ma'am.'

'And what about your claim to the throne of Geathan?'

'My father should be heir, but the emperor forced him to disavow his claim when he married my mother.'

'And your mother is Princess Volena, correct? The younger daughter of the emperor?'

'Yes, ma'am.'

'Does she know that you are a Master?'

'No, ma'am. Only my father knows. Is that how you discovered the truth – from my father?'

'Yes. I spoke to him a few days ago. He is looking for you. He wants to take you away from Klef Mordain, for your own safety.'

'Is he still in the city?

'He is. I doubt that he will leave without you. How do you feel about that, Denny?'

'That sounded strange. I'm not used to hearing my own name anymore. As for my father, I would rather stay here.'

'Why? The city is facing a tremendous struggle.'

'For my classmates, ma'am – both the Masters and the Makers. I will not abandon them.'

Fyenna nodded. 'Thank you,' she said. 'That means a lot to me. What you did in the clearing that day, it will stay with me forever.'

'How is Nyli, ma'am?'

'She is still having nightmares, and Drummond's death has only made them worse. His death has brought everyone's spirits low.'

'It is the same in the Master school, ma'am. How did the Sanctians find out about him?'

'It wasn't the Sanctians who did it, Denny; it was traitors within Klef Mordain, traitors who would prefer this city to be ruled by the Sanctians. They know that the Masters and Makers represent a powerful defence, and so they are trying to eliminate us.'

'Is it true that they tortured him, ma'am?'

'Did Mister Tobold tell you that?

'No, ma'am. I am guessing based upon what Mister Tobold did not tell us.'

'You are old enough to know the truth, Denny. Yes – Master Drummond was severely tortured before his death. His suffering will haunt me for the rest of my days.'

'Then, they must have interrogated him?'

'We assume so.'

'Master Drummond would have told them nothing, ma'am.'

'That is easy to say, but most people crack under torture.'

'Master Drummond wasn't like most people.'

'Yes. I know.'

A tear slid down her cheek as she tried to compose herself. Denny passed her a handkerchief.

'Thank you,' she said. 'Please do not tell the others that I cried. I have to remain strong for the girls.'

'I won't mention it, ma'am.'

'You have already proved that you can keep a secret. Were you never tempted to reveal your true name, not once in the five months since you arrived at the school?'

'I was tempted many times. My oath has felt like a burden that I had to carry around each day, or a wall that kept me apart from the others. In a way, I am glad that someone knows.'

'I have yet to tell anyone else about this.'

'Am I allowed to remain a student, ma'am?'

'Of course. I wanted you to know, but I don't intend to take any action. I felt that you needed to know that your father has been in contact. Do you wish to see him?'

'Could that be arranged, ma'am?'

'I can't make any promises, but if you are willing, then I can look into it.'

Denny gazed at the carpeted floor. 'Yes. I would like to speak to him.'

'I will see what I can do. Now, would you be able to do me a small favour while you are here?'

'Name it, ma'am.'

'Would you visit the girls? Your presence would cheer them up.'

'Why?'

'Come now; you must have an inkling of the impact your actions have had upon your fellow students. Aren't the boys in the Master school as equally impressed as the girls here?'

'It was nothing, ma'am. What I did... I... Anyone would have done the same.'

'You risked your life to save three students, Denny – that wasn't *nothing*. You should be very proud.'

'I'm embarrassed, ma'am; and ashamed.'

'Ashamed? Whatever do you have to be ashamed about?'

'I left Abigone alone when I rushed off into the forest. I feel terrible about it. What if something had happened to her?'

'But you killed the man who charged at you and Abigone.'

'I didn't know he was dead.'

'Goodness; is this what you have been dwelling upon over the last month? Listen to me, Denny – you have absolutely nothing to be ashamed of. Make sure you speak to Abigone before the carriage takes you back to the Master school. She will assure you that your feelings of shame are misplaced. Shall we visit the girls now?'

'As you will, ma'am.'

They got to their feet, then Fyenna led him from the room and up the stairs to the first floor. They came to a classroom, where the three first years were having a lesson. Reath and Nyli were standing next to Miss Vesta by a workbench, while Abigone was sitting by herself, reading a book.

'May I have your attention, class?' said Fyenna. 'We have a visitor.'

Vesta and the others turned.

'Shit on a stick,' said Reath. 'Look who it is.'

'Language, Reath,' said Vesta.

'Hello,' said Denny. 'I came to see if you were all well. How are you feeling, Nyli?'

The girl's cheeks flushed.

'She'll be a lot better now,' said Reath. 'What's happening at the boys' school?'

'Everyone is still sad about Master Drummond,' said Denny, 'and we all miss seeing the Makers. We are like one big family, and we need to help each other to get through this time.' He glanced at Abigone, then he remembered how he had managed to meditate successfully, and his mouth went dry.

'How are you, Valiance?' said Abigone. 'How is your shoulder?'

He turned to Fyenna. 'I want to tell her, ma'am,' he whispered.

Fyenna narrowed her eyes, then she nodded. 'As long as she promises not to spread the news around, I don't see why not. Miss Vesta, will you please excuse Abigone for a few moments?'

'Of course, ma'am,' said Vesta. 'Abigone, go with Lady Fyenna and Valiance.'

Abigone got to her feet, and walked to the doorway.

'The next classroom along is free,' said Fyenna. 'Talk in there. I will remain here to see what Reath and Nyli have been doing.'

Denny and Abigone walked along the corridor, then Abigone opened the door to another classroom. They went inside, then Abigone closed the door and turned to him.

'Yes?' she said. 'Did you want to speak to me?'

Denny nodded. 'Now that I have you here, I'm not sure where to begin.'

'Try at the beginning,' she said.

'All right. I'm sorry. Can you forgive me?'

'For what?'

'For leaving you alone in the clearing.'

'Are you still thinking about that? Valiance, if the same thing happens again, I would want you to act in exactly the same manner. There is nothing to forgive but, if it makes you feel better, then I forgive you.'

'I didn't know that man was dead.'

'Even if he had lived, he was hardly likely to get up and attack me. And, Valiance, even if he had, I can take care of myself. I would have summoned a stone dragon to crush him. You did the right thing by going off after Nyli; she isn't able to defend herself.'

'You would have summoned a stone dragon?'

'Yes. He wouldn't have been the first Westlander to die at my hands. Honestly, Valiance, think nothing more of this. I will not have you feeling guilty on my behalf.'

'Thank you. Now I have to somehow find the words to tell you what I need to say.'

'You mean there's more? Good. I am glad you didn't come all this way just for that.'

'My oath has lapsed,' he said.

'What does that mean?'

'It means that Lady Fyenna has discovered the truth about who I am; and now I want you to know.'

'I see. Is that what Lady Fyenna meant about me having to promise not to tell anyone?'

'Yes. Do you promise?'

'I do, but why do you wish to tell me in particular?'

'Because we're partners; one Master, one Maker.'

'I think those days are over. I doubt we shall be having any more joint exercises, not after what happened to Master Drummond.'

'All the same, I want you to know.'

'Very well; I am listening.'

Denny exhaled. 'My true name is Mor Dennahelm, Prince of Sanctos, grandson of Emperor Antonio, and twelfth in line to the throne of the Sanctian Empire.'

Abigone smiled.

'Well?' said Denny. 'What do you think?'

'Somehow, I am not surprised,' she said.

'But don't ever call me Mor Dennahelm,' he said. 'I go by Denny.'

'I think I might need to sit down,' she said.

They sat by a desk, and Abigone started to laugh.

'Is it funny?' he said.

'Yes, Denny, it is. I shall have to get used to calling you that; though I won't if there are others around. Prince Denny of Sanctos. I assume you must know Princess Hygilt?'

'I know her. She's my cousin; well, my second cousin, to be exact. She's one of my favourite relatives. Do you know her?'

'I know her quite well. My father abducted her last year, and we spent some time together in Upper Down.'

'Your father did what? Is she all right?'

'She's fine. Hygilt was the reason the Sanctians laid siege to Upper Down. I also met Count Sebastian.'

Denny smiled. 'Uncle Sebastian taught me how to swordfight. I went to school with his children.'

'And that was where you learned how to do all of the things you did in the clearing. Hygilt told me about the education she had received.'

'Emperor Antonio had us all drilled as if we were in his personal little army. It was exhausting.' His smile faded. 'They would all hate me if they knew I was a Master. Even Hygilt. I have no brothers or sisters; I grew up with my cousins.'

'Give Hygilt a chance,' said Abigone. 'She also loathed the fact that I was a Maker, but she had softened her stance by the time she left Upper Down. Why is it that you don't seem to be aware of the events that nearly caused the destruction of my homeland?'

'Before I arrived here, I was in hiding. We stayed away from large centres of the population, and didn't hear any news. Our sole aim was to make it to Klef Mordain.'

'Do you think the empire knows that you are here?'

'No. They think I am in Geathan.'

'Why would they think that?'

'My other grandfather, my father's father, was the last king of Geathan, before the Sanctians annexed it. If a throne of Geathan existed, then I would be its heir. My father wants me to use my Master abilities to reclaim what he sees as my inheritance.'

'You are not only a Prince of Sanctos, but the rightful King of Geathan? This gets better. What is Geathan like? I don't know much about it.'

'I have never been there. I had never left Sanctos until my father and I fled last year. He discovered that I was a Master; no one else on Sanctos knows. My father talks about Geathan as though it were some lost paradise, crushed underfoot by the wicked Sanctians. He thinks the people there would explode with joy if I arrived with a crown on my head. He's wrong, though. Nothing is ever as simple as that.'

'You are half-Sanctian.'

'Yes. I loved the concept of the Sanctian Empire when I was growing up – right until the moment I realised I was a Master. That opened my eyes to my grandfather's folly. He is lashing out at what he doesn't understand. Do you recall what you said to Lady Fyenna, during the lecture on the Golden Era of Masters and Makers? You told her that the emperor hates us for religious reasons, and you weren't wrong about that, although I didn't want to say so at the time. He sees us as sacrilegious – walking blasphemies. How can you argue with someone who believes that? There is no logic that can persuade the zealot. I just hope he dies soon.'

Abigone furrowed her brow. 'Can you say that about your own grandfather?'

'He is not a nice man, Abigone. I have seen him enraged, and have never been more frightened. All of my cousins would hide if he was in a bad mood. His eldest son Prince Mikel is far more reasonable; so too is his brother Prince Valentino. Either would probably repeal the law against Masters and Makers if they came to power. Until then, we are stuck with Emperor Antonio.'

'My father was also a wicked man,' said Abigone, 'though I refused to believe the evidence that was before my eyes. The truth came to me as a slowly-growing realisation. Anyway, what does Lady Fyenna intend to do with you now that she understands who you are? Please don't tell me that you are leaving Klef Mordain.'

'She isn't going to do anything about it, and I don't want to leave. I have missed being with you this past month; I mean, I have missed seeing all of the Makers.'

Abigone gave him a smile. 'I have missed you too, Denny.'

'Even though I was terrible company? I could see how annoyed you were that I wouldn't tell you the truth.'

'I was annoyed, but I still preferred your company over that of Reath and Nyli, though I am fond of them both.'

'I am relieved that I can be honest with you. I hated that damn oath.'

'Yet you kept your word.'

The door to the classroom opened, and Lady Fyenna walked in. 'Valiance, it is time for you to leave.'

'Can he stay a little longer, ma'am?' said Abigone.

'I'm afraid not. You need to get back to your studies, Abigone. Have you discussed the matter?'

'We have, ma'am,' said Denny. 'Abigone now knows the truth about me.'

'And did she promise to keep such information to herself?'

'I did, ma'am,' said Abigone. 'I will keep my word as well as Prince Denny kept his.'

'See that you do not refer to him by that name once you have left this room.'

Denny and Abigone got to their feet. They looked at each other a little awkwardly, as though neither was sure how to part. Denny wanted to embrace her, then he realised that he actually wanted to kiss her.

'When will I see you again?' he said.

Abigone glanced at Fyenna.

'I am arranging for the Makers to visit the Master school a few days from now,' Fyenna said. 'You won't have long to wait.'

'But I thought there were to be no more joint lessons, ma'am?' said Abigone.

'There are to be no more excursions outwith the walls of the two schools. We are still permitted to visit each other.'

Abigone turned back to Denny. 'That pleases me.'

Denny inclined his head. 'Your Highness.'

Fyenna rolled her eyes. 'Enough. Oh, for a world without kings and queens. Come, Valiance; your carriage is waiting.'

CHAPTER 21
IDLE HANDS

Old City, Klef Mordain – 6th Day of Lamenta 108

Amery stared out of his living room window at the people on the street.

'You don't look well, sir,' said Annalise. 'You are drinking too much, not getting enough sleep, and I wish you would sit down and eat a proper meal. There are folk going hungry in this city, and we're lucky to have any food at all.'

'It isn't luck,' Amery said. 'The Sanctians are smuggling in shipments of food for the Second Empire Association to distribute to their friends and allies.'

'I don't understand. Are you saying that the food that arrives at the townhouse every few days comes from the Sanctians?'

'They bring it in by ship. With pro-Sanctians in charge of the commercial harbour, there's no one to stop them. It then gets transported to the office of the Second Empire Association for distribution among a select few. As a senior employee, I get my share at a reduced price.'

The housekeeper frowned. 'Isn't that illegal, sir?'

'And now you are complicit,' said Amery.

'But you're a lawyer, sir. Shouldn't you be upholding the law?'

'The statutes of Klef Mordain are no longer worth the paper they are written on,' he said. 'But don't worry, we are protected. The secret police have been told not to touch us. You won't be going to prison.'

'There are no prisons in Klef Mordain, sir.'

'Quite right. Well then, you won't be gutted and strung up from a lamppost.'

'Are you certain that we are safe? I heard there was trouble in Nether Hall again yesterday; folk fighting over a few scraps at the market. I saw smoke on the horizon.'

'The walls of the Old City will keep out the hungry mobs,' he said. 'Is my coffee ready?'

The housekeeper narrowed her eyes at him. 'Yes, sir.'

'Are you disappointed in me, Annalise? Did you think you were working for an upright citizen?'

'I knew you liked to cut corners, sir; but this? If it weren't for Princess Abigone, I would say that we should leave Klef Mordain. It is getting too dangerous here. People are being killed on the streets, and decent folk are staying in their houses with all of the doors locked.'

'It will calm down when the Sanctians take over.'

'Is that what you want, sir – the Sanctians to come here and rule the city?'

'It's what my employers want. No, my employer, singular. There is only Lord Tain now.'

'I will fetch your coffee, sir.'

Amery continued to gaze out of the window. He considered not going in to work that day. The convivial atmosphere in the offices of the Second Empire Association had dissipated into a grim and sullen bitterness since Lady Ursula's assassination, and Lord Tain had become less concerned with maintaining the appearance that their activities were within the bounds of the law. Consequently, Amery and his small legal team had little to do on a day-to-day basis, and there was only so much shuffling of papers to go round. Did it matter, so long as the wages kept coming? The Sanctian warships were bringing more than food to the quays of the commercial harbour. They had also filled the coffers of the Second Empire Association with gold, as well as delivering some undocumented crates that were sitting in the basement. Amery had been told not to go near them, but he could guess their contents – weapons.

He heard a noise behind him.

'Place the coffee onto the side table,' he said.

'I'm not your fucking coffee boy,' said Lothar.

Amery turned. 'What are you doing here?' he said. 'Why are you back from work so early?'

Lothar glared at him, then he sat down on a couch, an enraged look in his eyes.

'Well?' said Amery.

'I've lost my job,' he said. 'The commercial harbour has closed the southern warehouses – there's not enough work any more. Three hundred dockworkers were told to go home and not come back, and I was one of them.'

'Oh.'

'Damn the Sanctians, and damn the Corse,' said Lothar. 'I curse them both. A few months ago, there were dozens of ships coming and going every day, and now? The harbour is like a fucking graveyard.'

Annalise came in with a tray.

'Lothar has lost his job,' said Amery.

'I know,' said Annalise. 'I could hear him cursing and swearing from the kitchen. Mister Lothar will have to clean himself up and go out to look for another job.'

'Where?' said Lothar. 'There's no work, and there are thousands of men like me with no job. Take a look at any street corner, and you'll see them. And I'm a damn foreigner here; I have no chance.'

'My salary will cover us all,' said Amery. 'Unless... No. Hmm.'

'What are you wittering about?' said Lothar.

'I was contemplating getting you a job at the Second Empire Association,' said Amery. 'They currently have a need for able-bodied men with a military background.'

'Forget it!' Lothar snapped. 'I refuse to work for that shower of bastards. And I know what kind of work they'd give me. I'd be a bodyguard for some hopeless traitor, or worse; I'd be roaming the streets with an armed mob, beating up anybody who disagrees with them.'

'It was only an idea.'

'Well, you can take that idea and shove it up your arse.'

'Show a little gratitude,' said Annalise. 'We are all dependent upon Mister Amery's generosity. He has four of us to pay for.'

'Fuck this city,' muttered Lothar. 'All I want to do is find Princess Abigone and go back to Upper Down. If I knew where she was, I'd take her out of Klef Mordain today.'

'There are literally dozens of agents looking for the whereabouts of Princess Abigone,' said Amery. 'If they can't find her, then I doubt that you would be able to do it.'

Lothar eyed him. 'And why are they looking for her? Tell us, Amery – what would the Second Empire Association do with Abigone if they found her? And don't give me any of your weasel excuses. Tell us in plain language.'

'Uh...'

'They would kill her, wouldn't they?' Lothar went on. 'Your beloved employer, the people who keep us fed and able to live in a fucking mansion – they would murder our princess if they got their hands on her.'

'We don't know that for certain.'

'The entire city knows that the Second Empire Association is working for the damn Sanctians; don't try to deny it.'

'I'm not. So, Lothar, about the dockworkers – who are they blaming for their misfortunes?'

'I'm not playing this game, Amery.'

'But who do they blame more – the Sanctians, or the Corse?'

'Do you think dockworkers are stupid? They all understand what's going on. They see the Sanctian warships coming and going, and they know that the Corse has made a mess of things. The reservists are mustered, then they are all sent home again. Crimes are being committed openly, and no one is being punished. It's more dangerous to hold the wrong opinion than it is to rob someone in the street. Like everyone else, the dockworkers are tired of it. Some of them actually long for the Sanctian army to get here, so then at least it will be over.'

'Would they fight if the Sanctians arrive?'

'I don't know. Some would, some wouldn't, I suppose. There's no leadership coming from the Corse, only confusion.'

Amery downed his coffee. 'I had better go.'

'Will you be working late tonight, sir?' said Annalise.

'Probably not. I will see you both later.'

Amery walked to the front door. He took a coat from a peg and stepped outside. His carriage was waiting for him, and the two drivers were standing by one wheel.

'Good morning, sir,' said one. 'The association?'

Amery nodded, then he climbed aboard. The drivers stepped up onto the bench, and the carriage got underway. A few armed men were standing by a junction, protecting the elegant neighbourhood from rioters and thieves, and Amery wondered who was paying them to be there. The next group of men he saw were unemployed workers. Just as Lothar had stated, large numbers of them were lingering by several street corners, and several of them eyed the carriage as it passed. Further on, Amery watched as a man was punched and kicked to the ground by three others, while onlookers did nothing to intervene. Amery tried to imagine what it would be like if thousands of Sanctian soldiers were patrolling the streets. They would restore order in a matter of hours, wouldn't they? But what if rebels and insurgents hid in the tunnels? Assassins were already using the vast underground network to appear and disappear at will. For the first time, Amery seriously considered leaving Klef Mordain. He could make for the south, and into the civilised and peaceful domains of the Central Provinces. He would have to get past the Sanctian army encamped along the Great Northern Highway, but he was still in possession of identity documents that marked him out as a citizen of the Sanctian Empire, so he would probably be allowed through. He would have to leave Lothar and Annalise behind, as they would no doubt insist upon waiting for Princess

Abigone, but his two drivers were from Lesser Down, and he might be able to convince them to make the journey back to their homeland.

The carriage stopped fifty yards from the entrance to the alley leading to the offices of the Second Empire Association. Four armed men employed by the association caught sight of Amery as he stepped down to the cobbles, and they escorted him to the front door, where more armed men had gathered. Amery squeezed past them, and entered the building. He walked to the small office where the legal team worked, and found them sitting at their desks with nothing to do.

'Good morning, Mister Amery,' said Loryn, standing. 'Is there anything for us today?'

'I don't think so,' said Amery, 'but I want to speak to Lord Tain, to ask him.'

'I'm amazed that we still have jobs, sir,' said the other notary. 'We've had little to do for over a month.'

'Are you thinking of leaving us?' said Amery.

'No, sir. Besides, no one else would employ us now, not after we've worked for the association.'

'Have any of you seen Lord Tain this morning?'

The team shook their heads.

'Might I have a discreet word, sir?' said Loryn.

'Of course.'

She smiled at him, and he tried to keep his eyes on her face.

'That's a nice dress you're wearing today,' he said, as they walked into an empty room.

'Thank you, sir.'

He closed the door. 'What is it you wanted to talk about?'

'I did happen to see Lord Tain this morning, sir.'

'Why couldn't you mention this when we were with the others?'

'I didn't wish to cause any upset.'

'You're speaking in riddles, Loryn.'

'I went down to the basement to collect some paper when I got here, sir, and that was where I saw Lord Tain. I don't think he saw me. He had… well, sir, he had blood on his hands. He opened a door, and I heard someone inside a room. A man. He was in pain, sir. Then Lord Tain went inside and locked the door.'

'I see.'

'Do you, sir?'

'Perhaps Lord Tain is administering treatment to a wounded colleague.'

'Perhaps, sir. Or…'

'Or what?'

'Do I need to say it, sir? It appeared to me as though Lord Tain was in the midst of torturing someone in that room.'

'You should be careful not to make any wild allegations, Loryn. And don't mention this to anyone else.'

'As you will it, sir.'

'Torture is illegal,' Amery said, 'and the Second Empire Association does not participate in illegal activities. Is that understood?'

'Yes, sir.'

'Now, the basement, you say? I had better go down there. I need five minutes with Lord Tain.'

Loryn reached out and placed a hand onto his arm. 'Sir, I am starting to get a little… concerned about recent developments. I was followed on my way home from work yesterday by three men wearing hoods. I couldn't sleep all night. I cannot abide the thought of thugs knowing where I live.'

'Did you lock your doors and windows?'

'Of course I did, sir, but would that really deter someone who wished to do me harm? I do not want to be killed because I work for the association.'

'I'll rustle up a few men to guard your home.'

'No, thank you. The thugs who work for the association are every inch as bad as those working for Lord Metrius.'

'Then what do you want from me, Loryn?' He laughed. 'Do you want me to find you a spare room in my townhouse?'

'That would be wonderful, sir; thank you so much. I shall move in this evening.'

'What? But, I was only...' He sighed. 'Fine. I have plenty of space, after all.'

They walked out of the room, and Amery took a flight of stairs down to the basement. He muttered a few curses. It was bad enough having Loryn around the office all day, distracting him with her uncommon good looks; how would he cope with her in his home as well? And he could imagine Lothar's response to her arrival.

He reached the basement level, and wandered the corridors for a few minutes, looking for any signs of Lord Tain. He came to where the paper supplies were kept. If Loryn's recollections were accurate, Lord Tain should be close by, but there were several doors in the vicinity, and he might be behind any of them. Amery stood still, and listened. After a few moments; he heard a muffled cry coming from a door to his right, and he walked up it. He cupped his ear against the door, and heard another cry, then a voice raised in anger.

Amery knocked on the door. 'Lord Tain, sir? Do you have a moment?'

The door opened a fraction, and Tain peered out.

'What is it, Amery?' he said. 'I'm in the middle of something.'

'Well, sir, I was wondering if you want me to get started on the new contracts for the property leases. They have been outstanding for a few weeks, and they need your approval for...'

'I couldn't give a shit about any of that, Amery.'

'But, sir, some members of my team are starting to get a little anxious, as the work has recently dried up, and...'

'None of them are going to lose their jobs, if that's what's worrying you,' said Tain. 'I don't care if they have nothing to do; we can afford them. Send them home if you want. And go home yourself. I'll send for you if I need you. And yes, before you ask, everyone will continue to get paid.'

'Are you sure there's nothing I can help you with, sir?'

Tain rolled his eyes. 'Are you any good at interrogating suspects?'

He opened the door a bit further, and Amery saw a man lying on the stained and filthy floorboards of the room inside. He was covered in blood and bruises, and his hands had been bound behind his back.

'This bastard knows the location of the secret schools; I'm sure of it,' said Tain.

Amery suppressed a wave of nausea. 'Should you be doing this yourself, sir? I thought you had people for this sort of thing.'

'My sister was butchered in the street, Amery. I am entitled to take my revenge.'

'And is this the man who murdered Lady Ursula, sir?'

'No. He's a lowly blacksmith, but his brother was a Master by the name of Drummond. He was a tough one to crack, and no mistake. No matter what I did to him, he refused to talk. In the end, I had to stab him in the heart.'

'You killed a Master, sir?'

'I did, and not just any Master. Drummond was the one who helped Fyenna at the Battle of Hader Pull all those years ago.'

'How did you find him, sir?'

'Fyenna's husband gave his name to one of Lord Penny's agents. If anyone knew the location of the secret schools, it was Drummond; and yet he preferred to die an agonising death rather than tell me anything useful. That's why I had his brother brought up from the cells. He's already admitted that he knew Drummond was a Master. No matter how long it takes, I am going to find out whatever he knows.' He turned to face the cell. 'Do you hear me, Heston? I'm going to hurt you, and I'm going to enjoy it.' He faced Amery again. 'Now piss off, and let me get on with my job.'

'Yes, sir.'

Tain closed the door, and Amery heard the key turn in the lock. A moment later, an anguished cry of pain sounded from within the room, and Amery backed away. He turned, and hurried up the stars to the ground floor of the building. He entered the office of the legal team, and sat down, his head in his hands.

'Are you all right, sir?' said a scribe.

'No. Everyone – go home.'

The others glanced at each other.

'Have we lost our jobs, sir?' said the scribe.

'No. You are all still employed by the Second Empire Association but, as there is no work for you at the present moment, you are to return to your homes. You will still be paid in full. I will send you a message when it's time to come back to the office.'

Three of his team rose to their feet. They collected their coats, and filed out of the room.

'Why are you still here, Loryn?' Amery said.

'Well, sir,' she said, 'as I will be residing with you, I thought it better to wait until you are ready to depart.'

'Oh, right. I had forgotten that.'

'Are you planning on remaining here for the rest of the day, sir?'

'No, I'm going home, too. I just need a minute. I bumped into Lord Tain in the basement, and I had the misfortune to get a clear look at what he was doing.'

'Oh. Do you know the identity of the... other party?'

'Sorry, Loryn, but I'm not at liberty to disclose what I saw or heard down there.'

'I understand, sir.'

Amery stood. 'Let's go. I need to get out of here.'

'Yes, sir.'

She passed him his coat, and they walked to the front of the building. The men on duty allowed them to pass, then a few others escorted them to Amery's waiting carriage.

'Back home,' Amery said to the drivers, then he helped Loryn climb into the carriage.

'Who else lives in your house, sir?' Loryn said, as the carriage set off.

'I have a housekeeper, the two drivers, and a... butler. Well, he isn't actually a butler, more of a handyman, or a bodyguard. He worked down at the commercial harbour, but he lost his job.'

'Then there will be six of us in the same house?'

'It is a very large house, Loryn. There will be plenty of room for you.'

'I want to thank you again for allowing me to stay with you, sir. I already feel much safer. I presume that you have no objections if I work in the house?'

'None. You can do what you like. Well, not quite. I would rather you didn't invite anyone over. The fewer people who know where I live, the better.'

'Perhaps your handyman might be willing to go to my home, sir, to collect some of my possessions?'

'I can ask him.'

She glanced out of the window. 'So many out-of-work men,' she said. 'What a tragedy for the city. The blockade is strangling us a little more each day. Are the markets well stocked close to your house?'

'We don't need to go to the market,' he said. 'Food is delivered to us twice a week.'

'From where, sir?'

Amery hesitated. Loryn wasn't supposed to know about the secret shipments of food from the Sanctians to the Second Empire Association, but then he remembered that he had already told Annalise about it.

'We get our food from the Sanctians,' he said. 'Their ships smuggle it to shore, and certain members of the association are given the food at a discounted rate.'

Loryn's eyes narrowed. 'That is against the law, sir.'

'So is what I just saw in the basement, Loryn. What do you want me to say? I am supporting four other people; five now, with you coming to stay. Would you rather we all starved?'

'No, sir.'

'Is this going to be a problem? Tell me now, and we can stop the carriage.'

'It won't be a problem, sir.'

. . .

One of the drivers opened the side door of the carriage when they pulled up in front of Amery's townhouse.

'Will that be all for today, sir?' said the driver.

'Most likely,' said Amery.

'This is a very elegant neighbourhood, sir,' said Loryn, as she gazed at the tall, stone buildings.

'It's one of the best,' said Amery. 'Come inside and I'll show you around.'

He gave her a quick tour of the lower floors, then they met Annalise, who was preparing food for that evening's dinner.

'Annalise,' said Amery, as the housekeeper glanced up from the stove, 'this is Miss Loryn. Loryn, this is my housekeeper.'

Annalise wiped her hands on her apron. 'I'm delighted to meet you, Miss Loryn; will you be staying for dinner?'

'She will be staying indefinitely,' said Amery. 'She's moving in; her old house has become unsafe.'

Annalise raised an eyebrow.

'Is Lothar in?' said Amery.

'No, sir. He went out to see if he could find a shop that sells whisky.'

'But we have about fifty bottles of wine in the house.'

'He says he won't be drinking wine again. He said... well, he was rather uncomplimentary about many things, then he stormed off. He is still upset about losing his job. So, Miss Loryn, do you work with Mister Amery?'

'Yes, ma'am,' said Loryn. 'I am a notary in his office.'

'We shall need to find her a room,' said Amery.

'There is a spare bedroom on the top floor, next to mine,' said Annalise. 'If you like, I can get it ready for someone to move in. It will take a few hours, though; we have been using it for storage.'

'You do that, thank you,' said Amery.

'I will let you know when it's ready, sir.'

'We shall be in my study.'

Amery and Loryn left the kitchen, and went up another flight of stairs to where Amery's little-used study was located. They walked in, and Amery gestured to a chair.

Loryn sat.

'Now, what shall we do?' said Amery. 'We have no work for the rest of the day.'

'This may sound selfish, sir,' said Loryn, 'but couldn't we just relax for a few hours? My nerves are a little frayed. Is that a bottle of wine on the shelf?'

'It is. Would you like a glass?'

'Would that be all right, sir?'

'Before we go any further, we are not at work, so there is no need to call me sir. And of course it's all right. I might have a glass myself.'

He took the bottle from the shelf, and found two glasses in a cabinet. He filled them, and passed one to Loryn.

'Annalise seems nice,' Loryn said, as Amery sat down next to her.

'She has been very helpful.'

'Is she discreet? Is she likely to gossip?'

'She rarely leaves the house,' said Amery. He sipped some wine. 'That's better. We should probably only have the one glass, though.'

Four hours later, Amery and Loryn were both drunk. So drunk, in fact, that Amery had told Loryn everything that he had seen and heard in the basement with Lord Tain, even though he knew he wasn't supposed to. Loryn had gasped when he had told her that Tain had slain the Master who had helped Fyenna at the Battle of Hader Pull, and she had put a hand to her mouth when Amery had mentioned that the Master's brother was the one currently being interrogated. Despite the breach of confidentiality, it had pleased Amery to think that he had managed to keep Loryn's rapt attention. Four empty bottles of wine were sitting on the desk in Amery's study, and Loryn was laughing as Amery regaled her with stories about Duke Hector of Upper Down.

'But Kilbride wasn't having any of it,' Amery said. 'She told me she'd rather die than marry that great oaf. And so, I helped her to escape.'

Loryn smiled. 'That was brave of you.'

'I have my moments.'

'Did I ever tell you that I find you very attractive?'

Amery blinked. 'What?'

'It's true. I have had a crush on you since I started working for the association.'

'That's just the wine talking.'

'It's the wine that's making me talk, but the wine didn't create my feelings for you, Amery.'

'Uh, well... thank you, I guess.'

'Do you ever picture us together?'

'I try not to.'

'Don't you like me?'

'No, I like you, but... we work together, Loryn.'

'I don't care. Do you know what I want to do right now? I want to tear your clothes off, and then I want to...'

The door opened. 'That's the room ready, sir,' said Annalise.

Amery turned. 'What?'

'The room, sir; it's ready for Miss Loryn.' Her eyes narrowed at the sight of the wine bottles. 'That's all I came to say, sir. I will leave you two alone. Dinner will be two hours from now.'

'Uh, thank you.'

Loryn laughed as the housekeeper closed the door, then she gazed at Amery. 'Will you show me to my room, sir?'

'If you like,' he said.

He stood, then swayed a little. 'I might have done that too quickly,' he said. He picked up the glasses and another bottle of wine, and led Loryn up to the top floor of the townhouse. He opened the door to the spare room, and saw that it had been thoroughly cleaned and aired. There was a flower in a vase, and fresh sheets and blankets had been placed onto the bed. They went inside, and Loryn closed the door.

Amery walked up to the bedside table, and placed the bottle and the glasses onto it.

'Would you like more wine?' he said.

He turned, just as Loryn was slipping the dress from her shoulders.
'I, uh... Are you sure about this, Loryn? The wine... maybe...'
'Shut up, Amery,' she said.
'All right. I can manage that.'
She took his hand, and pulled him onto the bed.

CHAPTER 22
COMPROMISED

Old City, Klef Mordain – 7th Day of Lamenta 108

Abigone and the other Makers climbed the stairs of the Master school towards the classrooms. As Fyenna had promised, only a few days had elapsed after Denny's visit for the girls to travel to the boys' school.

Mister Tobold was waiting for them at the top of the stairs. He inclined his head towards Fyenna.

'Welcome back to the Master school, my lady,' he said. 'How was your journey?'

'Slow and tiring,' she said. 'We went through the tunnels rather than risk the streets. Are the boys gathered together?'

'They are, ma'am. This way.'

Tobold led them along a passageway, and they entered the study hall, where all of the young Masters were waiting. Constans raised a hand to greet Raewyn, while Abigone smiled at Denny, who smiled back.

'Take your seats, girls,' said Fyenna. 'Sit on the right-hand side of the room, as the boys are on the left. Head Master Tobold and I would like to say a few words.'

Vesta joined Fyenna and Tobold and they walked to the far end of the room, from where they could see all of the students. Abigone sat down next to Stanza and Raewyn, while Reath and Nyli took their places behind them.

'Eyes to the front,' said Fyenna. 'You will have time to talk to each other later. A lot has happened since we were last gathered together. The death of Master Drummond has been a terrible blow to us all, but I want to assure you that we will try our best to keep things as normal as possible. I know that you have concerns, but let me be clear – your safety is my primary objective. For years, this city has sheltered young Masters and Makers from all over the Central Provinces, and beyond, and it is my fervent hope that we shall continue to do this long into the future. Disregard any rumours you might hear; Klef Mordain is not on the verge of collapse. It is true that the blockade by land and sea has caused some measure of suffering among the populace, but this does not mean that we are ready to capitulate to the Sanctians. Far from it. Our resilience only grows. I would also like to formally announce that Mister Tobold's promotion to the position of Head Master is now permanent. He is the youngest Head Master in the history of this school, but I have no doubt that he will excel in the role. Master Tobold, would you care to say a few words?'

'Thank you, my lady,' Tobold said. 'I am under no illusions that I can fill the shoes of Master Drummond. Our former Head Master was an exceptional man, and I considered him a mentor and a good friend. I may make some mistakes, as I grow into my new role. If I do, then I am sure you will point them out to me. With only one teacher in the Master school, however, some things will have to change. From now on, Constans shall act as my assistant in the classroom. He will supervise the younger first years, Ignatius and Salus; while I concentrate on the older boys. I will also be passing some administrative responsibilities on to the broad shoulders of Valiance. In this way, by relying on the two oldest boys in the school, I am confident that we can nurture a safe and rewarding teaching environment.' He glanced at Fyenna.

'Thank you,' said Fyenna. 'We, the teachers, are now going to leave you all for a short time, so that you can talk among yourselves. I'm sure you have much to say to each other.'

The three teachers strode from the room, and Vesta closed the door. At once, a hubbub of noise arose from the students. Constans got up, and Abigone moved out of the way so that he could sit next to Raewyn. Reath also got up, and wandered over to the front row of boys, where Marlow and Aplin were. Abigone went and sat down by Denny, who was sitting alone at the back of the room.

'Hello,' she said.

'Hello, Abigone. There was something I was supposed to do when I last visited the Maker school, but I forgot.'

'Yes? What was that?'

'I was meant to see how Eshia was doing. As soon as I got back here, Master Tobold asked me, and I had to confess that it had slipped my mind.'

'I suppose you had other things to think about. Eshia is heartbroken, as you would expect, and we haven't seen much of her. Lady Fyenna asked her if she wanted to come along with us today, but she declined the invitation. Did you tell anyone about...?'

'No. I'm still Valiance to everyone in the Master school. No one here knows.'

'I want to say your real name,' she whispered.

'I want to hear you say it.'

She gazed at him, then looked away. 'I wish we had more time to get to know each other. We first met over five months ago, and yet we've barely had a chance to talk alone.'

'I know what you mean. I have a confession.'

She smiled. 'Another one?'

'You might be able to guess this one. The truth, Abigone, is that I haven't been able to stop thinking about you. I see your face when I close my eyes, and I spend all day hoping that I will see you again. If this is too soon or too much, then tell me. I don't want to push you away.'

Abigone raised an eyebrow. 'It is a little soon for that sort of declaration; or I think it is. To be honest, I don't have much experience in this field. Are you saying that you wish to court me?'

'If that's the correct expression, then yes. It's odd; I was brought up to expect an arranged marriage. My grandfather has had a say in every marriage within my family for decades. I never imagined that I might have a choice in the matter. Now that I... have met someone I like, I have no idea what to do next.'

'I know exactly how you feel. I was betrothed to Prince Henry for months, and I never once laid eyes on him. My father chose my sisters' husbands, and he selected my brother's wife. It was all I knew. You are not alone in your uncertainty, so at least we understand each other.'

'May I court you, Abigone?'

She smiled. 'You may.'

He smiled back at her. 'That wasn't too difficult.'

Reath cackled with laughter. 'Abigone and Valiance are courting each other! I just heard them say it.'

'You shouldn't have been eavesdropping,' said Abigone.

'It's too late for that, Abigone,' said Reath. 'Did you hear that Nyli? You were too slow, sister; Valiance is taken.'

Abigone frowned as everyone in the study hall turned to stare at her and Denny.

'Courtship between students is forbidden,' said Stanza. 'You are going to get into trouble.'

'Oh shut up, Stanza,' said Raewyn. 'It's none of your business what they do.'

'Thank you, Raewyn,' said Denny. 'Frankly, I don't care what any of you think. Abigone and I are eighteen, and no one can stop us.'

'I think Lady Fyenna might have something to say about that,' said Stanza.

Reath groaned aloud. 'Are you going to tell her, you little telltale?'

'Someone has to tell her; the rules are there for a reason.'

'What about Raewyn and Constans, eh? They're always together.'

'Stanza has mentioned this to Lady Fyenna on several occasions,' said Raewyn. 'Haven't you, Stanza?'

'It's not my fault,' said Stanza. 'It's our duty to report those who break the rules.'

'But nobody else feels the need to go running off to Lady Fyenna,' said Raewyn. 'You should mind your own business.'

'Stop arguing,' said Marlow. 'You girls are like cats fighting in a bag.'

'Is that right?' said Reath. 'At least we don't stink. When's the last time you had a bath, Marlow?'

Marlow narrowed his eyes. 'I had a bath this morning.'

'I told you,' said Nyli. 'It's the soap he uses.'

Marlow sniffed his armpits. 'What's wrong with my soap?'

Constans laughed. 'It does have a rather odd aroma. Did you carry it all the way from Subnestia?'

'I bought it in a market in Lesser Down.'

'Are you sure it's actually soap?' said Reath. 'It smells like the stuff you use to clean toilets.'

Abigone glanced at Denny. He caught her gaze, and moved his hand under the desk to take hold of hers. They intertwined their fingers, and the simple gesture made Abigone shiver with joy. He had told her that he couldn't stop thinking about her and, in truth, she had also been thinking of him. She studied his face. He had kind eyes and an open, almost boyish expression; and he was a prince. Was that why her feelings towards him had changed? No, it went back to that day in the clearing, when they had sat together on the grass before the Westlanders had arrived. She remembered her annoyance when Master Tobold had suggested that she find a new partner; she hadn't wanted to be separated from Denny, even though at the time she couldn't have explained why. And then... well, then Denny had killed a Westlander and charged off into the forest to rescue Nyli. After that, she knew he would never have to prove himself to her; he had revealed his true worth in a few moments of reckless courage. His being a prince hadn't formed her feelings, but it had legitimised them in her mind. Her father had always said that only a prince would be good enough for her, and part of her had believed him.

'I would like you if you weren't a prince,' she whispered, 'but I'm glad you are.'

At the front of the study hall, Reath was still baiting Marlow, much to the boy's irritation.

'No girl will ever want to go near you if you smell like that,' she said.

Marlow shrugged. 'Do you think I want you coming anywhere near me?'

'Sit down and be quiet, Reath,' said Raewyn. 'Everyone is tired of you playing the fool.'

'What was that?' said Reath, turning. Her fists clenched. 'Are you calling me a fool? I will punch that smug expression off your face, you stuck-up bitch.'

'That's quite enough,' said Constans. 'There is no need for such vulgar behaviour.'

'Shut your mouth, Constans,' said Reath. 'You're just as bad as Raewyn. The two of you think you're so superior to the rest of us. *My daddy is an aristocrat, and you others are merely peasants.* That's what you think, isn't it? Well, Marlow might be a stinky peasant, but at least he didn't shit his pants when a few Westlanders turned up. We all saw you, Constans, quaking and trembling. Marlow's weird soap will wash off, but nothing will change the fact that you're a coward. Are you not embarrassed for him, Raewyn? You should be. If my boyfriend did something like that, I'd die of shame.'

Constan's face turned red, and he jumped to his feet and charged down to the front of the room to face Reath. He drew back a hand to strike her, then Marlow barged into him, pushing him back.

'Leave her alone!' Marlow cried.

The study hall stilled.

'Get out of the way,' said Constans. 'Reath deserves what's coming to her. For months, she has been insulting and threatening everyone. She treats us as though we were a joke, and look at the things she's said about you, Marlow.'

'I don't care,' said Marlow. 'You don't hit girls.'

'You can't beat me in a fight, Marlow.'

'Maybe not, but at least one of my punches will land.'

Denny released Abigone's hand and walked down to the front of the room. Constans launched his fist at Marlow's face, and Denny raised an arm to block it.

'What are you doing?' cried Constans.

'I'm preventing you from making an idiot of yourself, Constans. Reath is fourteen years old. Yes, she has a tongue on her that could crack granite, but you don't use violence against words.'

'She called me a coward.'

'What you are doing now is far more cowardly than the way you behaved in the clearing. No one knows how they will react when armed horsemen charge at them.'

'You knew,' said Nyli. 'You knew what to do.'

'I have faced dozens of horses charging at me,' said Denny. 'Do you think that was the first time? I had to practice that move, over and over again, even though I got bruised and beaten down into the dirt more times than I can recall. The first time a horse charged at me? Well, let's just say that I hardly behaved with much honour or dignity. It was Marlow and Stanza who showed true courage that day; I was reacting to years of training. Think on that, Constans. Use what happened in the clearing as a lesson, and pledge to do better next time.'

'I wasn't brave,' said Stanza in a low voice.

'You pushed Reath behind you,' said Denny, 'even though she has hardly been kind to you. It is easy to fight for your friends, far harder to defend those who belittle you. Would you agree, Reath?'

Reath nodded. 'I suppose so.'

'Has Stanza not then earned a tiny amount of respect from you for her selfless act?'

'She's not all bad, but she is a telltale; you can't deny that.'

'I don't care if she tells Lady Fyenna about me and Abigone. Why should you?'

'Maybe Abigone cares,' said Reath. 'Did you think about that?'

'Thank you for thinking of me, Reath,' said Abigone, 'but Valiance is right. Let Stanza run to Lady Fyenna. It seems to me that Stanza is worried that she will get into trouble if she doesn't tell the Head Maker, but I'm not concerned about that.'

'Tell the Head Maker what?' said Fyenna, as she walked through the doorway. 'Class, return to your seats at once. I have an announcement.'

The young Masters and Makers went back to their benches and sat down. Stanza raised her hand.

'Make it quick, Stanza,' said Fyenna.

'Ma'am,' she said, her gaze lowered, 'Abigone and Valiance are courting.'

Fyenna frowned. 'First of all, let me say that I am hardly shocked by this revelation. Secondly, why would you feel the need to bring this up with me? Are you not concerned that your classmates will grow to mistrust you, Stanza?'

'But, it's against the rules, ma'am.'

'They are eighteen,' said Fyenna. 'I am prepared to overlook the rules in this case. Now...'

'What about Constans and Raewyn, ma'am?' Stanza went on. 'They aren't eighteen.'

'Some things are more important than the rules, Stanza,' said Fyenna. 'No more interruptions. We are going to practise our evacuation procedures. We are going to pretend that the Master school is under attack by armed agents. You will remain calm, and you will listen carefully to any instructions. Everyone, with the exception of Abigone and Valiance, will now make their way to the top of the stairs, where Master Tobold and Miss Vesta are waiting for you.'

The rest of the students filed out of the study hall, leaving Abigone and Valiance alone with Lady Fyenna.

'Close the door, Abigone,' said Fyenna.

Abigone rose from her seat and shut the door to the study hall.

'What I am about to say is not to be repeated,' said Fyenna. 'This is not a practice. I have received information from a reliable source that the location of this school may have been compromised. Note the emphasis on *may*. We might be in no danger at all, but I am not going to take any risks. We shall progress down to the tunnels, and then we shall make our way in an orderly fashion to the Maker school, where we shall stay until we better understand the situation. Is that clear?'

'Yes, ma'am,' said Denny.

'Why are you telling us, ma'am?' said Abigone.

'Because you are both adults,' said Fyenna. 'I will be relying on you. I need you to keep an eye on the younger students. Reassure them that all will be well, and make sure none of them get lost. And, if it comes to it, defend them with your lives. You have both faced peril before, so I trust that you will be able to remain calm and clear-headed. Miss Vesta and Master Tobold know that I am telling you this, so pay particular attention to any orders they give you.' She nodded. 'Let us depart.'

Abigone and Denny followed Fyenna out of the study hall, and they joined the others, who had assembled by the top of the stairs.

'Miss Vesta and I shall lead,' said Fyenna; 'followed by the girls, with Abigone at the rear. Valiance shall lead the boys, and Master Tobold shall come last. Master Tobold, ensure that all doors and hatches we pass through are firmly closed and locked behind us.'

Reath raised her hand. 'Where are we going, ma'am?'

'Haven't you read the evacuation plan, girl? Miss Vesta, did you show the plan to the first years?'

'Yes, ma'am.'

'I don't remember it,' said Reath.

'We are going to the tunnels,' said Fyenna. 'You see, this is why we have to practise this. If a real emergency occurs, we should all know what to do. Follow me.'

The students and teachers formed themselves into a long line, then Fyenna led them down the stairs to the ground floor of the school. Abigone and Denny found themselves next to each other in the line as they descended, then they waited as Fyenna unlocked a door close to where her office lay.

'This is better than classes,' said Ignatius, who was standing behind Denny on the stairs.

Reath rolled her eyes. 'So says the one who needs to attend classes more than anyone else. Can you write your name yet?'

'Yes,' said Ignatius.

'Quiet there,' said Tobold, from the rear of the line.

'You will need to listen to instructions, Reath,' said Abigone. 'If you talk, then you might not hear them.'

'It's only a practice,' said Reath.

'You should treat it as though it's the real thing,' said Denny.

Reath narrowed her eyes, but said nothing. The line began to move again, as Fyenna and Vesta passed through the unlocked door into a storeroom. Abigone had reached the bottom of the stairs, when they halted again, as Fyenna placed a key into another lock. They shuffled forward a few feet, then Miss Vesta began handing out oil lamps to a few of the young Makers.

'Take this, Raewyn,' Vesta said. 'The tunnels are in pitch darkness, so watch your step.'

Raewyn took the lamp, then Vesta passed another one to Stanza.

'Follow Lady Fyenna through the hatch in the storeroom,' said Vesta. 'Off you go, girls.'

The young Makers began filing into the room that lay next to Tobold's office. A small waist-high hatch had also been unlocked, and Abigone could see Fyenna crouching on the far side of it with a lamp in her hand.

'This way,' said Fyenna.

Raewyn passed through the hatch, followed by Nyli and Stanza.

There was a tremendous noise along the hallway as the front door of the school burst open, its locks shattered by a blow from a battering ram. Hooded men with crossbows charged into the building, and several of the students cried out in panic.

'Keep moving!' Vesta yelled. 'Don't stop. Move!'

Abigone shoved Reath towards the hatch, then she turned and saw that Denny had raced to the rear of the line to stand side by side with

Tobold. The armed men saw the fleeing students, then three of them fell to one knee, raised their unwieldy crossbows, and loosed. Denny dived to the side of the hallway as Tobold raised his hand, then the teacher was struck twice in the midriff. Tobold let out a scream of agony, as blood poured from his waist. The men dropped their crossbows, drew daggers, and charged. Abigone remained where she was, as the last of the student Makers passed into the tunnel. She pulled Salus's arm, and shoved him through the hatch, then Aplin, Constans and Ignatius also crawled through, followed by Marlow. Abigone turned, trying to catch a glimpse of Denny, but Vesta pushed her back.

'Into the hatch, Abigone,' said Vesta.

'But...'

'Do as I say,' Vesta cried. 'Follow the plan.'

Vesta shoved Abigone down and forced her through the hatch, then she followed a moment later. Vesta closed the hatch but left it unlocked, then the two young women edged back a few yards through the darkness.

'Valiance and Master Tobold are still in the school,' Abigone said.

'I know, Abigone. It was cruel timing.' She lit a lamp. 'Do you see the ceiling of this tunnel?' she said. 'You and I will wait here. If assassins come through that hatch, we will summon stone, and collapse the tunnel. Are you up to it, Abigone?'

Abigone stared at the wooden hatch, her heart torn.

'Focus, Abigone,' Vesta hissed. 'I know you can do it. Think of your stone dragons.'

Abigone glanced over her shoulder. In the distance she could see a faint light bobbing up and down as the others students followed Fyenna through the maze of tunnels.

'How did they find us?' she whispered.

'I'm not sure,' said Vesta. 'A messenger arrived when you were all talking in the study hall, but he spoke alone with Lady Fyenna.'

'If Valiance dies...'

'Don't think that; not yet. We cannot allow any agents to follow us through the tunnels. If they find the Maker school, then it's over; do you understand? All that matters now is doing our job.'

The seconds passed, each as slow as an age to Abigone, as she stared at the hatch in the flickering lamplight. She could hear nothing from the far side, but she knew that the assassins must have seen them enter the storeroom.

The handle of the hatch turned, and it began to open.

'Help us, blessed spirits,' Vesta whispered.

The hatch was pushed aside, and Denny crawled into the tunnel. Abigone rushed forward, and pulled him close with her arms.

'Help me,' he said. 'I got one of them.'

He turned and dragged a body through the hatch.

'Where are the others, Valiance?' said Vesta.

'I killed one,' he said. 'The rest are in the hallway. I locked the door of the storeroom, and they are fetching the battering ram.'

'And Master Tobold?'

Denny shook his head. 'I'm sorry, Miss Vesta. I couldn't save him. He's dead.' He closed the hatch, and pulled the body further into the tunnel. 'This one is still alive, I think,' he went on. 'What should we do with him?'

'We will take him to Lady Fyenna,' said Vesta. 'Abigone, bring down the roof of the tunnel.'

Abigone made sure that Denny, Vesta, and the body of the unconscious assassin were out of range, then she raised her hand.

'Blessed spirits,' she said, 'with your permission, summon for me a stone dragon.'

A crack ripped through the ceiling and walls of the tunnel entrance, then chunks of stone fell into the space by the hatch, flooding the tunnel with rubble and dust.

Vesta coughed, as the light from her lamp was extinguished by the flow of air.

They retreated, making their way along the dark tunnel, while Denny dragged the body along with them. After ten minutes of struggling in the pitch darkness, a lamp bobbed towards them, and Stanza's face appeared through the gloom.

'I'm here to look for you,' she said. 'Is everyone all right?' She glanced down at the body. 'Is that Master Tobold?'

'Master Tobold is dead, Stanza,' said Vesta. 'Valiance captured one of the assassins. Is Lady Fyenna far?'

'No, miss. Just a few minutes away.'

'Did she send you to find us?' said Abigone.

Stanza started to weep. 'Is... is Master Tobold really dead?'

'Don't cry, girl,' said Vesta; 'not yet. There will be plenty of time for tears once we are all safe. Lead us to Lady Fyenna.'

Stanza wiped her eyes, then she turned and began retracing her steps. The others followed her as she descended a flight of rock-cut stairs. Stanza made a series of turns at various junctions, then, after another few minutes, they emerged into a cavern, where Fyenna and the others were waiting.

'Praise the spirits,' said Fyenna, a lamp in her hand. 'I feared the worst.'

Denny collapsed panting against the wall of the cavern. 'Master Tobold sacrificed himself to save the rest of us,' he said.

'I thought you had dragged him here, Valiance,' said Fyenna. 'Tobold is dead? Did you see this with your own eyes?'

'Yes, ma'am. One of the assassins gutted him from neck to waist. I killed the man who did it, then I struck the man you see at my feet. I think he's still alive, but I might be wrong.'

'How did you get away?' said Fyenna.

'I managed to lock the door of the storeroom.'

'And the tunnel entrance? Miss Vesta?'

'Abigone collapsed the tunnel by the entrance, ma'am. No one will be able to follow us until it has been dug out.'

'May the spirits preserve the soul of Master Tobold,' Fyenna said. 'He did his duty, and laid down his life for those under his care. Let us give him a moment of silence, students, to show our respect, and to offer our thanks for his actions.'

The students bowed their heads, and Abigone saw tears running down the face of Miss Vesta.

After a minute had passed, Fyenna raised her head. 'Valiance, check the status of the man you brought with us. If he lives, bind his wrists and blindfold him, and I shall question him upon our return to the Maker school.'

'Yes, ma'am.'

'And, Valiance,' she went on, 'it has not escaped my notice that you disregarded our instructions earlier. You were supposed to remain at the front of the boys, to lead them into the tunnel. Instead, you left your position to assist Master Tobold.'

'Yes, ma'am; I did. I was concerned that assassins might reach the rear of the line before everyone had passed through the hatch.'

'Have you truly no fear, boy?'

'No, ma'am. I was terrified.'

Fyenna turned to Abigone. 'Well done, girl, for collapsing the tunnel. I would now request that you speak to your errant partner in courtship. Perhaps you could use your influence over him to ensure that he obeys orders from now on. As for you, Valiance, as the oldest boy, I am now appointing you interim Head Master. Secure the body, and we shall leave as soon as you are ready.'

'Yes, ma'am,' said Denny. He crouched by the body, then he ripped a section from the man's sleeve, and used it to bind his wrists together.

Abigone crouched down next to them.

'Is he alive?' she said.

Denny nodded.

'You are always going to rush off like that, aren't you? It's your nature to run towards danger, when everyone else is running the other way.'

'It's what I was trained to do,' he said. 'I don't consciously decide these things. My instincts take over, and I move before my brain realises what I'm doing.'

'Were you really terrified?'

Denny bound another strip of fabric round the man's eyes. 'Yes.'

'And you killed another man?'

Denny paused, and he wiped a tear from his eye. 'That, I did for Master Tobold.' He stood. 'The captive is ready, ma'am. Might I have Marlow to help me carry him?'

'You may,' said Fyenna. 'Marlow, do as your Head Master instructs. Students, we will now make our way to the Maker school. Follow me.'

CHAPTER 23
BURDENED

Old City, Klef Mordain – 8th Day of Lamenta 108

Fyenna sat in silence in the empty cavern, her lamp flickering on a stone bench next to her. She kept her eyes fixed on the entrance to the cavern, while, behind her, the metal rungs of a ladder reached up to a trapdoor in the floor of the Maker school. Fyenna couldn't remember a time when her spirits had been as low. The effort to maintain a brave face in front of Eshia, Miss Vesta and the students was exhausting, but she knew it had to be done.

Another lamp appeared by the entrance, and Lord Metrius stepped into the cave, with Portia by his side.

Fyenna got to her feet.

'Greetings, Lady Fyenna,' said Metrius.

'Greetings to you, my lord,' said Fyenna, inclining her head, 'and to you, Portia.'

The other woman said nothing.

'I heard there was one casualty,' Metrius said. 'Is that correct?'

'Yes, my lord,' said Fyenna. 'Master Tobold was slain while defending the students.'

'What a blasted shame. Another Master, dead. I also heard that you had captured one of the assassins? Does he live? Has he been securely detained?'

'Yes, my lord. He has been shackled in an adjoining cavern.'

'Have you questioned him yet?'

'No, my lord. My time has been taken up with finding room for the young Masters within the school. Some of the younger ones have been frightened by recent events, and I wanted to reassure them. Might I thank you for sending the messenger? The outcome would have been far worse if we had been taken unawares.'

'I wish I could have got the message to you sooner. My agent in the Second Empire Association placed herself into a very precarious situation in order to collect that information. There is a good chance that Lord Tain will now suspect that he has an informant working for him. It was Heston who supplied the address of the Master school, as we had feared. Lord Tain has been personally torturing him, and poor Heston is likely dead. It was also Lord Tain who murdered Master Drummond. It seems that the Second Empire Association is no longer even attempting to remain within the bounds of the law. My retaliation shall be swift and thorough.'

'Did Tain kill Drummond with his own hands?' said Fyenna. 'Lord Tain? I hadn't thought him capable of such depravity.'

'Life is a mystery, Fyenna; who knows what drives people to act like that?'

Portia frowned. 'It was revenge for Lady Ursula. Lord Tain seems to have taken exception to the murder of his sister.'

Metrius eyed Portia for a few moments.

'Is that true?' said Fyenna. 'Were we responsible for Lady Ursula's death, my lord?'

'Weren't you present in the catacombs when I announced the list of those whose lives I deemed forfeit?' said Metrius. 'Do not act surprised that I kept to my word. Lord Asquith's death was also my doing. Drowning in a bathtub is one of Portia's specialities. This coming night, there will be more casualties. If there is justice in the world, then Lord Tain will be among them.'

'Do you mean to strike at the Second Empire Association?'

'Naturally. They are traitors, Fyenna. Did you know that the Sanctians are secretly smuggling food and gold to them? They use the docks at the commercial harbour, which, as you know, is under the control of Lord Penny, who is another target on my list.'

'The Sanctians are supplying them with food?'

'Despicable, isn't it?' said Metrius. 'They gorge themselves, while their fellow citizens go hungry.'

'What are the thirty doing about all of this, my lord?'

'The thirty has ceased to exist as a coherent body. In effect, Klef Mordain has no functioning government. We are entering the end days, Fyenna. We are waging a war we cannot win, and so my only objective is to make our enemies suffer as much as possible before it all comes tumbling down.'

'I cannot accept that, my lord,' said Fyenna. 'I must retain hope, if not for my sake, then for the young students under my care.'

'Continue to grasp on to your hope, if it makes you feel better.'

'Has there been any news of my husband?'

'Nothing that I could confirm.'

'Have you heard any rumours, my lord?'

'This city is full to the brim with rumours.'

'Will you please tell me what you have heard?'

'Very well. It seems as though your dog of a husband went running into the embrace of Lord Penny, seeking protection for his betrayal of Master Drummond. If rumours are to be believed, the Sanctian ambassador then furnished Selanius with a letter of safe conduct, and Lord Penny placed him on to a ship and allowed him to flee the city.'

'My husband has left Klef Mordain?'

'I cannot confirm this with any certainty. If it is true, then your treacherous spouse will be through the Sanctian blockade by now, no doubt sailing south towards the sanctuary of the Central Provinces. I curse him. May his blood turn to vinegar, and may maggots feast upon his liver.'

Fyenna lowered her gaze.

'I would initiate a quick divorce, if I were you,' Metrius went on. 'You don't want to be tainted by your husband's shame and guilt.'

'I have a favour to ask, my lord.'

'What do you require, my lady?'

'That prisoner I spoke to some time ago, could he be brought here, to this cavern?'

'You mean Mor Galthide?' Metrius said. 'Worry not, for Portia knows all there is to know about this matter. It was she who brought Mor Galthide to my attention.' He frowned. 'My dear Fyenna, are you about to confess that you broke my strict command?'

'Valiance had a right to know.'

Anger flashed over Metrius's features. 'That was not your decision to make! I gave you clear orders not to inform the boy about his father, nor to tell him that you knew his true identity. Why have you treated me with disrespect?'

'That was not my intention, my lord.'

'No? Tell me – what was your intention?'

'Valiance is an adult. More than that, he is an exceptional young man. The assassin we captured, that was his doing. He killed the man who slew Master Tobold, and brought me a live assassin. And do you remember how he acted when we were waylaid by Westlanders? He saved the lives of three students. He deserved to know the truth for that reason alone. I have been forced to appoint him as interim Head Master; if I can trust him with that, I can trust him with the truth.'

Metrius eyed her with a cold stare. 'And now he wishes to speak to his father?'

'He does.'

'His father will bring all of his powers to bear to try to persuade his son to flee the city with him. Did you forget that aspect?'

'No, my lord. I have asked Valiance if he wishes to escape Klef Mordain. He said he wanted to stay, in order to defend his fellow students.'

'Of course he would say that to you. It's what he says to his father's face than concerns me. Did you make any promises to the boy regarding this?'

'No, my lord. I told him I would make enquiries, but I promised nothing.'

'Good. There shall be no meeting between them.'

'I agree with Fyenna,' said Portia. 'Both father and son are now aware that the other is in the city. They might ally with our enemies if we keep them from each other.'

'And they might flee the city together if they meet,' said Metrius.

'And why would you care about that, sir?'

'You heard Fyenna – the boy has proved useful. Tell me, Fyenna – can he kill from a distance, as Drummond could? Can he transform water into salt?'

'All of the records from the Master school have been lost,' said Fyenna, 'and I have not yet had a chance to ask each of the boys about their abilities.'

'Find out with all speed. If *Valiance* can kill for us, then I intend to use him as an instrument of my revenge. It is time to unleash the Masters and Makers upon the pro-Sanctians of Klef Mordain.'

'I will not cooperate with this, my lord; not unless you allow the boy to meet his father first.'

'How dare you?' Metrius cried, his voice echoing off the walls of the cavern. 'You are severely trying my patience, Fyenna.'

'Listen to what she is saying, sir,' said Portia. 'She is agreeing that Valiance can be used as a weapon, if you were to grant her this one favour.'

'Confound you both,' Metrius snapped. 'My allies are more devious than my enemies.' He took a breath. 'Very well. I shall send someone to the Maker school if Mor Galthide agrees to my terms. They will let you know when the father will be here.'

'Thank you, my lord,' said Fyenna.

Metrius waved her away with a hand. 'You blackmail me, then you offer me your gratitude? After the father meets the son, I will expect your assistance and full cooperation in the coming days. I mean to wreak havoc among the pro-Sanctians. The streets shall run with the blood of traitors. Is that clear?'

'Yes, my lord.'

'Take me to your captive.'

Fyenna inclined her head, then she led Metrius and Portia to a side door. She unlocked it, and pushed it open. Inside, a man was sitting against the wall of a small, rough cavern. His arms were bound behind his back, and an iron ring had been fastened to his left ankle. The ring was attached to a chain, the other end of which had been hammered into a wall.

The man glanced up, and he blinked in the lamplight. 'Metrius?' he whispered.

'The very same,' said Metrius.

The man stared at the floor. 'I am not frightened of you.'

'No? Then perhaps you might be frightened by the woman standing next to me?'

Portia stepped out from the shadows, and the man's face paled.

'No,' he gasped. 'Please, not Portia.'

'Adamnul?' said Portia. 'I might have guessed. Are you working for the Second Empire Association now? Shame on you.'

'Do you know this man?' said Fyenna.

'Of course,' said Portia. 'He was once a member of the secret police.'

'I earn money doing the same thing you do, Portia,' said Adamnul. 'There's no difference between us.'

'I wouldn't say that,' said Portia. 'I doubt that I would have allowed myself to be taken alive by an eighteen-year-old boy.'

'That bastard was strong, and fast. Look – there's no need to torture me. I'll talk. I'll tell you whatever you want to know.'

'That's the spirit,' said Metrius. 'Confirm for me the name of your employer.'

'It's Lord Tain, of the Second Empire Association. He supplied our team with the address of the secret Master school yesterday morning, and told us to kill everyone inside the building. It was nothing personal; just a job.'

'I see. As far as you know, is Lord Tain aware that I have placed a spy into his employ?'

Adamnul narrowed his eyes. 'A spy? No, I... Is there a spy in the Second Empire Association? Is that why the Masters were fleeing the building when we arrived? Did someone tip them off?'

'So Lord Tain does not know about the spy?'

'He'll be able to guess soon enough. He'll want to know why the operation failed.'

'Do you know the employees of the association well?'

'I know some of them.'

'If you had to guess, who would you name as the spy?'

Adamnul fell silent for a few moments. 'I would probably guess that it was one of the new recruits from the remnants of the secret police. The association has hired a few dozen of them recently, to carry out various tasks. Is it one of them?'

Metrius smiled. 'It is not. Do you happen to know any members of the legal team?'

'I'm aware of a Mister Amery. He has a few scribes and notaries assisting him, but I don't know their names.'

'Excellent. With any luck, the identity of my spy will remain hidden for a little longer.'

Adamnul spat on the floor. 'Shit. I've just realised what's happening. You wouldn't have said any of that if you were intending to let me live.'

'Your powers of deduction are commendable,' said Metrius. 'You are indeed destined to die this day.'

'What if I pledge to work for you as another spy? Send me back to the association, and I'll find out what I can, and report back to you. And, if your spy does get caught, then you'll still have me.'

Metrius laughed.

'Please,' said Adamnul. 'I have a wife and two small children.'

'Some of the student Masters are only fourteen years old,' said Metrius, 'yet you were willing to murder them all yesterday. It is a little late to try to play to my sympathy.'

Adamnul started to weep. 'I beg you; I appeal to your mercy. Pardon my crimes, and allow me to serve you, Lord Metrius. Think of my children. Would you leave them without their father?'

'I would,' said Metrius. 'You, Adamnul, are a traitor to Klef Mordain, and you deserve to die. When Portia has finished with you, I will send your head in a box to the entrance of the Second Empire Association, as a gift for Lord Tain. I want him to wallow in his abject failure.' He turned to Portia. 'You shall have twenty minutes; no more, no less. Make him suffer as much as you can in that short time. Do unto him what Lord Tain did to Master Drummond, then sever his head and give it to a courier to deliver to the association. Dump what remains in the harbour, and I shall see you in my office one hour from now.'

Portia inclined her head. 'Yes, sir.'

'No, please!' cried Adamnul. 'Please!'

'Come, Fyenna,' said Metrius; 'unless you wish to witness what occurs in the next twenty minutes?'

'No, my lord,' said Fyenna. 'I do not wish to see it.'

'A wise choice. One requires an iron constitution to observe Portia at work.'

Metrius and Fyenna left the small cavern, and Metrius closed the door behind them.

'I will leave you now,' said Metrius. 'As I mentioned, I will send someone later with details regarding Mor Galthide's arrival. I remain angry with you for your breach of faith; you are fortunate that you are indispensable to me, my noble lady, very fortunate. Farewell.'

Fyenna watched him leave the large cavern, then she walked over to the ladder, and ascended the iron rungs to the top. She eased herself through the trapdoor, then she closed and locked it. She sat on the floor of the small room for a few minutes, going over everything that had happened, while trying not to think about what Portia was doing to Adamnul at that moment. With Drummond and Tobold's deaths coming in quick succession, and with her traitor husband having fled the city, in many ways her life was already in ruins. Despite his bluster, it was also clear that Metrius was close to despair, and that he was lashing out before he was dragged down. He believed that their defeat was inevitable, but Fyenna refused to agree. Something would happen, something that would change the fortunes of Klef Mordain for the better; something that would chase the Sanctians away for good.

'Make it so, blessed spirits; grant my prayer,' she whispered.

She got to her feet and walked out into the hallway on the ground floor of the Maker school. She ascended the stairs, and walked into the dining room, where the students from both schools were eating breakfast. Vesta and Eshia were seated at a table on their own, their heads together in hushed conversation, while most of the students seemed stunned, as though they were in a daze.

Fyenna forced a confident smile onto her face and walked towards the serving hatch. One of the kitchen staff peered through.

'Just some coffee for me, thank you,' Fyenna said.

The old woman poured her a fresh cup of coffee, then Fyenna took it and gazed down at the students. She walked over to the table, and sat down next to Constans and Raewyn, with Stanza and Abigone opposite her. Denny was sitting to Abigone's right, and they glanced up at her.

'This is the first time I have ever sat down in the dining room with the students,' said Fyenna, 'but I wanted to speak to each of you, to find out how you are all feeling.'

'Constans is angry with you, ma'am,' said Stanza.

Constans sighed and looked away.

'Is this true?' said Fyenna. 'Do you have a grievance, Constans?'

'No, ma'am,' he muttered.

'That's not what you were saying a moment ago,' said Stanza.

'I think it's my fault, ma'am,' said Denny. 'Constans has been at the school for much longer than me, and yet I have been appointed as interim Head Master.'

'You are the oldest boy,' said Fyenna.

'But he can't even transform metal, or stone,' cried Constans. 'He can barely transform wood. How can a first year become Head Master?' His features flushed. 'Sorry. I mean, ma'am.'

'It isn't fair, ma'am,' said Raewyn.

'I did not make the appointment based upon Valiance's abilities as a

Master, more on his other qualities,' said Fyenna. 'We all saw what he did in the clearing, and we all saw what he did when the Master school was attacked. You are a fine young Master, Constans, but Valiance has a wider range of experience. Would you agree with that statement?'

Constans stared at his plate.

'I think you made the right choice, ma'am,' said Marlow. 'I trust Valiance.'

'Me, too,' said Aplin.

'Are you saying you don't trust me?' said Constans. 'I can kill someone by raising my hand.'

'That is true,' said Fyenna, 'but you failed to do so when the Westlanders attacked, and you failed to go to Master Tobold's assistance in the Master school. Possessing an ability is quite different from having the will to use it. This is not a criticism of you, Constans. Master Drummond was effusive in his praise of your potential, but that is all it is at the moment – potential. I have no doubt that you will develop into a powerful Master, but that time has not yet arrived. Be patient.'

Constans leaned his elbows on the table and put his head in his hands. 'I feel so useless,' he said. 'We have been twice tested, and I have been found wanting.'

'You can't compare yourself to me,' said Denny. 'I underwent ten years of intensive training to get where I am today. It was a miserable childhood, one that I wouldn't wish on anyone else. When I was eight, I was taken into the woods twenty miles from home, and left there with a knife, a blanket and a flask of water, and told to make my own way home.'

'Why would they do that to you?' said Abigone.

'They said it was to toughen me up. I have a hundred more stories like that one. Be glad that your family loves you, Constans.'

'I will spend some time working out what level the Masters have attained,' said Fyenna. 'Apart from Constans, can anyone else kill from a distance?'

'Valiance and I managed it once, ma'am,' said Marlow. 'I mean, we didn't kill anyone, but we transformed some water into... slightly salty water.'

'And you have just done this the once?'

'Yes, ma'am.'

'What about you, Aplin?'

'I have done it a few times, ma'am,' he said. 'I still can't convert all the water to salt, though; there's always some left over.'

'And can you all meditate successfully?'

'I'm still terrible at it, ma'am,' said Salus. 'I can never empty my head of thoughts.'

Fyenna smiled. 'Meditation was always a mystery to me. As a Maker, I have to fill my head with thoughts, not empty it. I always admired Master Drummond's ability to clear his mind at a moment's notice. He told me that he would concentrate on something beloved to him, rather than try to think of nothing, which seems an impossible task.' She glanced over at the other table. 'It was Eshia,' she said. 'He used to think of Eshia's face when she was a little girl.'

'That's so sad,' said Raewyn.

'I think of Abigone's face,' said Denny.

'What?' said Abigone. 'You didn't tell me that.'

'It works,' said Denny. 'Does that bother you?'

'Uh, no, I don't think so,' said Abigone. 'Not if, you know, not if it works for you.'

Fyenna smiled. 'You are remarkably frank with your feelings, Valiance. Perhaps you should keep some in reserve, lest you frighten Abigone away.'

'I don't really know what to say or do, ma'am,' he said. 'I've never courted anyone before.'

'And there you go again,' said Fyenna. 'I see Abigone has her work cut out for her.' She got to her feet. 'I shall leave you in peace for now, and I will catch up with the other students a little later.'

She walked to the doorway, then she turned to look back at the students. They were her students now, all of them – the boys as well as the girls. She felt her shoulders sag a little from the responsibility, then she strode away.

That evening, Rupert knocked on the door of Fyenna's office as she was poring over the school's evacuation plan.

'Yes?' she said.

'Lady Niscoll of Mordana is here to see you, ma'am,' her secretary said. 'Shall I show her in?'

'Please do.'

Rupert bowed his head, then he left the room. Moments later, Niscoll walked in and sat down. The two friends gazed at each other for a long, still moment.

'There isn't much to say, is there?' Niscoll said. 'It's just one calamity after another – your husband, Drummond, the Master school. And those are only your problems. I won't burden you with mine; we would be here for hours.'

'Is it true that the thirty have disbanded?'

'Did Lord Metrius tell you that? We haven't officially disbanded; we just don't meet anymore. It has been well over a month since we were all in the same room together. No – the pro-Sanctians have their own meetings, in secret, while we do the same.'

'Where did we go wrong?'

'I am too deeply immersed to get a clear view, Fyenna.'

'Would you like a coffee, or perhaps some wine?'

'I'm afraid I can't stay. I am here in my capacity as Metrius's messenger. His words were cryptic, so I hope you understand them. He told me to tell you that the package has been successfully delivered to the front door of the Second Empire Association. He also said that the father will be below your feet two days hence, an hour after dawn. Does that make any kind of sense to you?'

'It does, thank you. Two days from now?'

'Yes. Lord Metrius has also issued a general warning not to be on the streets this coming night. Blood is going to be spilled in great quantities, and it won't be safe outside.'

'Lord Metrius believes that we have already lost.'

'I know.'

'And yet he continues to send out his assassins.'

'He does. I have attempted to rein him in, but he refuses to listen to me. I think the desire for vengeance is all that's keeping him going.'

'We can't go on like this.'

'Nothing lasts forever, Fyenna. You and I have sworn oaths to Lord Metrius, and neither of us would survive a Sanctian occupation. What can we do but remain faithful to our vows?'

'Do you think we still have hope?'

'I do. I will not capitulate until a Sanctian soldier thrusts his sword into my throat. There will be no negotiations, no surrender, and no running away. For Klef Mordain, we shall live, or die. Naturally, I would prefer to live, but if I must die, then I will do so fighting.'

She got to her feet. 'I shall see myself out,' she said.

Fyenna tried to smile. 'Farewell, old friend.'

Niscoll inclined her head. 'Steel yourself, Fyenna; our beloved city is about to be bathed in blood.'

CHAPTER 24
FATHER AND SON

Old City, Klef Mordain – 10th Day of Lamenta 108

Miss Vesta opened the hatch in the ceiling, and the students filed out onto the roof after her. Denny gazed around at the view.

'We never went up on to the roof of the Master school,' he said to Abigone.

'That's because it wasn't flat,' said Aplin.

Ignatius gasped. 'Look at all the smoke.'

'Never mind the smoke,' said Reath. 'Look down at the street – there's broken glass everywhere, and... is that blood?'

'What a mess,' said Miss Vesta. 'There must be half a dozen fires in the Old City alone, and I can see more smoke coming from Nether Hall and Cliephus.' She pointed. 'Look over there – do you all see the smoke and flames coming from that building, the one just to the right of the dome? That's the Master school. The pro-Sanctians must have decided to set it alight.'

Denny stared at the burning building. 'How many people have died over the past two days?'

'It will be a while before anyone knows the answer to that question,' said Miss Vesta. 'The situation is still too chaotic.'

'Why is the city fighting itself, ma'am?' said Ignatius.

'Do you know nothing?' said Constans. 'The pro-Sanctian traitors wish to sell Klef Mordain to the Sanctian Empire, while the patriots are trying to stop that from happening.'

'Yes, but why are they killing each other?'

'It's complicated,' said Miss Vesta.

'It looks as though both sides have blood on their hands,' said Abigone.

'And what would someone from Upper Down know about the politics of Klef Mordain?' said Constans.

Denny opened his mouth to tell Constans to be more respectful, but Abigone silenced him with a glance.

'Are you aware, Constans,' she said, 'that I was a sovereign regent of an entire realm before I came here? I have some experience of politics. The Sanctian Empire also wished to swallow us up, and we were fortunate to remain an independent nation.'

Reath laughed. 'That'll teach you to be an arrogant pig, Constans. Hey – do you see those men down there, at the end of the street? What are they doing?'

'They appear to be manning a roadblock,' said Miss Vesta.

'Then the Old City is divided?' said Denny. 'How is food going to reach the people if they can't walk the streets safely?'

'Very little supplies are coming in through the commercial harbour,' said Miss Vesta. 'Do you see the long breakwater down in the bay? That used to be full of masts; now it's empty. Any food that reaches the Old City will now be coming in through the suburbs.'

'How are our stocks, ma'am?'

'We had enough to last us months,' said Miss Vesta, 'but that was before the boys arrived from the Master school. I suspect that there will be hidden caches of food down in the tunnels and caverns, so let us hope that Lady Fyenna is able to tap into that resource.'

Denny turned to the north. He saw the twin statues marking the ends of the Celestial Bridge and, next to it, he could see five Sanctian warships, all with their cannon-bearing flanks aimed at the Old City.

'What will the Sanctians do next, do you think?' said Abigone.

'I don't think they need to do anything,' said Denny. 'The Second Empire Association is already doing their dirty work for them. If they were to land soldiers, they would most likely claim that their objective is to restore law and order.'

'Why don't they land soldiers?' said Reath.

'That would be illegal,' said Denny. 'The Sanctians do not want to gain a reputation in the Central Provinces for acting beyond the law. They could easily invade, and overwhelm the city in a few days, but they need a valid reason. If they do it on a whim, they will lose the support of their allies in the south.'

'But they are already blockading us,' said Raewyn. 'Isn't that an act of war?'

'They are not blockading us, not officially,' said Denny. 'They are hunting pirates and smugglers; well, that is what they will be telling everyone. If I had to guess, then I would say that they are waiting for something to happen. Perhaps they hope that the Corse will be overthrown by a hungry, rioting mob. If that happens, a new government, sponsored by the Second Empire Association, could invite the Sanctians into Klef Mordain. After that, annexation is a mere formality.'

'How do you know about this stuff?' said Reath.

'It's what the Sanctians did to Mylos,' he said. 'Fifteen years ago, they accused Mylos of flouting a trade agreement, and so they placed troops around its entire border to enforce the payment of tariffs. Mylos is landlocked, so it was like a siege, albeit on a far grander scale. It took three years to wear down the food reserves of the Mylians. Their king abdicated when his people were on the brink of starvation, and the new governor requested Sanctian assistance.'

'How do we beat them?' said Marlow. 'There has to be a way.'

'The black powder,' said Denny. 'Sooner or later, someone else will discover how to mix the black powder correctly, and the Sanctian's main advantage will be negated. The Sanctians know this, which is why they guard the secret so fiercely.'

Lady Fyenna joined them on the roof.

'Ma'am,' said Miss Vesta, inclining her head, 'Valiance was just giving us a most enlightening talk about the motives and tactics of the Sanctians.'

'I'm sure he was,' said Fyenna; 'however, I happen to need Valiance for a short while. Do you mind if I borrow him?'

'Not at all, ma'am,' said Miss Vesta.

Fyenna gestured towards the hatch, and Denny followed her back into the building.

'We are going all the way down to the ground floor,' Fyenna said, as they descended the stairs. 'I hope you weren't revealing too much of your knowledge on the roof. If you appear to know everything about the Sanctians, then some might start to suspect you.'

'Would it matter if they all knew, ma'am?'

'Possibly not. However, the more people that know, the more likely it is that this information will leak to the pro-Sanctians in the city. Their reaction to your presence is unpredictable.'

Denny shook his head. 'I think I know what they would do, ma'am. I was just talking about this on the roof. I told the others that the Sanctians are waiting for a legal reason to enter the city. If they discovered my presence here, then I would be used as the reason. They would claim that a prince of the imperial household is being held as a hostage, and they would send the troops in, ostensibly to rescue me.'

Fyenna frowned at him.

'Did I say something amiss, ma'am?'

'No, Valiance. It has just occurred to me why my superior did not want me to tell you that I had discovered your identity. Why did I not see it before? You are correct – you would give the Sanctians the perfect excuse to intervene militarily.'

'And the Central Provinces wouldn't be able to complain,' said Denny. 'It would all be justifiable and within the law.'

They reached the bottom of the last flight of stairs, and Fyenna led Valiance into her office.

'Don't sit,' she said; 'this won't take long. I have arranged for you to meet with your father this morning.'

Denny smiled. 'Thank you, ma'am.'

'Before I take you to where he is due to meet us, I must warn you that your father will most likely try to persuade you to flee the city with him.'

'I understand, ma'am. Where has my father been staying?'

Fyenna averted her gaze. 'He has been held in confinement.'

'What – in a dungeon?'

'His knowledge regarding you was deemed too dangerous by my superior to allow him to mingle freely within Klef Mordain. As you yourself stated, if the Sanctians discover that you are here, they could use it as an excuse to invade.'

'But my father hates the Sanctians, ma'am. He would never tell them that I am here. That's why he told me to use a different name.'

'I know, Denny, but there are many spies and informers in Klef Mordain, and it would take but one loose word for the Sanctians to see the truth. My superior did not want to take the risk.'

'You keep referring to your superior, ma'am. I think I would like to meet this man or woman, so that I can make my thoughts plain to them. How dare they imprison my father? Tell me this, ma'am – after today's meeting, will he be placed back into his cell?'

'I would assume so.'

Denny groaned aloud, and put a hand to his face. 'If I refuse to flee with him, then I will be responsible for him being imprisoned; that's if your *superior* would even allow us to flee. He might throw me into a dungeon as well.'

Fyenna said nothing.

'I don't know what to do,' said Denny.

'Speak to your father,' said Fyenna. 'See what he has to say, and then perhaps your path will be clearer.'

Denny nodded. 'All right.'

'This way,' said Fyenna.

She led him out of the office and into the small room that lay next door. She crouched by a trapdoor, and unlocked it. She eased it open, and Denny peered down into the darkness.

'I will go down first and light some lamps,' said Fyenna. 'When you see light, follow me down.'

Fyenna climbed down through the hatch, and Denny saw that metal rungs had been hammered into the side of the stone wall of the cavern. Fyenna disappeared into the darkness, and Denny waited, as his thoughts spiralled from anger to anticipation. It had been over five months since they had last seen each other – would his father blame him for his confinement? Would he be angry?

A lamp flickered from below, and Denny began to make his way down into a large cavern, closing the hatch as he went. Fyenna lit more lamps as he descended, and the cavern was filled with light by the time he reached the bottom.

'When will my father get here, ma'am?' he said.

'We are on time, Denny. All we have to do now is wait.'

'Did he look well to you, ma'am?'

'I think so. I could only see his face.'

A door in the cavern opened, and two armed men walked in. They took up positions by the sides of the entrance, and raised their crossbows. Mor Galthide strode into the cavern. His wrists were bound before him, but his head was held high. Two more armed men followed him in, their crossbows aimed at Mor Galthide's back.

'My son!' Mor Galthide cried. He crossed the cavern floor, and Denny walked forward to meet him halfway.

'No closer,' shouted one of the armed men.

'You can't tell me what to do,' said Denny, as he reached out and embraced his father.

'Did you hear that, you vile dogs?' shouted Mor Galthide. 'My son takes no orders from the servants of Lord Metrius.'

The four armed men tensed, but said nothing.

'Let me look at my boy,' said Mor Galthide. 'You appear fit and healthy. How have they been treating you?'

'I have been treated well, Father,' said Denny. 'I have learned much.'

'Have you learned enough?'

'There is always more to learn, Father.'

'You know the meaning of my words, Mor Dennahelm. Have you learnt enough to drive the Sanctians from our homeland?'

'I have not.'

'That is a pity, but we are driven by necessity and must leave this doomed city at once.'

'I heard that you have been confined to a prison cell, Father.'

'I made the mistake of knocking upon the door of Lord Metrius, and he had men subdue me and place me into a dark and dismal dungeon.'

'Lord Metrius? Who is this man?'

Mor Galthide nodded in the direction of Fyenna. 'Ask the woman. She works for him.'

'I must tell you, Father; I do not wish to leave Klef Mordain.'

'Have you lost your senses, my boy? The Sanctians will soon be dancing upon the grave of Klef Mordain. Do you remember what happened to Mylos? Recall you the subjugation of Subnestia? History is repeating itself, here in this city. If we do not leave, and soon, we shall be ground underfoot, and our homeland shall never be free.'

'I understand, and yet I wish to stay.'

'Why? Give me your reasons and, if I can, I shall rebut each in turn.'

'I have grown fond of the other students. I do not want to abandon them.'

'You owe these foreigners no allegiance. Your loyalty belongs to Geathan, not to strangers.'

'I wish to fight the Sanctians.'

'Then do so, but not here, in this doomed place. There will be other battlefields where you can earn glory. The greatest battlefield of all lies in Geathan – save your strength for your homeland.'

Denny glanced down. 'I have met a girl.'

Mor Galthide hesitated. 'Ah.'

'I am courting her, Father.'

'And is she worthy of your great name and lineage, son?'

'She is a princess of royal blood.'

'To which realm does she belong?'

'To that of Upper Down.'

'They are allies of the Sanctian Empire, are they not?'

'They are an independent and sovereign realm. The Sanctians tried and failed to annex them last year; and the princess of whom I speak performed great and noble acts to preserve the freedom of her realm.'

Mor Galthide nodded. 'Then she is indeed worthy. Goes she by the name of Abigone?'

Denny frowned. 'You have heard of her, Father?'

'Rumours about her fly through Klef Mordain. Some say that she arrived here only to be slain by the Corse; others that she is a hostage or a prisoner.'

'She is a Maker. She attends the school.'

Mor Galthide laughed aloud. 'Did I say she was worthy? Worthy is not strong enough a word. Have you proposed marriage to this girl?'

Denny's face flushed. 'No, Father. In truth, we have not long begun our courtship. To her, for many months I was merely Valiance, but now she knows the truth about me. And I did not know if I would need your blessing.'

'For her, son, you have it. Marry her; do you hear me? Marry this girl as soon as possible. Is she a suitable age?'

'She is the same age as me; but I shall not propose until I am sure that I love her, and that she loves me in return.'

'Love? Ha. Be not overly concerned with love. This could be a most profitable match. You would have a royal queen when you reclaimed the throne of Geathan; a Maker queen, and a Master king. Antonio would quake in his boots. When we leave the city, we shall take her with us.'

'I suspect you do not understand the situation, Father. Klef Mordain has been blockaded. The Sanctian army is encamped upon the Great Northern Highway, blocking any escape to the south by land, and their warships have sealed off the harbour. The only way out is via the north and west. We would have to travel through hundreds of miles of territory occupied by the Westlanders to reach the pass at Upper Down.'

'Is that so?' said Mor Galthide. 'I had not realised the extent to which we had been penned within this city. We cannot take a princess on such a perilous journey, and yet we shall not leave her here. Very well; this reason of yours for staying I shall not attempt to rebut. You have convinced me, son. Abigone must stay, and therefore you and I will also stay. Lord Metrius asked me if I would be willing to fight the Sanctians here in Klef Mordain, and I scorned his question. Now I think I will change my stance.' He glanced at Fyenna. 'Woman, come hither.'

Fyenna frowned and walked over to where Denny and his father were standing.

'Woman,' Mor Galthide went on, 'do you recall Lord Metrius asking if I would bear arms for this city against the Sanctians? Inform him that I shall indeed do so. My son has convinced me to stay.'

'I know,' said Fyenna. 'I could hear you from the other side of the cavern.'

'Does this woman mock me, my son?'

'No, Father,' said Denny, 'and she has a name.'

'A name she refused to give me the last time we met.'

'You didn't ask me my name,' said Fyenna.

'I heard Lord Metrius command you not to give it, and you showed your obedience to that cur.'

'Didn't you say you would fight for him?'

'I will not fight for Lord Metrius; I will fight for my son and his beloved.'

'Abigone is under my protection,' she said.

Mor Galthide bowed his head. 'Then in lieu of the girl's parents, I shall give you the respect due to her mother. My lady, will you allow my son to court Princess Abigone?'

'I will not forbid it.'

'You may now send me back to the darkness of my prison cell, my lady,' said Mor Galthide, keeping his head inclined, 'or, if it pleases you, you will permit me to abide in the school, in order to stand guard over the students. I understand the Sanctians, and I know what they will do to the young Masters and Makers of this city if they are discovered. Take me into your service, so that I can watch over my son. I will not interfere in your work, and I will obey your commands. I have fought in many wars and campaigns; and if you permit me to sit by the front door of the school, I will be your sentry and your shield. No one shall pass. Let me do this, and I shall be your faithful and humble servant; this I solemnly pledge.'

Fyenna narrowed her eyes. 'I do not have the authority to accept your offer, tempted though I am.'

'Are you not in charge of this school, my lady? Are you not responsible for the safety of the children who dwell here? Lord Metrius has already requested that I defend the city; would you not be obeying his command if you allowed me to defend the school?'

Fyenna said nothing for a moment, then she gestured to Denny. 'A word, alone.'

Denny followed Fyenna to the side of the cavern.

'Tell me, Denny,' said Fyenna; 'can your father be relied upon? Would he obey my orders if I were to allow this?'

'He would, ma'am,' said Denny. 'For many years, he was a celebrated and renowned knight of Sanctos. The Emperor sent him to fight in many campaigns in the Central Provinces, and my father returned from each one with his reputation enhanced. He was reluctant to serve the Sanctian Empire, but he swore an oath to Antonio when Geathan was conquered.'

'And then he broke that oath.'

'Only to save my life, ma'am. I think he longed for an excuse to fight the Sanctians.'

'And how would you feel if your father lived in the school?'

Denny frowned. 'He... is my father. I do not want him put back into a dungeon.'

Fyenna lowered her gaze. 'The school could use another protector, but Lord Metrius might disagree.'

'Is he the superior you mentioned, ma'am?'

'He is. Lord Metrius is likely the most powerful man in the city, and he is already angry with me. He did not want you to meet your father, in case you were persuaded to leave Klef Mordain.'

'Why would Lord Metrius care if I left, ma'am?'

'Because I have told him of your abilities, Denny. Lord Metrius wishes to use you in the fight against the Sanctians.'

'You could tell him that I demanded my father's presence as my condition for acquiescing.'

'Lord Metrius will require you to kill for him.'

'I understand, ma'am.'

'Will Abigone welcome this? How would you feel if her father moved into the school?'

'I don't know. Uncomfortable, maybe. I thought my father would laugh when I told him I was courting someone; I wasn't expecting him to embrace the idea so quickly.'

'I saw his eyes light up as soon as you mentioned that she was a princess and a Maker. The easy thing to do would be to send him back to his cell, but he has done nothing wrong.'

'Please let him stay, ma'am. If my father had been present when the Master school was attacked, then he could have held the entrance on his own. Much of what I know I learned from him.'

Fyenna nodded, then they walked back to where Mor Galthide was standing.

'My lady,' the older man said, bowing his head again.

'Will you respect the privacy of the students if I allow you to stay?' she said. 'And will you respect Abigone? I do not want you meddling in her life. If you live in the school, then you must behave as a gentleman.'

'You have my word,' Mor Galthide said. 'I shall restrict myself to the areas of the school that you deem permissible, and I shall behave with humility and discretion. If I see Abigone, I will bow my head and wish her *Good Day*.'

'Your son has advocated on your behalf,' Fyenna went on, 'and so I will allow it.'

Mor Galthide fell to one knee in front of her. 'Then I swear by the spirits to serve you, my lady. Thank you for this privilege.'

Fyenna glanced at the four guards. 'Go back to Lord Metrius without this man. I will be taking him into my personal custody.'

'But, ma'am,' said one, 'we were ordered to return him to his cell.'

'I am overriding that order,' said Fyenna. 'I am the Head Maker of Klef Mordain, and I take full responsibility for this decision. Inform Lord Metrius that Mor Galthide will be employed to protect the school. Tell him that this alone has persuaded his son to fight for the city. If Lord Metrius disagrees with my decision, then I will answer to him. Be gone.'

The four guards glanced at each other, then they turned and left the cavern.

Mor Galthide laughed as he got back to his feet. 'Well said, my lady. Now, will you cut my bonds and give me your name?'

'It is Fyenna,' she said, taking a knife from her belt.

'I have heard this name in the taverns of the city,' said Mor Galthide, as Fyenna cut the cords around his wrists. 'You defeated the Westlanders in a battle, did you not?'

'I did not fight the Westlanders alone,' said Fyenna.

'It will be an honour to serve one who has already distinguished herself in battle, my lady. I am now your humble servant; command me, and I shall obey.'

'Very well; I command you to bathe, dress in clean clothes, and then rest and eat. I will find a room for you by the front entrance of the school, and from there you will remain on guard.'

Mor Galthide bowed low. 'It shall be so.'

'It will only take a few minutes, ma'am,' said Denny.

Miss Vesta frowned. 'You are not supposed to enter the floor where the girls stay, Valiance.'

'Lady Fyenna said it was all right. I need to speak to Abigone.'

'Then I will fetch her. Remain here on the stairs.'

Denny leaned against the wall as Vesta walked along the corridor. She stopped at a door and knocked.

'Abigone? Could you come here, please?'

The door opened, and Abigone glanced out.

'Valiance wishes to talk to you,' said Vesta. 'He told me it was urgent.'

Abigone slipped out of the room and closed the door, then Miss Vesta escorted her to the top of the stairs where Denny was waiting.

'Five minutes,' said Vesta. 'The students are supposed to be studying.'

'Yes, ma'am,' said Denny.

Vesta walked away.

'What is it?' said Abigone.

'I just met my father,' he said. 'Lord Metrius had him confined to a dungeon.'

'Why?'

'Because he was looking for me. He wanted to take me out of Klef Mordain. He thinks the city is doomed.'

'What did you say to him?'

'I told him I wanted to stay to defend the school, and I told him that there was no way to escape Klef Mordain without passing through the regions occupied by Westlanders. Then I told him about you, and that changed his mind. Lady Fyenna is allowing him to stay within the school.'

'He will be living here?'

'Yes.'

'What did he say about me?'

'He was a little... over-bearing.'

'He disapproves of us?'

'The opposite.'

Abigone frowned, then she glanced over her shoulder. 'Miss Vesta has gone.'

'She has.'

'Do you want to come into my room for a moment? I'd rather no one overheard us. Reath has ears like a bat.'

Denny nodded, and Abigone led him along the corridor. She looked both ways, then placed her fingers on the handle and opened the door. She and Denny walked into the small bedroom, and a grey cat looked up from the bed.

'Meg,' said Abigone, as she closed the door, 'this is Denny.'

'I didn't know you had a cat,' said Denny.

'She isn't mine,' said Abigone; 'not really. The kitchen staff brought her into the school to catch rats, and I volunteered to look after her.'

'There were hundreds of cats in the palace where I grew up,' Denny said. He crouched down by the bed and extended a hand.

'Remain still,' Abigone said. 'She's a little nervous. Let her come to you.'

Meg edged forward, then she sniffed Danny's hand. She allowed Denny to stroke her head, then she backed away again, hissing. Abigone scooped her up in her arms.

'Don't hiss,' she said. 'Why don't you see if there is any food for you in the kitchen, Meg?'

Abigone carried the cat to the door. She opened it, then she set Meg down in the corridor, and closed the door again.

'Sorry about that,' she said. 'Meg hisses at the kitchen staff, too. The only one she seems to like is me.'

'That's all right,' he said. 'She'll get used to me.'

'What did you mean before?' Abigone went on, as she sat down on the bed. 'Is your father in favour of us courting?'

'Yes,' said Denny. 'It was a little disconcerting, to be honest. It's because you're a princess and a Maker. Lady Fyenna made him promise not to bother you while he's here. He's going to live downstairs, by the front door.'

'I should probably meet him at some stage.'

'I'll take you to see him when you're ready. I'm not going to allow him to push us together; we'll go at our own pace.'

'At what pace should we be going? We have been courting for three days, and all we've done is hold hands, once.'

'I would like to do more.'

'Such as?'

'I would like to touch you, and I would like to kiss you. Is that too forward?'

She gazed up at him. 'No.'

He sat down next to her, and placed his hand on her waist.

'My father...' Denny said.

'Forget him,' said Abigone. 'This will be my first kiss, and I don't want you thinking about your father.'

Denny leaned forward until their lips were almost touching. 'Don't worry, Abigone,' he said; 'you are all that is on my mind.'

CHAPTER 25
PILLAR TO POST

Old City, Klef Mordain – 12th Day of Lamenta 108

Amery awoke as sunlight flooded his bedroom. He groaned, and pulled the blanket over his head.

'It's time to get up,' said Loryn, as she drew the curtains open. 'You shouldn't lie around in bed all day.'

'What time is it?' he said.

'An hour after dawn.'

'It's hardly the entire day,' he cried. 'Why are you waking me up so early?'

Loryn sat on the bed and pulled the blanket back. 'It is unseemly for a man in your position to be indolent.'

His gaze lingered on her, and she smiled.

'We should go into the office,' she said.

'What? I can't think of anything worse. Why don't you take that dress off and get into bed?'

'Annalise has made fresh coffee.'

He reached out to touch her, and she stood. 'Get washed,' she said, 'then we shall have the coffee that Annalise has gone to the trouble of making, and go to the office.'

'You are a cruel woman,' he said.

'Someone has to keep you right, Mister Amery.'

His eyes followed her as she walked out of the room, then he sighed and got out of bed. He spent a few minutes washing his hands and face in the tepid water of a basin, then he pulled on his office clothes. When he walked through to the living room, Loryn was sitting on a couch with Lothar, and both were laughing. A twinge of envy shot through Amery's mind, and he narrowed his eyes.

'I owe you a sovereign,' said Lothar. 'You were right – he's actually awake at a decent hour.'

Loryn got up from the couch and kissed Amery. 'I will get the coffee.'

Amery mumbled his thanks, then he sat down opposite Lothar, as Loryn left the room.

The former Mountain Ranger shook his head at him. 'How the fuck did you get her, Amery? If I hadn't seen her, I wouldn't believe it. She's far too pretty for you.'

Amery shrugged. 'Just lucky, I guess.'

'Then it had nothing to do with the fact that you live in an enormous house and have tons of money?' He laughed. 'I have to say that I'm slightly jealous. Well done; but, if you fuck it up, just know that I'll be waiting. She can cry on my shoulder any time.'

Amery glared at him, then Loryn and Annalise came into the room. The housekeeper set a tray down onto a low table, then she shooed Loryn away.

'I will serve the coffee, Miss Loryn,' Annalise said. 'You are a guest in this house.'

'But I would like to help,' said Loryn.

'I know, I know, but it's my job to look after you all. Sit, girl.'

Loryn sat down, as Annalise filled three cups with coffee.

'Will you be needing any breakfast, Mister Amery?' said the housekeeper.

'No, thanks.

'Might I say how good it is to see you up and about at a respectable hour? Do you intend to go to work today?'

'Yes, unfortunately.'

Annalise smiled at Loryn. 'You are a good influence on him, young lady. Should I have the drivers prepare the carriage, Mister Amery?'

'Yes, thank you.'

Annalise inclined her head and strode from the room. Loryn leaned forward. She stirred two sugars into a cup, and handed it to Amery.

'Thanks,' he muttered.

Lothar smirked. 'I take one sugar in mine, Loryn.'

'You can fix your own coffee, Lothar,' she said.

'It's like that, is it? You're breaking my heart.'

'I'm sure you'll survive.' She picked up her own cup and took a sip. 'Am I the only one here who feels a little guilty that we are drinking coffee that the Sanctians smuggled into the city? Thousands are going hungry, and most won't have tasted coffee in weeks; yet here we are, living like royalty.'

Lothar shrugged. 'Well, we wouldn't want the coffee to go to waste now, would we? If we weren't drinking it, then it would go to people who actually like the Sanctian Empire.'

'That's an interesting way to look at it,' said Loryn. 'How do you know that I don't like the Sanctian Empire?'

'Because you don't seem like an idiot,' said Lothar. 'The city is collapsing all around us, and it's the fault of the Sanctians. If we don't flee soon, we'll have lost our chance for good.'

'Then why don't you flee?'

Lothar glanced at Amery. The former Mountain Ranger had been told not to mention anything to Loryn about Abigone and, as far as Amery knew, he had remained true to his word.

'I'm here to protect this house and the people in it,' Lothar said. 'While Amery stays, I stay.'

'We should get our carriage,' said Amery, as he finished his coffee.

'Certainly, sir,' said Loryn, getting to her feet.

'Have a lovely time at the office,' said Lothar. 'Give my regards to the arsehole traitors who work there.'

Loryn laughed, then she and Amery left the room and descended the stairs to the ground floor. They went through the back door, and found their two drivers waiting by the carriage.

'Where to, sir?' said one of them.

'The association,' said Amery.

'That, uh, might be tricky, sir,' said the driver. 'There are roadblocks all over the Old City.'

'There must be a route we can take.'

'We could loop round via the eastern coast,' said the other driver.

'That will take about an hour, instead of the usual fifteen minutes.'

'That will do,' said Amery.

He helped Loryn up into the carriage, then he climbed in after her and the side door was closed.

'Is something wrong, sir?' said Loryn, as they sat down in the carriage.

'Why would you think that?'

'Well, you seem a little distant today.'

'Lothar annoys me sometimes; that's all. Must he flirt with you all the time?'

'I wouldn't say that was flirting, sir. He was just being friendly. Would you prefer it if he was hostile towards me?'

'I don't know; maybe. And the way he looks at you...'

'I can handle Lothar, sir. You don't need to worry.'

'I can't help it. You, uh... well, you...'

'Yes, sir?'

'You're so beautiful, Loryn, and I... well, I sometimes wonder why you are with me.'

'I didn't know you were insecure, sir.'

'I've never had much success with the ladies; whereas Lothar... He's a big, strong soldier-type.'

'Yes, but he's not my type, sir. You are one of the cleverest people I have ever met; is that not enough?'

Amery shook his head and gazed out of the window as the carriage moved off. 'I never thought I'd ever be afflicted by jealousy. It's not a nice feeling.'

'I don't mind that you're jealous, sir. It means you like me.'

'I thought that was obvious.'

'Maybe to you. I worked next to you at the association for weeks, and you never once tried to make any approaches towards me.'

'I wanted to, but I thought it would be inappropriate. It might have been construed as taking advantage of my position.'

'But I was giving you hints and signs, to let you know that it would be fine with me.'

Amery narrowed his eyes. 'Were you? If you were, then they were far too subtle for me.'

'Your job deals in subtlety, sir.'

'The law I can understand. Women? – not so much. My default assumption is that women aren't all that interested in me, and so I need plain, clear guidance.'

'You should try to be more confident, sir. Insecurity can be a little off-putting.'

'All right. Message received.'

Loryn's eyes widened as the carriage pulled into a main road. Smoke was rising from burning piles of rubbish, and a dozen men with staves were guarding a roadblock consisting of three overturned carts. Along the length of the street, almost every window was smashed, and several houses had been gutted by fire. The carriage came to a halt, then the drivers began to turn it round, as the men by the barricade watched.

'The city,' said Loryn. 'My beloved city.

'These are rough times,' said Amery.

'Not for you, sir. You are insulated from the calamities afflicting Klef Mordain. Do you even care what happens to the people who live here?'

Amery blinked. 'I... well...'

'Sorry, sir,' said Loryn. 'That was uncalled for. I know that none of this is your fault.'

'That's all right, Loryn; I...'

'It's the fault of the Second Empire Association,' Loryn went on. 'Our employers are responsible. Are we implicated, sir, because we work for them?'

'No. We have tried to keep the association within the bounds of the law.'

'By falsifying documents and lying on the minutes, sir?'

'You said that you had no moral qualms about that. You told me this at your interview.'

'I know I did, but look out of the window and see what they have done to Klef Mordain. Where will it end?'

'It will end with the occupation of the city by the Sanctians. And both sides have been resorting to violence. You were there when Lady Ursula was murdered; you saw it happen.'

'Does that mean both sides are equally to blame? If someone strikes you, and you defend yourself, are you also the aggressor?'

'I'm not going to discuss this any further. It was your idea to travel to the office today, not mine.'

'Look into your heart, sir. I refuse to believe that you can't tell the difference between good and evil.'

'Good and evil? Come now; no one is either completely good, or completely evil; that's why we have the law, to decide between the innocent and the guilty.'

Loryn's eyes flashed with anger. 'But...'

'But what?'

'Nothing, sir. Forgive me; I spoke out of turn.'

'You are not yourself this morning,' Amery said. 'I didn't realise that the sight of the troubles would affect you like this. Perhaps we should go back to the townhouse.'

'No, sir. I will behave professionally.'

The carriage got under way again, and the drivers selected a different route.

. . .

Two hours later, the drivers halted the carriage close to the Second Empire Association. Some of the neighbouring buildings were showing signs of fire damage, and several dozen armed men were patrolling the street. A few rushed towards the carriage, then they stopped when they saw Amery and Loryn stepping down to the cobbles.

'Mister Amery, sir,' said one. 'You'd best come inside quickly. The streets around here aren't safe.'

The armed men escorted Amery and Loryn to the alleyway, and they were bundled through the guarded entrance and into the association. More armed men were packing out the ground floor, and Amery had to squeeze his way through to the office where the legal team had worked.

'Lord Tain is in the basement, sir,' said a clerk. 'Is he expecting you?'

'No,' said Amery. 'We came to offer our assistance. We shall go downstairs and see if we can speak to him.'

Amery led Loryn down into the basement, where more armed men were resting. Lord Tain was holding court in a large room, where maps of the city had been laid out onto a long table. A dozen others were there, receiving their orders.

'I want the road between the commercial harbour and the association patrolled night and day,' Tain was saying. 'The route must be kept open. If anyone hinders you, kill them.'

'Yes, my lord,' said a man.

Amery raised his hand, and Tain glanced in his direction.

'Ah, my lawyer,' Tain said. 'What are you doing here? I told you I would call for you if I needed you.'

'We came to offer our help, if any is needed, my lord,' said Amery.

'*We?*'

'Yes, my lord. I have brought Miss Loryn, my notary.'

Tain nodded. 'Everyone will have to excuse me for a moment or two,' he said. 'I wish to speak to my legal team in private. Amery, this way.'

He gestured towards a side door. Amery and Loryn walked through the crowd, as Tain opened the door. They went into a smaller room, the walls of which were stacked with crates of crossbows. Tain closed the door.

'We have a spy in the association,' said Tain.

'A spy, my lord?'

'Don't repeat my words back to me, Amery. Our attack on the secret school for Masters was foiled because they had advance notice of our intentions. They were evacuating when my men turned up.'

'I see, my lord. Wait – did you attack one of the schools?'

'Heston finally succumbed to my questions,' said Tain. 'It took a while, and a considerable quantity of blood, but he got there in the end. I need you to think very carefully, Amery, about who the spy might be. I have many other plans, and I can't afford any more mistakes. The Sanctians were deeply angered that I was unable to dispatch the young Masters. Well? What do you think?'

'I would have to look through the list of employees, sir. There have been many new recruits in recent days, and I am unfamiliar with some of them.'

'Then make a guess.'

'Very well, my lord. I know that the association has been hiring from among the old secret police. Perhaps one of them might actually be secretly working for your enemies? That seems to me to be the likeliest suggestion. Are all new employees properly vetted?'

'The more we hire, the harder it gets to vet them all thoroughly. But what am I supposed to do? I need manpower, and I need people who know the city, and who aren't afraid to get into violent situations. Where am I to find people like that, if not from the ranks of the secret police?'

'Lay a few traps, my lord. Feed select groups contradictory information, and observe which of your false plans, if any, are betrayed to the enemy. That will narrow down the list of suspects.'

A voice groaned from a nearby room, and Amery jumped in fright.

'What was that, my lord?' said Loryn.

'It's only Heston,' said Tain.

'Heston is still alive?' said Amery.

'You say the stupidest things when you're nervous, Amery. Do dead men groan? Of course he's still alive – he remains useful to me. Yesterday, he gave me another extremely valuable piece of information.' He smiled. 'I have discovered what has happened to the missing princess. We were so close to actually apprehending her. She was at the forge when my agents captured Drummond and Heston – can you believe that? My men, idiots that they are, completely ignored her.'

'Are you talking about Princess Abigone, my lord?'

'Who else? She's a student at the secret school for Makers. I have yet to inform the Sanctian ambassador of this development, but I think he might be interested to learn this. After all, the Sanctians are desperately searching for a legitimate reason to occupy this city, and Abigone might be exactly what they need.'

'I don't follow, my lord.'

'Abigone is a princess of Upper Down, and Upper Down is an ally of the Sanctian Empire. Why wouldn't the Sanctians intervene to rescue an ally? The Central Provinces could hardly complain about that. Ideally, I would find Abigone's school for Makers first, and kill all of the little brats that live there – the Masters and the Makers. Then, when the Sanctians find the bodies, we could blame their deaths on Metrius. The Corse will have murdered an allied princess; it's perfect. The Sanctians would be duty bound to take over the running of the city.'

'And have you found the secret school for Makers, my lord?'

Tain opened his mouth, then he smiled and closed it again. 'I think I shall be keeping that information to myself. Until the spy is identified, I need to be very careful. I'm sure you understand, Amery.'

'Of course, my lord.'

'Go home,' said Tain, 'and remain there. If the Sanctians intervene militarily, then I will need your help in drawing up the transitional constitution. You, too, Loryn – stay available.'

'Yes, my lord,' said Loryn.

Amery bowed low. 'I will be ready, my lord.'

He and Loryn left the room, and hurried up the stairs. They made their way through the crowds of armed men by the entrance, and went back out on to the street. Moments later, they were seated in their carriage, and were heading away from the association.

Amery put his head in his hands. 'Dear spirits, what have I done?'

'Sir?' said Loryn.

'He was talking about murdering children, Loryn.'

'I know, sir. What did you think the Sanctians wished to do to the young Masters and Makers who attend the secret schools?'

'I tried not to think about it. I tried to remain ignorant. Now, we are accomplices.'

'Yes, sir. We are.'

'How can you be so calm?'

'The methods employed by the Second Empire Association come as no surprise to me, sir.'

The carriage turned into another road, where there were no barricades.

'What do I do, Loryn?' Amery whispered.

'As your conscience demands, sir.'

Amery glanced out of the window, then he rapped on the access hatch. One of the drivers opened it and peered through.

'Yes, sir?'

'Stop the carriage,' said Amery; 'I'm getting out here.'

The drivers pulled on the reins, and the carriage ground to a halt.

'Where are we going, sir?' said Loryn.

'You are going back to the townhouse,' he said, as he opened the door. 'Drivers, take Miss Loryn back to the house. I will make my own way there later.'

'Are you sure, sir?' said one of the drivers. 'The city isn't safe at the moment.'

Amery stepped to the cobbles. 'I'm sure.'

'Take care, sir,' said Loryn.

Amery gazed at her, then he closed the side door. The drivers glanced down at him, then the carriage got underway again, leaving

Amery alone on the street. Amery waited until it had disappeared from view, then he began to walk.

'Well, well,' said Metrius. 'I wondered when you would come crawling back to me, Mister Amery.'

Amery stared at the carpeted floor of the large office.

'So,' Metrius went on, 'how is life at the Second Empire Association? Is Lord Tain well? And Lady Ursula? Oh. Wait a moment; Lady Ursula died in a most unfortunate accident a little while ago, didn't she? How forgetful of me. Be sure to send my deepest condolences to her most noble brother.'

Amery remained silent.

'Are you ever going to say anything, Mister Amery?' said Metrius. 'Do you have a message for me? Is the association using you as their errand boy?'

'No, my lord,' Amery said in a small voice.

'Speak up, boy. Was that a *no*? Then why are you here?'

'I... I was wondering if...'

'Yes?'

'I was wondering if I might be in a position to help you, my lord.'

'*You* help *me*? How droll. And how do you think you can help me, Mister Amery?'

'I have information.'

Metrius chuckled. 'Do you, indeed? Well, there's a surprise. Have you decided to betray your esteemed employer, eh?'

'The association are traitors, my lord.'

Metrius leaned his elbows on his desk, and rested his head on his hands. 'Yes, and? Why don't you tell me something I don't know?'

'It was Lady Fyenna's husband who betrayed Master Drummond, my lord,' said Amery, his words coming out in a tumble; 'and it was Drummond's brother Heston who betrayed the location of the secret school for Masters. But, the two cases aren't similar. Heston is being tortured for information. Yesterday, he revealed to Lord Tain that Abigone is attending the secret school for Makers. Lord Tain intends to slaughter all of the students and blame it on the Corse. He is receiving food and gold from the Sanctian warships at night; and weapons – crates of crossbows. The Sanctians are waiting for a legitimate reason to intervene militarily, and Tain thinks that Abigone might be the excuse they need. Lord Penny and Lord Harrow have been giving away the Corse secrets to the Sanctian ambassador, and…'

Metrius raised an eyebrow. 'Carry on.'

'Well, uh, I think that was about it, my lord. Oh, wait; no – Lord Tain thinks there is a spy working in the association.'

'I see.'

'I am giving you this information because I can't bear it any longer. The association is using illegal tactics to undermine the city of Klef Mordain, so that the Sanctians can take over.'

'Oh, Mister Amery; my poor, deluded Mister Amery. If only you had come to me some months ago, then I might have put you to use. Unfortunately for you, that time has passed.'

'But…'

'Did you seriously believe that I didn't already know every detail you have just told me?'

Amery stared at him. 'But how?'

Metrius sighed. 'I shall wait until it dawns upon you.'

'The spy? Lord Tain is right – there is a spy?'

'Well done. Is Lord Tain close to finding the spy?'

'I don't think so. Today, he asked me for advice on what to do about looking for him or her. I told him to concentrate on the new recruits who came from the secret police.'

Metrius laughed. 'Now, that amuses me.'

'Lord Tain wants to murder all of the students of the secret school! Children.'

'Yes, yes, I know. What surprises me is that you seem surprised by that. You are a Sanctian citizen, are you not? And you are a so-called expert on the law? Surely you knew that the Sanctians wish to execute every Master and Maker within their territories?'

'Yes, but...'

'But what?'

'I didn't think Lord Tain agreed with that policy. I thought there would be a compromise that allowed the children to live.'

'Your naivety is almost charming, Mister Amery. However, that does not excuse the fact that you are an accomplice to a series of horrific crimes. You have aided and abetted the Second Empire Association in all manner of illegal acts. How long did it take before you broke your first law of Klef Mordain? Did Lord Tain make you falsify the records of the association? From such humble beginnings, you have grown into a veritable monster – the man who covers up the treachery of others.'

'I am prepared to testify in court against my employers, my lord.'

'Pah. What rot. As if there will ever be a trial. It is too late for arrests, courts and trials. We are facing civil war and ruin, thanks to you and your association. Do you realise that, if I clicked my fingers, agents loyal to me will burst through that door behind you? They will drag you off into a dark alleyway and cut you to pieces, as a just reward for your criminal behaviour.'

'But I'm trying to make amends!'

'Stop wailing; it's pathetic. You know, it occurs to me that you are the worst sort of fool. When you had a chance to do the right thing, you spurned it. But now, when the end is nigh, that is when you decide to have a conscience. Did you not realise that all you had to do was keep your head down for a few weeks longer, and then the Sanctians would sweep through the city? As we know, the Sanctians always reward their friends, and you, dear Amery, have been a most useful friend to them.'

'Do you believe the cause is lost?'

'It was lost as soon as the eleven pro-Sanctians were elected on to the thirty,' said Metrius, 'and then all doubt vanished when the Sanctians began blockading our harbours. What can the Corse do when its numbers have been infiltrated by traitors? What can our galleys do against warships equipped with cannon? What can our part-time army of peasants and farmers do against the professional regiments of the Sanctian army? Do you have the answers, Mister Amery?'

'I could still be of use to you.'

'Nonsense. The only decision before me is whether to have you executed now, or leave it to Lord Tain.'

Amery trembled.

'Hmm, let me think,' said Metrius. 'On the one hand, I would derive considerable pleasure from watching you beg for mercy as you are tortured to death; but I have to consider the practicalities. Perhaps you were seen entering the building? That would be unfortunate. While, on the other hand, I would savour the rich irony of Lord Tain disembowelling you when he discovers what kind of man you really are, which he indubitably will, sooner or later.'

'Are you going to tell him that I came here, my lord?'

'No. That would be far too easy. I will say nothing to Lord Tain about your betrayal of him this day. Perhaps, when my anger cools, I may even decide that you should be allowed to provide me with information. It's unlikely, but possible.'

'Then you will let me live?'

'Yes. For now, at any rate. Run, Mister Amery. Leave quickly, before I change my mind.'

Amery fled from the office, and nearly ran into three agents who had been waiting outside the door. One of them, Portia, gave him a cold smile, then they allowed him to pass. Amery raced down the stairs and back out on to the main road. He staggered to the edge of the pavement, put his hands on his knees, and vomited into the gutter.

An hour later, after hurrying through the streets alone and in fear of his life, Amery walked through his own front door. Loryn was sitting in a chair by the entrance hall, and she jumped to her feet and rushed towards him.

'Thank the spirits that you got home safely, sir,' she said. 'I've been so worried.'

'You should leave while you can,' he said. 'I am a dead man.'

'What? Did something happen, sir? Where did you go?'

'I can't tell you, Loryn. The knowledge would endanger your life. I tried to save us, but I failed.'

She put her arms round him, and he sobbed into her hair.

'Everything will be all right, Amery,' she said.

'No, it won't. The city is doomed, Loryn, and so are we.'

CHAPTER 26
PAYING WHAT IS OWED

Old City, Klef Mordain – 14th Day of Lamenta 108

Abigone smiled the smile of someone in the first flushes of a new romance, then she immediately felt guilty. The city was in a terrible state, and yet she was happier than she had been in a long while. She told herself to keep her expression neutral as she walked towards the dining room. She knew that Denny would be there, but so would every other student from the two schools. For days, Reath had been bombarding her with questions about their fledgling relationship, from the banal to the downright vulgar, while Nyli had been wrapped in silent envy, almost refusing to speak to Abigone on occasions. Raewyn affected not to care; after all, she had Constans – and so she pretended not to be remotely interested in what Abigone and Denny had been doing. Stanza had continued to complain to Lady Fyenna, and walked around with a permanent frown, unable to understand why none of the adults in the school were acting to stop Abigone from seeing Denny.

As for the boys, well, Abigone didn't care what they thought.

She walked into the dining room, and Denny glanced up at her. He had already filled a tray for her with that morning's selection of breakfast foods, and he stood as she approached, and pulled out a chair for her. She sat down, and Denny sat next to her. At the same table were Aplin, Marlow and Ignatius, the three boys who seemed to look up to Denny the most, along with Reath, who had taken to sitting with them at mealtimes.

'I wish a boy would fetch my food for me,' Reath said. 'Valiance treats you like a princess, Abigone.' She glanced around, but no one responded. 'You were supposed to say, *That's because she is a princess,*' Reath went on. 'Do I have to supply the endings to my own jokes?'

'You do if they aren't funny,' said Marlow.

'Did you sleep well, Abigone?' said Denny.

'I did,' she said, 'though it was colder this morning.'

'It's autumn,' said Aplin. 'It'll be getting darker in the evenings soon.'

'Why?' said Reath.

'I don't know; it just does,' said Aplin. He glanced at Denny. 'What are we doing today?'

'Lady Fyenna wants us to practice transforming water into salt again,' said Denny. 'That's what the boys will be doing.'

Marlow leaned forward. 'She's getting us ready,' he whispered; 'ready to kill people if we're attacked again. She knows that Constans freezes, so she's relying on the rest of us. Well, not on Salus.'

'Poor Salus,' said Ignatius. 'He tries, but he can't clear his mind. That's why he's always in a foul temper.'

'I thought it was because his city is being destroyed,' said Reath.

'It's my city, too,' said Ignatius.

'Salus and Constans are aristocrats. They think they own the city. You're just a peasant.'

'Hey!' Ignatius cried.

'I'm a peasant, too,' said Reath. 'It's nothing to be ashamed of. Everyone in my village was a lot friendlier than the people in Klef Mordain, and more generous, too. Abigone, what are the folk like in Upper Down?'

'I don't know,' she said. 'I spent most of my life not being allowed to leave my father's palace.'

'That sounds like a prison,' said Reath.

'The palace has a large walled garden at its back. No, more like a large park. I could go there whenever I wanted to get outside, but I was forbidden from leaving the grounds. I didn't ever speak to many of the ordinary people. On the rare occasions when I did see them, they used to stare at me.'

'Have you met Valiance's father yet?' said Marlow.

'I've seen him, but we haven't had a proper conversation.'

'Lady Fyenna asked him to keep away from the floors where the classes take place,' said Denny.

'Why is he here?' said Ignatius.

'He has been employed to defend the school,' said Denny.

'Yes, but why is *your* father allowed to stay? My parents are probably going hungry in the Arnos Bank. Why can't all our families move into the school?'

'Mine live thousands of miles away,' said Reath.

'But mine don't,' said Ignatius. 'The Arnos Bank is only three or four miles from here. My mother is probably boiling shoe leather and river weeds again.' He gazed down at his breakfast tray. 'While we eat like lords and ladies.'

'Good morning, everyone,' said Fyenna, as she strode into the dining hall with Miss Vesta and a man in thick, dark robes. 'We have an honoured visitor in the school today. Lord Metrius, I would like to introduce you to the school's young Masters and Makers.'

The robed man smiled, but it seemed forced. 'Thank you, my noble lady,' he said. 'How good it is to be here. I daresay that I haven't set foot into the Maker school for nigh on ten years. First of all, I want to say that Lady Fyenna has told me how brave you have all been, following the unfortunate incidents that claimed the lives of Masters Drummond and Tobold. An awful tragedy. The stark truth is that the Sanctians wish to exterminate Masters and Makers as though they were naught but vermin. They see you as little better than rats or cockroaches. What can one do against such people but resist them? Klef Mordain has nurtured you, clothed you, fed you and taught you; and now, when the city faces its moment of direst peril, I call upon you to repay a little of that debt. Be ready to fight the Sanctians, just as we have protected you for decades. If we stand together, we shall prevail.'

A slight frown flashed over Fyenna's face before she could compose herself.

'Thank you for those kind words, Lord Metrius,' she said. 'Now, his noble lordship would like to speak to Abigone and Valiance. Will you please come forward?'

Abigone and Denny got to their feet as the other students gazed at them. Lord Metrius stared at them both as they walked to the front of the dining hall.

'We shall conduct the meeting in my office,' said Fyenna. 'If you would please follow me? Miss Vesta, stay here to supervise the other students.'

Fyenna led Metrius, Abigone and Denny down the stairs to the ground floor. At the end of the hallway, Mor Galthide was sitting upon a wooden bench next to the front door of the school, and he rose to his feet at the sight of the others.

'My son,' he said, 'and fair Abigone, good day to you both, and to Lady Fyenna.'

Metrius rolled his eyes.

'Good morning, Father,' said Denny, inclining his head.

'Good morning, sir,' said Abigone.

Fyenna opened the door to her office, and Metrius strode in, followed by Denny and Abigone. Fyenna began to follow them, then Metrius raised his hand to block her.

'You may remain outside for now,' said Metrius.

Fyenna narrowed her eyes.

'Remember your promise to me,' said Metrius. 'I allowed the boy's father to lodge here without complaint; and now it is time for you to uphold your end of the bargain.'

He closed the door in Fyenna's face.

Abigone turned, and saw that another woman was already in the office, standing in the shadows by the shuttered window.

'This is Miss Portia,' said Metrius.

'We have met before, my lord,' said Abigone, 'on the day I arrived in Klef Mordain.'

Metrius made no acknowledgment of her words as he walked round Fyenna's desk and sat in her chair. He frowned, and gazed up at the two students.

'Somehow,' he said, 'royalty is never as impressive in the flesh as its reputation suggests. Here you are, scions of two illustrious houses, yet to my eyes you look more like spoiled children.'

'Why did you imprison my father?' said Denny.

'I will be asking the questions and giving the orders, Prince of Sanctos,' said Metrius. 'Abigone, my first words concern you, and then you may leave. I have received information letting me know that the Sanctians have finally discovered your whereabouts from Master Drummond's brother. I know not if your presence here will be sufficient to spark a full military intervention by the forces of the Sanctian Empire, but, if they do come, it will not be to rescue you. They know you are a Maker, and if they discover the location of this school, they will butcher you along with the others. Do you have anything to say?'

'I am a signatory of a peace treaty with the Sanctians,' Abigone said.

'That will not save your life, girl,' said Metrius. 'The Sanctians will blame the deaths on the infighting caused by the civil conflict; they will no doubt loudly mourn your passing, using your death to prove to their allies that their intervention was just and legal. That is all I wished to say to you; you are dismissed.'

Abigone felt anger ripple through her. 'What do you want with Denny?'

'Denny, is it?' said Metrius. 'How charming that you use his pet name. I sense that you are fond of this runaway Prince of Sanctos. However, the task I have for Mor Dennahelm does not concern you.'

'I know you want us to fight for you,' Abigone went on. 'If you are sending Denny away to do something, then I will be included. You will not leave me here.'

Metrius chuckled. 'Am I hearing this right, Portia? Did this girl just presume to tell me what to do?'

'It appears that way,' said Portia.

Denny caught Abigone's gaze. 'I don't want you to endanger yourself for me.'

'I know you don't, Denny,' she said, 'but I would rather die than see you face peril alone. Lord Metrius, I appeal to your wisdom. Denny and I are a team – a Master and a Maker; and we have trained together. I destroyed the cannon of Prince Valentino, and I am ready to fight again, if you will allow me to stand by Denny's side.'

'Let her go with him, my lord,' said Portia. 'She might prove useful.'

'Do you think so?' said Metrius. 'I had imagined this task as better suited for one person to carry out alone; could it be done with two?'

'I sense that they will fight for each other, my lord. Sending two would only increase the likelihood of success.'

'You make a reasonable point, Portia,' said Metrius. He turned back to examine Abigone and Denny.

'What is the task?' said Denny.

Metrius ignored him. 'So be it, Portia,' he said. 'We shall send both. Go outside and distract Lady Fyenna and Mor Galthide. I have a feeling they may object to what I have in mind.'

Portia inclined her head, then she strode to the door and left the office.

'What if I refuse to do your bidding?' said Denny.

'Then I shall reveal the location of this school to the Sanctians,' said Metrius. 'Do you have any idea how much the secret schools have cost this city over the years – and for what? What benefit or return on our investment have we seen? How many students from the Central Provinces have passed through the doors of these schools, and then returned to their homes, giving nothing back to the city that protected them, and nurtured their skills? Were it not for the respect in which Lady Fyenna is held by the population of this city, the schools would have been closed down years ago. It is about time, I think, that you began to pay your way.'

The door opened again. 'The way is clear, my lord,' said Portia.

Metrius got to his feet, and then he led Abigone and Denny out of the office. They entered the storeroom next to the office, where the trap-door was lying open.

'Down you both go,' said Metrius, 'into the murky depths. Portia will escort you to where you need to be, and she will provide you with your instructions. I will remain here to see the expression on Lady Fyenna's face when I tell her what you are about to attempt. May the spirits bless your endeavours.'

Portia gestured to the iron ladder, and Denny began to descend into the cavern that lay below the school. Abigone went next. She climbed down into the darkness, then Portia followed, a small oil lamp grasped in her left hand. They reached the bottom, and Portia eyed the two students.

'Follow me,' she said, then she set off.

Abigone and Denny followed Portia through the maze of tunnels and rock-hewn chambers for twenty minutes, then she stopped when they arrived in a small, square cavern.

Portia pointed towards a set of stairs leading upward to a wooden hatch. 'That is where you will emerge into the city streets,' she said.

'Will we need armour or weapons?' said Denny.

'No,' said Portia. 'Your civilian clothes will help you blend in, and you may be searched when you arrive at your destination. What you must do shall be done with your Master and Maker abilities. At the top of the stairs, you will enter the rear of an abandoned house, damaged in the recent troubles. Go out through the front door, and you will appear on Cornmarket Road. The Sanctian Embassy will be a hundred yards to your right.'

'The Sanctian Embassy?' said Abigone.

Portia eyed her. 'Do not interrupt me again. Your chances of surviving this day are slender, and what I say might make the difference between life and death. When you reach the front entrance to the embassy, you will be stopped by armed men working for the Sanctian ambassador. You, Mor Dennahelm, will reveal your true identity to those men. You will tell them that you have escaped confinement, and you will beg for sanctuary. Abigone, you will pretend to be his young wife. Ask to speak to the ambassador. As soon as you are in his presence, use your abilities to eliminate him. Then, make your escape. I will post an agent here, in this cavern, to wait for you. If you lead soldiers to this cavern, you will be abandoned. If you try to make your way back to the school on foot, you will be abandoned.'

'Killing the ambassador will provoke the Sanctians into a full invasion,' said Denny.

'Do not question the strategy of Lord Metrius, boy. It is time for you to pay your dues. Go.'

Abigone glanced at the stairs. 'How many soldiers are guarding the embassy?' she said.

'Over a hundred,' said Portia. 'None of our agents can get close enough to the ambassador to kill him.'

Abigone nodded. 'Come on, Denny; let's get this over with.'

Denny gazed at her, then they began to climb the stairs, leaving Portia standing in the cavern. Denny pushed open the hatch at the top of the stairs, then he and Abigone climbed into a small room with a high window.

Abigone closed the hatch.

'I wish we had never met,' said Denny.

'Why would you say that?' said Abigone.

He took her hand. 'I don't think we're meant to come back from this task alive, Abigone. Lord Metrius doesn't care if we survive. Because of me, your life is in danger. If we hadn't met, then you would be safe.'

'I meant what I said before – we are a team. We work better that way. Alone, either one of us would likely die, but together?'

'We are about to walk into the Sanctian Embassy.'

'Then we had better get our stories straight. If I am you wife, then where did we meet, and where was I born? Would a Prince of Sanctos have married a commoner? They might question us separately, and we need to know what to say. Where is your father, for example? Did you flee from him because you are loyal to the emperor?'

'You're right,' he said. 'We'll work out the details, and then we'll go.' He lifted a hand, and brushed his fingers against her face. 'If you die and I live, I will kill Lord Metrius.'

'I will do the same if I live and you die.'

'We are about to start a war.'

'Then let's make sure we get it right.'

Twenty minutes later, Abigone and Denny hurried along the street towards the embassy. They had decided that, if they were meant to be fleeing, then they couldn't just stroll towards the building.

Four men with long, steel-tipped pikes moved out to block their way.

'This part of the street is restricted,' one cried. 'Step away.'

Denny raised his empty hands. 'I am here to beg for sanctuary with my wife,' he said. 'Listen to my accent – am I not from Sanctos? I am a citizen of the empire.' He glanced over his shoulder, as though he was fearful of being followed. 'We have escaped from our captor,' he said. 'Please help us.'

A sergeant narrowed his eyes. 'Name?'

'I would rather tell that to the ambassador in person,' said Denny. 'My name is known.'

'You must tell us, or you will never set foot inside the embassy, boy.'

'Very well,' said Denny. He straightened his back. 'I am Prince Dennahelm of Sanctos, grandson of the Most Exalted Emperor Antonio, abducted from my home by my traitorous father. It is from my father that my wife and I have escaped.'

The soldiers stared at him, and more gathered round.

The sergeant got down to one knee and bowed his head. 'Your Imperial Highness,' he said; 'forgive me for calling you *boy*. I spoke in ignorance.'

'Are we sure he's telling the truth, sergeant?' said another soldier.

'He has his mother's eyes,' the sergeant said. 'I have served in Princess Volena's household; this is her son.'

'You served my mother?' said Denny, his eyes widening. 'How is she? I have not seen her since I was taken from Sanctos.'

'She mourns your loss deeply, Your Highness. And your royal cousins also miss your company.'

'As I miss theirs,' Denny said. He reached into his tunic, and pulled out a silver chain that hung round his neck. 'Here is my signet ring, the stamp of my imperial seal.'

The other soldiers stared at it, then most bowed their heads.

'It is the lost prince,' one whispered.

The sergeant wiped a tear from his cheek and stood. 'Get them inside, quickly. Get them off the street.'

The soldiers formed up around Denny and Abigone and escorted them at a brisk pace towards the front doors of the embassy.

An officer on duty raised a hand. 'Who are these people, sergeant?'

'The man is Prince Mor Dennahelm, sir,' said the sergeant, 'and the woman is his wife. They have escaped the clutches of Mor Galthide.'

Denny held out his signet ring for the officer to inspect.

'By all the spirits,' the officer cried. He bowed low. 'Your Highness, I am at your service. Please, come into the embassy, where we shall protect you with our lives.'

They entered a large hallway, where more soldiers had set up a barricade by the stairs.

'Your Highness,' said the officer, 'are you hurt, hungry? Does your noble wife require anything? I did not know that you were married.'

Denny gestured to Abigone. 'We wed last year, when my father took me through Mylos. This is Lady Cordelia, daughter of the Duchess of Fellbrook.'

Abigone held out her hand, and the officer kissed it. 'We are indebted to your generosity,' said Abigone. 'For long months, Prince Mor Dennahelm and I have been in fear of our lives. His father is looking for us.'

'Is Mor Galthide in the city, Your Highness?' said the officer.

'He is,' said Denny. 'My wife and I were brought here by my father, as he wished to aid those opposed to the Sanctian Empire. He met with a man... I think his name was Lord Metrius. I overheard them talk about plots and conspiracies. I can fully debrief you later, but my wife is tired. Might she sit?'

'Of course, Your Highness. Come this way – there is a small anteroom where you may rest.' He gestured to another officer, who was walking down the stairs. 'Sir! May I have a moment?'

The two officers conferred by the base of the stairs, while the sergeant led Abigone and Denny to a chamber that lay by the entrance hall. Abigone sat down, feigning exhaustion, and Denny placed a hand on her shoulder.

'You have been so brave, my darling,' he said to her. 'We are safe now. My father cannot reach us here.'

The officers walked into the room, and the elder of the two eyed Denny with suspicion.

'Your Highness,' he said; 'please forgive me, but I must ask you a few questions to confirm your identity.'

'Have I not already shown the other officer my signet ring?' said Denny. 'Do you doubt the word of the Prince of Sanctos?'

'No, sire, and yet the ambassador will require proof. Klef Mordain is experiencing grave troubles, and it would not be beyond the wit of our enemies to have sent an imposter here, pretending to be our beloved prince.'

'Ask your questions. I shall not be daunted.'

'Thank you, Your Highness,' the officer said. 'Firstly, what type of tree does your mother sit under when she takes her tea in the Western Court of the palace?'

'The same beech I fell from when I was six,' said Denny.

'And what colour are the eyes of your cousin Prince Francesco?'

'They are dark green.'

'Thank you, sire. My final question – what token did Count Sebastian gift you on your twelfth birthday?'

Denny smiled. 'He gave me my first sword. He had my name engraved upon the hilt.'

The officer fell to his knees and bowed his head. 'It is he. We are in the presence of an imperial prince. Can you forgive my questioning, sire?'

'You are forgiven,' said Denny. 'Please, stand.'

The officer got back to his feet. 'I shall now escort you to the ambassador, sire. He is on the rooftop loggia, taking refreshments. There will be food and drink there for you and your noble wife.'

'You have our thanks,' said Denny.

He helped Abigone stand, and they made their way to the upper floors of the embassy, passing courtiers who bowed before them, news having spread through the building quicker than they could climb the many stairs.

They reached the guarded rooftop, which had a long wooden loggia stretching over half of it. Sitting under the shade of the loggia were several people, all clustered around an older man in fine robes. The officer rushed forward, and whispered in the older man's ear. The older man's eyes widened, and he gazed up at where Denny and Abigone were standing. He got to his feet, then bowed low.

'Your Highness,' said the officer, 'may I present to you His Eminence Ambassador Tertius?'

Denny nodded. 'Well met, Ambassador.'

'Your Imperial Highness,' said Tertius; 'your eyes give you away, for I see the likeness of Princess Volena in them. But who is your bride? She is from the Duchy of Fellbrook, or so I am told?'

'Fellbrook is my noble mother's inheritance, Your Eminence,' said Abigone. 'I was brought up in the castle there.'

'And how did you meet Prince Mor Dennahelm, my lady?'

Abigone smiled. 'His father was passing through Mylos, before word had reached us that he was a wanted fugitive. Naturally, my mother offered him and the noble prince hospitality. It was there that I came to know Prince Mor Dennahelm, or Denny, as I call him.'

The ambassador smiled. 'That is indeed the name by which the prince was known upon Sanctos. Welcome, my lady.' The ambassador gestured to a few chairs. 'Please be seated, my prince, and my prince's fair wife. There is food and drink enough for all.'

Denny whispered a few hushed words under his breath. Abigone glanced at the ambassador, but nothing had changed.

One of the ambassador's colleagues coughed and spluttered. 'Don't touch the food, I beg you,' he cried. 'It has been ruined by too much salt.'

The ambassador frowned, then he tasted a morsel from a dish, and grimaced. 'Who prepared this food? I will have them flogged.' He sipped from a glass of red wine, then he gestured to a servant. 'Take it away; at once! Your Highness, I do apologise. We shall have fresh food brought here.'

Denny glanced at Abigone, and she nodded.

'Blessed spirits,' she whispered, 'with your permission, summon for me ten dragons of stone, and ten of wood.'

The loggia exploded, showering the ambassador and his colleagues with fragments of wood, then tons of stone were ripped from the fabric of the building. Denny grabbed Abigone and they dived for cover as the sky began to rain with great boulders and blocks of wood. Half of the roof gave way, collapsing into the floors below. The ambassador screamed, then a boulder fell on him, crushing his body beneath its weight.

Denny and Abigone scrambled for the stairs.

'Halt,' cried an officer. 'Your wife, sire; she is a Maker!'

Denny launched himself at the officer. He crouched, grasped on to the man's leg, then hurled him up, back and over the low wall that ran around the edge of the roof. The officer screamed as he tumbled through the air, then he collided with the pavement in front of the embassy, his head splitting open when it hit the cobbles.

Denny and Abigone raced down the stairs, as the building trembled and swayed. Tiles and masonry were raining down on the soldiers in the street.

'The roof has collapsed!' Denny cried as they reached the next floor down. 'Evacuate the building!'

A mixture of servants and soldiers stared at him.

'The ambassador is still up there,' Denny shouted, as he pointed at the stairs. 'Go to his aid!'

Several soldiers obeyed, and they raced for the stairs.

Denny gestured to the others. 'Get downstairs – save yourselves.'

Abigone unhooked a wall lamp as soon as the hallway had cleared, then she opened a door and threw it inside. It smashed against a table and burst into flames. The fire reached a set of curtains, and within moments smoke was belching out of the room.

Denny took Abigone's hand, and they ran off, as part of the ceiling cracked and fell. They made it down two more flights of stairs before their way was blocked by a panicking mob of courtiers trying to flee the collapsing building. Denny gestured to a window at the deserted end of the corridor, then he picked up a piece of broken masonry from the carpet and hurled it through the glass, smashing the pane into a hundred pieces. He and Abigone ran to the window and looked down.

'Can you climb?' he said.

'We could jump from here.'

'And if we twist our ankles?'

The sergeant from before ran over to them. 'My prince!' he cried. 'Come with me; we will get you out of the building.'

Denny pulled a knife from the man's belt and drove it into his heart.

'Sorry, sergeant,' Denny said, as the man stared at him. Denny let go of the hilt, and the man fell to the floor.

More soldiers appeared at the end of the hallway. They glanced at the body of the sergeant, then at Abigone and Denny.

'Blessed spirits,' said Abigone, 'with your permission, summon for me ten dragons of stone.'

The entire façade of the embassy collapsed, sliding from the building and taking with it a dozen screaming courtiers and soldiers. More boulders fell, smashing the hallway to pieces as Denny and Abigone clambered through the open window. Denny began to climb down, and Abigone took a chance, and let go. She fell fifteen feet, and landed on the body of a man lying face down on the pavement. She felt a pain in her left leg, but managed to get to her feet as Denny reached the cobbles next to her.

'Walk, don't run,' Denny said, as he took her hand.

'Ow,' Abigone muttered. 'My leg.'

'You are going to have to learn how to climb, my dear wife,' Denny said, as they walked away from the building. 'You're limping.'

An embassy soldier barged into them.

'Watch where you're going,' Denny said in his most imperious tone. 'You could have knocked over my wife.'

'Sorry, sir,' said the soldier, as he sprinted towards the embassy.

Denny and Abigone reached the far pavement, and kept walking. They had gone forty yards when the ground shook, and a roar of noise rose up, followed by a great cloud of dust. They turned. The Sanctian Embassy was in ruins, its upper floors collapsed into rubble.

'There are bodies everywhere,' said Abigone.

'I feel sorry for them,' said Denny. 'It was a wicked thing we were asked to do.'

They reached the house with the hatch leading to the tunnel. They went into the back room, where they had made their plans earlier, and Denny crouched by the floor. He tried to lift the hatch, but it wouldn't move.

'What's wrong?' said Abigone.

'It's locked,' he said. 'The bastards have locked us out.'

'They expected us to die.'

'We still might, if we are caught here.' He stood. 'I know how to get to the Maker school.'

'Do you? How?'

'I worked out the school's location when we were on its roof with Miss Vesta and the others.'

'Portia told us that we would be abandoned if we tried walking there on foot.'

'We have already been abandoned, Abigone. You were right – they did not expect us to survive. If we can get to the school, then my father and Lady Fyenna will protect us.'

They went back to the front of the house and peered out through a window. To their right was a scene of chaos and destruction. Bodies were being dragged away from the collapsed ruins of the embassy, while others were staggering over the cobbles, covered in blood.

Denny lowered his gaze. 'What have we done, Abigone?'

'I think we may have provoked the Sanctians into invading Klef Mordain,' she said.

'We killed a lot of innocent people.'

Abigone said nothing.

'Thank you for coming to my assistance on the roof,' Denny went on. 'I tried to transform the water in the ambassador's body to salt, but... I don't know what went wrong.'

'We did it together, Denny.'

'Are you ready to walk through Klef Mordain in broad daylight? We'll have to stick to the back streets, and try to avoid the roadblocks.'

She kissed him. 'I'm ready, Denny.'

CHAPTER 27
DECLARATION

Old City, Klef Mordain – 15th Day of Lamenta 108

Mor Galthide emerged from the room and closed the door.

'How is he?' said Fyenna.

'Tired but unharmed, my lady,' he said. 'May I speak freely?'

'You may.'

Mor Galthide's expression darkened. 'If ever I see that dog Metrius again, I will rip his head from his shoulders. How dare he send my son and his beloved to the Sanctian Embassy?'

'They both got back in one piece. We should be grateful.'

'I am grateful, my lady; but my anger burns as bright as any fire. Metrius did not care if they lived or died; in fact, he assumed they would die. My son told me that the hatch they were supposed to use in their escape was locked.'

'I am just as angry, Mor Galthide,' Fyenna said, 'but we must be careful. If Lord Metrius knows the extent of our ire against him, he could send agents to harm us.'

'Would he be so spiteful?'

'He believes the fall of Klef Mordain is inevitable. He had Denny and Abigone assassinate the Sanctian ambassador, knowing full well that the Sanctians will have to respond. It was an act of war. The Sanctians now have a legitimate reason to invade.'

'This is wrong of me,' said Mor Galthide, 'but I cannot but help feel some measure of pride in my son's actions. To walk into a heavily-guarded embassy, strike down the ambassador, and then escape without a scratch?'

'He did it with Abigone's assistance.'

'Of course, my lady. I did not mean to take anything away from her achievement. My son told me that it was she who destroyed the embassy building, and it was she who delivered the killing blow to the ambassador. Crushed by a falling rock, while sitting on a roof? Ha. I wish I had seen it. You visited Abigone earlier – does she flourish?'

'She hurt her leg jumping from a first floor window,' said Fyenna, 'then she made it worse by walking through half of the Old City. She will need a few days to rest.'

'May I speak with her, my lady?'

'Only if you agree to me being present.'

'I acquiesce. Lead on.'

They went up a flight of stairs, and went to the door of Abigone's room.

Fyenna knocked. 'May Mor Galthide and I come in, Abigone?'

'Just a moment, ma'am,' came a voice from within. 'All right.'

Fyenna opened the door. Abigone was lying on her bed, while above her, the window was open, letting in the warm sunshine.

'Mor Galthide wishes to say a few words to you,' said Fyenna.

Abigone sat up in bed. Mor Galthide strode in, placed his hands on his hips, and grinned down at her.

'You, my young lady, are a blessed marvel,' he said. 'My son has told me all that you did, and I wanted to thank you in person. My son loves you, I think, and I could not be happier with his choice. I want the best for my son, and you match that requirement with distinction. You are brave, resourceful, and beautiful – everything a young noblewoman of royal blood should be.'

Abigone's cheeks flushed a little. 'Thank you, sir.'

'However,' Mor Galthide went on, 'I am also enraged by what that vile cur made you do. I speak of Metrius, of course, may his name be cursed. If that dog returns here, he will not be leaving with his head.' His expression softened. 'My son also told me that you pretended to be his wife. How I long for the day when pretence becomes reality. If I live to see you wedded to my boy, I will die a contented man. Has he spoken to you yet of marriage?'

Abigone's face flushed a deeper colour.

'Perhaps we should leave her to rest,' said Fyenna. 'Let's not put any pressure on our young couple.'

Mor Galthide inclined his head. 'As you will, my lady. I shall go to the kitchen, and prepare some food for my son.'

He left the room, and Fyenna closed the door. 'Pay no heed to his talk of marriage, Abigone,' she said. 'It's a little early to be thinking of that.'

'Is it?' said Abigone. 'My father used to arrange betrothals after interviewing candidates for less than ten minutes. My betrothal to Prince Henry was conducted by letter.'

'Perhaps, but you will have to make up your own mind this time. No one is arranging things for you anymore. You are free to decide how fast, and how soon you want things to progress. I was engaged to my husband for two years, and we knew each other for a long time before that.' She glanced away. 'Of course, you shouldn't follow my example. My marriage ended in disaster.'

'Thank you for giving me advice on this, ma'am,' said Abigone. 'Normally, I would ask Kilbride about these things. I miss her.'

'I am happy to give you advice, and I will act as a shield between you and Mor Galthide, if you wish. He has sworn to do as I command, and so I will keep him away from you, if you think he is too overbearing.'

'I don't know what I think. Did you know when you were in love with your husband?'

Fyenna smiled. 'Yes. I knew.'

'How?'

'I had seen a few other men before I met him and, to me, it was obvious. I thought about him all the time; I wanted to be with him; I was attracted to him. I even got jealous when he spoke to other women.'

'I feel all of those things about Denny.'

'Yes, but you are young.'

'I am almost nineteen, ma'am.'

'Exactly. Don't worry about marriage at the moment, just enjoy being together. If he likes you as much as I think he does, then he will ask when the time is right.'

Abigone started to cry.

'What's wrong?' said Fyenna.

'I don't know,' she said. 'I can't control it. I'm happy, then I'm sad. I keep thinking about some of the people Denny and I killed. There was a sergeant, who was so glad to see Denny that he shed a few tears; then, later, Denny had to kill him. The way the sergeant looked at Denny... It was horrible.'

'I'm relieved to hear you say that. If you enjoyed killing, then I don't think I would be able to look you in the eye. Witnesses are claiming that over sixty people died when the embassy collapsed.'

Abigone wiped the tears from her face.

'Listen to me,' said Fyenna; 'you were placed into that situation by Lord Metrius. If you hadn't acted in the way that you did, neither you nor Denny would have made it back to the school alive. On the one hand, I am very glad that you survived the ordeal, and not a little proud; but, on the other, I am furious with Lord Metrius. He came to talk to me after Portia had taken you both away into the tunnels. He told me what he had commanded you to do. Had I been a Master, his blood would now be salt. I told him to get out of my school, and he laughed. I fear that my relationship with him will never recover, for how could I ever forget this betrayal?'

'Denny asked him what he would do if we refused to undertake his task.'

'And what did he say?'

'He said he would give the location of the school to the Sanctians, ma'am.'

Fyenna felt her shoulders sag. 'Get some rest,' she said. 'I… I need to… think.' She stood, and went to the door. 'I will see you soon, Abigone.'

She left the room, closed the door, and put a hand against a wall to steady herself. Abigone's words echoed through her mind. She tried to wave them away as nothing more than a vain threat, not something that Metrius had meant sincerely, but she remembered the way he had laughed in her face when he had told her where he had sent Denny and Abigone.

She hurried down the stairs, and ran into Mor Galthide, who was carrying a tray.

'My lady,' he said.

She leaned in close. 'Say nothing of this to anyone but, if we were to evacuate all students out of this city, then where should we go?'

He gazed at her. 'Do you mean leave Klef Mordain, my lady? If so, then we should journey to the west, to the pass at Upper Down. That would be my advice.'

'That route is too long, and too dangerous for the younger students. The Westlanders would raid us day and night.'

'Then what do you suggest, my lady?'

'I don't know, but be ready.'

Mor Galthide inclined his head, then Fyenna went down to the ground floor and entered her office. She gazed up at a map of Klef Mordain and the surrounding area. If Metrius no longer wished to protect the school, then Fyenna's first objective would be to get the students out of the Old City. That would be difficult enough, but where could they go after that?

She felt close to despair. If Metrius truly believed that the end was inevitable, then he might lash out at everyone around him, creating a cataclysm for the Sanctians to inherit.

The door opened, and Lady Niscoll glanced at Fyenna.

Fyenna's eyes narrowed. 'If Metrius has sent you here, then…'

Niscoll raised her palms. 'Lord Metrius did not send me; I am here of my own accord. Might I come in?'

Fyenna gestured to a chair. Niscoll edged past her, and sat.

'I heard about what happened,' said Niscoll. 'The entire city knows that the Sanctian Embassy collapsed, killing the ambassador, but I know what actually happened.'

'Did Metrius tell you?'

'He did. You have my deepest commiserations, Fyenna. Lord Metrius told me that you had taken the news rather badly, my old friend.'

'He sent two of my students off on a task that he assumed would kill them both.'

Niscoll blinked. 'Assumed? You mean... are they alive?'

'Alive and well. They made it back here on foot, abandoned and betrayed by those who sent them on their way.'

'Ah. Then, do you remain angry with Lord Metrius? He said that you lost your temper with him.'

'Of course I am angry. My students are children, and he used them as though they were weapons. Worse than that, because he assumed they would die, he did not see fit to lend a hand with their escape. He locked the tunnels against them, forcing them to flee on foot.'

Niscoll narrowed her eyes. 'I can see how enraged you are, Fyenna, but haven't you often spoken in the past about using the students to defend the city?'

'Assassinating the Sanctian ambassador is not the same as defending the city. The Sanctians are liable to react; how can they not?'

'They have already reacted,' said Niscoll. 'I have it on good authority that the Sanctian admiral upon the *Bitter Respite* – the flag ship anchored out in the estuary – has already sent a message to the twenty thousand soldiers upon our southern frontier, ordering them to advance into our territory with all haste.'

Fyenna collapsed into a chair.

'That is why I am here, to tell you this,' said Niscoll. 'Well, it was one of the reasons. Another was to offer my profoundest sympathies for the loss of your two students, but it seems that none are required. I must say, it was remarkably proficient of them to get back here in one piece. Clearly, they are a credit to your abilities as a teacher.'

'I fear that had little to do with it. How long will it take for the Sanctian army to get here?'

'It is a mere four-day march from the border with Lesser Down to the boundaries of the city, but it will take time for the message to reach them, and more time to put their affairs in order. If the message was sent yesterday, then we perhaps have another nine or ten days.'

'Nine days? Dear spirits. Why? Why did Metrius do it? He must have known that the Sanctians would retaliate in strength.'

'They reacted exactly as he hoped they would. He wants the Sanctians to invade. He told me that he would rather see the city burned in a conflagration, than be slowly starved to death. Needless to say, I do not agree with him, but you and I swore oaths to obey his commands.'

Fyenna shook her head. 'I cannot, in all good conscience, continue to adhere to that oath. Metrius will make a bonfire of Klef Mordain, and for what? His pride? The Sanctians will crush us.'

'Your response disappoints me, but there is nothing that can be done, my old friend. Each of us must accept the fate the spirits decide to bestow upon us.'

'I cannot accept that. I have eleven students under my care, along with Eshia and Miss Vesta. Their safety is my responsibility. I love them. In some ways, I love them as much as I loved my own son. I certainly love them more than I loved my husband.'

'I have some information regarding your husband.'

'You do?'

Niscoll nodded. 'Word reached us some time ago, from Campsie,' she said. 'That is where your husband disembarked the ship he was put on by Lord Penny. Selanius has been given shelter by the local Sanctian administrator. It seems he is safe and well.'

Fyenna narrowed her eyes. 'Of course he is. He gets to live in safety, while the city he betrayed burns.'

'I have more news about Selanius, if you wish to hear it.'

'Not particularly.'

'It concerns you; otherwise, I would not trouble you with it. As you may know, Lord Penny temporarily confiscated all of your husband's assets when he placed him on to that ship, pending a further investigation into Selanius's accounts. According to Penny, there were a few discrepancies.'

'I know about those. Selanius told me.'

'Well, the outcome was that nine-tenths of your husband's wealth has been formally requisitioned by Lord Penny, to cover the taxes, fines and expenses incurred. The remainder has, by law, gone to you.'

'The entire city is collapsing around us, and yet the tax department is still functioning?'

'It has become Lord Penny's main source of wealth, since he was elected to the thirty. He is now the richest man in the city, and four hundred armed soldiers guard his mansion. However, that is not the point I was trying to make. The one-tenth of Selanius's wealth that has passed to you is not inconsiderable.'

Fyenna rolled her eyes. 'Will I be able to spend it all in nine days before the Sanctians get here?'

'There was no money involved, just physical assets. You now own a small house in Nether Hall, for example.' Niscoll pulled a rolled-up document from her robes. 'The details are listed here.'

She passed the scroll to Fyenna, who placed it onto the desk without reading it.

Niscoll gazed at her. 'If you meant what you said about reneging on your oath to Lord Metrius, then this might be the last time we meet, my old friend,' she went on. 'I have decided to remain by his side, despite the recklessness of his recent decisions. For your sake, though, I will not mention to Lord Metrius what you said about the oath.'

'Does it matter? Lord Metrius and I will never trust each other again. Will you warn me if he intends to do harm to the school or the students?'

Niscoll smiled sadly. 'Lord Metrius would never harm the school, Fyenna.'

'Are you sure about that?'

'Quite sure. He is angry with you, as you are angry with him, but he understands that we face a common enemy. At the very least, he knows that you and the students will resist the Sanctians with all your strength. Why would he throw that away?'

'I want to believe you.'

'Then do so.' Niscoll got to her feet. 'This parting saddens me. I came here to mourn the loss of two students, and I leave with the renunciation of your oath ringing in my ears. In time, your anger may cool, and you might reconsider. If that turns out to be the case, then my door will always be open to you.'

Fyenna stood, and the two women embraced.

'May the spirits watch over you and your students,' Niscoll said. 'Farewell, Fyenna.'

The older woman strode from the room. Fyenna glanced at the rolled-up documents sitting on her desk. What use did she have for a cottage in Nether Hall, when the Sanctian army would be arriving in a matter of days? She shook her head, then left her office. It was time to give Raewyn and Stanza a lesson on summoning metals, and she was already five minutes late.

She hurried up the stairs to the classrooms. The all-conquering army of the Sanctians might be approaching, but the school would continue to do as it had always done.

'Very good, Raewyn,' Fyenna said. 'Your steel is improving. Did you finish that chapter on removing impurities?'

Raewyn smiled. 'Yes, ma'am. I read it twice yesterday evening.'

'Why is Abigone not in class with the first years today, ma'am?' said Stanza.

'You noticed that, did you?'

'Yes, ma'am. I saw Reath and Nyli with Miss Vesta, but Abigone wasn't there.'

'She hurt her leg,' said Fyenna. 'She is resting in bed.'

'How did she hurt her leg, ma'am?'

'She fell.'

Raewyn and Stanza glanced at each other.

'Why don't you girls tell me what you have heard?' said Fyenna; 'for it seems clear to me that you have heard something.'

'No one saw Abigone or Valiance after Lord Metrius took them away yesterday, ma'am,' said Raewyn. 'They were gone for the whole day. Then, last night, there was a noise in the corridor outside my door. It sounded like Abigone being helped to her room.'

'Why did she come back late at night, ma'am?' said Stanza.

'Damn those creaky floorboards,' said Fyenna.

Stanza opened her mouth to ask another question, then she stopped as a low rumble shook the building. It was quiet at first, then the volume of noise increased.

Mor Galthide appeared at the door, as dust fell from the ceiling. 'My apologies for entering the girls' floor, my lady,' he said, 'but the Sanctian warships are bombarding the shore of the Old City.'

'Are you sure? Might it be another... what was it called – a salute?'

Mor Galthide cocked his ear to the rumbling. 'That is a sound I have heard a hundred times before, my lady. Stones are being torn asunder, and masonry ripped apart. No cannon ball can reach as far as the school, but I fear the waterfront is taking a pounding. Shall we hasten to the roof?'

'Can we, ma'am?' said Stanza.

Fyenna gripped the back of a chair as the building shook again. 'Very well,' she said. She glanced at Mor Galthide. 'Summon the students and the staff, and ask them to go up onto the roof.'

Mor Galthide inclined his head. 'Yes, my lady.'

Stanza frowned. 'Valiance's father is like a giant. Why is he allowed to stay in the school, ma'am? It's against the rules for the relatives of students to live here.'

'Ask me that another time, Stanza. Come, girls; follow me.'

Raewyn and Stanza got to their feet and walked out of the classroom with Fyenna. They went to the stairs, and ascended to the floor where the boys had been found rooms. They ascended again, passing the level where the girls slept, then they reached the hatch that led on to the roof. Fyenna opened it, and the noise of the cannon increased. She led Raewyn and Stanza onto the roof, and they walked to the northern edge of the building. Smoke was rising from the five Sanctian warships anchored in the estuary, and more smoke was coming from a long strip of buildings along the waterfront facing the vessels. The barrage of cannon fire was being staggered by the Sanctians. One ship would fire, then the one to its left, then the next, and so on, that by the time the fifth had fired, the first was ready to do so again. A tall building by the shore collapsed in a roar of noise, its smashed masonry tumbling down onto the cafes that littered the wide esplanade.

The other students arrived, led by Miss Vesta and Mor Galthide, followed by Eshia, Fyenna's secretary and the three women who worked in the kitchen and laundry-room. Even Abigone was there. She was limping, and Denny was helping her walk.

Mor Galthide raised his arms. 'Witness the power our foe brings to bear!' he shouted over the noise of the cannon. 'No stout wall, no proud fortress, no building of stone can withstand it. All crumble to dust.'

'Are they going to destroy the whole city?' cried Reath, her eyes wide.

'Be at peace, little one,' said Mor Galthide; 'the mighty cannon of the Sanctians cannot reach this school, so how would they be able to pound the other parts of the city? No, child, this is a warning, or a declaration. They are delivering a message unto us.'

The cannon fell silent.

'And thus the message ends,' said Mor Galthide, lowering his arms.

'Give me your attention,' said Fyenna. 'Everyone; listen.'

The students and staff turned to face her.

'Valiance's father is correct,' she said. 'That was merely a message and, if my interpretation of it is sound, then it can mean only one thing – a declaration of war. As of this moment, Klef Mordain is at war with the Sanctian Empire.'

She waited for her words to sink in.

'Yesterday,' she went on, 'the Sanctian ambassador to this city was assassinated. What you have just seen and heard is their response to that act. There is more to come. To our south, twenty thousand Sanctian soldiers will soon begin their march across our frontiers; they will be entering the city in a matter of days.'

Nyli burst into tears, and several other students looked close to panic.

'Some of us suspected this day would arrive,' Fyenna went on, 'and our fears have come to pass. As Head Maker, know that I will never abandon you; I will never stop fighting for you, and I will never give up hope that we will endure this crisis. While you continue with your studies, I shall be working hard on your behalf. Now, go back to your classrooms, and carry on with your lessons. This school will continue as normal, until I command otherwise. Dismissed.'

The students stared at her.

'Listen to the Head Maker,' said Miss Vesta. 'Back to work, everyone, or I'll ask Valiance's father to chase you down those stairs. Reath, help your sister. Marlow, lead your classmates back to their lesson.'

Fyenna watched as Miss Vesta and Mor Galthide cajoled and herded the students towards the stairs. She glanced back at the waterfront. A fire had broken out in one of the damaged buildings, and flames were rising over the rooftops.

Eshia approached. 'We should flee, ma'am,' she whispered, 'before it is too late.'

'The Sanctian army advances from the south,' Fyenna said; 'their warships are blocking all routes to the east, and the Westlanders roam the lands to the north and west.'

'We don't need to leave Klef Mordain, ma'am; we could hide in Nether Hall. We could pretend to be ordinary civilians, and take shelter while the fighting rages around us. If we stay in the Old City, we will be trapped.'

'I fear we are already trapped, Eshia,' she said, 'but if a solution exists, I will find it.'

Fyenna turned away from the scene of destruction by the waterfront, and made her way back down the stairs.

When the lesson on metals had concluded, Fyenna sent Raewyn and Stanza off to get washed for dinner, then she returned to her office. Alone, her mask of confidence slipped from her features, and she sank into a chair, her hands trembling with pent-up frustration and fear. She took a map from a drawer, and laid it out on her desk. Unlike the one pinned to her wall, the map covered the entirety of the old Northern Provinces, and Fyenna's finger traced out the distance between Klef Mordain and the pass through the mountains that led to Upper Down. Thanks to Kilbride, that pass was now open to traffic, but how would the ruler of Upper Down react if Fyenna brought eleven young Masters and Makers on to her territory? Would it breach the terms of the treaty Kilbride had signed with the Sanctians? Fyenna shook her head in despair. Reaching Upper Down would be almost impossible. They would first have to cover the hundreds of miles that lay between; lands infested by roving bands of Westlanders. They would need wagons, and a large supply of food and water; horses, tents, weapons. They would be a slow-moving target, easy prey that would be irresistible to any nearby Westlanders.

She turned away from the map, and noticed the rolled-up scroll that Lady Niscoll had left. Might there be wagons and supplies listed somewhere within the document? She cracked open the wax seal with her thumb, and flattened the pages.

The first items listed were under a heading marked *Fixed Property*, and Fyenna's eyes scanned over the various farms, buildings and workshops. She went to the second page, and saw a list of part-shares. Her husband's assets had included shares in a wide selection of industries, some of which Fyenna knew to be bankrupt or closed down. Fyenna went to the third, and final page. She saw a heading marked *Moveable Property*. Under it were lists of cattle, paintings and furniture, but no wagons. At the bottom of the list, three ships were noted – two trading carricks, and one small ferry for carrying passengers across the estuary.

Fyenna's eyes narrowed as she read the accompanying details. According to the document, the three vessels were tied up in the commercial harbour. Their crews had been disbanded following the confiscation, but the ships themselves were described as sound and seaworthy.

Ships.

Fyenna placed the document back onto the desk. Three ships. Could it be done? Did the dangers of the Sanctian navy outweigh the dangers of the road to Upper Down? There was only one way to find out.

She would need to visit the harbour.

CHAPTER 28
THE LITTLE GHOST

Old City, Klef Mordain – 20th Day of Lamenta 108

Denny opened the hatch and stepped onto the roof of the Maker school.

'There you are,' he said to Abigone, who was sitting by herself gazing out at the city. 'I was looking for you.' He walked over. 'Would you rather I left you in peace?' he said. 'Do you want to be alone?'

She gazed up at him. 'No. I'll be glad of some company.'

'I need to talk to you,' he said, as he crouched down next to her.

Abigone said nothing.

'I hate what we did,' Denny went on. 'We abused our abilities. Will the spirits ever forgive us?'

'I don't know,' she said, lowering her gaze. 'At the time, all I wanted to do was make sure we left the embassy alive.'

'I wish I hadn't killed that sergeant. Why did I do that? Why couldn't I have knocked him unconscious?'

'He would have died when the building collapsed.'

'I know, but... the way he looked at me, when I drove his own knife into his heart. The pain of betrayal might have hurt him more than the blade.'

'I have killed before,' she said. 'You must try to put it out of your mind, Denny. Dwelling upon it will not help.'

'I, too, have killed,' he said, 'but each time it was because I was being attacked. This time, we were the aggressors. We persuaded people to trust us... and then we murdered them. It was a wicked act.'

'We did it together. We will shoulder the blame and guilt together.'

'I don't know if I can,' he said. 'Seeing you reminds me of what we did; of what I did. I see my shame reflected in your eyes. How can you bear to look at me?'

Abigone frowned.

Denny sat down on the roof next to her. 'I tell myself that, if we hadn't done it, then someone else would have; but that isn't true, is it? There was no one else who could have done what we did. If we hadn't entered the embassy, the ambassador would still be alive, and the Sanctians wouldn't be sending soldiers to invade the city.'

'Lady Fyenna told me that we shouldn't blame ourselves; that the fault lies with Lord Metrius.'

'My father said the same thing to me. They are trying to protect us.'

'Yes,' she said, 'but I don't need them to protect me. You know, Denny, I wish I could go home. I want to see my sister again, and the palace in Torrent, and I want to walk under the branches of the trees in the parkland. I want to read my old books of Elestian sonnets, and not another volume about how rust forms, or how an oak grows from an acorn, or how metals combine to form alloys.'

'Do you wish you had never come here?'

Abigone turned her head to look at him. 'I am glad I met you, but apart from that, I am not sure. If what we did was wicked, Denny, then do you believe me to be wicked at heart, a cruel and manipulative murderer? When I now think of marriage, I remember pretending to be your wife in order to slay the unsuspecting; I remember how well I acted; how easily I lied. Yet, at the same time, I know that the Sanctian ambassador wished to see all Masters and Makers dead. He wasn't innocent. If he had arrested us, he would have executed us. If he had found the school, he would have given orders that the students be slaughtered.'

'Are we now as bad as he was?' said Denny.

'We can still redeem ourselves,' said Abigone.

'The ambassador can't. Nor can the innocent embassy staff and soldiers we slew.'

'Instead of damning ourselves,' she said, 'might we not strive to make amends by protecting those unable to protect themselves? We might never be able to wholly purge ourselves of these feelings of shame and guilt, but we still have a duty to perform; and that duty isn't to Metrius, it is to Reath, Ignatius and the others. They are relying on us.'

Denny put his head in his hands. 'I wish that weren't true.'

Abigone kept her gaze on him. 'Denny,' she said, 'do you wish to break off our courtship?'

Denny said nothing for a few moments, then he shook his head.

'No,' he said. 'My feelings towards you are confused, but I cannot talk to anyone else the way I can talk to you. My heart both soars and sinks whenever I see you, but our guilt is shared, and that fact consoles me a little.' He took her hand, and kissed it. 'What we did together haunts my thoughts, but I would be bereft without you. You are the greatest joy in my life. Had you not been there, and had I dared to enter the embassy alone, then I would have drowned in despair by now. We are murderers, you and I, but I love you.'

'You love me?' she said. 'Lady Fyenna thinks we are too young to understand love.'

'And my father thinks love is unimportant. They are both wrong. If what I feel for you isn't love, then I don't know what to call it.'

'Then I pledge myself to you, Denny, for I love you, too.'

'I must warn you,' he said; 'our road will not be without obstacles. What we did has littered it with thorns and ripped up the cobbles. My thoughts waver between hope and despair, and there will be times when I will be unable to stand being in your company. If I am cold to you, or distant, you will know why. It is not you that I hate, but what we did. Despite that, your pledge means more than I can say. If we can endure this, we can endure anything, my love.'

They kissed, then he held her in his arms as they sat on the roof together.

'Am I interrupting?' said Reath, a hint of laughter in her voice.

Denny and Abigone turned.

'This isn't my fault,' said Reath; 'I didn't want to come onto the roof, knowing what you might be doing up here on your own. Miss Vesta has asked us all to assemble in the study hall.'

'Why?' said Denny.

Reath shrugged. 'I don't know.'

Denny stood, then he helped Abigone to her feet. They followed Reath to the hatch, and descended into the building.

'How's your leg, Abigone?' Reath said, as they went down a flight of stairs.

'It's still sore,' she said.

'How exactly did you fall?'

'I'm not very good at climbing.'

Reath eyed her, then they entered the study hall. All of the other students were present, along with Eshia and Miss Vesta. Denny noticed his father standing by a wall, and he inclined his head in his direction.

'My son has arrived with the fair Abigone,' Mor Galthide said, his voice filling the hall. 'Now, if you please, Miss Vesta, will you tell us why we have been summoned so? And where is Lady Fyenna?'

'Lady Fyenna is on an errand at the moment,' said Vesta. 'Settle down, boys and girls. Face the front, and be quiet. Miss Eshia wishes to speak to you.'

Eshia nodded at Vesta, and took a step forward. 'Good morning,' she said. 'Thank you for looking after me here since the death of my father. Seven weeks have passed since he was taken by agents of the pro-Sanctians, and the pain remains strong within me. You have all helped me recover, and I am grateful for your love and support. Today, I had an idea. It should have occurred to me earlier, but my thoughts have been clouded in grief.' She paused for a moment, as the others gazed at her. 'Raewyn mentioned something to me,' Eshia went on. 'She told me that she was working on steel, and I realised that I had a chance to repay some of the debt I owe the school.'

She lifted her gaze a little. 'I was never any good at summoning wood, but steel? Steel, I can summon with my eyes closed. With the army of the Sanctians approaching, we have a need for steel. Valiance has proved he can fight, and his father is a warrior, and yet neither have weapons or armour. Allow me to summon them. I can create any type of steel armour, at any size you need – breastplates, helms, greaves; and I can make weapons. Give me a list of all that is required, and I will summon it. I will need help from a Master, to transform base iron to steel for me, and then I can get to work.'

'Bravo,' cried Mor Galthide. 'I can dictate my list here and now. I shall require a halberd, three throwing spears, a war axe, and two daggers, as well as a full panoply of armour. Thus equipped, I shall be more than a match for enemies who dare to cross the threshold of this school.'

'I can manage all that,' said Eshia.

'Are there any Masters here willing and able to transform steel for Miss Eshia?' said Vesta. 'Constans? How about you? You are skilled at transforming metals.'

Constans glanced up. 'I can do it, ma'am.'

'We shall make a lesson of it,' said Vesta. 'Constans will take the Masters to my classroom, as there are supplies of iron there, and Miss Eshia shall instruct the Makers until the steel is ready. Valiance, do you require anything?'

'A short sword and a breastplate will suffice, thank you,' he said. 'I do not wish to be weighed down.'

'Wise words, my boy,' said Mor Galthide. 'I shall be the heavy infantry, and you the light. Do any of the other boys or girls know how to fight? Speak up.'

No one raised their hands.

Mor Galthide shook his head. 'What manner of education did you all receive? One insufficient to our current needs, or so it seems. It matters not – my boy and I will be more than enough to hold the line. You have my thanks, Miss Eshia.'

'Could you and Valiance remain behind when the Masters leave the study hall?' Eshia said. 'I need to measure you for the armour.'

'Constans,' said Vesta, 'take the Masters downstairs, and begin work on the steel. Make it as high quality as you are able, and fashion as much as you can from the iron.'

Constans got to his feet, then he led the other boys out of the study hall. Denny also stood, then he walked down to the front of the hall to stand next to his father.

'I thought Valiance was tall,' said Reath, 'but he looks tiny standing next to his father. Are you part-bear, Valiance's father?'

Mor Galthide laughed. 'Maybe I am, child, or maybe it is the noble blood of Geathan that flows through my veins.'

Reath frowned. 'Geathan? I thought Valiance was from Campsie.'

'He is, yes,' said Mor Galthide quickly. 'My ancestors hailed from Geathan… a long time ago. Yes.'

'Nyli and I passed through Campsie on our way here,' Reath went on, 'but you don't speak much like the folk there.'

'By all the spirits,' Mor Galthide cried; 'sickened am I by the lies I tell. Here is the truth, girls; listen to it well – my son comes not from Campsie. He is the heir to the throne of Geathan, and the grandson of the wicked Emperor Antonio of Sanctos. His real name is Mor Dennahelm, and I am Mor Galthide. There. I have said it.' He put his hands on his hips. 'If Lady Fyenna wishes to punish me for the crime of honesty, that shall be her business.'

The Makers stared at him.

Denny raised a hand to his eyes.

'Is that true?' said Miss Vesta.

'Every word,' said Mor Galthide.

'It's a secret,' said Denny. 'We're not supposed to tell anyone.'

'No kidding,' said Reath. 'So you… you're royalty, too; just like Abigone?' She nudged Nyli with her elbow. 'It all makes sense now. I'll bet you the world that Abigone knew about this.'

Stanza turned in her seat to stare at Abigone. 'Did you know?'

'I did,' said Abigone.

'He's a Sanctian,' said Raewyn. 'Valiance is a Sanctian prince.'

'I am still the same person,' said Denny. 'I haven't changed. I am half Sanctian, half Geathan, but my loyalty lies with my father, Abigone and the school. I fled Sanctos before the emperor could discover that I was a Master.'

'It was I who bore him away,' said Mor Galthide. He glanced at Eshia. 'Now, miss, I am ready to be measured.'

Three hours later, Denny was standing with his arms held out as Eshia and his father removed the new breastplate from his body. The laundry room had been ransacked for linen sheets, which had been used to pad out the armour, and rolls of it were lying next to the assorted weapons. The news about Denny had spread throughout the school, and many of the young Masters and Makers in the classroom were whispering to each other as they stared at him.

Fyenna strode into the classroom. She glanced at the heaps of steel armour and weapons summoned by Eshia, and raised an eyebrow.

'What is going on here?' she said.

'Good afternoon, ma'am,' said Vesta. 'Eshia kindly offered to make equipment for... Valiance and his father.'

Reath coughed. 'That's not his name.'

Fyenna glanced at her, but said nothing.

'Did I do something wrong, ma'am?' said Eshia.

Fyenna shook her head. 'No, girl. Thank you for your efforts. However, I need to speak to both Valiance and his father, alone.'

'I am at your service, my lady,' said Mor Galthide. 'I have tried on my new armour, and wielded my new weapons.'

Fyenna frowned. 'Come with me.'

She led Denny and Mor Galthide to another classroom and closed the door.

'You have my apologies, my lady,' said Mor Galthide. 'I spoke the truth, as I could no longer bear to utter so many lies. If this has inconvenienced you, then I am deeply sorry.'

'What in the world are you talking about?' said Fyenna.

'Then you have not summoned us to berate me for my indiscretion?'

Fyenna rolled her eyes. 'Is that what Reath was referring to? Did you tell the students the truth about you and your son?'

'I did, my lady.'

'No matter. That is not why I want to speak to you.'

Mor Galthide slapped his son on the back. 'Do you see? Her ladyship is not offended. We should have told them earlier.'

'I am too tired to be offended,' said Fyenna, 'and I will deal with the repercussions later. I need to ask you a question – do either of you know how to sail?'

Mor Galthide laughed. 'Did you hear that, son? Her ladyship asks if I can sail.'

'Is that a yes or a no?' said Fyenna.

'It is a resounding yes, my lady. I was piloting boats when I was twelve, sailing the coastal waters off Geathan long before the Sanctians devoured my homeland. I am a better sailor than I am a warrior.'

'Why, ma'am?' said Denny. 'Are you thinking about sailing somewhere?'

'I might be,' said Fyenna. 'My husband's assets have been seized, but I was left a few items. Among them are three ships – two large, and one small. That is where I have been today, visiting the harbour in order to see them with my own eyes. They appear to be in a decent condition but, unlike many in Klef Mordain, I have never been to sea. Can you sail, Denny?'

'Not as well as my father can. I think Constans has sailed on his family's merchant ships.'

'Constans has been on many voyages,' said Fyenna, 'but as a passenger, not a sailor. I need you to take a look at my ships, and tell me if any are capable of sailing a distance of several hundred miles. I also need to know how many crew I shall require.'

'My lady,' said Mor Galthide, 'I think I am beginning to grasp your intentions. You spoke to me of evacuating, and I suggested the western route. Are you thinking otherwise? Do you plan to sail out of Klef Mordain? The Sanctian warships anchored in yonder estuary might have something to say about that.'

'Two of the Sanctian warships have departed the estuary for now,' she said.

'The *Bitter Respite* alone would be enough to block any escape, and that vessel remains by the Celestial Bridge.'

'Let me worry about the Sanctians. All I need from you is an evaluation of my three ships. If they are unfit to sail, then the rest is irrelevant.'

'As you will, my lady. When shall we depart?'

Fyenna eyed them. 'Now.'

The sun was low in the sky when Fyenna led Denny and Mor Galthide out of the maze of tunnels and into the streets close to the commercial harbour. Most of the offices of the shipping agents were closed, and only a few taverns were doing business. Fyenna took the two men down a few side streets, and they emerged on to the long quayside, where gulls were idly pecking at the remains of a crow. A few dozen vessels were tied up along the piers that ran out from the quay, but the harbour felt deserted.

'There used to be hundreds of ships here,' said Fyenna. 'Those which have left have not returned, either captured and requisitioned by the Sanctian fleet, or not daring to attempt the return voyage. The same goes for the crews. Thousands of sailors from Klef Mordain are being held in camps in Lesser Down, and the others are out of work.'

'The empty berths by each pier outnumber those occupied, my lady,' said Mor Galthide. 'This is indeed a mighty harbour, brought low by the depredations of the Sanctians.'

'I will take you to my three ships,' said Fyenna. 'They are tied up in a row, so we won't have to travel far.'

They turned left, and walked along the wide quayside, passing a few taverns, from where light and noise were emanating. They reached a long pier, and Fyenna led them to where three vessels were tied up, bow to stern.

'Here they are,' said Fyenna, gesturing to them. 'What do you think?'

Mor Galthide and Denny walked closer to the vessels, and they spent a few minutes looking them over in silence. Denny tried to remember all that he had been taught about sailing. With Sanctos being an island, learning how to sail had been one of the many skills thought important by Emperor Antonio, and all of the imperial children had been given some lessons on the subject.

They returned to where Fyenna was waiting.

'Would you care to hear my evaluation, my lady?' said Mor Galthide.

'Very much,' said Fyenna.

'Very well. The carrick on the left would sink long before it left the harbour – its boards are warped and rotten from months of neglect and ill-maintenance; its ropes are frayed, and its sails in tatters. It should be picked over for spare parts, towed to a lonely beach, and allowed to decompose in peace. The middle ship, another carrick, is in a far better condition – the best of the three – but it will require work to be fit to sail a distance of several hundred miles. That was your requirement, was it not, my lady? Its greatest problem, however, is that it needs a crew of forty. Sixty would be better, but forty would suffice. Carpenters, sailmakers, a bosun and his mates, and a dozen sturdy lads to climb the rigging. Had we a month to spare, I would pick the middle carrick.'

'We don't have a month,' said Fyenna. 'And I doubt I'd be able to find forty skilled sailors willing to risk the voyage I am imagining.'

'Then I select the cutter, my lady. It requires a crew of eight, and it remains seaworthy. That would be my choice.'

'The cutter?' said Fyenna. 'That shabby little boat on the right? It's used as a ferry, to take people to the other side of the estuary.'

'Mean you to cross the wild ocean, my lady?'

'No. I was thinking of taking it south, down the coast.'

'Again, I suggest the cutter. It is small, and it would be cramped, but it could take twenty passengers, as well as a crew of eight. Its size would handle well in coastal waters. I would skipper and pilot, and my son would be my midshipman.'

'And what is a midshipman?'

'It means he will do whatever I tell him to do, my lady. We would require but six others with seafaring skills. Best of all, it does not require much work. Its life as a simple ferry has kept it in good working order, despite its poor looks. If you wish to flee Klef Mordain by sea, that is the ship to take.'

Fyenna frowned as she gazed at the small cutter. 'Will it remain afloat in a storm?'

'Not an ocean storm,' said Mor Galthide, 'and one can never guarantee that we will not encounter such a storm along the coast. Such is the nature of sea-going, my lady. Ships sink, ships ground, and ships founder. If the business was easy, then merchants would not get rich off the risks they run.'

'It has a shallow hull,' said Denny. 'It will be able to sail in waters too dangerous for Sanctian warships. It is also fast.'

'My son is correct on both points. Swift and agile. A tricky bugger to handle in a cross wind, but light of foot, and able to make a quick escape. One ball from a cannon, though, and its sailing days are over. How might we get past the *Bitter Respite*, my lady?'

'I will deal with that aspect,' said Fyenna. 'Now, where will I find six willing sailors?'

Mor Galthide gestured towards the taverns. 'Give me but a few coins for an ale or two, and I will find them for you. I know exactly what we require. How much could you pay them, my lady?'

'I don't know. I was never concerned with these matters.'

'I shall discover the usual rate, and double it. Once I have my recruits, I shall order them to berth on the cutter. They can spend their hours cleaning and repairing until we are ready to depart. Shall I do this for you, my lady?'

Fyenna passed him a purse. 'There is enough in there to give an advance sum to each sailor you find.'

Mor Galthide inclined his head. 'You have my thanks. One last thing – by what name does the vessel go?'

'It's called the *Little Ghost*.'

'A most propitious name, my lady, for we shall need to be as silent as a ghost to escape the estuary. I shall return when I am successful.'

Denny watched as his father strode off towards the nearest tavern. 'May I go aboard, ma'am?' he said to Fyenna.

'We both shall,' said Fyenna.

They walked up to the cutter, and Denny stepped down onto the deck of the *Little Ghost*. Fyenna boarded the vessel after him, and they inspected the rest of the ship. It had a single, small cabin, but the hold beneath the main deck was large enough for several dozen people. It had been fitted out with benches, for the passengers who had crossed the estuary. They went back up onto the main deck and took a look at the ship's wheel, which was located in front of the cabin. Denny put his hands on the wheel for a moment, and imagined he was out at sea.

'How goes it with you and Abigone?' Fyenna said.

Denny took his hands from the wheel. 'We... It's been hard, ma'am. We dwell too much on what happened in the embassy, and it has caused some ill-feeling between us. We are pledged to make it work, though; we are not giving up.'

Fyenna eyed him. 'When Abigone first arrived at the school, I saw nothing but a spoiled, entitled girl who had never worked a day in her life.'

'I hope your opinion has changed since then, ma'am.'

'It has. When Lord Metrius told me that he had sent you to the embassy to kill the ambassador, I was more angry than I have been in many years. Part of that anger was aimed at the injustice of it all, but part was because I realised something. I have, unwittingly, become rather fond of Abigone these past months. I have seen her try and try again, when before, I believed that she would give up at the first hurdle. And now I see her struggle with what you and she did that day. I see her burdened with guilt and shame, and it pains me to watch her so anguished. You must be patient with each other, lest your regret at what you did sours what you share.'

Denny leaned against the railings running along the side of the vessel.

'I hope you don't think I'm interfering,' said Fyenna.

'No, ma'am. I agree with what you said. May I tell Abigone what we have been doing this evening?'

'If I say no, will you tell her anyway?'

'Are you going to make me swear an oath?'

'No, Denny. Tell her if you want, but make sure she doesn't spread it around the school. I don't want the younger students to know what I am planning.'

'Are we evacuating? I thought we were needed here, to help defend the city.'

'Our army of reservists has all but disintegrated. A few regiments will muster along the southern flank of Klef Mordain, but not nearly enough. We can join the fight, but the end result will be the same – we will lose, and the Sanctians will march into the city.'

'And say we make it past the warships by the bridge – what then? Where will we go?'

'I don't have an answer to that question yet.'

'If my father is piloting the *Little Ghost*, then I know which destination he will suggest.'

'Geathan?'

'Yes, ma'am.'

'Wouldn't that entail sailing around the island of Sanctos?'

'It would, ma'am, but that won't stop my father suggesting it.'

'What are your feelings about this? Do you want to be King of Geathan, assuming that you were able to conquer the territory?'

'The Sanctians would immediately send an army to re-take it.'

'You didn't answer my question, Denny.'

'If I tell you the truth, will you promise not to say anything to my father?'

Fyenna eyed him. 'I see. You need say nothing more. I happen to think that your father's dreams about Geathan are little more than wishful thinking. He has placed a great burden onto your shoulders.'

'I cannot tell him how I feel about it. His hopes would be crushed.'

'You will have to tell him at some point.'

'Yes, but not now.'

Fyenna glanced up. 'Here he comes.'

'And with six men trailing him.'

Fyenna shook her head. 'How does he do it?'

'He was raised as a prince. Giving orders comes easily to him.'

Denny and Fyenna waited on the deck as Mor Galthide led the six sailors along the pier.

'There she is,' said Mor Galthide. 'The *Little Ghost*. Do you think this old ferryboat could sail the coastal waters of the Central Provinces? I shall man the helm, and you lads will be my crew. Double rates, and a bonus upon arrival at our destination.'

The six sailors eyed the vessel.

'Mister Galthide,' said one, 'you haven't told us how we'll get past the Sanctian warships, nor where our destination might be.'

'Well observed,' said Mor Galthide. 'Move your gear on to the cutter this very night, and you shall be paid in full from today.'

'It's easy money,' said another sailor. 'We get paid for sleeping on board, and carrying out a few repairs by day, and then we can go back home; because this old boat ain't going nowhere. Where do I sign?'

Fyenna stepped up onto the pier. 'And what if the boat does sail?' she said. 'Will you remain true to your contracts?'

'Who's that?' said a sailor.

'I am the owner of this vessel,' said Fyenna. 'Are any of you married? Do you have young children? If so, then you're no good to us; for if we leave, we will not be returning.'

'I have ensured that not one among them has any dependents, my lady,' said Mor Galthide.

'Is this a serious offer, ma'am?' said a sailor. 'Are you going to attempt to run the blockade?'

'I have a plan to get us past the Sanctian warships,' she said. 'I ask again, will you sail with us? If you sign up to serve aboard the *Little Ghost*, will you remain faithful and true to your word?'

'And it's double the usual rates, ma'am?' said one.

'Who cares about the rates?' said another. 'If it means getting out of Klef Mordain before the Sanctians get here, I'm in.'

The others nodded their agreement.

Fyenna smiled. 'Take their signatures,' she said to Mor Galthide. 'I think we've found our crew.'

CHAPTER 29
MISTAKEN IDENTITY

Old City, Klef Mordain – 21st Day of Lamenta 108

Amery felt sick with worry as he sat in the little hall next to the front door of the townhouse. For nine days, he hadn't left the building, too fearful to step outside.

A key turned in the lock, and Amery jumped to his feet. The door opened, and Loryn walked in.

'Where have you been?' Amery cried. 'I thought something terrible had happened to you. I was so worried, but now... now, I'm just angry.'

Loryn closed and locked the door behind her. 'I was out,' she said.

'Clearly. Where?'

'I told Annalise that I was going out. Did she not tell you?'

'She told me. You didn't tell her where you were going, nor did you think to mention how long you would be.'

She hung her coat up on a peg by the door. 'I was visiting my parents, Amery. With everything that's been going on, I wanted to check that they were all right. Is that fine with you?'

'You should have told me. I thought you'd run off.'

'There is nowhere to go. The Sanctian army is close to the southern edge of the city. They'll be entering Nether Hall tomorrow. I couldn't run away even if I wanted to.'

She strode along the hallway, and Amery hurried after her.

'Why didn't you tell me where you were going?' he said.

'Because you were still sleeping when I left.'

'You could have woken me.'

'I tried. It's not my fault you had too much to drink last night, and were dead to the world this morning.'

'You could have left me a note.'

Loryn halted at the foot of the stairs. 'Amery, I told Annalise that I was going out; there is no need for an interrogation. I was concerned about my parents, so I went to see them. That's all. I don't know why you are reacting in this manner.'

'People are being murdered in broad daylight, Loryn!' he cried. 'Pro-Sanctian mobs rampaged through the commercial district only yesterday, and then the anti-Sanctians came out on to the streets to fight them. It isn't safe out there. You could have been killed. Am I not allowed to worry about you?'

'I am sorry I caused you so much concern. Is that better?'

Amery followed her up the stairs. 'So, how are they?' he said.

'Who?'

'Your parents?'

'They are fine. They have a shelter dug out of the rock beneath their house, and they have been moving clothes, bedding and food down there. That's where they will hide when the Sanctian army gets here.'

They reached the top of the stairs, and Loryn walked into the living room, where Lothar was sitting with his feet up on a stool.

'They asked me if I wanted to take shelter with them,' Loryn went on.

'And what did you say?' said Amery, following her in.

'I thanked them for the offer, and told them that the townhouse had a more-than-adequate cellar.'

Amery nodded. 'Good. Our cellar is big enough to hide us all. There are only four of us, after our two drivers fled. They were faithless cowards for running away, but it means that we will have more food to spare.'

'They weren't cowards,' said Lothar. 'They did the sensible thing.'

'Fleeing south is the opposite of sensible,' said Amery. 'They will have run smack right into the Sanctian army.'

'They have papers showing that they are citizens of Lesser Down. The Sanctians will have allowed them through their lines.'

Amery snorted. 'Yes, after relieving them of their carriage and horses.'

'So?' said Lothar. 'That seems like a fair trade to me, if they managed to get out of Klef Mordain with their lives. I'd donate a horse for that.'

Loryn sat. 'Is that coffee fresh, Lothar?'

'It's about ten minutes old,' he said.

'Then it's fresh enough,' said Loryn. She poured herself a cup, then she unlaced her boots and pulled them off.

'Were the streets busy?' said Lothar.

'They were practically deserted,' said Loryn. 'The Great Northern Highway was busy, though, with wealthy foreigners trying to leave Klef Mordain. They were queuing up to get out of the Old City.'

'I carried four mattresses down into the cellar this morning,' Lothar went on, 'and I rigged up a curtain to divide the sleeping area in two – one half for me and Amery, and the other for you and Annalise.'

'Thank you,' said Loryn. 'Do we have enough lamps and candles?'

'Plenty. Enough for at least five days and nights, if we're careful. A food delivery arrived when you were out, and I've moved most of it down there. There's no toilet, though – we'll either have to take a risk and run upstairs, or go in a bucket. If we decide on the bucket, then I can hang up another curtain for privacy.'

'I don't like the idea of a bucket,' said Loryn.

'It won't be too bad if we're only down there for one night,' said Lothar. 'Anything beyond that, though? The cellar will start to stink, and that won't do much for anyone's mood.'

Amery frowned as he watched Loryn and Lothar talk as though they were old friends. He sat down on a chair opposite them, and poured himself a coffee.

'Does anyone snore?' said Lothar.

'Amery does,' said Loryn.

'I do not,' said Amery.

'And how would you know?' said Loryn. 'You aren't awake to hear yourself. It's worse when you have been drinking, which, let's face it, is pretty much every night.'

'Lothar snores, too,' said Amery.

'Perhaps,' she said, 'but I'm not sleeping with him.'

'More's the pity,' said Lothar.

Amery glared at him.

'It was just a joke,' said Lothar. He smiled. 'Or was it?'

Loryn rolled her eyes. 'It sounds as though the cellar is almost ready. I can help decorate the bare walls. We can hang up some of the smaller tapestries, to make it seem a little more welcoming.'

'We can go down after lunch,' said Lothar, 'and I'll give you a hand.'

'Thank you.'

Amery sipped his coffee in silence, as envy coursed through him. He imagined a situation where poor Lothar got accidentally locked out of the cellar when the Sanctians arrived. What a terrible shame that would be. Loryn would be sad, and Amery would have to comfort her.

Annalise strode into the living room.

'Mister Amery, sir,' she said. 'There are several gentlemen at the front door asking for you.'

Amery's mouth went dry, and he dropped his cup of coffee, spilling it over the rug.

'Relax,' said Lothar. 'If they were assassins, would they have bothered to knock at the door? Do you want me to go downstairs and ask them what they want?'

Amery's hands shook. 'Would you do that for me?'

'I'll go down,' said Loryn, getting to her feet. 'How many men were there, Annalise?'

'Five, miss. I'd best fetch a napkin to clear up that spill.'

The two women walked from the room, and Lothar shook his head at Amery.

'Are you letting your woman go down there alone?' he said. 'What the fuck does she see in you, Amery? It's a mystery to me.'

Amery stood. 'Fuck off, Lothar,' he mumbled.

Lothar laughed, as Amery hurried out of the room.

'Wait for me, Loryn,' Amery called out, as he ran down the stairs.

He saw Loryn approach the front door, where the men were standing. She started speaking to them as Amery crossed the hall.

'Lord Tain wants you,' said one of the men.

'Me and Mister Amery?' said Loryn.

'That's right. We have a carriage waiting to take you both to the association.'

'Why?' said Amery, coming up to stand next to Loryn. 'What does Lord Tain want?'

One of the men narrowed his eyes. 'How should we know? We were only sent to fetch you. Are you ready to go?'

'I think so,' said Loryn.

'Wait,' said Amery. 'How do we know that these men are who they say they are? They might be working for Lord Metrius.'

One of the men patted his waist, where a knife sat tucked into his belt. 'If I worked for that old dog Metrius, and he wanted you dead, then, well, you'd already be dead. Lord Tain mentioned that this place was undefended, and he wasn't kidding. You should be more careful. Anyone after you could easily get in through a window, and it would take but a single kick to break down your back door.'

'We're wasting time,' said another man. 'The longer that carriage is parked out on the street, the more likely it is that someone will recognise it. We should get going.'

'Do we need to bring anything?' said Loryn.

'Just yourselves.'

She glanced at Amery, who shrugged.

'I need to get my boots on,' Loryn said. 'Give me a moment.'

There was a shoe rack close to the front door, and Loryn selected a pair of black ankle boots. She crouched down and laced them up as the men watched. Amery took a coat from a peg, and held it over his wrists to conceal his trembling hands.

Loryn stood, and reached for her own coat, then she walked back to the stairs.

'Mister Amery and I are going to the association,' she called out in a loud voice.

Lothar appeared at the top of the stairs. 'Duly noted, miss,' he said.

'Does he work in the legal team?' said one of the men.

'He's my butler,' said Amery.

'Right. Well, he can stay here. Let's go.'

Loryn and Amery followed the men out on to the street, and Amery closed and locked the front door of the townhouse. They walked a few yards to where a carriage was sitting, and one of the men opened the side door. Amery helped Loryn ascend, then he stepped up after her, and they sat down inside the carriage. The door was closed, and the five men climbed on to the outside of the carriage, with three on the driver's bench. The horses were whipped, and the carriage set off at speed, its wheels racing over the cobbles.

'Are you all right?' said Loryn.

'What a ridiculous question,' said Amery. 'Of course I'm not all right. What does Lord Tain want with us?'

'Presumably, he is in need of some legal advice.'

'Ha! I wish. It's more likely that he thinks I'm the spy.'

'Why would he think that?' said Loryn. 'Are you the spy?'

'Of course I'm not the damn spy!' Amery cried.

'Then you have nothing to worry about. Think. If the Sanctian army is due here any day, what might the Second Empire Association want with its legal team? Perhaps they wish to discuss the mechanics of a provisional government with us, or maybe they want to make some sort of declaration. Most of the ambassador's staff were killed alongside him when the embassy collapsed, and they are probably short of a lawyer or two.'

'Buildings don't just collapse, Loryn.'

'I am aware of that. The ambassador was assassinated; that much is clear.'

'We could have been inside the embassy. Why did they have to kill so many people? Why didn't they stop with the ambassador?'

'You've heard the same rumours as I have,' said Loryn. 'If it is true that the assassin was a Maker, then she would have had every reason to hate the Sanctians. Maybe she was also hoping to kill the prince that turned up that day.'

'The so-called prince might have been working with the assassins. His body was never recovered from the rubble.'

'Maybe.'

Amery lowered his head and closed his eyes. He had read the descriptions of the young woman who had walked into the Sanctian Embassy. She had been in the presence of a man who had claimed to be a missing Prince of Sanctos. Surviving witnesses had described how the young couple had been taken up to the roof loggia to meet with the ambassador, just before the building had started to collapse. And then, they had vanished.

It was Abigone – it had to be.

Amery had mentioned none of his suspicions to Lothar or Annalise, and he had also kept quiet about it to Loryn, even though she had read the same descriptions. If it was true, then didn't it prove that Metrius had resorted to using the student Masters and Makers to carry out his dirty work – and what work! Over sixty dead, and an entire building reduced to ruins. Was the Abigone he had known in Upper Down capable of such an atrocity? The ambassador might have been a target on Metrius's list, but what about all of the staff who had worked there?

And now Amery was on his way to the Second Empire Association, where Lord Tain would certainly be a target for assassination. What if a Maker brought that building down while Amery and Loryn were inside? Amery felt sick at the thought.

Their carriage slowed at a roadblock, then the men guarding the barricade waved them through. They sped down another street, and halted outside the association, which had come to resemble a fortress.

Armed men crowded the street, and more were up on the roof, watching all approaches to the building. Amery and Loryn alighted the carriage, then they were escorted down the narrow alleyway and in through the front door, where a clerk was waiting to greet them.

'Mister Amery and Miss Loryn,' he said, 'thank you for coming. Lord Tain is waiting for you upstairs.'

Amery gasped with relief. 'Upstairs? Excellent.'

The clerk eyed him, then he led them both up a flight of stairs and into a large conference room. Two men were sitting at the end of a long table, and they glanced up as Amery and Loryn walked in.

'Amery!' said Tain, rising from his seat. 'And Miss Loryn, too. How good it is to see you. Have you been receiving the food parcels without any trouble?'

'Uh, yes, sir,' said Amery.

'It was very generous of you to think of us, sir,' said Loryn, curtsying.

'Not at all,' said Tain. 'Think nothing of it. If I can't look after my legal team, then who would? Come. I have a critical task that requires your expert attention.'

Amery and Loryn approached the end of the table.

'This is Captain Pontus of the Sanctian Navy,' Tain said, gesturing to the other man. 'The admiral has appointed him as liaison officer to Lord Penny.'

The naval officer stood. He shook Amery's hand, then kissed Loryn's. 'It is a pleasure to meet you both,' he said. 'Lord Tain has informed me of the great work you have done for the association. Lord Penny is also grateful, and he sends you his greetings.'

'Sit,' said Tain.

All four took their seats.

'I shall order coffee, wine and food shortly,' Tain said, 'but first, I wish to go over what it is that I need you to do for us this day. Do you see the document in front of Captain Pontus? It is the draft of a transitional constitution. As soon as the first Sanctian soldiers arrive in Klef Mordain, Lord Penny will declare that this new constitution is in effect. Lord Penny will then be appointed as Lord President of a provisional government, a government that the Sanctian Empire will immediately recognise. As Lord Penny's first act, he will formally invite the Sanctians to restore law and order within the bounds of the city. His second act will state a willingness to enter into negotiations with the Sanctian Empire regarding the status of Klef Mordain. If all goes well, this city will be formally welcomed into the empire within a month or two.'

Tain smiled. 'We are so close to achieving all that we set out to do. For many long years, the association has toiled to bring us to this great moment in history, and I only wish that my dear sister was here to see it.' He opened a drawer and withdrew two leather pouches. 'This is for you two – one each. Call it a little bonus for all of the hard work you have done these past months.'

'Thank you, sir,' said Loryn. 'You are too generous.'

Tain waved her away. 'You both deserve it for the long hours you have put in. You will be putting in more hours today, for I need the constitution thoroughly checked, and amended, if necessary. It was drafted by one of Lord Penny's scribes, and Captain Pontus and I have already noticed a few errors.'

'What happened to the draft handed over by the Sanctian admiral, sir?' said Amery.

'All copies were lost in the destruction of the embassy, sir,' said Pontus. 'Hence, it has been re-drafted from scratch. The ambassador had several staff with sharp legal minds working for him but, alas, they were killed in the Maker attack that destroyed the building.'

'The loss of Ambassador Tertius has been a terrible blow,' said Tain. 'The only good thing to come of it was that it has given the Sanctians a perfectly legal reason to move their forces into the city. Now, I need this document ready by sunset. Shall we leave you to it? Captain Pontus and I can see to other matters while you work, and I will keep you well-supplied with food and drinks.'

'We can begin work on it now, sir,' said Amery.

'That's the spirit,' said Tain.

He and the naval officer got to their feet.

'We shall be in my office if you need us,' said Tain.

Loryn opened one of the leather pouches as soon as Tain and Pontus had left the conference room.

'There is a lot of money in here,' she said. She smiled at Amery. 'Are you feeling a little more relaxed now, sir? There was nothing to worry about.'

'So it seems,' said Amery. He slid the draft of the constitution over the table towards him. 'I suppose we had better get to work.'

Amery and Loryn toiled over the document for the next eight hours. Some sections required a light edit, while others were almost incomprehensible, and had needed to be completely re-written. Food trolleys came and went, and Tain and Pontus had popped in occasionally to see how they were doing.

Both Tain and the naval officer entered the conference room as the sun was setting. The captain had put on his outer coat, and was carrying a briefcase, as though he was ready to leave.

'Might I ask?' said Tain, as they walked towards the table.

Amery smiled. 'We have just finished, sir. It's done.'

Tain beamed. 'What did I tell you, Captain? These two cost me a fortune, but they are worth every coin.'

Pontus glanced down at the document, and leafed through the pages. 'This is good work for such a short time,' he said. 'I'll have Lord Penny's scribe write out a fair copy this evening. Thank you, Mister Amery and Miss Loryn; your assistance this day has been very useful.'

He picked up the draft, and placed it into his briefcase.

'I will be travelling back to Lord Penny's mansion now, Lord Tain. Thank you for your help.'

'It was my pleasure,' said Tain.

The two men shook hands, and then the officer strode from the room.

Tain sat. 'Another step closer,' he said. 'By the spirits, I could do with a drink.'

'Do you require us for anything else this evening, sir?' said Loryn.

'I don't think so,' said Tain. 'Get yourselves home.'

'Thank you, sir,' said Amery.

Amery and Loryn got to their feet and started to walk towards the door.

'Actually, Amery, could you stay a moment?' said Tain.

They both halted by the door.

'Not you, Miss Loryn,' said Tain. 'In fact, Loryn, why don't you take the carriage back to the townhouse? I will organise another carriage later for Mister Amery.'

Amery and Loryn glanced at each other, then Loryn curtsied.

'As you will, sir,' she said, then she walked from the room.

'Close the door, Amery,' said Tain, 'then come back to the table.'

Amery did as he was bid.

'Sit down,' said Tain, smiling, 'and don't look so nervous. I'm not going to eat you.'

Amery sat, his hands clasped together.

Tain got to his feet, and began to pace up and down. 'I wanted to ask if you have had any more ideas about the possible identity of the spy. I worry that they might try to sabotage the Sanctian takeover.'

'Oh,' said Amery. 'Well, I…'

Tain swung a clenched fist into the side of Amery's head, knocking him off the chair. Amery fell to the thick carpet, and Tain kicked him in the stomach.

'You filthy fucking traitor!' Tain screamed in his face. 'How could you do this to me?' He kicked him again, and Amery groaned in agony. 'I am going to make you suffer,' Tain went on. 'You saw what I did to Heston – that was nothing compared to the tortures I shall inflict upon you.'

'But, sir…' Amery gasped. 'I am not the spy.'

Tain grabbed him by the throat. 'You lying piece of dogshit. I know it was you, because your real employer has been in contact. Do you want to see the evidence? Let me show it to you, before I pluck out your eyes.'

Tain released him and straightened his back, and Amery squirmed on the floor. Tain removed an envelope from a pocket.

'This arrived three days ago,' he said, 'but I needed one more day of work from you. You have no idea how hard it was to not lose my temper earlier.' He withdrew two notes from the envelope. 'This is a letter from Lord Metrius, in which he mocks me for hiring you. He makes out as though he is doing me a favour by informing me of the identity of his spy – that blasted dog.'

'He's lying, sir,' groaned Amery.

'Shut up,' said Tain. 'Do you think I would have believed him if the letter was the only thing he had sent me? He included something else – a short note. I recognised the handwriting immediately, from the countless documents that you have written for the association. Shall I read the note to you? Shall we see if it sparks your memory?'

He unfolded a smaller piece of paper and held it out.

'It goes: *Lord Metrius, greetings. I have a Maker for the city. Your loyal friend, Amery of Yearl.*'

Amery stared up at him.

'At least you are not denying that you wrote it,' said Tain. 'You delivered Princess Abigone into the hands of Metrius, and then you lied to me about it. You said that you had no idea what had happened to Abigone, and like a fool I believed you. My sister is dead because of you. The ambassador is dead because of you. The student Masters and Makers are alive because of you. Every step I have taken has been reported to Lord Metrius, allowing him to hinder us at every turn. I trusted you, Amery, and your betrayal feels like a knife in the heart.'

'Please... I...'

Tain crouched down next to him, and placed his hands on his throat.

'How I yearn to drag out your death,' Tain whispered. 'How I long to eke out every last morsel of suffering, until you are utterly spent and broken, until you crawl across the floor to beg for death.' His grip tightened, and Amery's hands flailed around. 'That's it,' said Tain. 'Struggle. I want you to struggle.'

Amery closed his eyes. His hands tried to pry Tain's fingers from his neck, but the other man was far stronger.

'You will fall unconscious soon,' whispered Tain, 'and when you awake, the real torture will begin.'

There was a sharp gasping sound, and Tain's fingers came away from Amery's throat. Amery opened his eyes, and saw Loryn standing behind Tain, her hand wielding a knife. Blood came from Tain's lips, then Loryn stabbed him a second time, driving the blade into the back of Tain's neck. Tain fell to the carpet, blood pouring from the two wounds. Loryn released the knife, and crouched by Amery.

'Stand up,' she hissed. 'We need to leave.'

'Loryn...'

'Thank me later. Get up.'

Loryn held out her hand, and helped Amery stand. He swayed.

'You are going to have to walk out of the building as though nothing was wrong,' Loryn said.

'I don't know if I can.'

'You will,' she said, her eyes piercing him. 'If we are caught, we die. Do exactly as I say, and we will live.' She released him. 'Walk by my side, and nod to everyone as though you are happy to work here. The carriage is waiting for us; the drivers know nothing of what just happened. They are expecting to take us home, and we shall allow them to do so.'

Loryn walked to the door, and Amery limped after her. He straightened his back, and forced himself to tread normally, despite the pain.

'That's better,' she said, opening the door.

They strode out of the conference room, and headed straight down the stairs.

'Are you leaving, Mister Amery?' said the clerk.

'I am, yes,' said Amery. 'Lord Tain has no more work for us today.'

'Well, all the best, and to you, too, Miss Loryn.'

Loryn smiled. 'Thank you.'

Amery and Loryn carried on. The armed men at the front door eyed them, then allowed them to pass out into the alleyway. They walked to the main road, and the five men gathered next to the carriage saw them.

'Back to the townhouse?' said one.

'Yes, thank you,' said Loryn.

'No problem, miss.'

The side door was opened, and Amery and Loryn climbed in.

Amery collapsed into a chair the moment they were back in the townhouse.

Loryn went to the foot of the stairs. 'Lothar! Get down here.'

The former Mountain Ranger appeared at the top of the stairs. 'What is it?'

'We need to block all doors and windows,' Loryn said, 'and then we need to hide in the cellar.'

'What, now?'

'Yes, now. Fetch Annalise, then start working on the entrances. Block every damn one.'

Lothar hurried off, and Loryn returned to where Amery was half-sobbing, half-trembling on the chair.

She crouched by him. 'What did he do to you?'

'Some kicks, some punches. He tried to strangle me.'

'No broken bones?'

'Do you think I could have walked out of the building with broken bones?' he cried. 'Sorry. I didn't mean to shout. Thank you, Loryn; thank you for saving my life.'

'Why did he do it?' said Loryn.

'He thought I was the spy.'

Loryn frowned. 'That doesn't make any sense.'

'Metrius sent him a note I wrote months ago.'

'And what did the note say?'

'I... I wrote a note to Metrius, telling him that I had brought Abigone to the city to be trained as a Maker.'

Loryn stared at him. 'That was you?'

'Tain took it to mean that I have been spying for Metrius this entire time; but you have to believe me, Loryn – I'm not the spy. I swear it to you.'

'I know, Amery. I believe you.'

'You do?'

'Of course I do.'

'How can you be so sure?'

She smiled at him. 'Because, my sweet Amery, I am the spy.'

CHAPTER 30
HEARTLESS

Old City, Klef Mordain – 22nd Day of Lamenta 108

'But if you remove every impurity, Abigone,' said Eshia, 'you will be left with nothing but iron.'

Abigone frowned at the iron blade she had summoned. 'And what is so wrong with iron?'

'Iron is brittle; steel yields.'

Raewyn rolled her eyes. 'It's easy, Abigone. You just need to remember to include a little charcoal when you form the steel in your mind. And, then add some wood for a handle.'

'A week ago,' said Abigone, 'I couldn't even summon iron, and now you want steel from me? We're moving too fast.'

'We are,' said Eshia, 'but I make no apologies for that. The Sanctians are on the doorstep of the city, and this might be your last lesson in the school.'

'That's why you're studying with me, and not the other first years,' said Raewyn. 'We're lucky to have Miss Eshia to teach us.'

'If things had been different,' said Eshia, 'then you would have had plenty of time to learn at my uncle's forge. I'll give you a few minutes, Abigone. Read the chapter again while I show Raewyn how to summon gold.'

Eshia and Raewyn moved over to another workbench, and Abigone glanced down at the large volume on steelmaking that was lying open in front of her. She had already read the relevant chapter three times, but the information didn't seem to be penetrating her head. There were too many thoughts already whirling around inside her mind – thoughts of Denny and what they had done together in the embassy; thoughts of what Denny had told her about the three ships tied up in the harbour; and thoughts of the approaching Sanctian army. To quell the chaos in her mind, she tried to imagine what Kilbride would say. Her sister had the ability to cut through the chaff to find the wheat. Decide what is most important, she would say, and then focus on those things one at a time. Trying too much at once leaves all tasks unfinished; better to get the important things right, leaving the less important to look after themselves.

It sounded easy, but Abigone knew she wasn't the same kind of person as her sister. Abigone remembered the aftermath of her destruction of the Sanctian cannon in Upper Down. She had felt no regret and no remorse about what she had done that day; she had certainly not shed any tears over it; so why did she feel so guilty about the things she and Denny had done in the embassy? It was partly because Denny had seen her kill. She had tarnished herself in front of him, showing him how proficient she could be at lying and killing; and he had done exactly the same in her presence. They had each revealed a side to themselves that neither had wanted to show. Was that so bad?

She got up from her seat.

'May I be excused for a moment, miss?' she said to Eshia.

'Yes, but don't be too long,' said Eshia. 'I want a steel blade out of you before the end of today.'

Abigone inclined her head, then she walked out of the classroom. She ascended a flight of stairs to an upper floor, where a few spare rooms had been found for the Masters to hold their lessons. Fyenna's secretary was busy with a woman from the laundry room, packing up books and other items into crates, and they both glanced at Abigone as she strode past them. She came to a classroom, where Denny was sitting with Ignatius and Salus, helping them meditate. Abigone watched them for a few moments, then Denny glanced in her direction.

He stood. 'Keep at it,' he said to the two boys. 'I'll be by the door.' He walked over to Abigone. 'Did you want to speak to me?'

'Yes,' she said. 'I want to tell you something that I have only just realised. It may sound heartless, but you should know the kind of person I am. You may change your mind about loving me after you hear it.'

'I doubt that, Abigone,' he said.

'We shall see, Denny. Here it is – I am not ashamed of what I did in the embassy.'

He narrowed his eyes. 'But...'

'I know I said I was ashamed, and I am. My shame is not due to my actions, but the fact that you saw me do them. Had I been alone, and had I killed everyone inside the embassy, from the highest ranked to the lowest, then I would not be feeling this way. I would probably be feeling nothing. My fear is that you will think me a monster.'

Denny said nothing.

'I don't want to feel this way any more,' Abigone went on. 'I love you, but I must be honest with you. You can accept me as who I am, as I accept that you are also capable of violence; or you can decide that you would do better without me.'

'Then,' he said, 'you don't regret all those deaths?'

'No. I regret that you witnessed what I did, but, in truth, I feel no need to redeem myself. I do not enjoy killing, but nor do I loathe myself for being a killer. My concern was that you would loathe me. I think we did what we had to do, in order to survive. I would do it again, Denny, if I had to. You should know that.'

Denny glanced away.

'Do you need time to think over my words?' she said.

'I... I don't know if I will be able to make my peace with what you have said to me, Abigone. How can you not regret what we did?'

'It was us or them, Denny. Either we lived, or we died, and I wanted us both to live. If that makes me a monster in your eyes, then I am a monster.'

'No. You are confused.'

She smiled. 'For the first time since it happened, my thoughts are clear. By telling you how I feel, a burden has been lifted from my shoulders. I could not say this to you before, because I felt guilty about not feeling guilty. I felt judged. Now, I feel liberated.'

'Maybe you are not the person I thought you were,' he said.

'For months, you pretended to be someone you are not. Perhaps we are only now realising what kind of people we each are. We are capable of kindness, and we are capable of murder. I can live with both sides of your character; indeed, I love you as you are, Denny. It is better that you know who I am. If this knowledge persuades you that I am unworthy of your love, then I will have to accept that, too. I had better return to class. Miss Eshia will be needing me.'

She turned from him and went back down to the floor where the Makers had their lessons. She walked back into the classroom and went to her desk. She glanced at the pages of the book in front of her, then she smiled.

'Blessed spirits,' she said, 'with your permission, summon for me a steel dagger, with an engraved wooden handle.'

The air rustled, and a perfectly-formed dagger appeared in the air before her. She reached out and caught it by the hilt before it could fall to the desk. Miss Eshia and Raewyn came over to look.

Raewyn laughed. 'See, Abigone? I told you it was easy.'

Eshia took the dagger from Abigone's hand. 'This is... very impressive,' she said. 'From rusty iron to perfect steel in one leap. How did you manage it, Abigone? I notice you didn't re-read the chapter.'

'The knowledge was already in my head, miss,' she said. 'I just needed some clarity before I could find it.'

. . .

At lunchtime, the student Makers all filed into the dining hall. Abigone glanced over at the tables where the boys were sitting, but there was no sign of Denny among them.

'Where's the cook?' said Reath. 'Why isn't she here? Who's going to serve us lunch?'

'The cook is busy packing up supplies,' said Miss Vesta. 'You can go into the kitchen and help yourselves to lunch today.'

'They must think we're stupid,' Reath whispered, as the girls walked into the kitchen. 'Something's going on. They keep saying that the school is carrying on as normal, so why is everyone packing up as though we're about to leave?'

'Maybe we're going to hide in the caverns when the Sanctians get here,' said Stanza.

'What – and live down there forever?' said Reath. 'No. They're planning something; they're just not telling us what it is.'

'Abigone probably knows,' said Nyli, as she cut a piece of bread from a loaf.

Abigone took an apple from a bowl, and pretended she hadn't heard.

'Abigone made a steel knife this morning,' said Stanza. 'I can't do that, and I'm in second year. The handle was even engraved. It's not fair.'

'It is fair,' said Raewyn. 'It's not Abigone's fault that you're incompetent, Stanza. Did you see me summon gold?'

Stanza snorted. 'It was barely a farthings-worth.'

'So? It was gold, Stanza – real gold.'

'That's nice,' said Nyli, 'but shouldn't we ask Abigone if she knows what the plan is?'

Abigone walked back into the dining room with her apple, and the other girls followed her.

Reath narrowed her eyes. 'Where have Miss Eshia and Miss Vesta gone?'

'They went downstairs,' said Marlow. 'We've been left to fend for ourselves.'

'And Valiance?' said Reath. 'Oops. I mean Prince Denny – is he helping them?'

Marlow shrugged. 'I've no idea where he is.'

'I think he went to his room,' said Ignatius. 'He was in a foul temper.'

'He's been in a foul temper for days,' said Constans. 'Ever since he and Abigone disappeared for ages.'

'His mood was even worse today,' said Ignatius; 'especially after Abigone came upstairs to speak to him.'

Abigone sat at a table, and the other girls sat down next to her.

'What did you say to Denny?' Reath said. 'Have you cast him aside like a smelly old sock?'

'Ignore her, Abigone,' said Raewyn. 'Your courtship with Denny is none of her business.'

'Aren't you going upstairs to see how he is?' said Nyli.

'No,' said Abigone. 'I can only be who I am.'

Reath laughed. 'What is that supposed to mean?'

'It means they've had a falling-out,' said Stanza. 'Abigone did something that Denny didn't like.'

'Ahh,' said Reath. 'Did he demand your flower, and did you refuse to give it to him?'

Abigone got to her feet.

'Why must you be so vulgar, Reath?' said Raewyn. 'Abigone, where are you going?'

'To my room,' she said.

She walked out of the dining hall and strode towards the stairs. She was about to ascend, when Mor Galthide called out her name. She halted on the steps, and the huge figure hurried over to her.

'What did you say to my son, girl?' he said. 'Have you broken off the courtship?'

'I have not, sir.'

'Did he dishonour you in some way?'

'He did not, sir.'

'He spoke to me as though the fires of your love have been extinguished. Might what has broken between you be repaired?'

'My love for him remains as strong as ever, sir. It is his love for me that I doubt.'

'Why, sweet Abigone? What has turned his thoughts from you?'

'I told him, sir, that I did not regret the deaths we caused in the embassy. I told him that my shame was due to your son's presence as a witness to my actions. I think he now considers me cruel and heartless.'

'Alas, he is too sensitive. Were I betrothed to a woman with a heart of fire, one capable of great and terrible deeds such as those carried out by your fair and pitiless hand, I would never let you go. He has inherited this softness from his mother. Let him simmer for a time, Abigone. I have been called to visit the *Little Ghost*, to oversee our preparations. When I return, I will attempt to straighten his course.'

Mor Galthide inclined his head towards her, then he turned and made his way back down the stairs. Abigone climbed the steps, and strode towards her room. She opened the door, and Meg appeared from under the covers of the bed. Abigone picked her up and cradled her like a baby.

'Dear Meg,' she said, kissing her. 'I may have lost Denny, but I have found myself.'

When classes finished that day, Abigone gathered up the clothes from her room that needed to be laundered. She placed them into a basket, and walked downstairs to the laundry room. She pushed open the door, but the chamber was deserted. Piles of bedding had gone from their usual shelves, and the washing tubs were empty.

Abigone set her basket onto a table, then she heard the unmistakeable sound of Mor Galthide's voice coming from the next floor down. Abigone walked out of the room, and gazed over the banister. Mor Galthide was gesticulating with his broad arms next to Fyenna, whose head was bowed. Abigone went down the stairs, and saw Denny standing close to his father.

'I could not approach,' Mor Galthide said. 'Had I done so, I would have been discovered.'

'What's wrong?' said Abigone, as she descended the stairs.

'Armed men have impounded Lady Fyenna's vessels, fair Abigone,' said Mor Galthide. 'I fear that one of the sailors must have given away our scheme to escape the city.'

'How many men are on the quayside?' said Fyenna.

'Four dozen, at the least, my lady,' said Mor Galthide. 'I clung to the shadows of an alleyway to observe them. They have closed off the pier that leads to the *Little Ghost* and the two carricks. What is to be done?'

'Give me a moment to think,' said Fyenna. 'I have even worse news. Miss Vesta, the cook, and my secretary have disappeared.'

'How so, my lady?'

'Rupert and the cook were down in the tunnels, arranging supplies to be taken to the cutter, but they did not return when they were due. I sent Miss Vesta after them, to fetch them back to the school, but she has not returned, either. I have searched the caverns, and I found a few crates where they had been working, but I saw no sign of them.'

'They might be lost, ma'am,' said Abigone. 'The tunnels are like a maze.'

'All three of them knew the tunnels well enough, girl,' said Fyenna. 'Unfortunately, our enemies also know them well.'

'Might these two incidents be connected, ma'am?' said Denny. 'If so, then the school might be in danger.'

'I don't know,' said Fyenna. 'Your father is probably correct about the ships – it is likely that a sailor with a loose tongue has unwittingly divulged too much information – but to whom? Both the pro-Sanctians and Lord Metrius have cause to stop us from leaving Klef Mordain. The same could be said about the tunnels. If Miss Vesta and the others have been taken by agents of the Second Empire Association, then it is only a matter of time before one of them reveals the location of the school. But, if they were taken by those working for Lord Metrius, then… I don't know.'

'Should we summon the children, my lady?' said Mor Galthide.

'No,' said Fyenna. 'They would only panic, and we must keep them calm if we are to remain together and alive. All that matters to me now is saving the children from the Sanctians. Mor Galthide, stay by the front door; Denny, watch the hatch that leads to the caverns below. I will inform Miss Eshia.'

Fyenna strode away, leaving Abigone with Denny and his father. Mor Galthide regarded them both, then he turned and walked to the bench by the front entrance of the school, where he sat, his gaze on the door.

'Can we talk, Denny?' Abigone said.

'What is there to say?' he said. 'You told me how you feel.'

He began to walk to the storeroom, where the hatch was located.

Abigone went after him. 'Are you breaking off our courtship,' she said, 'after I pledged myself to you?'

'When you made that pledge,' he said, 'your eyes were shedding tears of shame and regret. Now, it turns out that your only regret was that I witnessed you murder without shame.'

'I cannot help the way I am,' she said. 'My tears were genuine, and so is my lack of shame at what I did.'

'What you have brushed off so easily weighs heavily upon my soul.'

'Truly? Does this mean you will forswear violence forever? Are you so appalled by what we did that you will stand and do nothing if we are attacked?'

Denny walked into the storeroom.

'Answer me,' she said.

He sat by the open hatch, saying nothing.

'I am a Maker,' Abigone said. 'I did not wish to be one, but I am. If our enemies come here, then I will do all I can to kill them. Will you?'

'Have you no pity?'

'I have none for those who would see us dead, Denny. None. If my answer displeases you, then perhaps I am better off alone. I would not wish to be an encumbrance upon your conscience.'

'Then go, for I shall not be with one whose cruelty engenders no regret. I will fight if our enemies attack, but I shall do so reluctantly. You kill, and you do not care. I thought my heart mirrored yours, but now I see that you are heartless.'

'And I see that I was right to think that you were judging me. Consider my pledge withdrawn.'

Abigone walked away, and ran into Fyenna at the bottom of the stairs.

'Careful where you step, girl,' said Fyenna. 'I almost knocked you over.'

'Denny and I have broken off our courtship. I thought you would want to know, ma'am.'

Fyenna peered at her. 'How did this come about?'

'He thinks I am heartless, because I told him I feel no regret for what I did in the embassy.'

'What? After all those tears you spilled? You told me that you felt great shame and guilt over your actions. I don't understand.'

'It has taken me time to see my true feelings, ma'am. It occurred to me that I would have felt neither guilt nor shame if Denny had not witnessed my actions.'

'You are cold, girl.'

'Denny also thinks that, ma'am. Regardless, I am ready to fight again, if needs be. I shall not shrink from my responsibilities.'

A low rumbling commenced.

'Did you hear that?' said Fyenna. 'Come with me to the roof, Abigone.'

They hurried up the stairs, passing the floors where the classrooms and students' quarters lay, and went up onto the flat roof of the school. Abigone followed Fyenna to the southern edge of the roof, and they peered out into the distance.

'Smoke, there, on the horizon,' said Fyenna. 'The Sanctian army has arrived on the outskirts of Klef Mordain.'

'Are they firing cannon, ma'am?'

'What else could cause such a roar at that distance? Our army of reservists has been digging defensive ditches for the last few days on either flank of the Great Northern Highway, but they will be no match for the Sanctians.'

'Should we go there, ma'am? Should we help with the defence of the city?'

'If I were alone, I would go, but I am not alone. I have eleven children under my care.'

'But the Sanctians will break into the city without us.'

'That knowledge pains me, too, Abigone, but I have the future to think of. How many Masters and Makers remain on this continent, do you think? A few dozen, or fewer? Some will be hiding in the mountains, or some may have fled to the lands beyond the reach of the Sanctian Empire; but I have eleven to look after. Eleven young Masters and Makers. If the Sanctians get their hands on them, then there will be no future for our kind.'

'But the boats, ma'am; and Miss Vesta. What shall we do?'

'I wish I knew, girl. I have prayed to the spirits, begging for their advice, and their aid. I don't know if they heard me. I have never felt such despair.'

'Do you want me to go south to fight the Sanctians, ma'am? I am willing to go on my own.'

Fyenna stared at her. 'You would do that? Oh, Abigone, I was so wrong about you. But I cannot let you go. I need you here, to protect the other students. We might have to storm the quayside, and try to overcome the armed guards that have cut off the pier. Some of us will probably die, but I cannot think of another way out.'

'I understand, ma'am.'

'Your ruthlessness may have lost you Denny, but it is precisely what I need from you if we are to survive. Will you kill upon my command?'

'Yes, ma'am. I will follow whatever orders you give.'

'Then let us plan our next steps.'

They descended from the roof, and the rumbling noise diminished as they re-entered the building. When they reached the ground floor, Mor Galthide was speaking to a man by the school entrance.

'Who is that?' said Fyenna.

Mor Galthide turned. 'This scoundrel claims to be a messenger from Lord Metrius, ma'am. Shall I tickle the cur's throat?'

'Not yet,' said Fyenna. 'Let him speak.'

The messenger inclined his head towards Fyenna. 'My noble lady,' he said, 'I bear tidings, and a summons, from Lord Metrius, the man to whom you swore an oath of loyalty.'

'He thinks to summon me, does he?'

'He does, my lady. He also bade me deliver this message. He said that if you want your ships and your crew back, you will have to speak to him first. He will not allow you to flee the city without his permission.'

'So it was he who sent armed men to the harbour?' said Fyenna.

'It was, my lady. He also demands that the one known as Valiance accompany you to the meeting with his lordship. I have a carriage waiting outside to take you both to where Lord Metrius can be found.'

'My son belongs not to Lord Metrius,' Mor Galthide cried. 'How dare he...?'

Fyenna raised a finger to quieten him. 'Hold, please,' she said. She turned back to the messenger. 'You say you have a carriage? Did you bring it to the front door of the school? Are you sure you were not followed? You might have betrayed us all by this lapse of secrecy.'

'The streets are empty, my lady,' said the messenger.

'And the pro-Sanctians mobs?'

'The Second Empire Association has ordered them into the tunnels and caverns beneath the city, to await the arrival of the Sanctian army. There was no breach of secrecy, my lady; the streets are the safest way to travel.'

Fyenna gestured to Abigone and Mor Galthide. 'A word with you both, in private.'

She led them to the door of her office, while the messenger remained by the entrance to the school.

'I will go,' Fyenna said, 'and Denny shall go with me.'

'You shall not take my son into the jaws of a trap,' said Mor Galthide.

'Lord Metrius has the power to release our ships,' said Fyenna. 'I will perform whatever task he asks of me, in return for him allowing us to sail from this city.'

'He will want Denny to do something for him, ma'am,' said Abigone.

'If it is a cold-blooded killer he wants, then he has picked the wrong student. Mor Galthide, please fetch your son.'

Mor Galthide glared at her, then he strode into the storeroom.

'Should I go in Denny's stead, ma'am?' said Abigone.

'No. You will stay here, and get ready to lead the students to the harbour. From the messenger's words, I now believe Miss Vesta and the others to have fallen into the hands of Lord Tain's men. If that is the case, then all hope for them is lost. You may have to take the students by road, rather than by tunnel, but you will have Mor Galthide and Miss Eshia with you.'

'How will we know when to leave, ma'am?'

'I will send a signal, if I can; otherwise, I leave that up to your judgement.'

'*My* judgement, ma'am? But Miss Eshia is older than me, and Mor Galthide...'

'You said you would obey my orders.'

'And I shall, ma'am.'

'You have what I need, Abigone. Be as ruthless as you were in the embassy; do you understand?'

Abigone nodded, as Mor Galthide emerged from the storeroom with Denny. Abigone glanced at them, but Denny looked away.

'Denny,' said Fyenna, 'you and I have been summoned into the presence of the only man in the city who can allow the *Little Ghost* to sail from Klef Mordain. Will you come with me?'

Denny bowed. 'I shall, ma'am. If by going, Lord Metrius will allow us to leave, then I am at your service.'

'This is folly, son,' said Mor Galthide.

'What is the alternative, Father?' said Denny. 'If I do not go, we shall have to fight dozens of men to reach the ships.'

'So be it; I am not afraid.'

'You swore to serve my will,' said Fyenna. 'I order you to protect the students, Mor Galthide. I shall be leaving Abigone in charge of the school during my absence. You will accept her orders as you have accepted mine, and when she commands you to escort the children to the harbour, you will obey.'

Mor Galthide lowered his gaze. 'Damned by my own oath. Take good care of my son, Lady Fyenna. When we meet again at the harbour, I shall expect Mor Dennahelm to be by your side.'

Fyenna gestured to Denny, and the two of them walked over to where the messenger was standing.

'Lead us to Lord Metrius; we are ready,' said Fyenna.

The messenger bowed, then he escorted them out of the school.

Mor Galthide turned to Abigone. 'It seems that my life is now in your hands, sweet Abigone, as my son's fate now lies in the hands of Lady Fyenna. What are your orders?'

'Gather the students and the remaining staff in the study hall,' said Abigone, 'and fetch your armour.'

CHAPTER 31
WITHOUT A PLAN

Old City, Klef Mordain – 22nd Day of Lamenta 108

Fyenna gazed out of the carriage window as it passed through the empty streets of the Old City. Barricades were blocking some of the roads, but the armed men who had been guarding them had gone. Every front door was closed, and every window either broken or shuttered. The carriage turned left at a junction, and Fyenna saw a family pulling a laden cart along the cobbles, in the direction of the commercial harbour. Two young children were sitting on the back of the cart, along with piles of luggage, while the elder children were helping their parents drag or push it along the street.

'Abigone has broken off our courtship,' Denny said, from the seat opposite Fyenna.

'I know,' she said.

'She... she feels no regret for what we did in the embassy.'

'I heard you called her heartless.'

'How else was I to respond, ma'am? I don't understand why she doesn't feel any pity towards those we murdered.'

'Perhaps you should remain focussed on our meeting with Lord Metrius.'

Denny eyed her with suspicion. 'You want her to be ruthless, don't you? I mean, you're happy that Abigone can kill without hesitation or remorse. That's why you left her in charge.'

'She can stay calm in a crisis,' Fyenna said; 'as can you. You have both proved yourselves competent when faced with danger. You are not as dissimilar as you think.'

'I may be able to react, thanks to my training, but there is a big difference between us. I kill when faced with no other choice.'

'Are you saying that Abigone kills gratuitously; that she enjoys it?'

'No, but...'

'But what, Denny? The only difference I can see is that she doesn't wallow in shame after the deed has been done. You did what you had to do, and Abigone has the ability to put it behind her and move on; whereas, you?' She shook her head. 'I don't want to get involved in this. You are both young. I can give advice, but it is up to you and Abigone to work it out between you.'

Denny's eyes darkened. 'Do you think I am wallowing in shame? Is it weak to feel regret for some of the things I've done?'

'Will that regret prevent you from fighting, if you are called upon to do so?'

'No, ma'am.'

'Then you can feel whatever you like.'

Denny closed his mouth and turned to look out of the window.

The carriage took another turn, and Fyenna saw dozens of people on the street, next to the building where Lord Metrius had his office. Some were trying to force their way through the entrance, while armed guards were stopping them. The carriage came to a halt by the edge of the crowd, and the messenger, who had travelled up on the driver's bench, gestured to a few of the armed men. Scuffles broke out as several guards barged through the crowd, using their pikes to clear a path between the carriage and the front door of the building. The messenger opened the side door of the carriage, and Fyenna and Denny were escorted into the entrance hall of the office block. The messenger led them to the rear of the building, and they crossed an internal courtyard, where a huge heap of documents was being burned on a bonfire. Clerks were throwing sheaves of papers into the roaring flames, and smoke was spiralling upwards in the autumn breeze.

The messenger gestured to a doorway, then he led Fyenna and Denny up a narrow staircase into a square tower. More officials were clearing out their offices, packing crates, and dropping documents out of the windows, to be added to the bonfire below. On the top floor, the messenger knocked at a door, and was told by a voice within to enter.

The messenger bowed low as he opened the door. 'My lord,' he said, 'I have brought lady Fyenna and the boy known as Valiance to you, as requested.'

'Thank you,' said Metrius. 'You may leave us.'

Fyenna and Denny strode into a large, comfortable sitting room, where Metrius was reclining on a long couch with a glass of wine in his hand. The messenger bowed again, then he left the room, closing the door behind him.

'The Sanctians are drawing ever closer,' Metrius said.

Fyenna said nothing.

'Every available reservist has been sent south to hinder their progress,' Metrius went on, 'but the Sanctians are nothing if not efficient. The walls of the Old City will most likely be breached by nightfall, demolished by cannon fire, and overrun by soldiers. Tell me, Lady Fyenna; in this hour of peril, why are you not assisting our brave troops on the front lines? Are you not a war hero?'

'I have other responsibilities, my lord,' she said.

'Responsibilities greater than the preservation of this city, Fyenna? Have you forgotten your oath? While Klef Mordain cries out for help, you, instead, make plans to flee by ship?'

'I have eleven children under my care, my lord; children that represent the future of Masters and Makers upon this continent.'

'And I can see one of these so-called children standing in front of me. You did a fine job in the Sanctian Embassy, Mor Dennahelm. What else might you be able to achieve? I wonder.'

'I am not your weapon,' said Denny.

'Then what use are you to me?' said Metrius. 'The entire purpose of the secret schools was to prepare a line of defence for the city, in case the worst happened. Well, the worst is happening before our eyes, and where are our renowned defenders? After all the money and time we have lavished upon our Masters and Makers, where are they when we need them?'

'We cannot force fourteen-year-olds to fight in a war, my lord,' said Fyenna.

'Why not? Why did we bother having the secret schools if we cannot call upon them? Don't answer that; I have no desire to listen to your equivocations. You are here now, and that is all that matters.'

'I ask that you allow our ship to sail, my lord,' said Fyenna.

'And what will you give me in return? Will the two of you pledge to join the battle for the walls of the Old City? I need time; can you provide it?'

'Time for what, my lord?'

'Time to destroy my records, for one thing. I assume you saw the little bonfire in the courtyard? It is imperative that the Sanctians do not get their hands on the archives of the Corse; otherwise, all five thousand members of that august body will be hunted down and arrested as soon as the Sanctians assume power. If you fight, I will order my men to release your boat. Does that sound fair?'

Fyenna narrowed her eyes.

'I see that you do not trust me, my lady,' said Metrius. 'Do you think me so spiteful that I would promise to release your ship, and then not do it? One question has piqued my curiosity – why have you decided to flee by sea, and not by land? The Celestial Bridge is open, and I believe that many of our fellow citizens are using that route to escape north.'

'Many of those citizens will be able to return to Klef Mordain, once the fighting dies down. No such opportunity exists for my eleven young Masters and Makers. In order for them to be safe, I will need to take them somewhere out of the reach of the Sanctians.'

'I understand that, but you still haven't answered my question. Why not take them overland to Upper Down? I am sure that Princess Kilbride would welcome the return of her younger sister.'

'That journey would take over a month, my lord; and the lands between here and Upper Down are riddled with marauding bands of Westlanders.'

'But the harbour entrance is being guarded by three Sanctian warships, Fyenna,' said Metrius. 'That tells me that you must have a plan to get past them.'

Fyenna said nothing.

'Come now; what is your plan?' said Metrius.

'Why do you wish to know, my lord?'

'Call it professional curiosity. I cannot believe that you are leaving this to chance.'

'It has not escaped my attention that you own many ships, my lord; and some of them are tied up in the commercial harbour.'

Metrius waved a hand at her. 'What of it? I am far from the only member of the Corse who has taken an interest in shipping.'

'I saw some of your clerks placing valuables and documents into crates.'

Metrius laughed. 'And from that have you deduced that I, too, intend to flee by ship? Did I not pledge to remain here unto my death?'

'You did, my lord, but pledges made in haste are often broken.'

'How dare you? I would slap you across the face, were it not for the fact that you are correct. I have two vessels ready to leave the harbour as soon as I arrive. I shall be upon my favourite – the *Lasting Fealty*; while I have outfitted the *Good Will* to be used as a fire ship. There. I have revealed to you my plan. I know we have had our differences, Fyenna, but could we not work together? If we each aid the other's efforts, might not we increase our chances of escaping the blockade? Join the battle by the walls of the Old City. Earn us a few more hours, and then we shall leave the harbour in a single group. By fighting the Sanctians, you would not only be helping me, you would be helping your students. Once we are in open waters, we can go our separate ways. Do we have a deal?'

'Do I have a choice?'

'Of course you do. You can reject my offer, and I will instruct my men at the harbour to cripple your vessel.'

'You would leave the students here to die?'

'I feel no moral compunction to save them. What have the Masters and Makers ever done for me? I, on the other hand, have kept them provided with food, clothes and books. I have protected them from spies, and shielded their secrets. I did this on the understanding that they would rally to our defence – shall you now prove me a fool? Did I shelter the students for nothing?'

'I will fight,' said Denny.

Metrius turned to regard him. 'Well said, boy. I see your pragmatism outweighs your obvious loathing for me. Your actions at the embassy set in motion the events that will lead to the deaths of thousands.'

'You ordered him to kill the ambassador,' said Fyenna.

'I did. It is better that the agonies of the city be over within a few days, rather than the citizens endure months of starvation. I made that choice. Our defeat was inevitable, and my only recourse was to quicken it, to lessen the suffering of the masses. You see, Fyenna, I do care. I tried to overcome the pro-Sanctians, and I failed. All that was left was to put Klef Mordain out of its misery in the most efficient way possible. Now that the end is approaching, however, I do not intend to be strung up from a lamppost. Tell me your plan for getting past the *Bitter Respite*.'

'I will tell you when we are all safely in the harbour.'

Metrius laughed again, but it was a hollow sound. 'Very well, my lady; keep your secrets for now. Does this mean you will fight? Delay the Sanctian advance by any means necessary – give us until sunset, or midnight, preferably. Hold them at the ancient walls of the Old City. Will you do this?'

Fyenna nodded. 'I will.'

'Excellent. I will instruct my men at the harbour to welcome your students and staff when they arrive. I will follow on later, and then we shall await your return from the front lines. If the Sanctian soldiers arrive first, then I regret to say that we shall leave without you. A clerk will now show you to a detachment of reservists – they will accompany you to the walls. Dismissed.'

Fyenna turned without bowing, then she and Denny walked out of the chamber.

Denny shook his head as they descended the stairs. 'He doesn't seem to realise that it was Abigone who did most of the killing in the embassy, not me.'

'He believes what he wants to believe.'

'I hate him.'

'That was clear from the look on your face.'

'Are we really going to help him escape?'

'There will no doubt be several ships trying to leave the harbour this night, all desperate not to be here when Klef Mordain falls. We may need to help each other if we are to get past the blockade.'

'But what about your plan?'

Fyenna eyed him. 'What plan? I am improvising as I go along, Denny. I will decide what to do when we are aboard the *Little Ghost*.'

A clerk gestured to them as they reached the bottom of the stairs.

'Lord Metrius indicated that there would be a detachment waiting for us,' said Fyenna.

'Yes, my lady,' said the clerk. 'This way.'

They went back through the internal courtyard, where the flames from the bonfire were rising high, and passed through to the rear of the building. Some forty men had gathered there – a mixture of bowmen, and soldiers with pikes and armour.

'Are you Lady Fyenna?' said an officer.

'I am she,' she said.

'Then we are honoured to act as your personal guard, my lady,' he said. 'What are your orders?'

'We shall take the road south, until we reach the walls of the Old City. From there we shall link up with the rest of the defence, and ascertain our next step.' She gestured to Denny. 'This is Valiance. He shall be acting as my squire and assistant.'

'Yes, my lady,' said the officer. He turned to his men. 'Form up on the street.'

Denny eyed Fyenna as the soldiers exited through a gate in the wall of the building. 'Why did you not mention that I am a Master, ma'am?'

'Can you turn someone's blood into salt?'

'No, ma'am.'

'Can you create a ditch, by transforming stone and earth into wood or metal?'

Denny lowered his gaze. 'No, ma'am.'

'Then you have your answer. You have a sword strapped to your belt; stay close to me, and use it if necessary.'

They followed the soldiers out into the street. The men-at-arms flanked Fyenna and Denny, while the bowmen remained at the rear.

'To the walls,' cried the officer, and the soldiers set off.

They passed through a crowd of angry civilians, and the men-at-arms pushed them aside.

'Who are they?' said Denny. 'Why are they here?'

'They are most likely loyal clients of Lord Metrius,' said Fyenna; 'demanding to know what his lordship is going to do to save them from the Sanctians.'

They strode away from the crowds, and took a main road leading south. They passed a small procession of families with carts. Some were making for the Celestial Bridge, while others were walking in the direction of the commercial harbour.

'Tell me something, Valiance,' said Fyenna. 'You know the Sanctians better than most. What will their soldiers do when they arrive? Will they rampage through Klef Mordain?'

'It depends upon their orders, ma'am. In some cases, they have been given a day to loot and murder without any repercussions, and then they restore order. But, that's usually after a long siege, when their soldiers have suffered. The Sanctians won't want to damage the city too much, nor slaughter its inhabitants. Their officers will have lists of those to execute, and those to protect.'

'I know which list will contain my name,' she said.

A low rumbling from the south made the soldiers glance up.

'The cannon are approaching the Old City walls,' said one.

'How?' said another. 'How could they get here so quickly?'

'Quiet,' said the officer. 'Our job is to protect the Maker. Take heart, lads. Lady Fyenna defeated the Westlanders at Hader Pull, and the Sanctians have no idea that she's coming.'

Fyenna caught the gazes of a few soldiers, and she kept her expression calm, despite the turmoil roiling through her.

After walking for another twenty minutes, the walls of the Old City became visible above the roofs of the houses. The ancient defensive line ran east to west for a mile, cutting off the peninsula where the Old City lay. Its stonework, turrets and battlements had protected the Old City for five hundred years, but they appeared dilapidated and flimsy next to the might of the Sanctian cannon. A stream of wounded soldiers was entering the Old City through one of its gates, but the walls themselves were unmanned.

The officer brought the men-at-arms and archers to a halt by the gate, and they stood by the side of the road as the wounded passed them.

'We are at the gates, ma'am,' said the officer. 'Shall we proceed to the battle?'

'Let's find out what's going on first,' said Fyenna. 'Can one of your men scout ahead, and bring us some information on the disposition of the enemy?'

The officer gestured to an archer. 'You heard the Maker. Get through the gate and find a sergeant or an officer, then report back.'

The archer shouldered his bow and raced off through the open gate. Another round of rumbling began, and Fyenna could make out the individual sounds made by each cannon as they fired. The ground shook beneath her feet. Whatever was going to happen next, this was no Hader Pull. That day, the Westlanders had attacked the armed forces of Klef Mordain across a flat, open field; perfect for their heavy cavalry, but also perfect for the tactics Fyenna and Drummond had deployed against them.

The archer returned to the detachment, a young sergeant by his side.

'Over here,' said the officer. 'Sergeant, what can you tell us about the enemy?'

The sergeant saluted. 'The Sanctians are advancing along six different routes into the city, sir; and each has their own brigade of cannon. We stop them in one place, and the others advance to outflank us.'

'Six? How far are they from the Old City?

'Less than a mile, sir.'

'I don't understand. Why wouldn't they concentrate their forces and make for the main gate? This strategy will do nothing but slow their advance.'

'They are expecting Masters and Makers to be here,' said Fyenna. 'They know that if they concentrate their army, a single Master or Maker could wreak untold damage upon them. How many cannon are in each brigade, sergeant?

'Around a dozen, I think, ma'am,' said the sergeant. 'Each brigade is being supported by two regiments of foot soldiers. They are fanning out through every alley and back street, attacking us from every direction. Should we retreat behind the walls and bar the gates?'

'Their cannon would breach the wall in minutes,' said Fyenna. 'We have to stop them before they are in range of the Old City.' She glanced at the officer. 'Captain, escort us down the Great Northern Highway. We shall strike that way first, and slow down the advance.'

The captain eyed her. 'Could we speak alone for a moment, ma'am?'

Fyenna nodded, then she and the officer walked a few yards away.

'Our situation is hopeless, ma'am,' the officer whispered. 'If we march down the Great Northern Highway, we shall be outflanked and surrounded. If the walls of the Old City cannot contain the Sanctians, then the prudent course of action would be to surrender, to save the lives of the men and women in our army.'

Fyenna narrowed her eyes. 'What would Lord Metrius think, were he to hear your words, Captain?'

'Everyone who works for him knows he is planning to flee the city, ma'am. Why should we die for someone who is attempting to abandon us? If we keep fighting, the Sanctians will drive us into the sea. It is over, my lady.'

'And what will happen to me if I surrender?' she said.

The officer glanced away.

'Answer me, Captain,' she said. 'What will happen to me?'

'I don't know, ma'am.'

'Don't lie to me. You know what the Sanctians think of people like me. If I surrender, my corpse will be swinging from a lamppost. If I wish to live, I have no choice but to fight.'

'But the same is not true of my men, ma'am. If they fight, they will die – but if they surrender, the Sanctians will allow them to live. Look at them – part-time archers and men-at-arms – what chance do they have against a professional army with cannon? They just want to go back to their homes and families. Could you not beg Lord Metrius to allow you to board his ship?'

'You must do as your conscience dictates, Captain. I shall be fighting this day.'

They walked back to the others.

'Our orders,' said the officer, 'stated that we were to accompany Lady Fyenna as far as the gates of the Old City. We have done so. To now throw ourselves into a losing battle would accomplish nothing but our deaths.' He took a long breath as he gazed at the frightened faces of the soldiers in front of him. 'Klef Mordain has fallen. With only one Maker to defend the Old City, its capture is inevitable. Therefore, I am ordering you to return to your homes. When you get there, lay your uniforms and weapons to the side, and dress as you would for your normal occupation. Then lock your doors and windows, and await the arrival of the Sanctian army. You are dismissed from your service. Go.'

'Wait,' said Fyenna, as the soldiers began to disperse. 'Klef Mordain has been free for a hundred years – does that mean nothing to you? Where is your patriotism? Stand and fight; defend your city from the invaders.' Her fury grew as the soldiers ignored her. 'Had I run away at Hader Pull,' she cried, 'the Westlanders would have ravaged our lands and homes. Cowards; come back.'

She stared at the soldiers as they hurried away from the vicinity of the gates. The officer raced after his men and, in a few moments, all of them had disappeared from sight.

'Damn them,' said Fyenna.

'There are still plenty of soldiers resisting on the other side of the wall, ma'am,' said Denny.

'Yes, but for how long?'

'Do you think we should leave and go to the harbour?'

'We can't. We still have to hinder the advance of the Sanctians, or there won't be enough time to get the students to the *Little Ghost*. Dear spirits, let Abigone hear my plea – take them to the harbour.' A tear fell down her cheek, and she wiped it away. 'If I fall, Denny, run to the quayside. If the students are there, set sail immediately. If not, find them and escort them to the *Little Ghost*. Do you understand?'

'Yes, ma'am. And if I fall, tell my father that I love him, and tell Abigone...'

'Yes?'

'Tell her I wish things had been different.'

'I will.'

'Thank you, ma'am. What's the plan?'

Fyenna smiled. 'Didn't you hear me earlier, Prince of Sanctos? I'm making this up as I go along.'

She set off for the open gate, and Denny walked by her side. They passed a cart loaded with wounded soldiers, and left the Old City. Fifty yards to their right, the Great Northern Highway ran in a straight line towards the southern outskirts of the city, while, ahead of them, dozens of Klef Mordain soldiers were slowly retreating.

'We shall start here,' said Fyenna, as she gazed at the buildings on either side of the street. 'We shall block this route, then move onto the next one. If we cannot stop the Sanctians, we shall slow them down for long enough to give the young Masters and Makers the time they need to get to the harbour. Are you with me?'

'Yes, ma'am,' said Denny, a hand on the hilt of his sword. 'I'm ready.'

CHAPTER 32
SON OF SANCTOS

Old City, Klef Mordain – 22nd Day of Lamenta 108

Denny steadied his breathing as he followed Fyenna down the street towards the retreating Klef Mordain soldiers. His gaze took in their surroundings. The buildings lining the street were two and three-storey, and they looked like a less expensive version of the houses in the Old City. They passed a bakery that had wooden beams nailed over its windows. Behind the beams, two pairs of eyes watched as Fyenna and Denny strode down the middle of the road. They ran into the first of the retreating soldiers, and Fyenna put a hand on a bowman's shoulder.

'How far away are the Sanctians?' she said.

'Their cannon blew our barricade to pieces,' the bowman said, 'then their archers loosed, and their infantry charged.'

'How far?' said Fyenna.

The man brushed her hand away, and hurried towards the walls of the Old City.

'Turn and fight!' cried an officer. 'Get back in line!'

A few soldiers halted, but the rest seemed oblivious to the officer's words.

'I want archers by each side of the road,' the officer said, as he cajoled a few stragglers. 'Shields in the middle. Form a new barricade.'

A man with blood coating his face and shoulders staggered by, his uniform in tatters.

'Quickly!' the officer went on. 'We have ten minutes before those bastards have moved their cannon into range of the walls.'

Fyenna approached the officer.

'Get off the street, ma'am,' he shouted.

'I am Fyenna of Hader Pull,' she said. 'I am here to help.'

He flashed a bitter smile at her. 'You're a little late, ma'am; the Sanctians have been pushing us back since yesterday evening.'

'Where are the rest of your men?'

'Dead, injured, fled,' he said. 'Half of them ran at the sound of the first damn cannon. Every time we make a stand, Sanctians move through the alleyways on either side of the road and outflank us. It's the same on their other approach routes. They have four columns moving through Nether Hall, and another two coming up through Cliephus. They advance a few hundred yards, re-position their cannon, and fire while the other columns move forward.'

Fyenna gazed down the street.

The officer pointed. 'There, ma'am, by the fountain – do you see the Sanctian scouts? The rest of them won't be far behind.'

'Get your men out of the way,' Fyenna said. 'I will block the road.'

The officer gazed at her, then he nodded. 'Move up to the bakery,' he shouted at the men left on the street. 'Form defensive lines and take cover. The Maker of Hader Pull is here!'

Denny remained by Fyenna's side as she walked forward, leaving the soldiers behind. Denny's eyes went to the scouts, and he saw four of them crouching by the fountain, which sat in the middle of a crossroads.

'The scouts have seen us, ma'am,' he said.

'I want them to see us,' said Fyenna. 'I want them to know that Klef Mordain has a Maker. It might make them pause.'

They kept walking, until they were just out of bow range. In the distance, the rest of the two regiments were advancing up the street towards the fountain, dragging over a dozen cannon with them.

Archers and crossbowmen were keeping to the flanks, while small squads of soldiers were peeling off into the alleyways on either side of the road. One of the scouts by the fountain scurried back and re-joined the main body of soldiers, then he pointed up the street to where Fyenna was standing.

Fyenna raised her hand, and the Sanctian archers were ordered forward at a run.

'Ma'am,' said Denny.

'I see them,' said Fyenna.

She whispered a few words, and a cloud of dust arose as buildings were stripped of their stonework, and hundreds of cobbles were ripped up from the surface of the road. A massive stone wall began to form between the fountain and Fyenna, layer upon layer of rock, until it stood ten feet high, and stretched across the entire road. A flurry of arrows was loosed by the Sanctians. They soared into the air over the newly-summoned wall, and came down upon the place where Fyenna and Denny were standing. An arrow clipped the ground by Denny's right foot, then Fyenna raised her hand again, and a large shield appeared in front of them. Denny picked it up, and they crouched beneath its shelter as the arrows rained down upon the street.

Fyenna glanced at Denny from the shadow cast by the shield.

'Get ready to run,' she said. 'We'll move north to the next main road, and do the same.'

'The cannon will smash through your new wall,' he said.

'I know,' she said. 'All we can do is slow them down. Now. Run.'

They got to their feet as the arrow storm petered out. Fyenna led Denny to a narrow alleyway, and they raced up it, Denny still grasping the heavy shield in his left hand. They reached the alleyway, which ran between rows of brick walls at the rear of the terraced houses. Four Sanctian soldiers burst out from an alley on their left, and Denny raised the shield, as he pushed Fyenna behind him. Denny charged into the four men, and the boss of his shield struck one in the face, breaking his nose. Denny ducked under a sword swing, then he felt his shield take the impact of a crossbow bolt. He tried to draw his own sword, but a soldier lunged at him with a spear. He parried it with the shield, then Fyenna raised her hand, and a stone gargoyle formed in the air above the Sanctians. It fell, hitting two of them. One collapsed with a crushed skull, and the other rolled away screaming and clutching his arm. Denny got space to draw his sword, then he jabbed forward, slicing across the last Sanctian's arm. The man retreated, and Fyenna grabbed Denny by the shoulder and pushed him forward. Denny sheathed his sword and picked up a discarded spear as he ran. Sweat was getting into his eyes, and they paused for a moment in the empty rear yard of a house. Denny panted for a moment as he leaned on the spear.

'Do you need anything?' said Fyenna. 'A helmet?'

Denny shook his head.

'Are you all right?' she said.

'Yes, ma'am. Could you make the shield any lighter?'

'Place it against the wall,' she said.

He did so, and Fyenna raised her hand. The shield disintegrated, and a smaller, lighter version appeared in its place. Denny picked it up, then he nodded at Fyenna, and they set off again. They took a left, and headed further away from the walls of the Old City. Fyenna raised a finger for silence, and they crept along another alleyway. They came across a Sanctian scout, who was peering over a wall with his back to them.

Fyenna gestured at Denny, then at the man, and Denny nodded. He stole forward, the shield in his left hand and the spear in his right. When he was a yard away, the scout turned his head, and his gaze met Denny's. Denny lunged forward, and drove the spear into the man's chest. The man fell, wrenching the spear from Denny's grip, then Denny kicked him in the head, sending several bloody teeth flying. Fyenna joined him by the wall, and they looked over. They had reached another main road. Fifty yards to their right, the defenders of Klef Mordain had erected a barricade from barrels and carts, and a thick row of archers had taken up position behind it. To their left, a wall of Sanctian shields was making its way step by step towards the barricade. A few archers from both sides loosed, but the shields and the barricade absorbed most of the arrows. Behind the thick Sanctian shieldwall, soldiers were pulling six cannon. They set them down, and placed wooden wedges behind the wheels. More soldiers arrived, laden with iron balls.

Denny nudged Fyenna. 'Do you see the man with the leather shoulder pouch?' he whispered. 'That contains the black powder. Each team of cannon will have a man whose job it is to carry the powder. Eliminate him, and the cannon will not be able to fire until more powder is brought up from the rear.'

Fyenna nodded. 'I'm going to sow destruction upon the cannon,' she said. 'Steal the pouch, if you can.'

Denny exhaled, then he leaned the shield and the spear against the wall. Fyenna raised her hand, and her mouth formed the words of blessing. There was a great roar as huge shards of iron were torn from the six cannon, and from the balls being carried by the soldiers. Some Sanctians fell as the shrapnel pierced their bodies, then dozens of metal blades appeared in the air above the soldiers. They fell like hail among them, cutting down over two dozen as they sliced through leather armour and flesh. Denny put his hands onto the top of the wall and vaulted it. He ran out into the chaos, scrambling past the wrecked cannon and the writhing bodies of the wounded.

'They have a Maker!' he shouted in the accent of a Sanctian aristocrat. 'Pull back!'

He launched himself at the man carrying the leather pouch, and the strap keeping it to his shoulder snapped as they fell together. Denny gripped the man's hair, and battered the back of his skull off the cobbles, then he pulled at the pouch. A soldier punched him in the face as he tried to get to his feet, and Denny slipped on a pool of blood and crashed to the ground. He opened the pouch, spilling its contents into the blood, then a kick landed in his stomach. Denny gasped in pain, then he glanced up as the two men drew their swords. Something whistled through the air, and both men spiralled away as though in a dance, each pierced by arrows loosed by the defenders by the barricade. Denny lay on the ground with his hands covering his head as more arrows broke up the Sanctian formation. Denny crawled to the side of the road, then he clambered over the wall and fell into a heap on the other side, his chin aching from the blow he had received.

'Get up!' Fyenna cried. 'You were seen. Soldiers are in the alleyways.'

Denny pulled himself to his feet as a crossbow bolt struck the brick wall two feet to his left. He and Fyenna sprinted along the alley, racing towards the barricade. They turned a corner, and were nearly impaled by spears held by soldiers on their own side.

'Hold!' Fyenna shouted. 'I am a Maker. I am Fyenna of Hader Pull!'

Fyenna and Denny were ushered behind the barricade, and a soldier shoved a water skin into Denny's hands. He pulled out the cork and took a long drink, despite the pain in his jaw.

'All six cannon are out of action on this road,' said a sergeant. 'You, there – run back to the next retreat position and let them know.'

A soldier raced off down the street, and the sergeant crouched down by Fyenna and Denny.

'Thank you, ma'am,' he said. 'I don't suppose you could do that again another nine times?'

'Nine?' said Fyenna. 'I was told that the Sanctians were advancing along six routes.'

'They were, ma'am,' said the sergeant, 'but they've been dividing their numbers further, and they're using every street that leads to the walls of the Old City.'

'We disrupted their advance on Low Street,' Fyenna said. 'I summoned a stone wall to slow them down.'

'Then, ma'am, if you'll take my advice, you might want to do the same on the next road along. If you block the three central routes, the columns on the flanks might have to pause for a while. They won't want to leave a large gap in the middle of their lines.'

'The Great Northern Highway is the next road along.'

The sergeant nodded, then he gave her a wry smile. 'This is nothing like Hader Pull, is it, ma'am?'

'Nothing,' she said. She glanced at Denny. 'Let's go. One more road, and then we can rest for a while.'

Denny got to his feet.

'Do you require any more soldiers to watch your back, ma'am?' the sergeant said.

'My squire has done a good job so far,' she said, as she stood. 'I'll move quicker if it's just him and me.'

'May the spirits go with you, ma'am.'

'And you, sergeant.'

Fyenna and Denny hurried off, passing through the lines of archers and men-at-arms towards another alleyway. They sprinted up the narrow lane, then reached a blocked alley, where a dozen defenders of Klef Mordain were keeping their heads down.

'You can't go any further,' said one of the soldiers. 'The Sanctians are occupying the alleyways between here and the Great Northern Highway.'

'We have a job to do,' said Fyenna.

'But...'

'I am a Maker,' she said.

The soldier nodded, then he signalled to his archers. 'Ready a volley,' he said.

Eight archers drew arrows from a central bucket, and then each nocked their bows and pulled their right arms back.

'Aim high,' said the soldier. 'Loose.'

Fyenna and Denny set off as soon as the arrows were in the air, scrambling and jumping over the barricade. They landed on the far side, and ran. They raced at full speed along the alleyway, then, as they passed an entrance on their left, four Sanctians armed with crossbows aimed their weapons at them. Fyenna raised her hand, and summoned a thin stone wall that sealed off the entrance, then they carried on running. Denny drew his sword as they neared a corner. They ran round it and straight into three crouching Sanctian scouts. Denny yelled at the top of his voice as he charged. Two of the scouts fled in surprise, and Denny rammed the tip of the short sword through the last one's throat.

'Don't stop,' Fyenna said, as she pulled him by the arm.

They raced off again, then took shelter in a small garden at the rear of a house. They crawled to the back door of the house, and found it unlocked. They crept inside, their boots making the floorboards creak with every step.

'It looks empty,' said Fyenna. 'The Great Northern Highway should be right outside the front door.'

They came to a small parlour, which had a window overlooking the wide thoroughfare. The shutters had been closed, so Fyenna and Denny peered between the wooden slats. In the street outside, a squad of Sanctian soldiers were finishing off a small group of archers from Klef Mordain that had been cut off and surrounded.

'Should we help them, ma'am?' whispered Denny.

'No,' said Fyenna. 'Do you see the cannon?'

Denny pulled his eyes away from the carnage in front of him and gazed down the street to the left. Twenty yards away, over a dozen cannon were being hauled over the cobbles, while thick rows of armoured soldiers with heavy shields were acting as a barrier between them and the retreating defenders.

'Yes, ma'am,' he said.

'Is there a man carrying the black powder?'

'He'll be there somewhere, but I don't see him.'

'We need a better view,' she said. 'Follow me.'

Fyenna found the stairs, and they went up to the first floor of the house. In the bedroom, they found a man and a woman hiding under the bed, their eyes wide with terror.

Denny stared at them for a moment, then Fyenna pulled him away.

'Ignore them,' she said.

'But if we are seen, this house will be raided,' said Denny. 'We should warn them.'

'We have no time for that. Leave them. This is war, Denny. Harden your heart.'

He followed her to another set of stairs, and they ascended to the building's flat roof. They crawled to the edge, and peered down at the advancing Sanctians. Denny's eyes scanned the soldiers, until he saw a man carrying a large leather pouch who was walking behind the cannon.

'There,' Denny whispered, pointing.

Fyenna nodded, then she raised her hand. A huge chunk of masonry was ripped off a neighbouring building, and a gigantic gargoyle appeared in the air above the soldiers. A few screamed as it fell, then it landed on the man with the pouch, crushing him into the cobbles. The advance halted. Several men attempted to retrieve the pouch from under the enormous gargoyle, while others gazed up at the roofs and at the windows of the houses. A soldier pointed directly at where Denny and Fyenna lay, then several squads broke away from the others and charged towards the house.

'We need to go,' said Denny.

'Not yet,' said Fyenna, 'not when I have a dozen cannon in front of me.'

She raised her hand again, as soldiers loosed their crossbows at the roof. A terrible sound of grinding came from the street as iron was ripped from the cannon, until there was almost nothing left, then a long metal fence appeared across the road. Soldiers who had been standing in its path were impaled by the sharp iron spikes as they rammed themselves into the ground; then the road was blocked, the iron fence cutting across the entire width of the Great Northern Highway.

Fyenna and Denny crawled away from the edge of the roof, as the front door of the house was kicked in by Sanctian soldiers. A hail of bolts and arrows filled the sky, and Fyenna summoned a thick wooden canopy that she and Denny dived under. The projectiles struck the canopy, and others skittered off the flat roof. Shrieks and cries came from the floor below them, and Denny felt sick at the thought of the two civilians hiding under the bed.

The hailstorm of arrows and bolts ceased, and they got moving again. They raced for the stairs, then halted as a Sanctian solder rushed up to them. Denny kicked him in the face before he could climb the last few steps, and the man went tumbling backwards, knocking down one of his comrades.

'Jump,' said Fyenna. 'Aim for the vegetable patch.'

Denny and Fyenna ran to the rear edge of the roof and leaped down into the garden. Denny rolled as he landed, his trained instincts taking over, then he heard a yell of pain from Fyenna. He reached out and gripped her by the shoulder, then he helped her stand.

'Can you walk, ma'am?' he said.

'It's my elbow,' she said. 'My legs are fine.'

They raced through the garden, and vaulted a low wall, as the Sanctians burst through the back door of the house. Fyenna cradled her left elbow as they ran back the way they had come. They passed the body of the scout Denny had killed, and then the wall Fyenna had summoned, before reaching the barricade blocking the end of the alley. Klef Mordain soldiers reached out for them, and dragged them over the barrier. Denny fell, then he sat up and leaned against a wall, out of breath, aching, and with sweat in his eyes.

Next to him, Fyenna groaned in pain.

'Is it broken, ma'am?' said a soldier.

'I don't think so,' she said, 'just bruised. I destroyed the cannon on the Great Northern Highway, and blocked the road.'

The soldier grinned. 'Well done, ma'am. If only we had ten other Makers like you, then we might actually win this damn battle.'

Several hours passed. Reports reached Fyenna and Denny that their efforts had caused a complete halt to the Sanctian advance. With their three central routes blocked, and almost twenty cannon destroyed, they had pulled back in order to re-group, and a lull had settled over the approaches to the Old City. Denny and Fyenna had been taken to a house close to a barricade, and, as Denny had recovered, Fyenna's condition had deteriorated. Her elbow had become swollen, and she was unable to move her left arm without it causing her pain.

'I'm forty-seven years old,' she said to Denny, as they sat on the floor of the abandoned house. 'Too old to be sprinting through gardens, vaulting over walls and jumping from roofs. I haven't run like that since I was in my twenties.'

'What you have done this day, ma'am,' he said, 'I will never forget.'

'Thank you, but what was it all for? To steal a little time from the Sanctians' advance? It has made no difference to the outcome, and I don't know if I can run again. My arm will take weeks to heal.'

Denny glanced out of the window. 'The sun will be setting soon.'

'If the Sanctians do not renew their attacks within the next few hours,' Fyenna said, 'we should start to make our way to the harbour.'

'Can I ask you something, ma'am?'

'Of course.'

'Why gargoyles?'

Fyenna smiled. 'I'm not sure why, but they're easy for me to remember. The Corsehall has dozens of them, and I used to look up and see them whenever I went there. Most of the people who walked past the building had no idea that it was used as the meeting place for the Corse – there were several secret entrances and hidden doors for us to use. Sometimes, I would arrive by tunnel, and I wouldn't catch a glimpse of the gargoyles, but I always remembered them. Abigone does something similar, when she summons her stone dragons.'

'I saw her do that in the embassy,' he said. 'I miss her. I don't want to break off our courtship.'

Fyenna eyed him for a moment. 'You have been through a lot today, Denny,' she said. 'You have fought and killed, and you have watched me take the lives of several dozen Sanctians; and yet you are sitting here, asking me about gargoyles. You don't seem to be stricken with guilt or shame. Perhaps you are not as different from Abigone as you like to imagine.'

Denny narrowed his eyes. He wanted to say something that would contradict Fyenna's words, but he could see the truth in her claim. He had accused Abigone of being heartless, yet he was hardly filled with regret for what he and Fyenna had been doing. Had he been holding Abigone to a higher standard, or had his accusations reflected fear about his own actions?

'Did my words offend you, Prince of Sanctos?' said Fyenna.

The sergeant from the barricade ran into the house before Denny could respond.

'We have to move,' the sergeant cried. 'The Sanctians have launched another attack.'

Fyenna frowned. 'I hear nothing coming from the street.'

'They are advancing rapidly on both flanks, ma'am,' the sergeant said, 'while their centre remains where it is. Our defences both north and south of our position have already been pushed back. If we stay here, we'll be cut off and surrounded.'

Denny got to his feet. He extended a hand for Fyenna, and helped her stand. She groaned as she nursed her left arm, then they followed the sergeant out on to the street. The soldiers by the barricade were picking up their weapons and equipment, and a column was already hurrying off in the direction of the walls of the Old City.

'Don't run,' the sergeant called out to those who remained. 'Keep your discipline during the retreat. Head for the gates of the Old City, and stay in formation.'

He gestured to the north-east, and the last of the soldiers by the barricade began to move off, with Fyenna and Denny in their midst. Denny heard the rumble of cannon somewhere to his left, followed by the sound of buildings being hit. The soldiers marched up the middle of the road, their eyes scanning the alleyways on either side. More cannon fire roared from somewhere to their right, and a few of the soldiers almost broke and ran.

'Stay together!' the sergeant shouted.

'Movement,' cried another soldier. 'The windows on our left!'

A hail of crossbow bolts spat out from a building on the northern flank of the road, and three soldiers fell, their bodies pierced. A few of the others panicked and fled, sprinting along the road.

'Run,' Denny said, 'before they have a chance to reload.'

A column of Sanctians burst out from an alleyway on their right, and the flurry of crossbow bolts ceased. Denny drew his sword as the Sanctians lowered their pikes and charged at the formation of defenders. Denny deflected a pike that was aimed at him, but he couldn't get close enough to the Sanctians to inflict any damage of his own. Another soldier of Klef Mordain fell, the pike passing through his chest, then the formation disintegrated as every defender fled towards the Old City. Denny shoved Fyenna along after them as the pikes jabbed out. One pike went for Fyenna's head, and Denny parried it with his sword, his arm aching from the juddering impact.

They sprinted along the street, but the Sanctians made no attempt to chase them, choosing instead to regroup their ranks, ready for the next measured advance. When Denny and Fyenna came into sight of the ancient walls protecting the Old City, hundreds of fleeing defenders were already there, crowding round the gates to get through. Cannon fire rumbled, and the area around one of the gates was pounded by iron balls. Chunks of masonry were ripped from the walls, and the soldiers below were showered with the splintered fragments. One iron ball hit a tightly-pressed group of fleeing defenders, and several were dismembered, their bodies torn apart. Another struck the arch directly above the gate, and the keystone fell, along with tons of rubble. Screams of pain and despair echoed off the ancient stonework as the barrage intensified.

Fyenna halted by the side of a building as the carnage went on by the gates.

'We can't get back into the Old City, ma'am,' said Denny.

Fyenna stared at the wall and the damaged gate. Dozens of bodies were littering the ground, along with rubble and ripped up cobbles.

'Can you still run?' she said.

'Yes, ma'am.'

'Then I shall try to keep up.' She pointed at a narrow street leading off to the left. 'Take that lane, and don't stop until you reach the waters of the bay. Go.'

They set off, heading away from the devastation by the gate. They entered the narrow lane, and Denny slowed down, keeping by Fyenna's side. They came out onto another main road. The narrow lane continued on the other side of the street, but a detachment of armoured Sanctians were advancing from the left. Denny and Fyenna bolted across the street, in full view of the Sanctians, but the armoured men let them pass.

'They must have thought we were civilians,' Denny gasped, as they ran onwards down the lane.

'We were lucky they weren't archers,' Fyenna said.

They began to slow further as the minutes passed, Fyenna unable to maintain the pace. Denny stayed by her side, his eyes scanning every alleyway and every window, as they made their way to the north. They emerged from the lane onto a long esplanade, with the dark waters of the bay in front of them. A hundred yards to their right, the walls guarding the Old City rose up from the shoreline, while in the distance ahead of them, Denny could see a faint line that marked one of the breakwaters of the commercial harbour.

Fyenna stared at the still waters of the bay. 'It'll be cold,' she said.

'Are we going to swim across to the Old City, ma'am?'

She nodded, as she cradled her left arm. 'Can you swim, Denny?'

'Yes, ma'am. Can you?'

She smiled. 'It's been a while.'

'I mean your arm, ma'am; will you be able to swim?'

She glanced back and they listened to the sounds of the battle behind them.

'We have no choice,' she said. 'It's only a hundred yards or so to the far bank. Do you see those lights by the shore? We shall make for them.'

Denny unlaced his boots, then he tied them over his shoulders. He dumped the sword and its sheath, and removed his outer coat. The sun was setting at that moment, and the western sky was a deep shade of red.

'By the time the sun rises again,' said Fyenna, 'the Old City will be in the hands of the Sanctians.'

'We should make sure we're on a boat by then,' said Denny. 'Are you ready, ma'am?'

She nodded, and they stepped off the road and began to wade out into the bay. The water had lost all of the warmth of summer, and was bitterly cold. When it reached their thighs, they both dived in. Salt-water engulfed Denny for a moment, then he rose to the surface, and started to swim.

CHAPTER 33
OUT OF THE CELLAR

Old City, Klef Mordain – 22nd Day of Lamenta 108

Amery coughed. 'The smoke from the oil lamp is getting into my throat,' he said.

'Would you rather sit in the darkness?' said Lothar. 'I don't mind either way.'

'I prefer there to be some light down here,' said Annalise. 'How long should we stay hidden? Do you think the Sanctians have arrived yet?'

'Who knows?' said Lothar. 'The cellar walls are so thick that I can't hear what's going on up on the street.'

'I think we should give it another day,' said Loryn, her face partly hidden in the shadows. 'We have enough food and water, and there's plenty of oil for the lamp. It's what happens afterwards that worries me. Sanctian soldiers will be occupying the entire city, and they will be hunting for everyone who tried to stop them.'

Lothar eyed Amery. 'He'll be all right; he fucking helped them take over the city.'

'I was doing my job!' Amery cried. 'I did what I would do for any employer – I acted like a professional.'

'Then why do you always pick such bastards to work for?' said Lothar. 'First Duke Hector, and then the Second Empire Association.'

'You worked for Duke Hector, too, or had you forgotten?' said Amery.

'And I learned my lesson,' Lothar said. 'Did you?'

Amery glared at him.

'Please don't argue,' said Annalise. 'It's bad enough being stuck in this cramped cellar without having to hear you shout at each other.'

Amery clenched his fists to stop himself weeping. 'We should have gone to the Celestial Bridge,' he said. 'Why didn't we leave the city when we had the chance? I'm truly fucked. As soon as the Sanctians realise that Lord Tain is dead, and that I had a hand in killing him, I'll be strung up from the nearest lamppost.'

'It was I who killed Lord Tain,' said Loryn. 'If anyone is going to be strung up, it will be me.'

Lothar eyed her. 'Were you really working for Lord Metrius the entire time?'

'Yes,' she said. 'He paid for my education at the Consideral, because my family couldn't afford the expense. I didn't realise at the time that he would use that debt to call upon my services once I had qualified as a notary. He sent me to apply for the vacant position at the association.'

'Your duplicity led to Lady Ursula's death,' said Amery.

'Yes, but it also led to the attack on the school for Masters being foiled,' said Loryn. 'I passed on information to Lord Metrius, but I wasn't responsible for deciding what to do with that information. I didn't know that Lady Ursula was going to be assassinated that day.'

'I trusted you,' said Amery.

Loryn regarded him. 'Have you forgotten that I saved your life? Lord Tain was going to torture and murder you for delivering Abigone to Lord Metrius. I stopped him. I didn't have to. Lord Metrius wanted you dead, do you know that? That's why he sent the message to Lord Tain, so that he wouldn't have to kill you himself. I went against his orders when I saved you.'

'Do you think Metrius has fled over the bridge?' said Annalise.

'No,' said Loryn. 'He was committed to dying for the city. He would never try to run away; he has too much honour. He told me that he would die fighting the Sanctians.'

Amery narrowed his eyes. 'I hope his death is long drawn out, and exceedingly painful.'

'You didn't know him,' said Loryn. 'Lord Metrius is a good man. He has been fighting for this city his entire life. I was proud to serve him.'

'He betrayed me to Lord Tain.'

'You betrayed yourself, Amery, by lying to Tain and Ursula. You were lucky you got away with it for so long.'

'Fine,' muttered Amery; 'then I guess we'll both be swinging from lampposts when the Sanctians arrive.'

'Quiet,' said Lothar. 'Someone's upstairs.'

The cellar fell into silence as all four inside gazed up at the ceiling. Amery heard nothing at first, then the sound of footsteps came to him from the floor above.

'Spirits preserve us,' whispered Annalise.

Lothar crept over to where he had laid a sharpened staff against a wall. He picked it up with both hands, and edged towards the hatch. The footsteps from above fell silent.

'Maybe they've gone,' said Amery.

The hatch buckled as something hit it, then it was ripped upwards. It fell open, and four men pointed crossbows down into the cellar.

'Everyone out!' cried one of the men. 'You, big guy, drop the spear, or I'll loose a bolt into your eye.'

'Do as he says!' hissed Annalise, her hands in the air.

Lothar cursed, then he let go of the staff and raised his palms.

'One at a time,' said the man, 'climb out of the cellar.'

The men edged back a little to make room for them.

'Those aren't Sanctian accents,' Amery whispered, as they moved towards the hatch.

Lothar was the first to climb up, followed by Loryn and Annalise. Amery extinguished the oil lamp, and climbed up after them. He emerged into a back room on the ground floor of the townhouse, and saw the men line up the others by a wall.

'Name?' one of the men said.

'Lothar of Upper Down,' said the former Mountain Ranger.

'Upper Down?' said the man.

'That's right,' said Lothar.

'And you?'

'Annalise of Upper Down. Lothar and I work for...'

'Shut up,' said the man. 'You?'

'Loryn of Cliephus,' she said.

'She's on our list,' said another man. 'We were told she might be here.'

The first man nodded. 'And what about you?'

'Amery of Yearl.'

The men laughed. 'You're also on our list,' said one.

'Not the same list as Loryn, though,' said another. 'Grab him and take him outside.'

Two men took hold of Amery's arms and started to haul him towards the door. Lothar took a step forward, and another man pointed a crossbow at his chest.

'Stay where you are!' the man shouted. 'Mister Amery has an appointment with a lamppost.'

Amery struggled in the grip of the two men, but they were stronger, and he was dragged out of the house and on to the street, where three other armed men were standing in the night air.

'We found him,' said one of the men holding Amery. 'This is the traitor Lord Metrius wants dead.'

'Is that what we write on his placard – traitor?' said another.

'It'll do. Hold him down on the cobbles, and we'll gut him neck to groin.'

Amery screamed in fright as hands forced him to the ground.

'Leave him,' Loryn cried.

'Be quiet, girl,' said a man. 'Don't you know how lucky you are? Lord Metrius has a place for you on board the *Lasting Fealty*. As soon as we've done with Amery, we'll take you to the harbour.'

Loryn stared at them. 'Is Lord Metrius fleeing the city?'

'Indeed, he is, girl.'

Lothar lunged forward. He grabbed one of the men holding Amery down, and threw him to the cobbles. He reached for another, and a man clubbed him on the back of the head with the butt of his crossbow. Lothar sank to his knees and groaned in pain. He put a hand to his head, and it came away red with blood.

'Should we kill him?' said one of the men.

'Leave him and the woman,' said another man. 'We have no quarrel with Upper Down.' He pointed at Amery. 'Let's get this over with so we can get out of here.'

Amery screamed again. 'Help!'

Lothar, Annalise and Loryn were pushed back against the outside wall of the townhouse, as a man drew a knife and approached Amery. He crouched down next to him, as Amery was pinned to the cobbles.

The man with the knife looked into his eyes. 'This is what happens to traitors, you piece of shit.'

The air thrummed with crossbow bolts, and four of the men fell. A second later, a volley of arrows struck the last three men. The man with the knife took an arrow in the side of his head, and his face was torn off by the impact, spattering Amery with blood and gore.

'Nobody move!' cried a voice with a Sanctian accent.

Amery lay on the cobbles, drenched in blood and shaking uncontrollably, as over three dozen Sanctian soldiers advanced along the street. They checked that the seven armed men were dead, then one crouched by Amery.

'We just saved you from a lynching, lad,' said one. 'What did those men want with you?'

'His name is Amery of Yearl,' Loryn cried.

The soldier glanced up at an officer, who withdrew a folded bundle of papers from his uniform.

'Amery of Yearl?' said the Sanctian officer, as he scanned the text written on the document. 'I see his name here. He works as a lawyer for the Second Empire Association. He is a friend.'

The soldiers helped Amery to his feet, and one of them passed him a water skin. Amery splashed some water into his face.

'Thank you,' he gasped.

'No problem, sir,' said the officer. 'Are you hurt? Do you require medical attention?'

Amery shook his head.

'Have the Sanctians occupied all of the Old City, sir?' said Loryn.

'Not yet, miss,' said the officer. 'We only broke through the walls twenty minutes ago, and we're fanning out towards the government district. You civilians should get back indoors, and stay there. There's going to be trouble until we've taken control of the entire city.'

'Yes, sir,' said Loryn.

The officer gestured to his men, and they began to re-form into a wide column across the street. Amery gave the water skin back to the soldier, who nodded.

'Take care, sir,' said the soldier.

They began to move north and, after a few moments, they were gone.

Lothar, Loryn and Annalise joined Amery on the cobbles.

'I can't believe they let us go like that,' said Annalise.

'They can't know that Lord Tain is dead yet,' said Loryn.

'Should we go back indoors?' said Annalise.

'Are you mad?' cried Amery. 'Is that your advice, that we should just wait for the Sanctians to find Lord Tain's body? They would come back for us. We have to run!'

'Where?' said Lothar. 'We'll never make it to the Celestial Bridge, not if the Sanctians have already entered the Old City.'

'The harbour,' said Loryn.

'What about the Sanctian warships anchored in the estuary?' said Lothar.

'You heard what that man said. Lord Metrius is planning to flee the city in the *Lasting Fealty*.'

'Is that the name of a ship?'

'Yes, Lothar,' she said. 'He must have some idea of how to get past the blockade.'

'But Metrius also wants me dead,' said Amery.

'I will plead for your life with him,' said Loryn. 'What choice do we have? The Sanctians will be seeking us when they learn of Lord Tain's death. They will execute us – you know this. Lord Metrius might listen to me.'

Lothar rolled his eyes. 'So, we stay here and definitely get executed, or we go to the harbour, where we'll probably be executed? What about Abigone? If you were working for Metrius, did he ever tell you where the school for Makers was located?'

Loryn shook her head. 'There were a lot of things he kept secret from me. I know it is somewhere in the theatre district, but I can't be any clearer that that. Anyway – how is your head?'

'Sore,' said Lothar. He went to pick up a crossbow lying next to one of the dead men.

'Leave it,' said Loryn. 'The Sanctians must have been ordered to kill every armed man in the Old City. If they see you with that thing...'

Lothar frowned, and straightened his back.

'Amery,' said Loryn. 'We can't stand out here on the street. We need to make a decision.'

Amery stared at the ground for a few moments. 'Both sides want to kill me.'

'I know,' said Loryn. 'Which side offers the best chance of survival?'

'How long will it take to walk to the harbour?' said Annalise.

'It's only ten minutes from here,' said Lothar. 'I know the way well.'

'Fuck it,' said Amery. 'Let's go to the damn harbour. Probably is infinitely better than definitely.'

Loryn smiled. 'Let's go.'

They set off along the dark street. Few lamps had been lit, and the rows of elegant townhouses on either side were silent, their windows shuttered and their doors barred. Lothar led the way, and they took a few short cuts, heading down dark alleyways towards the west. Lothar raised a hand when they reached a main road, and they waited in the shadows as a company of Sanctian soldiers raced north towards the Celestial Bridge.

Amery started to walk across the road, and Lothar raised an arm to stop him.

'There are more Sanctians coming,' Lothar whispered.

'Maybe we should take the tunnels,' said Loryn.

'No,' said Lothar. 'The tunnels will be full of people hiding from the Sanctians.'

They quietened as the soldiers approached from the left, and remained silent as they passed to the north.

'Now,' said Lothar, and they hurried across the street. He led them down another narrow lane between two vast warehouses, and they emerged at the northern end of the commercial harbour. Most of the piers were empty, but there were crowds of people on the main quayside, all trying to board whichever vessels were available. Some of the people had carts loaded with their families and possessions, while others were barefoot and dressed in their nightgowns. Lothar scanned the scene, as the others waited.

'Why are there no Sanctian soldiers here yet?' said Annalise.

'The government and bridge must be their priorities,' said Loryn.

'Either that,' said Lothar, 'or they don't believe anyone would be stupid enough to try to flee by ship. As soon as any vessel tries to sail under the Celestial Bridge, the *Bitter Respite* and the other two warships will open up with their cannon. Shit. Even if Lord Metrius is feeling merciful, this is not looking good.'

'Lord Metrius will know what he's doing,' said Loryn. 'He wouldn't sail if he didn't have a plan.'

'You claimed he wouldn't flee the city,' said Amery.

'I was wrong about that, it seems.'

'Then you could be wrong about this.'

'Yes,' she said. 'I might be wrong. Should we just lie down on the road and wait for the Sanctians to arrest us? Would that be preferable? I am open to suggestions. Does anyone have a better idea of how we're going to get out of Klef Mordain alive?'

The others said nothing.

'The *Lasting Fealty* is berthed by one of the southern piers,' Loryn went on.

'I think I might know the ship you're talking about,' said Lothar. 'Is it a big, three-masted galleon?'

'That's the one.'

Lothar frowned. 'It's not exactly inconspicuous. The Sanctians on the *Bitter Respite* will see it coming from a distance. They will have plenty of time to aim their cannon.'

Loryn shook her head. 'I despair. Amery, we've come this far. Shouldn't we at least try to find the ship?'

'You said you would plead for my life,' he said.

'And I shall,' said Loryn. 'I will get down on my knees and beg Lord Metrius to spare you, if that's what it takes. And you will also have to beg. Can your pride cope with that?'

'I don't know.'

'Then I have nothing more to say. I shall go to the *Lasting Fealty*, on my own if I have to. Are you coming?'

'I think we should do it,' said Lothar. 'What choice do we have?'

'I agree,' said Annalise. 'We cannot hide from the Sanctians forever. Once they realise that Lothar and I accompanied Princess Abigone here, they will arrest us.'

Amery put his head in his hands. 'Curse this city,' he groaned. 'Curse the Corse, curse Lord Metrius, and curse the blasted Sanctians. All right; let's try it.'

They emerged from the shadows onto the wide quayside, and Lothar and Loryn led the way to the southern piers.

'Take heart, Mister Amery,' Annalise said, as they walked behind them. 'We're not dead yet.'

'I wish I'd never come to Klef Mordain.'

'I doubt Miss Loryn would agree with that.'

'Loryn lied to me. She pretended to like me, so that I would give her information to pass on to Lord Metrius. It makes my skin crawl to think that she only shared my bed for that reason.'

'If that were true, then why would she be willing to plead for your life?'

'I don't know. Maybe she feels guilty. I should have guessed it was too good to be true.'

'I think you underestimate her. She could have abandoned us and gone off to the harbour; but she didn't. There is only one reason she is still with us, and that reason is you.'

Amery snorted.

They passed a large group of civilians who were trying to board a large carrick, despite the fact that the deck was already crammed full. Several smaller boats next to it were also over-crowded, yet more people were attempting to get on board. Lothar led the others round the group, and he picked up his pace a little when the southern piers came into view. Two piers were being heavily guarded. The one on the right had two carricks and a small cutter tied up, while the other had a huge galleon and a medium-sized freighter berthed alongside. The men guarding the two piers had set up barricades to stop anyone approaching any of the five ships, and the civilians were staying away from the area. Behind the barricade blocking off the pier on the left, dozens of workers were loading cargo on to the galleon and the freighter.

Loryn halted, then she raised a finger to point at the huge galleon. 'There it is – the *Lasting Fealty*.'

'The ship next to it is also being loaded, but I don't know why,' said Lothar. 'It's the *Good Will*, and it's in no condition to brave the ocean. It's in such bad repair, that it will be lucky to make it as far as the *Bitter Respite*.'

'Maybe Lord Metrius intends to use it as a distraction,' said Loryn. 'Perhaps that's his plan.'

Amery looked over his shoulder to make sure that no Sanctians soldiers were approaching, then they walked towards the two barricaded piers. As soon as they got to within twenty yards of the barricades, several crossbows were aimed at them.

Loryn raised her empty palms in the air. 'My name is Loryn of Cliephus,' she said. 'I was told to come here.'

A man with a crossbow peered over the barricade at them. 'Who are the others?' he shouted.

'Friends,' said Loryn.

'There's no space for them on board,' said the man.

'Is Lord Metrius here?' said Loryn. 'Could I perhaps speak to him for a moment?'

'His lordship is on his way, but he hasn't arrived yet,' said the man. 'As soon as he gets here, we're leaving.'

An older woman approached the barricade. 'What's going on here?' she said to the armed men.

'The young woman is Loryn of Cliephus, ma'am,' said the man with the bow.

'Then let her pass,' said the older woman. 'Lord Metrius has often mentioned her to me. She is a valuable agent.'

'What about the others, ma'am?'

'Search them,' said the woman. 'If they have no weapons, then allow them to come on to the pier. We can question them there without the entire harbour knowing our business.'

The man gestured for Loryn and the others to approach, then three men crossed over to the other side of the barricade.

'Hands in the air,' said one.

Amery, Lothar and Annalise raised their arms, and the men patted them down for weapons.

'They're not armed, ma'am,' said one.

'Bring them here,' the woman said.

Loryn led the others past the barricade, and the armed men followed them on to the boards of the wooden pier.

The older woman walked up to Loryn. 'Welcome,' she said. 'My name is Lady Niscoll. I am a close friend of Lord Metrius.'

Loryn bowed her head. 'I have often heard your name, my lady. It is an honour to meet you.'

Niscoll smiled. 'We shall make our proper introductions if we manage to sail past the blockade,' she said. 'Tell me – who are your companions? Did I hear you say that they were friends?'

Loryn gestured to the others. 'This is Lothar and Annalise of Upper Down. They have been very helpful and kind to me. Both will be arrested by the Sanctians if they remain here.'

'And why would that be?'

'They brought Princess Abigone to the city as a Maker, ma'am,' said Loryn.

Niscoll narrowed her eyes. 'I see. I think I can now guess the identity of the other man, but I would like you to say his name for me, Loryn.'

Loryn exhaled. 'His name is Amery of Yearl, ma'am.'

The armed men on the pier tensed, and several aimed their bows at Amery.

'This man is a traitor to Klef Mordain,' said Niscoll. 'Why have you brought him here, Loryn? Was it to hand him into our custody?'

Loryn got down onto her knees in front of Lady Niscoll, and raised her palms. 'I beg of you, my lady; show mercy upon him. He did not wittingly aid the Sanctians. He is merely a lawyer who was doing his job. He does not deserve to die.'

'You poor naïve fool,' said Niscoll. 'I think I see what has happened. Have you fallen in love with the man you were ordered to spy on?'

Loryn said nothing.

'Mister Amery was instrumental in the electoral success of the pro-Sanctians,' Niscoll went on. 'For that alone, I would not shed a tear to see his gutted corpse hanging from a lamppost.'

Amery got down to his knees on the pier next to Loryn.

'I am sorry,' he cried. 'I was just trying to be a good lawyer, and I didn't know that the association were traitors. Please, my lady, I beg you to spare my life.'

'If it were up to me,' said Niscoll, 'I would have these men rip your heart from your chest. You say you knew nothing about the treachery of the association? Well, I say that you are a liar. You sat with the Sanctian ambassador, and had meetings with Admiral Assanio on board the

Bitter Respite. You worked in the same building where Lord Tain tortured and murdered Master Drummond and his brother. Do not insult my intelligence, Mister Amery – I know exactly what kind of man you are. However, whether you live or die is a decision I will leave up to Lord Metrius. When he gets here, I am sure he will know what to do with you.' She turned to Loryn. 'You disappoint me, girl. I thought you had more sense than this.'

Loryn bowed her head.

Niscoll gestured to the armed men. 'Bind their hands behind their backs and keep watch over them until Lord Metrius arrives.'

'Should we bind Loryn's hands, too, ma'am?' said one.

'Yes. Her judgement has been found lacking. Let none of them stray from your sight.'

Lady Niscoll turned, then she strode along the pier. She stopped at a gangway, and ascended onto the deck of the *Lasting Fealty*. The armed men took cords, and tied the hands of Amery, Loryn, Lothar and Annalise. They were led to the side of the *Lasting Fealty*, and made to sit down on the pier. Two men remained to keep watch on them, while the others returned to guard the barricade.

Lothar shook his head. 'It was worth a try, I guess.'

'I'm sorry I got you all into this mess,' said Amery; 'and I'm sorry that you had to beg, Loryn.'

Loryn shrugged.

'You should have left us, and boarded the ship on your own,' Amery went on.

'I couldn't have done that,' Loryn said.

'Why not?'

'I wouldn't have been able to live with myself; not if I'd betrayed you.'

'Betrayed me?' said Amery. 'I don't understand. You betrayed me when you lied to me; you betrayed me by making me think that you liked me. All those nights we shared, and none of it meant anything to you.'

'That's not true,' she said.

'Which part?'

'It is true that I didn't like you at first, but...'

Amery narrowed his eyes. 'But what?'

'But it took me some time to realise how I felt. Lady Niscoll guessed right. I have failed in my service to Lord Metrius, because I fell in love with the man I was spying on.'

Amery's mouth opened. Too stunned to speak, he stared at her.

Lothar nudged him with an elbow. 'I told you she was too good for you.'

CHAPTER 34
THE DEATH OF HOPE

Old City, Klef Mordain – 22nd Day of Lamenta 108

Abigone stared through the hatch in the floor at the dark cavern beneath the school.

'Are you pondering which route to take, sweet Abigone?' said Mor Galthide. 'Those tunnels will be infested by Sanctian agents and spies – we heard Metrius's messenger say as much.'

'I know,' said Abigone, 'but to travel by the open streets seems foolhardy.'

'All courses open to us are foolhardy,' he said. 'If fight we must, I would prefer to do so out in the open, and not trapped within the confines of a dark tunnel. The children are waiting, and no word from Lady Fyenna has arrived at our door. It is time.'

Abigone closed the hatch and got to her feet. She glanced at the steel armour Mor Galthide was wearing, and the weapons he held in his hands.

She took a breath, and nodded. 'You are right, sir. It is time.'

She walked out into the corridor that lay next to Fyenna's office, and saw Miss Eshia and the two remaining women who had worked in the kitchens. They had organised the students into pairs, and Mor Galthide joined the other adults at the head of the column.

'I have decided,' said Abigone. 'We cannot stay here any longer to wait for a message from Lady Fyenna. The sun set two hours ago, and we need to be in the harbour.'

'I cannot go to the harbour, miss,' said one of the kitchen women. 'I have a husband and three children in Cliephus. I cannot abandon them.'

'And I have two children and four grandchildren,' said the other woman. 'I will not leave Klef Mordain.'

'Be you so faithless?' said Mor Galthide. 'Measly cowards.'

'Let them go,' said Abigone. 'Let them return to their families.'

One woman lowered her gaze, while the other performed a quick curtsey, then they hurried off to the back door of the school.

'Mor Galthide,' said Abigone, 'you and I shall lead the students through the Old City. Miss Eshia, please remain at the rear of the column.' She turned to the students. Constans and Raewyn were the first pair in the line. They were holding hands, but Abigone could see the fear in their eyes. Behind them were Reath and Marlow; then Ignatius and Nyli, followed by Aplin and Stanza; then Salus, who was the only child without a pair. 'Miss Eshia,' Abigone went on, 'please pair with Salus. That way each one of us will have someone to look after.'

The students quietened, and Abigone became aware that everyone was staring at her.

'I shall lead us all to the commercial harbour,' she said. 'A ship is waiting there to take us from Klef Mordain. We will meet Lady Fyenna and Denny on the quayside, and then we shall sail away.'

Several of the students cried out in anger or surprise.

'What about our parents?' said Constans. 'Raewyn, Salus and I have mothers and fathers living in Klef Mordain.'

'I do, too,' said Ignatius.

'How will we get past the warships in the estuary?' cried Stanza. 'I'm not leaving until Lady Fyenna and Miss Vesta get back.'

Reath chuckled. 'It looks like you have a rebellion on your hands, Abigone.'

Mor Galthide's eyes darkened with anger, but Abigone raised a hand before he could berate the students for their insubordination.

'Let me make something clear to all of you,' Abigone said. 'If the Sanctians catch you, they will kill you. They will cut your throats and hang you from a lamppost. This is not a game. If we do not run, we shall die. You have been protected by this school a little too well, perhaps, and you have lost sight of a few truths. The Sanctians hate you more than they hate anyone else upon this world. To them, Masters and Makers are nothing but vermin. From this moment forth, you will do exactly as I say, if you wish to live through this night. There is no time to say our farewells to any loved ones within the city; there is barely any time to flee to the harbour. One mistake, and we are all dead. Miss Eshia, Mor Galthide and I will do our best to protect you. We shall die for you if it comes to that, but you must obey my orders, and obey them without question.'

'Or what?' said Reath.

Abigone smiled at Reath, then she slapped her across the face with the back of her hand. The other students stared at her in silence, as Reath sobbed.

'Are there any more questions?' said Abigone. 'No? Then we shall leave. Mor Galthide, please open the front door of the school.'

'As you will, my lady,' said the huge man in armour. He walked up to the door, and loosened the many bolts that kept it locked; then he swung it open. The street outside was quiet and empty, and Abigone gazed in both directions. She gestured to the others, then she led them out into the still night air. Muffled sounds of fighting could be heard far off in the distance, but the area around the school was wreathed in silence. Abigone looked up, but every window above them was shuttered. She nodded to Mor Galthide, and they set off along the street towards the west. Behind them, the students marched in their pairs, with Eshia and Salus at the rear.

'That Reath child will never glance at you in the same way again, fair Abigone,' said Mor Galthide, as they walked.

'Did I go too far?' Abigone said. 'My words clearly had little effect on her.'

'She meant to test your boundaries, and she found her answer.'

'Maybe she will be able to forgive me if I get them out of this alive.'

They turned a corner, and ran straight into a Sanctian patrol of six soldiers. The armed men took one look at Mor Galthide's armour and weapons, and reached for their crossbows. Before any of them could loose, Mor Galthide charged into their midst, his long halberd held out on front of him. He skewered one soldier through the stomach, then punched another with a gauntlet-clad fist, breaking his jaw. He pulled the halberd from the first man's body, and swung it over his head, causing Abigone to have to duck. Mor Galthide's backswing scalped another soldier, the blade of the halberd slicing through the top of his skull. At that, the other three soldiers bolted down the street, fleeing the armoured warrior. Mor Galthide raised a boot, and crushed the head of the man he had punched, then he turned back to look at Abigone and the students.

'Gaze not upon me with such amazement, children,' he said; 'I fight, and I sail; there is naught else you need know about me.'

'Keep moving,' said Abigone. 'Step around the bodies.'

A few students glanced anxiously at Mor Galthide as he wiped the blood from the halberd's blade. Abigone gestured to Raewyn and Constans.

'You know these streets better than I,' she said. 'What is the quickest route to the harbour?'

'We shouldn't be going to the harbour,' said Raewyn. 'My parents live a few minutes from here. I want to see them.'

'Our parents allowed authority over us to pass temporarily to Lady Fyenna,' said Constans, 'not to you, Abigone.'

'Lady Fyenna passed that authority on to me,' she said.

'We have only your word for that,' said Constans. 'You are trying to scare the younger ones with dire tales of execution and exaggerated threats of violence.'

Abigone narrowed her eyes. 'What was exaggerated about Master Tobold's death? Did you not see him die at the hands of pro-Sanctians?'

'No,' said Constans. 'Denny told us that he had died, but we didn't see it. Besides, the pro-Sanctians are a thuggish and undisciplined mob. I say we turn north for my father's home. He will know what to do.'

'Your father will not be able to protect you,' Abigone said, as the other students watched them argue. 'If you stay in this city, the Sanctians will come for all of you.'

'I'd rather take my chances with my parents,' said Constans.

'I, too,' said Salus. 'Please take me home.'

Mor Galthide glared at them. 'This is worse than goat-herding. You children have but one task – to obey the orders of Mistress Abigone, yet I hear nothing come from your lips but recalcitrant disrespect. You will cross this road now, else you will feel a taste of my wrath.'

Constans glanced at the huge man in armour. 'My home is that way, anyway,' he said. 'We shall cross the road.'

Abigone led them to another alleyway that snaked off to the west, while Eshia cajoled the students forward from the rear. Abigone could hear the muttered complaints coming from the students as they hurried along the narrow lane. Reath was looking at her with venom in her eyes, and she was whispering to her sister Nyli.

They came to a small square with a crossroads set amid rows of terraced housing, where only one street lamp had been lit. Abigone glanced up, and saw the reason why. Hanging from the other five lampposts were bodies, each one of which had been gutted from chin to waist. Blood and gore had settled in pools beneath each corpse, and the students flinched at the sight.

'Don't look at them,' said Abigone.

'Miss,' said Marlow.

Abigone turned. 'Yes, Marlow?'

He pointed up at one of the bodies. Abigone's gaze rose to take in the sight of a young woman strung up from the central lamppost. Around her neck hung a placard with one word written on it in clear, bold letters – *Maker*.

'It's Miss Vesta!' Stanza cried, as Eshia and the students gathered round the base of the lamppost.

Nyli and Ignatius burst into tears.

'A sight to break the heart,' said Mor Galthide, as the students gazed up in horror.

Marlow's eyes narrowed with fury. 'Do you see?' he said to the other students. 'Do you see what Abigone has been talking about? None of you know anything about the Sanctians, but I do. I had to hide from their soldiers a dozen times on my way to Klef Mordain.' He pointed at the body. 'If they had caught me, they would have done to me what they have done to Miss Vesta. Do you think that being children will save you?'

Constans and the others lowered their gazes, and none replied to Marlow's words.

'I am sorry,' said Abigone; 'sorry I have been so strict with you, and sorry that I struck Reath. I am trying to prevent the Sanctians from stringing you up like slaughtered animals. If you want to survive, then you must listen to what I say.'

No one responded.

'I hear more boots behind us,' said Eshia.

'Raewyn,' said Abigone. 'Which route will take us to the harbour?'

Raewyn pointed to the lane leading off to their left.

'Thank you,' said Abigone. 'Follow me.'

They set off down the alleyway to their left, and Abigone picked up her pace. They left the housing district, and entered an area filled with warehouses and the offices of shipping companies. Sounds of fighting echoed off to their right, and then voices were heard ahead of them. They emerged on to the wide quayside, and Abigone halted. A crowd of civilians was trying to board a handful of over-crowded vessels by several piers, but there were no Sanctians soldiers in sight.

'The *Little Ghost* is to our left, fair Abigone,' said Mor Galthide. 'See you the barricades by those two piers? The pier on the right berths the three vessels of Lady Fyenna. Metrius's men have them under guard.'

'Is Lady Fyenna here?' said Aplin.

'Let's find out,' said Abigone.

Abigone strode over the paving slabs of the quayside, as the students followed her. They stayed clear of the desperate crowd of civilians by the few remaining boats, and made for the two barricaded piers. Abigone raised a hand for them to halt as they came within fifty yards of the blockades. Armed men on the other side of the barricades were eyeing them, and aiming their crossbows in their direction.

'We had a deal with Lord Metrius,' Abigone said. 'Let us reach our vessel.'

'We were told to allow no one to pass,' cried one of the men.

'On whose authority?'

'Lady Niscoll's,' said the man. 'If you want to get onto this pier, it is her you need to speak to. She is by the *Lasting Fealty*, at the next pier along.'

Abigone inclined her head slightly, then she led the students to the pier on the left, which had its own barricade.

'Is Lady Niscoll here?' she said aloud to the men blocking the pier. 'Please tell her that I wish to talk with her.'

The men glanced at each other, then one of them ran off towards the two large ships that were tied up behind them.

'That's the *Lasting Fealty*,' said Raewyn. 'Lord Metrius's vessel.'

'And the other ship?' said Abigone.

'That other ship will not be sailing far,' said Mor Galthide. 'It looks fit only to sink. And where are its passengers? I see cargo being loaded onto its deck, but no people.'

'What's happening?' said Stanza. 'Why aren't they letting us on to our ship?'

'They are protecting them for us,' said Abigone. 'We just need to talk to the woman in charge.'

There was movement behind the barricade.

'I am Lady Niscoll,' said a voice. 'What is your purpose here?'

'We were sent here by a friend,' said Abigone. 'She had a deal with Lord Metrius.'

'I know of no such deal,' said the voice.

'Is Lord Metrius in the harbour?'

'We await his arrival. If you wish to board a ship, I suggest you join the crowd of civilians by the central piers.'

Abigone cursed under her breath, and decided that the time for secrecy was long past.

'Lady Fyenna sent us,' she said. 'We are the students from her two schools.'

The voice behind the barricade fell into silence, then Abigone saw an older woman climb up onto the blockade to take a look at them.

'Lady Fyenna told you to come here, girl?' she said.

'She did, ma'am,' said Abigone. 'Her three vessels are tied up at the pier to your left, but the men there will not allow us to board them.'

'Where is your crew?' said Niscoll. 'How do you intend to sail without any sailors?'

'We had a crew,' said Mor Galthide. 'Metrius thought it best to incarcerate them.'

'Lord Metrius will be here soon,' said Niscoll. 'It is his decision. If he has indeed made a deal with Lady Fyenna, he will be able to confirm it.'

Marlow tapped Abigone on the shoulder, then he pointed towards the southern corner of the quayside.

'Sanctian scouts, ma'am,' he said. 'They are approaching the harbour.'

Abigone nodded, then she turned back to Niscoll.

'We are running out of time,' she said. 'If the Sanctians come, will you stand and watch as they kill these students? There are no teachers left to protect them. Master Drummond, Master Tobold and Maker Vesta are dead, and Lady Fyenna was summoned by Lord Metrius. Will you abandon these children, Lady Niscoll?'

'I wish you no harm, child,' said Niscoll, 'but I do not have the power to acquiesce to your demands.'

'I can charge the barricade blocking the way to our vessel,' Mor Galthide whispered to Abigone. 'With speed and strength I may overcome those standing against us. Say but the word, my lady, and they will feel the gentle touch of my halberd.'

'Thank you,' she said, 'but you are the only one of us that knows how to sail.'

'Without a crew, we shall not sail far,' he said.

'Abigone!' cried a man's voice from the far side of the barricade. 'Abigone – is that you I can hear?'

Abigone frowned. 'Lothar?' she called out.

'Yes, ma'am,' the voice called back. 'I am here with Annalise, and... our lawyer associate. Our hands have been bound, and we are awaiting Metrius's judgement upon us.'

'Is this true, my lady?' Abigone said to Niscoll. 'Are you holding my friends captive?'

'Mister Amery is a traitor to Klef Mordain,' Niscoll said. 'He and his companions are indeed in my custody. So, you are the fabled princess of Upper Down? At last we meet.'

There was a grinding noise a few yards away, and Abigone turned. To her left, a large paving slab was being lifted and moved, revealing the entrance to a dark tunnel. Two faces appeared, and Abigone recognised Portia, the woman who had sent her to assassinate the Sanctian ambassador. She climbed out of the opening, then she and a man reached down, and pulled Lord Metrius from the tunnel. Metrius's garments were ragged and wet, and they were giving off a reek of raw sewage. He glared around at the harbour, his misery and anger evident upon his features. His gaze took in Abigone and the students, then he caught sight of Lady Niscoll by the barricade.

'Lord Metrius is here,' cried Niscoll. 'Order the captain of the *Lasting Fealty* to prepare to sail.'

One of the men raced off towards the ships.

Metrius staggered up to Abigone, and she recoiled from the smell.

'Did you lead this rabble here, Abigone?' he said.

'I did,' she said.

'Is Fyenna here, girl?' he said. 'Where is she?'

'I don't know,' said Abigone. 'Where did you send her and Denny?'

'They were supposed to keep the Sanctian army out of the Old City until midnight,' Metrius snapped. 'They failed. The damn Sanctians are all over the streets, ransacking the offices of the Corse, and sealing off the Celestial Bridge.'

'Nevertheless,' said Abigone, 'did you or did you not have a deal with her?'

'She reneged upon that deal when she allowed the Sanctians to breach the walls of the Old City. I owe you nothing.'

'You hateful cur!' Mor Galthide cried. 'Faithless and craven dog. I ought to strike your head from your shoulders.'

Metrius hurried away to the barricade, and Portia drew a sword as she retreated away from Mor Galthide. The men behind the barricade shifted a barrel, and Metrius passed through.

'Amery?' he shouted. 'What is this traitor doing here?'

Abigone gazed through the gap in the barricade, and saw four people sitting on the wooden pier. Lothar was there, next to Annalise. By them sat Amery, along with a young woman.

'Execute him,' said Metrius. 'Wait – why are Loryn's hands bound? Who did this?'

'She got onto her knees and begged me to spare the life of Mister Amery, my lord,' said Niscoll.

'What? No,' said Metrius. 'Is this so, Loryn?'

The young woman bowed her head, and went down on to her knees. 'Please, my lord, spare Mister Amery and his friends. For all I have done for you, please do me this one favour.'

'I fear she is in love with him, my lord,' said Niscoll.

'Lord Tain was your enemy, was he not?' Loryn went on. 'Mister Amery slew him, within the offices of the Second Empire Association. Could you not spare him for that act, if you hesitate to spare him for my sake?'

'Tain is dead, is he?' said Metrius.

'He is, my lord.'

Metrius said nothing for a while, then he shook his head. 'What a damnable waste,' he muttered. 'I had high hopes for you, Loryn. Amery deserves nothing but a violent and painful end; nevertheless, you have served me well, and so, for your sake, not his, I shall grant your request.

Amery shall live, but he will not be allowed to board my ship. Neither will you, Loryn. As you have begged for his life, so you shall remain here with him.' He glanced at Niscoll. 'Have the *Good Will* raise anchor and cast off. We shall board the *Lasting Fealty*, and be gone within the next few minutes.'

'Yes, my lord,' said Niscoll, then she hurried off towards the ships.

'Wait,' cried Abigone. 'Will you order your men to allow us to reach our own vessels?'

Metrius turned, then he smiled at Abigone. 'Princess of Upper Down,' he said; 'there is no need for you to die here. I invite you to come aboard the *Lasting Fealty*, where you shall be an honoured passenger. I will return you to your sister in Lesser Down, and from there you may seek shelter in your own realm.'

'Will you allow all of us to board?' said Abigone. 'The students, and my friends?'

'Just you, Abigone. Save yourself. Do not be a cause for mourning to your sister Kilbride.'

'Kilbride would mourn if she learned I had abandoned those dear to me,' she said. 'If the others are not allowed to board, then I will not leave them.'

'This is your last chance, Your Highness,' Metrius said. 'Come with me, and I will deliver you from this catastrophe.'

'You brought this catastrophe down upon us,' Abigone said. 'I refuse your offer.'

Anger swept across the face of Metrius. 'So be it, you fool,' he cried. He turned to his men by the other pier. 'You there! Despoil the *Little Ghost*. Rip its sails, break its wheel, and toss the compass into the dark waters of the bay. Tear up the charts and cut the ropes.'

The men by the pier raced towards the small cutter. They leapt down onto its deck, and began destroying whatever was in sight. One went into the ship's only cabin, then he emerged with armfuls of maps. He dumped them into the bay, as two other men sliced through the sails and rigging with knives and swords. Another man hacked at the ships' wheel, cleaving it into pieces. Mor Galthide started to run towards the pier, and the men behind the other barricade raised their crossbows.

'Mor Galthide, no,' said Abigone. 'Stay where you are. Do not give them cause to kill you.'

Metrius laughed. 'Farewell, Princess Abigone, and farewell, my young Loryn. If you see Lady Fyenna, pass on my fondest regards.'

He turned and strode along the pier towards the gangway leading to the *Lasting Fealty*. At a signal from the ship's whistle, his men raced after him, abandoning the barricade. The ones on the *Little Ghost* withdrew from the cutter and ran up the other pier, and they boarded the large galleon. The gangway was pulled up, and the ropes securing the vessel to the pier were loosened. Ahead of the galleon, the *Good Will* was already moving off into the waters of the bay.

The pier fell into silence as the students watched the *Lasting Fealty* follow the *Good Will* away from the quayside. Abigone strode up to where Lothar was sitting, and Mor Galthide cut the bonds of the four prisoners.

Lothar got to his feet, and Abigone embraced him.

'I missed you, Lothar,' she said.

'It is good to see you alive and well, Your Highness,' said Annalise.

'And you,' said Abigone, as she embraced the woman.

'This is Loryn, ma'am,' said Lothar.

'We're doomed!' Amery cried, his eyes red with tears.

'We are not, Mister Amery,' said Abigone. 'Mor Galthide, take the students on board the *Little Ghost*, and see what can be done to repair the vessel.'

'I shall require some spare hands to help me scour the two carricks for parts, fair Abigone,' he said.

'I'd like to help,' said Lothar. 'Who are you?'

'This is Mor Galthide,' said Abigone. 'Mor Galthide, this is Commander Lothar of the Mountain Rangers, a trusted friend.'

'Alas; there are few ships in the mountains, my lady,' said Mor Galthide. 'Are there no sailors among us?'

'I can sail,' said Loryn.

'I thank you,' said Mor Galthide

'We must do what we can,' said Abigone. 'Take what you need from the carricks. If you cannot find what you need, Miss Eshia and some of the older Makers may be able use their abilities to summon the parts you require.' She turned to the students. 'Run to the *Little Ghost*, and do whatever Mor Galthide tells you. We have but minutes to repair our ship before the Sanctians get here.'

The children hurried away, then Mor Galthide leaned close to Abigone.

'I will render the cutter able to sail, but who will crew it, sweet Abigone? I cannot do so alone.'

'Let me worry about that,' she said.

'As you will, my lady,' he said. 'Commander Lothar and Miss Loryn, will you accompany me?'

He led them off towards the *Little Ghost*, where they joined the students. Mor Galthide shouted out a few orders, and they got to work. Abigone glanced at Amery.

'I see you have also earned the disfavour of Lord Metrius,' she said.

Amery wiped his face. 'It seems lawyering can be a dangerous occupation,' he said. He glanced around at the quayside. 'Are you in charge?'

'For the moment,' she said. 'Walk with me to our ship.'

Amery and Annalise accompanied Abigone as she went to the other pier. Mor Galthide and several of the students had boarded one of the large carricks, while Loryn was talking to Constans and Raewyn by the broken wheel.

'This is the *Little Ghost*,' Abigone said.

'This tiny boat?' said Amery. 'That can't be right. One cannon ball, and we will go straight to the bottom.'

'I am offering you a place on board,' Abigone said. 'You are free to decline, if you have something better to do.'

They watched as Mor Galthide, Lothar and Marlow carried a new sail down from one of the carricks. On the cutter, Eshia was directing some of the younger students to remove the ripped sail, while Constans and Raewyn were crouching by the wheel. Abigone silently urged them to hasten their efforts, despite knowing that they had no one but Mor Galthide and Loryn who knew the first thing about sailing. One step at a time, she told herself. When Denny arrived, they would have three able to sail, and that might be enough. She glanced over to her left. The *Good Will* and *Lasting Fealty* were inching their way north towards the high arches that passed under the Celestial Bridge, and several smaller vessels crammed with civilians had cast off from the central piers to join them.

Amery stifled a gasp. 'Abigone,' he whispered. 'They're coming.'

Abigone turned, and her hopes seemed to slip away. Two contingents of Sanctians soldiers were starting to flood into the harbour, one from the east, the other from the south. The crowd of civilians by the central piers screamed as the easterly contingent loosed a hail of arrows at them, then the men-at-arms charged, their pikes extended. They rammed into the civilians, cutting them down, and pushing them into the waters of the bay.

Mor Galthide dropped the sail onto the deck of the *Little Ghost*, then he and Lothar ran over to where Abigone was standing. Mor Galthide passed Lothar a sword, and they took up position by either side of Abigone, as the contingent coming from the south raced towards the pier where the *Little Ghost* was berthed.

'Stand fast!' cried Mor Galthide. 'Sing forth our blades, and let our end be glorious!'

Amery fled to the cutter, and Abigone readied herself.

She had tried her best. She had done all she could. She gazed at the approaching mass of Sanctians, and steeled her heart.

CHAPTER 35
INTO THE NIGHT

Old City, Klef Mordain – 22nd Day of Lamenta 108

Abigone raised her hand. The Sanctians charging across the harbour were organising themselves into detachments, with archers to their left and right, and armoured men-at-arms with shields and pikes in the centre. The students on the cutter had seen them, and several were crying out in alarm.

'Their archers will get us long before their men-at-arms are close enough to fight,' Lothar said.

'We shall shelter behind the barricade made by Metrius's men,' said Mor Galthide.

Eshia joined Abigone, Lothar and Mor Galthide by the end of the pier.

Abigone glanced at the daughter of Drummond. 'Can you summon stone?' she said.

'I will try,' said Eshia.

'Aim for the archers,' Abigone said. 'Blessed spirits,' she went on, 'with your permission, summon for me a dozen stone dragons.'

There was a cracking noise as tons of paving slabs were ripped into the air, then a dozen monstrous stone shapes appeared in the night sky above the Sanctians. They fell indiscriminately onto the advancing soldiers, crushing many, and gouging great holes in the quayside.

'Blessed spirits,' said Eshia, 'with your permission, summon for me a stone wall.'

More slabs were pulled up, and a low wall formed across the quayside in front of the Sanctian's left wing, blocking the progress of a company of archers.

'Build it higher!' cried Mor Galthide. 'They will loose at us from behind that wall at their leisure.'

'I am trying!' said Eshia.

The Sanctian men-at-arms regrouped, then continued their advance. As Mor Galthide had predicted, the left-hand company of archers took cover behind Eshia's wall, and began to loose arrows at the barricade blocking the entrance of the pier. Abigone and the others ducked behind the heaped rows of empty barrels as arrows fell around them. Eshia cried out as an arrow struck her right leg. She fell to the wooden beams of the pier, and Mor Galthide leaned over her, his armour protecting them both. He reached for the arrow and began to pull.

'What are you doing?' cried Lothar. 'Push the fucking thing through; don't try to pull it out!'

Mor Galthide caught his glance.

'Let me do it,' said Lothar. He grabbed the arrow in both hands, and drove it through Eshia's leg. The Maker screamed, then passed out. Lothar snapped the arrow in two, then pulled both ends away. He ripped off the hem of Eshia's skirt, and wrapped it round the wound, tightening the knot. He picked her up, and ran onto the deck of the cutter.

Abigone turned back to the Sanctians as soon as she realised that the hail of arrows had stopped. The men-at-arms were advancing towards the barricade at the end of the pier, their pikes extended. They charged, and thrust their pikes through the gaps between the barrels. Mor Galthide jabbed out with his halberd, and the blade swept across the torso of one of the soldiers, ripping his stomach open. The steel tip of a pike glanced off Mor Galthide's armour, then another found its way into a gap under his breastplate. He let out a grunt as the pike stabbed his waist.

'Blessed spirits,' Abigone cried, 'with your permission, summon for me a stone dragon.'

Stone from the quayside buckled under the boots of the soldiers, and several fell into the cold, dark waters of the bay. A misshapen lump of stone fell. It hit two soldiers, killing them, then it crashed into and through the wooden beams at the end of the pier, creating a hole in its centre. Sanctian soldiers raced round either side of the hole and clambered up onto the barricade. Mor Galthide thrust upwards with one of his spears, and its tip passed through the throat of a soldier. The Sanctians aimed down with their pikes, and Mor Galthide was impaled again, once through the thigh, and once through his left shoulder. A soldier drove his pike towards Abigone, and Lothar parried it with his sword. He dragged Abigone back and leapt in front of her, as more pikes came lunging at him. Two soldiers fell, their eyes crusting over with salt, as Constans stepped up onto the pier, then an arrow struck the young Master in the shoulder, and he collapsed back onto the deck. Lothar fended off three pikes, then four, until one got through his guard and struck him in the neck, slicing off an inch of flesh.

A Sanctian atop the barricade crowed down at Abigone. 'The spirits will laugh when they see you die, Maker!' he cried.

A rumble like thunder sounded in the distance, then the entire southern section of the quayside rippled as thousands of tons of stone were ripped upwards. Dozens of hideous, grey gargoyles appeared in the air, then they rained down upon the Sanctian soldiers, crushing them where they stood. Eshia's low wall folded up onto itself, then it burst into fragments that fell upon the archers who had taken shelter behind it. The Sanctians on the barricade gazed back at the destruction and slaughter on the quayside, then their metal weapons and armour were ripped from them. Jagged spears of iron appeared in the air, then they sliced down through the soldiers on the pier. One soldier jumped down from the barricade, and landed on his knees next to Abigone.

'Blessed spirits,' she whispered, 'with your permission, summon for me a knife.'

Wood and metal formed in the air next to her. She caught the blade by the hilt, and rammed it into the neck of the Sanctian soldier by her side. At once, the fighting ceased. The surviving Sanctians on the quayside were fleeing in panic, and only the groans of the wounded were left to fill the air. Abigone pushed herself up to her knees. Mor Galthide was groaning in pain on the beams of the pier, blood seeping from three separate wounds. Lothar was sitting next to him, holding a piece of cloth to his neck.

'Is it over, fair Abigone?' gasped Mor Galthide.

'I think we won,' said Lothar.

Abigone got to her feet and and gazed over the devastation. Two figures were approaching across the pock-marked and bloody quayside. One had a sword, and he was finishing off any of the wounded Sanctians who offered any resistance; while the other was clutching her left arm as though it was giving her great pain.

'Who came to our aid?' said Mor Galthide.

'Your son and Lady Fyenna,' said Abigone.

Mor Galthide unstrapped several pieces of his bloodstained armour, and pulled himself to his feet.

'My boy,' he said. 'Mor Dennahelm! Son of Geathan! To us!'

Abigone clambered up onto a barrel, then she eased herself to the far side of the barricade. She edged round the hole in the pier that her dragon had made, and strode to the quayside, as Denny and Fyenna approached. A Sanctian soldier gasped and reached for Abigone's ankle, and Denny drove the point of his sword into the back of the man's neck.

'Denny,' said Abigone.

He inclined his head a little. 'Sorry we're late.'

She glanced at his clothes. 'Did you swim here?'

'The walls of the Old City had fallen,' said Fyenna. 'We had no choice but to come by water.'

'Are you hurt, ma'am?'

'My elbow sustained some damage. Like you, Abigone, I fall badly.'

'Then how did you swim?'

'Denny assisted me. He has been protecting me since we set off to fight the Sanctians. Were it not for him, I would not be here.'

Abigone gazed at Denny, and their eyes met. 'He is a brave fighter.'

'He is,' said Fyenna.

Denny looked away.

'We have wounded,' said Abigone. 'Mor Galthide, Miss Eshia, Constans, and Lothar.'

'Who is Lothar?' said Fyenna. 'Is the cutter ready to leave?'

'No, ma'am. In his spite, Metrius had his men damage the *Little Ghost*. We were in the midst of repairing it when the Sanctians attacked. Lothar is an old friend from Upper Down. He was here with a few others, including Mister Amery of Yearl. Do you know him?'

'I know of him,' said Fyenna.

Denny helped Fyenna climb over the barricade. Lothar and Mor Galthide managed to stagger down to the deck of the *Little Ghost*, where the students were waiting. Several were in tears at the sight of Lady Fyenna, while Eshia and Constans were unconscious, and each was having their wounds bandaged.

Stanza ran up to Fyenna and hugged her, weeping.

'Please be careful, my child,' said Fyenna. 'My elbow is a little sore.' She gazed around at the others. 'Was there no sign of Miss Vesta? Did she not return to the school?'

'Miss Vesta is dead,' sobbed Stanza, still clinging on to Fyenna. 'We saw her body hanging from a lamppost.'

'Abigone led us here, ma'am,' said Marlow.

Fyenna said nothing for a moment, then she turned to Abigone. 'I owe you my gratitude,' she said. 'I asked you to lead the children here, and you did. Thank you. We are now on board, but we have no crew.'

'I shall pilot the craft,' said Mor Galthide. 'Strap me to the wheel, and prop me up with a chair.'

'But the wheel was broken,' said Abigone.

'Raewyn and Constans fashioned one anew,' said Mor Galthide.

'Mor Dennahelm, I am appointing you as my lieutenant – you shall skipper the vessel, and Miss Loryn shall be your midshipman.' He looked around at the others. 'Marlow, you shall assist Miss Loryn; you, too, young Reath. Do as she says.' Mor Galthide staggered over to the wheel. He collided with the side of the cabin, and nearly fell.

'Are you able to take the wheel in your condition?' said Fyenna.

'Fear not, my lady,' he said. 'My wounds have been bound by the hands of Stanza. Find me a chair, and I will steer us to freedom.'

Fyenna and Abigone crouched by Eshia and Constans, as Marlow hurried off to fetch a chair for Mor Galthide. Constans had regained consciousness, and his face mirrored the pain he was feeling.

'Constans killed two Sanctians, ma'am,' said Abigone. 'He took an arrow in the shoulder.'

'Brave lad,' said Fyenna. 'And Miss Eshia?'

'An arrow struck her leg,' said Abigone, 'but the bleeding has stopped.'

'What about your friend Lothar?'

'I would feel a lot better if there was any whisky to be had,' said Lothar, from where he was sitting on the deck, a hand clutching a bloody rag by his neck.

'I concur,' said Mor Galthide, as he sat on the chair Marlow had brought for him. 'A drop of brandy would do me well.'

'The cutter's new sail is ready,' Loryn shouted from the mast.

Mor Galthide gazed at his son. 'Mor Dennahelm, skipper of this vessel, we await your instructions.'

Denny stepped onto the low platform where his injured father sat by the wheel. He glanced up at the wind pennant, then gazed out over the harbour. Metrius's two vessels had reached the end of the bay, and were slowly turning east towards the Celestial Bridge, the half dozen civilian ships following them like baby ducks.

'Marlow,' Denny said, 'cast off the ropes. Reath, get the younger students down into the hold, then get back up here. We have a north-westerly, Miss Loryn, so raise the sail and get ready to tack into the breeze; and Father, take us out of the harbour.'

'Aye, Skipper,' said Mor Galthide.

Abigone remained by Fyenna as the small cutter began to edge away from the pier. The ropes were secured, and the sail raised. The wind caught the fabric, and their speed picked up. Denny bounded back and forth along the deck, helping out wherever necessary. He assisted Loryn with the sail, then he spent a moment showing Marlow and Reath how to adjust the ropes.

'What did I tell you?' Mor Galthide cried, as the cutter picked up speed. 'The *Little Ghost* might not be elegant, but she is fast.'

'Do we have a plan to get past the Sanctian warships, ma'am?' said Abigone to Fyenna.

'No, not yet.'

'We should wait to see what Lord Metrius does with the *Good Will*,' said Denny, as he joined them. 'Reath – tie those loose ropes down.'

He hurried off to help Marlow with something, and Fyenna watched him.

'You should speak to Denny when he has a spare moment, Abigone,' she said.

'About what, ma'am? He told me that he had nothing left to say to me.'

'Perhaps he required a day longer than you to work through his feelings. I was by his side all afternoon, and all evening. Not once did he flinch from doing what needed to be done. Without both of you, we wouldn't have got this far.'

Abigone said nothing as the *Little Ghost* raced past the northern breakwater.

'Due north, Father,' Denny cried, and Mor Galthide turned the wheel.

The cutter began to approach the slower-moving vessels as they clustered by the tall arches on the western side of the Celestial Bridge. The *Lasting Fealty* had come to a halt, and men could be seen racing over the deck of the *Good Will*. A whistle sounded, and the *Good Will* began to sail under the bridge's central arch. It disappeared from Abigone's sight for a moment, then the *Little Ghost* began to turn to the east, and she caught her first glimpse of the three Sanctian warships through the arches of the bridge. The *Bitter Respite* was anchored a hundred and fifty yards off the northern shore of the Old City, and two smaller frigates were positioned a little to the east of the flag ship.

As soon as the *Good Will* passed through the arch, flames started to rise from its decks. A few sailors dived overboard, and the burning ship began to drift towards the Sanctian vessels, its sails and deck ablaze. Smoke billowed up into the night sky, and the wind carried it over to the Sanctian flag ship. The *Lasting Fealty* got underway. It began to move through a narrower northern arch of the bridge, and the civilian vessels followed it.

Denny beckoned Abigone and Fyenna over to where Mor Galthide was holding the wheel.

'I think I know what Lord Metrius is doing,' Denny said. 'He plans to use the *Good Will* as a buffer, to shield his escape. If he sails to the north, and stays parallel to the *Good Will* as it drifts past the Sanctians, then he could raise every sail and speed out of the estuary.'

'Should we follow his lead?' said Fyenna.

'No, ma'am. The slower vessels behind the *Lasting Fealty* will be easy targets for the Sanctians' cannon as soon as the *Good Will* passes them. We should take the southernmost arch, and hug the coastline. The cutter's shallow hull will allow us to slip along by the esplanade. If the Sanctians have their eyes on the *Good Will*, then they might not see us.'

'But if they do,' said Mor Galthide, 'we are finished.'

'Yes,' said Denny. 'It's a risk. Can you see a better way, Father?'

Mor Galthide gazed at the approaching arches of the bridge as the *Little Ghost* raced over the dark waters.

'No,' he said. 'You are the skipper, my son. I accept your orders.'

'Do it,' said Fyenna.

Denny nodded. 'Make for the southern arch, Father, then stay close to the coast.'

'Aye, Skipper,' said Mor Galthide.

The craft began to turn, and Denny raced away to help Loryn and

Marlow adjust the sail. They approached the southern arch as the last of the civilian ships sailed through the northern arch in the wake of the *Lasting Fealty*. Through the arch, Abigone watched the flaming *Good Will* drift close to one of the Sanctian frigates. The two ships collided, and the fire spread to the frigate. Sailors dived overboard to escape the flames, but the collision had given the *Bitter Respite* a clear view of the *Lasting Fealty* and the small ships following it, and the sixteen cannon on its starboard flank opened up with a roar of smoke and noise. The *Little Ghost* raced under the bridge and entered the waters of the eastern estuary. Mor Galthide steered the cutter as close as possible to the coastline, as the *Bitter Respite* fired again. Several of the ships following Metrius's vessel were hit, and three sank within minutes. The *Lasting Fealty* was struck, and it began to slow.

'They haven't seen us,' said Fyenna.

'There remains plenty of time for that, my lady,' said Mor Galthide.

Another barrage from the *Bitter Respite* echoed across the estuary. Another two civilian ships were struck, then the main mast of the *Lasting Fealty* took a direct hit. The mast split in two, then the top half toppled over, taking the sails and rigging with it.

'Are you laughing now, Metrius, you cur?' cried Mor Galthide.

A further barrage was fired, and the last of the civilian ships was struck, while the *Lasting Fealty* was slowly sinking into the depths of the cold water. The cannon of the *Bitter Respite* fell silent, then the loudest explosion Abigone had ever heard sent her falling to the deck, as the black powder on board the burning frigate ignited. A great burst of flames erupted, and fragments of the frigate were flung out in all directions by the force of the explosion. Flaming beams of wood rained down onto the second frigate, then a great wave rippled over the estuary. The cutter bucked up and down, and Marlow fell overboard. Reath screamed, and Denny ordered his father to turn the cutter round.

'Throw him a rope,' Denny cried, as the vessel slowed and turned.

Loryn raced along the deck, and threw out a rope towards Marlow, who was floundering in the water. He reached for the rope, and wrapped it round his wrist. As Denny was trying to pull him in, the second frigate started to burn, its sails set alight by the fragments of the exploding ship. Its front anchor had been dislodged by the earlier explosion, and the frigate's bow drifted south, blocking the escape route of the *Little Ghost*.

Denny and Loryn pulled Marlow out of the water and dropped him onto the deck, and Reath crouched beside him. Denny glanced up, and saw the second frigate barring their way. Despair rippled over his features for a moment.

'What now, Skipper?' cried his father.

'Take us closer to the *Bitter Respite*,' said Fyenna.

'But if they see us, my lady, their cannon will obliterate this vessel.'

'There is no longer any way past without them seeing us, Father,' said Denny.

'Look,' cried Loryn. 'The *Lasting Fealty* is going down.'

Abigone glanced over, and watched as the huge galleon went down by the stern. A moment later, it had disappeared beneath the waves.

'Take us closer to the Sanctian flag ship,' said Fyenna. 'Trust me.' She glanced at Reath. 'Fetch Raewyn.'

Reath ran off to the lower deck, then Denny put a hand to his face. 'Take us alongside the *Bitter Respite*, Father,' he said. 'Quickly and silently.'

'Aye, Skipper,' said Mor Galthide, as he turned the wheel. 'We almost made it, didn't we, my boy?'

Fyenna gestured to Abigone. 'Stand by me at the bow.'

'What are we going to do, ma'am?'

'You will see.'

They walked towards the front of the cutter, and Raewyn joined them. The three Makers stood side by side as the *Little Ghost* approached the Sanctian flag ship.

'This might be your last lesson, girls,' Fyenna said; 'I will need your full attention.'

'What shall we summon, ma'am?' said Raewyn.

A whistle sounded on board the *Bitter Respite*, and sailors up on its high deck began pointing down at the *Little Ghost*.

'We have been seen,' cried Mor Galthide.

Fyenna turned her head. 'Keep on our present course.'

The hatches on the port side of the flag ship swung open – sixteen holes, for sixteen cannon.

'Raise your hands, girls,' said Fyenna, 'and make damn sure you hold them out in front of your body. Do not move your arms from side to side; is that understood?'

Abigone and Raewyn glanced at each other, then they lifted their right arms.

'Tell us what to summon,' cried Raewyn.

'Steady, girl,' said Fyenna.

Abigone gazed through one of the hatches in the side of the *Bitter Respite*. In the thick shadows beyond, men were busy preparing a cannon, loading an iron ball into its muzzle.

'Have you ever ridden a horse, Abigone?' said Fyenna.

'Yes, ma'am.'

'Picture them in your mind. Summon as many of them as the spirits will allow. A hundred. You, too, Raewyn. A hundred each should suffice.'

Raewyn stared at her. 'But, ma'am...'

'Do as I say, Raewyn. Summon a hundred horses. Do it now.'

'Blessed spirits,' the three Makers cried, 'with your permission, summon for me a hundred horses.'

The screams from the *Bitter Respite* were short-lived. Dozens of sailors had their bodies torn to pieces by the power of the summoning, as their flesh and bone was ripped from them to create a vast swirling mass of gore, which hovered above the waters of the bay between the *Bitter Respite* and the shore. No living horses were formed from the maelstrom of flesh, and it collapsed into the estuary, raining blood down upon Abigone and the others on the *Little Ghost*.

'Once again,' said Fyenna, 'but wooden beams.'

'Blessed spirits,' said Abigone, Raewyn and Fyenna, 'with your permission, summon for me a hundred wooden beams.'

A fierce noise of splintering wood came from the *Bitter Respite*. It began to list to port, then holes opened up along its flanks, as hundreds of wooden beams crashed down upon its deck. Its bow went down first, then the vessel disappeared into the dark waters of the estuary. The cutter rolled up and down on the waves, as everyone on the deck of the *Little Ghost* stared at where the *Bitter Respite* had been.

Raewyn broke down in tears, then she fell to her knees and vomited over the side of the boat.

Abigone glanced at her right hand. 'Horses,' she said. 'I will remember that.'

Fyenna eyed her. 'We did a terrible thing,' she said.

'Did we?' said Abigone. 'Are we not alive and free?'

'Take us through the gap, Father,' Denny cried. 'Full speed.'

'Aye, Skipper,' Mor Galthide cried back.

The *Little Ghost* began to pick up speed again, and it raced over the place where the *Bitter Respite* had been. A cry came up from the dark waters, and Abigone glanced down to see Lord Metrius clinging on to a broken beam of wood. Abigone glanced around, but everyone on deck was busy, and no one else had noticed him. Metrius raised his right hand in supplication towards her, and Abigone smiled at him, and shook her head. The *Little Ghost* turned for the open waters to the east, and Metrius faded out of sight.

Over to their right, the other frigate exploded, and the sky lit up for a second time. Abigone and the others turned to watch, as the flames rose up above the rooftops of the Old City. Abigone began to walk down the deck. She passed Raewyn, who was kneeling by the railing, her face pale and wet with tears, then she walked by Reath, who was placing a blanket over Marlow's shivering shoulders.

'I am sorry I slapped you, Reath,' she said.

Reath narrowed her eyes. 'Are you? You don't look very sorry.'

Abigone nodded, then she carried on walking. She passed Loryn, who was adjusting the ship's sail, then she came to where Annalise, Amery and Lothar were sitting. Annalise was fixing a bandage to Lothar's neck, and Abigone crouched down next to them.

'How is the neck, Lothar?' she said.

He shrugged. 'Another scar to add to the collection.'

'You did it, ma'am,' said Annalise.

'We all did it,' said Abigone.

'We failed,' said Amery. 'Every hope and dream we had when we arrived in Klef Mordain has evaporated. What are we now? Fugitives? Where will we go?'

'I don't have the answers,' said Abigone, 'but you are right – we failed. Sometimes, you can try your best, and still fail. Does that mean we should stop trying?'

She got to her feet and walked up to where Mor Galthide was handling the wheel.

He eyed her. 'I can see from your expression, sweet Abigone, that you believe me liable to keel over at any moment. Fear not, I will soon ask my son to take the wheel for a while, and then I shall rest. Before I do so, why don't you speak to him?'

'I don't think he has anything to say to me, sir.'

'We shall see about that. Skipper! My son, come here.'

Denny strode down the deck. He inclined his head towards Abigone, then turned to his father.

'Head due south as soon as we leave the estuary, Father,' he said. 'Stay close to the coast, until we find a deserted cove to anchor for the night. Does this ship have any charts?'

'It does, my son. We pilfered them from one of Lady Fyenna's carricks. I will do as you will, but you must also do something for me.'

'Yes, Father?'

'Yes, my beloved son. Abigone desires to speak alone with you in the cabin. She has something she wishes to say.'

Denny lowered his gaze. 'Very well.'

Abigone narrowed her eyes at Mor Galthide, then she followed Denny into the small cabin.

Denny closed the door. 'What is it that you wanted to say?'

'Your father is trying to push us back together, Denny,' said Abigone. 'I stated no desire to speak with you. You have made your feelings plain. You deem me heartless and without pity, and perhaps I am.

At this moment, Raewyn is weeping tears of remorse over what we did to the Sanctian sailors; whereas, I… Well, you can see me. Do I look distraught?'

'No,' he said.

'I will leave you now,' she said. 'I know you are very busy.'

She made for the door.

'Wait,' he said. 'Abigone… I'm sorry.'

'For what?' she said.

'I was wrong. Wrong about you, and wrong about me. I am the one without a heart. I killed many times today, and not once did I feel pity or regret for my actions. I… did what I had to do to survive. Those things I said to you – I would take them back if I could. We are fighters, you and I. We are ruthless at times, but there is more to us than that. There is more to you – much more.'

'We were a good team,' she said.

'Might we be so again? I love you, Abigone, and I never want to be parted from you. I accept you, as you accepted me. If you refuse me, then I will leave you in peace; but know that you will always have my love.'

'Do you mean those words?' she said.

'The blood, the death, the fall of Klef Mordain – none of it wounds me more than the pain that came from losing you. You are all I want.'

'Even when I show no remorse?'

'I am the same as you – that is what I have realised.'

Abigone smiled at him. 'We are the same?'

'We are. Do you still love me?'

'I do, Denny. I have never stopped loving you.'

'Then I am yours,' he said. 'Will you have me?'

She took his hand and smiled up at him. 'Yes, Denny. I will have you.'

AUTHOR'S NOTES

SEPTEMBER 2024

Thank you for reading ***The Making of Abigone***, the second book of the Masters & Makers series. Whereas ***Fall Seldom Kings*** flowed out of me in one long delirious rush of words, ***The Making of Abigone*** had to be dragged out kicking and screaming. The main reason for this was that, when I was about a third of the way through the draft, I decided to re-order the four points of view, thereby necessitating wholesale rewrites that sucked all joy out of the book for a while. All of the extra work was worth it in the end (I hope!), but there was a long road to get there!

I hope you enjoyed it.

JOIN MY NEWSLETTER

Building a relationship with my readers is very important to me. Join my newsletter for information on new books and deals and to keep up to date on my writing progress.

www.ChristopherMitchellBooks.com/Masters

ABOUT THE AUTHOR

Christopher Mitchell is the author of the Magelands and Masters & Makers fantasy series.

For more information:
www.christophermitchellbooks.com
info@christophermitchellbooks.com

Printed in Dunstable, United Kingdom

64120219R00296